DYER LANE

Marie Aitchison

This book is dedicated to my husband, mother, and daughters who have always supported my dreams of writing. Also, to my sweet boy Buddy. You're part of our pack forever and I am honored to have had you in our family.

CONTENTS

INTRODUCTION

The Dyer Lane that inspired this novel is an actual place. It's a one lane country road in Placer County, a suburban area in Northern California. Dyer Lane is linked to rumors of gangs, cults, and witchcraft along with a swirl of disturbing urban legends that have cropped up over the years.

I have personally heard numerous locals tell stories about going to Dyer at night and having something scary happen. It is a popular Halloween hangout and a place that teens like to go when they are up to no good, or looking for an adrenaline rush.

For some reason, people dump trash there...and bodies. True story.

However, the contents of this novel are not true. The characters and events of this story are fictional and any similarities to actual people or circumstances are coincidental and do not reflect reality other than Dyer Lane being a real place one can visit...and probably see some scary shit.

"Deep into that darkness peering, long I stood there wondering, fearing, doubting, dreaming dreams no mortal ever dared to dream before."

-Edgar Allan Poe: The Raven

"By the pricking of my thumbs, something wicked this way comes."

-William Shakespeare: Macbeth

CHAPTER 1

I have always lived my life like a shark, keep moving forward, or die.

Much like a Great White, stopping has never been an option for me. I don't give up, even when I feel crushed by the sheer weight of life. I just numb the bad stuff. This method may not be the healthiest way to move forward, but at least I'm alive.

Or so I tell myself.

I learned this fun fact about certain types of sharks suffocating if they stop swimming from a biology teacher I had in highschool. This same teacher told the class that Clown Fish can change their sex from male to female as needed. I thought this was amazing and it forever changed the way I watched the movie, *Finding Nemo*.

I smile to myself as I lift the almost empty handle of Captain Morgan to my lips and take a deep swig. The seven of us stopped measuring out shots about an hour ago, and moved on to passing the bottle around in a circle. The amber liquid also stopped burning as it went down around the same time we nixed the shot glasses.

I hold the handle in my lap and stare down at the leering face of the Pirate on the label. One booted foot is propped on a barrel that has been turned on its side, and his blue cape billows behind him. His surly features look proud of the fact that he's gotten us faded.

The smell of weed hangs in the air above our heads, thickening the atmosphere and the blaze of the setting sun trickles in through the gnarled branches of the trees like fresh blood through spread fingers. I feel like I'm floating above my body, looking down at myself.

I tilt another sip of the spiced rum into my mouth. It sloshes noisily as the bottle becomes lighter and a dribble trickles down the side of my face. I feel like being reckless.

"Cora! Save some of that C-Mo for the rest of us." I look over at Kate sitting on an adjacent tree stump. Her voice reaches my ears as if I am hearing her underwater. Kate's big brown eyes are opened wide and her raised hands repeatedly open and close at me like a toddler would when asking for a toy.

I pass the bottle over to her and she quickly takes it from me and lifts it to her ruby lips, draining most of the remaining alcohol. Kate lowers the handle and grimaces, "fuck, that burns."

"Still?" Noah asks. "We should be past that by now. My guess is you're like four shots deep. You must need another."

Kate shrugs in response and tilts the bottle so that the last of it drips down to her tongue as everyone begins to get up and head to the path that leads toward the house. I stay sitting, enjoying the soft haze that has settled over me like a weighted blanket, enveloping me in a false warmth. The seasons are rapidly changing from summer heat to fall crisp, and there is a bite in the air. I love this time of year. October is my favorite.

Suddenly, Avery stands over me. I didn't even notice him approaching. "You good?" He asks, eyebrows raised and hand extended toward me.

"Yeah," I reply and take his palm in mine, appreciating the way our skin colors mix into a swirl of dark and light when clasped together like this. He pulls me up to standing, and I brush off the back of my shorts. Small bits of bark from the log I was seated on scratch against my fingers as they loosen from the fabric.

I gaze out at the scenic golf course that Kate's house overlooks. Large pines dot the expanse of the perfectly manicured lawn, and there's a fountain gently spraying water into the air. Everything is as picturesque as a Thomas Kinkaid painting. This has to be one of the nicest views in all of Stone Bay.

Avery and I turn to join the group making their way toward the house. Mandy stumbles, her dark auburn hair spills down her back and sways with her movements. Kate is all giggles, and her delicate features radiate joy. Even Nikki looks like she is enjoying herself; her usually solemn face is flushed and her smile easy. She carelessly flips her shoulder length platinum hair as she strolls along with the group.

Each of us are loose-limbed and relaxed. We probably look like one of those prescription medication commercials of young healthy people boldly laughing and having a good time outdoors while terrible side effects are incongruously rattled off by the narrator. *Warning: Blah blah blah may heal you, or it may cause you to suffer serious issues such as bleeding ulcers, suicidal thoughts, fatal heart conditions, throat swelling, and death.*

I'm caught off guard by my own morbid thoughts and let out a small giggle. It attracts the attention of Leo, who responds as any stoner would, by passing me a joint. I inhale deeply, the herbal flavor of the tree filling my senses. I hold it in, and then release a cloud into the afternoon air. My exhalation is a bird fleeing a cage. *Freedom.*

The roses bordering the path are a bright display of baby pinks, red, and mauve petals. The blooms release a sweet floral fragrance as we pass them on the way toward the marketlight-bedecked patio. I savor the scent as it mingles with the marijuana.

We walk inside the house, and make our way to the kitchen. Leo heads straight for the pantry and takes a chip clip off of an extra large bag of nacho cheese Doritos. "How long are your parents gone for?" He asks, as he sets the chip bag down long enough to chew a handful and leans his palms down against the black and white granite counter. His toned tattooed arms flex with the pressure of holding himself up and orange Dorito dust clings to the tips of his fingers.

He gazes at Kate with half closed, bloodshot eyes. He looks high as fuck, but is probably the most sober out of all of us since he doesn't drink, and usually sticks to Mary Jane. He'll be our designated driver for the night.

"They are gone for an entire month. Jamaica. Living the life," Kate says with a wry grin and then chugs water from a glass she filled at the fridge.

"Fuuuck. You get this house all to yourself for that long?" Noah asks with raised brows.

"Too bad I'll be spending it studying most of the time," she says. "I should have moved out by now, but living rent free while I'm in the nursing program is just too sweet. Especially when they travel so much."

"Well you're lucky you don't live with the creeps I do. They are always watching films with subtitles and snorting stuff. I would choose this life for free over paying for that any day," Mandy says as she sways slightly on her feet, clutching the crystal necklace that she always wears. "It's still better than living with my mom though," she adds as an afterthought, scrunching her freckled button nose in distaste.

Kate shrugs "you're here most of the time anyway, you might as well just move in."

"You think your parents would let me? I'll pay rent."

"I don't know, probably. Or you can just keep staying here every night like you already do and not pay," Kate answers as she starts grabbing water bottles and handing them out. "We have to sober up a bit if you don't want to feel like death in the morning."

She also begins packing a tote bag, and fills it with extra waters, a couple flashlights, a portable phone charger, and several small bags of Cheezits.

"But we are bringing more Captain, right?" Noah asks, genuinely concerned even as his voice slurs and he has to close one glassy eye to focus.

"No man, we can't risk that in the car. Water only until we get back," Avery says.

Noah lifts his hands in a gesture of surrender, "fine. I'm ready. Let's go see some scary shit at Dyer Lane."

* * *

The sun has almost fully set now, and the sky remains a sherbert vision of pinks and yellows as it continues to sink lower. All of us pile into Kate's black Chevy Tahoe, and I start to giggle. The pot is smoothing everything over for me and making me want to laugh for no reason. Avery notices and turns to me, "care to share what's so funny?" He says.

"Well, first off, the fact that we are trying to be drunk ghostbusters right now is hilarious," I respond, and playfully arch an eyebrow at him.

"Oh, I know," he replies, "but everyone always says Dyer Lane is crazy and we are guaranteed to see something. We gotta check it out."

"Fine. Just don't leave my side," I whisper in his ear, as I grab his hand and interlock our fingers. I can feel the steady beat of his heart through his warm palm pressed against mine.

"I would never." He leans and places a soft kiss on the top of my head and then opens the back door for me. I am greeted by a marked new car smell as I boost myself up to climb into the SUV. The black leather is firm and cool beneath my hands as I head for the third row of seats, Avery following behind me. Nikki and Mandy sit in the row in front of us, and Noah implants himself between them.

"Ladies," he croons with a broad grin.

"Don't be getting fresh with my girl," Leo says flatly as he takes his place behind the wheel and starts the ritual of dropping Clear Eyes in. His head is tilted far back and mouth hangs open in concentration. Kate sloppily climbs into the front passenger side. The smell of rum clinging to her.

"She wasn't even in the car yet, but they don't call me Mr. Steal yo Girl for nothin,'" Noah says with a smirk.

Nikki rolls her eyes, "no one calls you that, Noah."

"Keys," Leo says, ignoring Noah and holding out a hand

to Kate expectantly.

"It's push to start," she answers as she adjusts herself in the seat.

"So, I don't need keys?"

"As long as the keys are in the car, it will start. They are in my purse." She pats her hand on a small black and gold bag in her lap. "We're good."

"Fuck, you're fancy," Leo says and makes a big show of pushing the start button. The Tahoe's engine comes to life and the doors automatically snap into lock with a smooth *snick* sound. The clicks start around the car as we all begin to buckle up and the vehicle smoothly departs down the tree lined driveway as we head out. The time display on my phone reads that it is 6:42 PM, and our destination is about an hour away. It will be full dark by the time we arrive.

We reach the gate at the end of the path and wait silently as it senses the vehicle and slowly opens to let us off Kate's property. It's as if everyone is holding their breath and the nerves in the car are suddenly palpable despite the lightness we were all feeling only seconds ago.

What are we getting ourselves into?

CHAPTER 2

"So," Nikki starts, breaking the silence that had settled over the car "what do you all actually know about this place? I've heard it's one of the most active paranormal sites in NorCal."

"I heard it's one of the most haunted places in ALL of California," chimes in Avery.

"I know there are farmer ghosts on the side of the road," Noah states. Nikki scoffs. "For real!" Noah says excitedly. "Everyone knows about the overall wearing farmers."

"I don't know why you would get stoked to go see something that lame, Noah. I heard it's a place that devil worshipers go...and there are spirits of witches and a grim reaper that walks along the paths," Nicki mumbles as she picks at her chipped black nail polish.

"Ok, this isn't Harry Potter. Get out of here," Noah says. Nikki gives him a smirk and then flips him the middle finger. I cringe wondering if they are going to be at each other's throats the entire car ride.

"My brother told me it's where gangs go to initiate people and the body count there has been pretty high," Leo adds.

"Oh, because your brother who works as a *graphic designer* knows so many gangsters," Noah says. "Makes total sense."

"Noah, my brother and I grew up in Placer County. We've

heard stories about Dyer Lane since we were kids, and even would go explore and play there sometimes. This place has a rep. There's a ton of messed up stories about it."

"Yeah, yeah. I'll believe it IF I see it."

I pull my phone out and begin to try and google Dyer Lane but the screen is unfocused and trying to read makes my head spin. I drop my hands to my lap and rest my head back on the soft seat with my eyes closed. I feel like I'm on a ship at sea with the way my world is tilting.

Damn you, Captain Morgan. I think as I picture that smug Pirate face framed by the long, dark, windblown hair.

Avery reaches over and squeezes my hand. "I knew we should have kept using the shot glasses. It's too hard to know when you drink too much if you stop...and you took that extra hit on Leo's joint..."

"Mmmm," is all I can manage through pursed lips.

"Kate, can you pass a water back here?" Avery calls up

"Uh, yeah. Is Cora ok? She better not get sick in my new car," Kate responds.

"Yeah, she'll be fine," he says as he side eyes me," I just want to give her some water."

Kate bends and grabs a water bottle from down by her feet. It makes its way into Avery's hands, and I crack one eye open to look at him. He breaks open the seal and offers the open bottle to me. Concern etches his features.

"I'm good, I'm good," I slur, straightening up and taking the cold bottle from him. The precipitation makes it slippery beneath my fingers, but I manage a small sip and hand it back without spilling. Avery caps it and then reaches up to brush a long blonde strand of hair off my face and delicately places it behind my ear. I look up at him and we both smile, then I lean my head back again and close my eyes.

Kate sighs, "I personally don't think Dyer is haunted. I think it's just a shithole country road. I've driven on it plenty of times. Nothing but trash, graffiti, and hicks. The stories are all just urban legends," she flips her glossy dark hair over her shoulder.

"When did you go?" Nikki asks. "Because if it was in the daytime, maybe that's not when people see stuff…" she trails off.

"Yeah, it was daytime. There were cows. It's literally just a regular country road. One lane going in both directions, some scraggly trees, tall grass...poorly maintained POS."

"I've been there a few times also on work calls, and it is pretty much exactly what Kate just described," Avery chimes in.

"Ok. I have intel," Noah interrupts holding up his phone. The screen casts ghostly reflections upon the glass. We've been driving for about ten minutes. The bright swirls remaining of the sunset that were just so recently gracing the sky have now been replaced by the violet clouds of dusk, which paint the dimming horizon in angry bruises as evening fully sets in.

"Basically, this place is super fucked up," Noah slurs as he squints down at his screen. "Tons of wild stories are popping up in the search."

How he is able to read his phone as drunk as he is, is beyond me. My interest is piqued though, and I listen silently in the back seat, my eyes remaining closed to ward off the spins.

"So, according to Professor Google, it all began in 1855 with William and Alice Dyer. They settled there with their family and had a ranch and slaughterhouse. William was a playboy and stepped out on Alice, which caused her to go mad with jealousy and rage. She butchered him and her entire family with a meat cleaver before burning her home down and shooting herself in the head with a shotgun...hashtag farmlifeprobs."

"Yeah, no. That was a dumb story," Mandy says. "But there are other ones too," she adds as she stares at her phone screen. "In the 1950's a police officer was pursuing a car suspected of fleeing the scene after a nearby home invasion and he took the 90 degree turn too fast and wrapped his car around a tree. He was ejected from the vehicle and his skull bashed in. Instant death. His body was found the next day and animals had already eaten his eyes. People say that when you drive on Dyer Lane at night a ghost cop can be seen racing up behind you and when it passes you, it will disappear into thin air. If you pull over, the car will pull up next to you and look inside and the police will be there in the front seat with no eyes."

"Lame," Leo mutters.

"I actually think that one is kinda creepy," Mandy says, wrapping her arms around herself.

"So, what? Is a guy with a hook for a hand going to murder us if we park on the side of the road and makeout?" Nikki asks.

"Are you implying you want to makeout? because..." Noah starts.

"OMG shut up, I'm just saying it sounds like the stories about Dyer Lane are just a bunch of urban legend rip offs."

"My point, exactly!" Kate agrees.

Avery stirs next to me. I open my eyes and glance at him. His phone is out too and his brow is furrowed as he navigates his search. "It just seems like a place that attracts bad incidents," He says. "Just as recently as 2017, the body of a man was found. He was reported missing and apparently murdered and dumped out there in the bushes among all the trash on the side of the road."

"That's sad," I say. "Do we even want to go somewhere like this? It's getting pretty dark out and it just sounds like a crime magnet."

"You're scared," Noah declares, casting me a judgmental look over his shoulder.

"No. I'm just not deranged," I say with a shrug and small shake of my head.

"It's like true crime. Don't you listen to Podcasts?"

"Yes, Noah, I do. That doesn't mean I want to go to the scenes of brutal murders to check it out first hand."

"You're not very fun," Noah mutters.

An awkward silence settles over the car. Everyone is thinking or unsure of what to say.

"I'm going to put some music on." Kate says decisively, and a moment later, *Candy* by Machine Gun Kelly starts to blare through the speakers.

"YES!" Mandy yells and rolls her body along to the beat. She loves this song because her name is in it. Noah begins rapping along with the lyrics.

Candy gives way to *Circles* by Post Malone. Song follows song off Kate's random playlist, and we are all in a comfortable silence. Everyone is on their phones looking at Instagram or Tik Tok. I've drunk almost all the water Avery gave me, but the spins are still lingering.

The streetlights are on until we turn down a narrow street and enter onto a country road that has dry grassy fields bordering either side for miles. It's completely dark outside now. We make our way further and further away from suburbia. Outside the window is a blanket of deep shadows punctuated by looming oak trees. I check the map app on my phone and see that we are now in the rural area bordering the cities of Roseville and Elverta.

Almost there.

CHAPTER 3

Dyer Lane is a long and winding road with a single lane going one way in both directions, divided by a yellow line that stretches into the darkness like a sleeping serpent. No one is traveling on the streets but us. There are large oaks on either side, the scraggly branches bending across the road to create a gnarled canopy, long twisted fingers reaching up to scratch at the indifferent sky above.

Leo reaches out to lower the volume of the music, and whistles through his teeth. "You have to admit, this place is actually pretty creepy."

I manage to watch out the window as we continue down the path and spot trash littering both sides of the narrow two lanes. My stomach lurches as we hit a sharp turn, but I can't drag my eyes away from all the litter cluttering the path. My vision singles in on an old couch that has been ripped to shreds. I wonder who would ever go out of the way to dump something like that here. I watch as we pass discarded tires, an old bed frame, soda bottles and crumpled fast food containers. Black bulging garbage bags have been discarded, and seem to be leaking some sort of fluid. There is even a grimy baby doll laying among the debris.

Bullet holes pepper a speed limit sign and there is spray painted graffiti on the street and marring the trees along the road. I see a swastika painted in white on a thick oak. There one minute and gone the next as we pass it by. The symbol makes me clench my jaw as I suppress my disgust along with the nausea I've already been battling.

"Like I said, this place is fucked," Noah mutters.

"Clearly," Nikki agrees. "Also, shut up, you've repeated that line like 10 times on an hour long car ride."

We silently continue down the road at a slower crawl, all of us looking out the window taking in the strangeness and straining to notice anything else unusual.

"Who would drag a barbeque out here like that?" Nikki asks as we pass by a large grill that has been dumped on the side of the road.

"The cannibals who eat human flesh, of course," Noah responds.

Nikki is gearing up to make a smart ass comment back to Noah, when red and blue lights suddenly begin to flash behind us and a motorcycle cop comes into view. Leo immediately signals and pulls over to the side of the road. "That didn't last long," he mumbles as he puts the car into park.

"You weren't doing anything wrong, why are we getting pulled over?" Kate adds, stress edging into her tone.

I reach over and squeeze Avery's hand, and he traces a thumb over the back of mine.

A slim figure approaches the car, shining a flashlight toward us as the officer closes in on the driver's side window. Leo takes a cleansing breath, and then shifts himself to the side in his seat so that he can reach his back pocket. He pulls out his license to have it ready, and rolls his window down.

A woman in uniform stands outside the window. From where I'm sitting I can see that she is tall and sturdy. Her hair is pulled back into a severe bun, secured at the nape of her neck.

"Hello, Officer," Leo says pleasantly. His Russian accent is suppressed as he attempts to sound American.

"License and registration, please," she requests. Her voice is clipped and firm with a smoky quality to it. Leo reaches his hand out to Kate, who hands him her registration and license and he passes all the documents out the window to the officer. "I'm driving my girlfriend's car," he informs the cop.

"Hi, Kate Andrada, here," Kate provides with a small wave, indicating she is the car owner. Her words are slurred and I clench my teeth willing her to shut up. The Officer glances up at Kate with narrowed eyes. I lean a little to my right and try to catch a glimpse of what's happening. At the same time, the cop uses her flashlight to sweep over the back of the car as she takes in the number of us in the SUV.

"Driving some friends home?" She asks, casually.

"Yeah, I'm just dropping everyone off."

"Do you know why I stopped you tonight…Leonardo Morozov?" she asks as she reads his full name off of his license in her hand, and then passes back the registration form.

"I am not sure..." Leo answers softly, and sets the paper in his lap, maintaining eye contact with the officer.

"You were driving ten miles below the speed limit," the officer responds.

"Oh. My apologies. I'm unfamiliar with the area and it's very dark on this road. Just trying to get home safely," Leo explains apologetically.

The silence in the car is heavy. Nobody is moving or even daring to breathe. We all are unsure of where this is going. *Is she going to notice that we all reek of alcohol? Can she smell the pot?* The what ifs of anxiety start to crowd into the back of my mind, wrestling for purchase.

As if sensing my thoughts, the Police asks, "are all passengers of legal drinking age?"

"Yes. We are all 21 or older," Leo answers.

"I'll have to check all the licenses of the people present to verify that. If everyone can please pass them forward to me."

We all start scrambling for our wallets. For some reason my heart is beating out of my chest. I purse my lips together and struggle to contain the nausea that threatens to overtake me. I grab my license and pass it forward along with Avery's, and Leo collects them all from us.

The Police Officer reaches her hand in through the front window to retrieve all the identification cards. I study her face as she reads the birth dates on each license. She has dark skin, high cheekbones beneath large, almond shaped eyes, and full lips. Even in this dim lighting, I can tell that she is beautiful.

"I'll give you this warning," she begins in that distinctly smoky voice as she hands back the bundle of licenses to Leo, "get off Dyer Lane and make sure you follow the speed limit. It is dark out here, so I understand the caution you're taking, but this isn't somewhere that you want to linger, okay?" She tilts her chin and gives Leo a pointed look, as if to say *you're full of shit, I know you were here to explore.*

"I will do that, Officer. Thank you," Leo replies.

"Have a good night," she says, and turns to stroll back to her motorcycle.

Leo rolls up his window as Kate reaches over to pluck her license and registration slip from him. She promptly puts them both back into the proper places. Then, she takes the stack of cards and starts passing them back to us.

I turn and crane my neck to see the cop gracefully climb onto her bike and make a U-Turn. She's going back the other way. *Strange.* I watch as her motorcycle quickly fades into the darkness behind us, swallowed by the night.

Avery nudges me and holds my license out for me to grab. I take it and slip it back into my wallet. Pursing my lips to fight back the nausea that has only intensified since being pulled over.

Leo shifts the car back into drive and we start rolling forward, further down Dyer Lane.

"Well, that went better than anticipated," Noah says. "I can't lie, I was sweating a bit. Even with weed being legal, and all. You tend to smell like a grow house, bro."

"Oh come on, you know I had it under control."

"Only *you* would get pulled over for driving too slow," Noah responds.

Leo still has both hands placed firmly on the wheel.

He looks stiff, like he hasn't yet let himself relax. He always gets nervous around law enforcement. *Maybe he worries they will profile him based on his accent or his full sleeves and neck tattoos,* I wonder to myself, trying to think of anything to keep my mind off the roiling in my stomach. I sit stone still, as acid claws its way up my throat. I swallow down the burning sensation, and try to focus on the headrest in front of me.

"Well, I guess that's it. She said to basically get the hell off this road so we should probably just follow it down to Watt Avenue and head out," Avery says.

"Are you kidding? We are here, and she turned around anyway. Let's explore a little," Nikki urges.

"I'm down," Mandy says, mischievously. Her white teeth shine in the dark as she smiles.

"Me too," Noah adds.

"Ugh. I'm with Avery, I just kind of want to leave," says Kate as she fidgets with her purse in her lap.

I start to give input, but all the alcohol and adrenaline catch up to me right as I begin to speak. I clench my mouth shut abruptly, creating a squeaking noise.

Avery looks up at me startled as I start gagging, struggling to keep the contents of my stomach from coming up. I slap my hand against my mouth, eyes wide as I stare back at him. I continue heaving against my firmly placed hand, and Avery calls out, "Leo! Pull over real fast, Cora is getting sick."

"Damn it! I told her not to barf in my new car!" Kate yells, as Leo quickly swerves down a dirt path on the side of the road.

He drives down a little ways and then parks, this time shutting off the engine. The lights blink on as Mandy opens the door and quickly climbs out so I can clamber from the back row and make my way to a nearby tree.

I double over with my hands braced against the rough trunk for support as the wood digs into my palms and release everything I have been trying so hard to contain during the entire drive. Nothing but liquid spews forth, since I haven't eaten much today. The sour stream burns as it pours out of my nose and mouth with eye watering force.

Avery quickly appears by my side, and begins holding my hair out of my face and rubbing my back. My vomit splashes off the ground and I continually mutter "I'm sorry," between each heave. Tears are involuntarily running down my face from the force of being sick.

Eventually the nausea subsides and my stomach is empty of its contents. I feel a little better, and go back to join the group. I lean against the Tahoe, still not fully trusting the spins to be gone. Luckily, Mandy has some baby wipes in her bag from the last time she worked a nanny shift, and I use them to clean my face off.

Avery hands me another bottle of water and I chug it absentmindedly wondering where I should go once I need to pee, because that is most certainly going to be coming up next. *Damn, baby wipes would be perfect for that situation as well,* I think as I grab a couple extra from Mandy's package and stick them in my front right pocket. Not caring that the wetness from the wipes is seeping through.

Everyone has exited the car and are glancing around at our bleak surroundings. It's difficult to see any further than a couple feet in front of us even with the cabin light on in the Tahoe. The blackness seems to move and breathe, and the silence is unnatural.

"Why did you take us into the boons?" Kate asks Leo.

"I pulled off the main road because I didn't want another cop to see us parked on the side. I saw this path and figured it would be safer," Leo explains with a shrug.

"Good thinking," Nikki says. "Now we can explore."

"You can have fun with that, I'm staying in the car," Kate says. "Plus, Cora is sick, I don't want to leave her." Kate lifts her phone and hits the stories button on her Instagram. She starts excitedly speaking into the screen about how she is having an adventure with friends on Dyer Lane. Once Kate is done with her story, she clicks off the car light above her head and begins scrolling her IG feed. The absence of the cabin light plummets us into an even deeper darkness than before. Mandy scrambles to grab her phone from her hoodie pocket and hits her flashlight icon. The night is so impenetrable that even the usually bright beam from her phone is insubstantial for more than a foot.

"I'll join you," Noah says to Nikki.

"Me too," Leo adds, and then bends down to give Kate a kiss on her head, which she barely notices because she is so focused on typing out a story to her followers about how a cop just pulled us over. The words are flying across her screen as she types, only slowing when she adds emojis in.

"I'm coming too!" Mandy says.

I look up at Avery and give a slight shake of my head. He nods.

"Are you two going to stay?" Leo asks.

"Yeah," Avery answers. "We will make sure Kate doesn't drive off and strand everyone here because a new Keeping Up With the Kardashians episode is coming on."

"Haha, you're so funny," Kate responds as she continues to scroll and respond to DMs. "Continue making fun of me, and I just might."

"You should make sure to take some flashlights." I croak. My throat feels raw, and I take another sip of water, savoring the soothing coolness.

"For sure. Here," Kate says as she hands Leo the gym bag with the extra waters and lights inside. "Oh, wait," She pauses to grab the portable phone charger and snacks out of it, and then continues to pass the bag out the window.

"Throw me one!" Noah says holding out a hand, and Kate tosses him a Cheez-It package.

"We are just gonna see where the path goes and then circle back. It shouldn't be long," Leo says to Kate as he helps himself to a snack pack.

"Love you," Kate calls out as she turns back to the screen of her phone in her lap.

Avery and I watch as Leo and Noah walk with lit

flashlights in hand toward Mandy and Nikki who are talking and waiting on the path. The beams of their lights dance off the woods and play across the ground as they go.

The brightness of the flashlights quickly fade away with their departure, and I tilt my head up against the car to stare at the sky. The absence of light pollution allows for a clear view, and the stars are radiant. I am transfixed on them, and try to pick out some constellations. I never get to see this in the city. Witnessing such an immense number of glistening stars is humbling and looking up at the night sky makes me feel small, but not necessarily in a bad way.

"You seem better," Avery comments, breaking the silence and interrupting my thoughts. I don't mind, though. "Yeah. It's all that water you've been making me drink," I say, as I lower my eyes from the stars and smile at him.

He smiles and then walks around to the side of the car where he asks Kate for a couple of the Cheez-It packages and returns with them in hand.

"Thanks for taking such good care of me," I say, taking a pack from him.

"Always," he says, softly.

We stand there in the cool night air munching on the cheddar crackers.

"These are good," I say between bites. "I always forget that I like these."

"How do you forget that you like something?" Avery laughs.

"I just haven't had them in so long, so then I forget that they taste so good," I respond, starting to giggle.

"Okay, I definitely think you got the alcohol out, but the high is still going strong," he says and I start laughing harder.

"Yup," he affirms. "Still high as a kite."

"You know what I was actually just thinking?" I ask as I lean into him. "I was looking at the stars and I started thinking how pretty they are. Then, I thought, what if those aren't really stars and they are just holes poked in the container so we can breathe?"

Avery pulls away to look at me with a wide expression. "So, we are some sort of pet for higher beings to observe? Is that what you're saying?" We are both silent for a beat and then burst out laughing. "I think I saw that in a meme once," I say, once I catch my breath.

"You're so weird!" Kate calls out the open window from her cozy spot in the passenger seat. "I know!" I call back, my cheeks feeling frozen and achy from smiling.

"But for real, what happens when we die? Is there some higher power that watches over us or not?"

"Ah, always your favorite question to ponder. My dark Cora," he murmurs as he wraps me in his arms. "You know that I think our spirits go to heaven. You change your mind all the time though, so what's your guess tonight?"

Avery holds me as I think, "I think we don't matter anymore unless there are people alive who still value our memories. Our entire existence just seems meaningless if not for the imprints we leave behind. I guess I'm in a nihilist mood tonight."

"Well, if that's what you think, then you better enjoy every moment you have," he whispers and kisses my cheek.

We stay like that for awhile, having more strange existential conversations, and laughing about random thoughts. Kate listens in and interjects sarcastic comments here and there. It feels like a long time has passed but my phone indicates it's only been about thirty minutes since everyone left up the path.

The moment I had been dreading finally arrives and all the water catches up to me. I have to pee. I tell Avery, and he hands me the flashlight that he was holding in his back pocket. It's small and has a wrist strap. Perfect.

I slip my hand into the loop and click it on. I walk in the opposite direction from the tree that I claimed as my personal barf spot earlier. I don't want to go far from the car because I really do get an uncomfortable feeling out here. I can barely see around me even while using the flashlight, but I make my way toward an area with some bushes a few feet away. I stand behind the shrubs, and pull down my shorts, grabbing onto a small tree trunk that I can anchor myself with as I squat.

I don't even use the baby wipes I took because there's nowhere to put them after, and I don't want to litter. I look around me at the trash others have left behind. There are numerous discarded red solo cups and a filthy used condom on the ground. I shudder in disgust. I guess a little more litter wouldn't hurt, but I can't bring myself to add to it.

Once I'm done, and have my shorts pulled back up, I return to the car. I'm feeling relieved but notice that the temperature has plummeted. It feels much colder than it did moments ago. I wish I had a sweatshirt. I also keep getting a strange sensation like strings are skimming across my legs, arms, and face, and wonder if I walked through a spiderweb.

When I get back to the car Avery is silently staring out into the grassy field to the left, lost in thought. His back is to me as I approach.

Past the nearby row of trees, the open field looks like an abyss that can go on into eternity. It's an otherworldly quality, like something that would be described in a macabre fairytale before the evil witch comes to claim the souls of children. My thoughts are turning dark and I picture a pale clawed hand thrusting forward to grab Avery and pull him into the inky black beyond. I shiver at the unwelcome image.

The old oak trees loom around us. It is menacing given the recent image my mind played out, and the distinct feeling of isolation. There are no sounds here. Not even the buzzing of insects. The world around us is holding its breath.

I approach and whisper into Avery's ear, "and when you gaze long into the abyss, the abyss also gazes into you."

He turns to me and says, "Nietzsche? That you?"

I laugh and wrap my arms around his waist. I tilt my head up to look at him and he bends to kiss my lips. I pull back before he can make contact, "I threw up, remember?"

"Oh, yeah. Okay," He says with a laugh. "Good lookin' out."

"I'll promise to kiss you as much as you want after I brush my teeth later," I say and rest my cheek on his chest. My head is turned so that I'm looking out at the vast darkness he had been staring into. My breath rises in front of my face like smoke billowing out to be lost in the night. "This place really is weird though, I want to go."

"Same," Avery replies. He begins to rub his palms up and down my arms to create warmth. " It's been getting colder and I don't even have a sweatshirt to offer you."

"Always the gentlemen," I say, smiling up at him, our exhaled clouds mingling together as we speak. The vapors of our breath remind me of souls leaving a corpse. I clench my teeth together, disturbed by my intrusive thoughts.

Despite Avery's calming presence I still notice that our surroundings are eerily silent and I feel on edge. The quiet feels manufactured, somehow. Abruptly, Avery slaps at his left arm. "Mosquito" he murmurs. "Or a spider web."

"I felt like I walked into one of those earlier. It could have come off of me." I glance around, "I actually haven't heard any bugs or birds at all the entire time we have been out here. Isn't that unusual for the country?"

Avery's brow furrows at my comment. "Yeah, it is. I noticed it was really quiet but now that you point it out, that's exactly what's missing," he says. He shifts his weight from foot to foot, and then says, "let's get in the car, it's freezing out here." I agree, and we turn toward the SUV together. I open the rear door, and the light automatically flashes on in the backseat as we climb in and the door thumps hard as Avery closes it behind us.

Kate sits forward with a gasp. Her hands clutch hard to the seat.

"Wow," I say. "Were you actually sleeping?"

Kate's face has the tell-tale seatbelt crease on her right cheek of a passenger seat car sleeper. "Yeah," she mumbles.

"You scared me. Are they still not back yet? When did it get so cold?"

"Nope, and it's way warmer here in the car than it is out there. The temperature kinda dropped out of nowhere," says Avery.

"What the hell," Kate says as she looks at her phone. "Leo sent me a few messages. Apparently there is a tiny abandoned house at the end of the path. Figures. He says it's super sus and they are all headed back now."

"When did he send that?" I ask.

"About ten minutes ago," she answers.

Then, there is a loud smack on the windshield toward the side that Kate is sitting on and she lets out a shrill scream that makes my blood freeze.

CHAPTER 4

Noah immediately starts laughing hysterically. He's standing outside of Kate's window, clearly very pleased with his ability to scare her.

"You should have seen your face! Aw man, I'll never forget that. It was so funny," he calls out as he's doubled over laughing. His warm breath is steaming into the night air.

"Ugh! Why do you get off on fucking with people?" Kate yells.

"Why does anyone? It's fun," Noah says, nonplussed.

"Noah you're such an asshole," Leo says, despite the grin on his face.

"What? All I did was hit her window, It's not a crime," Noah says grinning back at Leo.

Kate is frowning at Noah. Her face still creased on one side from her recent nap.

Noah stares back at her and says, "sorry, Princess Kate."

"Whatever," Kate says, bitterly. "I'm beyond ready to go. This place doesn't feel right."

"I'm ready to leave, too," Nikki agrees. A yawn escapes her as she climbs into the back seat. Her platform Doc Martin boots thump as she crawls to the opposite side of the car so that Mandy and Noah can follow behind her. Avery and I are already comfortably buckled in the very back. I'm also anxious to leave and feeling tired. It's only a little after 11:00 PM, but I am grateful that tomorrow is Sunday and I can sleep in before my overnight work shift starts.

Leo slides into the driver's seat and closes the door. He pushes the *start* button, but nothing happens. The car doesn't start. He looks over at Kate, a question upon his face.

She looks down at the gears, "it's in park," she notes. "Is your foot on the break when you hit the button?"

Leo tilts his head down and looks up at her exasperated. "I'm not dumb."

"What? You didn't even know it was push to start, I was just checking," Kate says. "Try it again."

"Well, your last car had keys! I didn't know. This is the first time I've driven your new one," Leo responds defensively as he reaches out and punches the button with his forefinger again. Still, nothing.

Kate snaps open her purse and begins rummaging through it. "I just want to make sure I didn't somehow take the keys out for something. I don't know why else it wouldn't start..." She pulls the fob out triumphantly, but her smile slowly turns to concern when she realizes this doesn't solve the problem because the keys are in the vehicle but the car is still not starting.

"Hit the button again," she commands.

Leo jabs at the start button. Nothing.

"This is why I don't trust these fancy new cars. Too unpredictable," Mandy starts to explain, but quickly stops mid sentence when Kate whirls around in her seat and glares before dropping her head forward in her hands.

"I can get out of the car and see if there's something going on under the hood..." Leo offers as he unbuckles his seatbelt and opens the door.

Leo pushes himself out of the car and takes a few steps toward the front of the vehicle, when the engine suddenly revs to life and the headlights flash on illuminating the rows of looming oaks surrounding us.

"What the fuck," Kate murmurs.

"That was so weird," Mandy adds.

"I'm just glad it's on so we can leave." Kate says, fatigue lacing her words.

Leo climbs back into the driver's seat, and shuts his door. "I guess it was just a bit delayed," he says with a sigh and rakes his hands through his shaggy blond hair.

"Yeah, maybe the ghost of that girl whose diary you took messed with the electrical shit in this car," Noah casually comments.

"*What* diary?" Kate asks, turning in her seat to face her boyfriend.

"Oh, you know, the creepy diary we found in the old abandoned house at the end of the path. Your lover boy insisted on bringing it along with us as some sort of souvenir," Noah supplies as he reaches into the bag they had taken with them and pulls out a book. He waves it in the air, showing it off, and then sets it down back into the bag.

"It was kind of cool," Leo says with a shrug of a shoulder. "The journal was just laying there in a cupboard. It was too dark to actually read it all, but I was curious, so I took it."

"Why would you do that?" Kate asks. "It wasn't enough to go explore a haunted house in the woods, but you had to take something from there, too?" She stares at him with wide eyes. Then, she puts a hand to her forehead and closes her eyes before quietly saying, "please just drive, let's go. I have a headache and I never want to come here again."

Leo puts the car into drive, and starts slowly rolling down the path toward the main road.

* * *

Noah fills Kate, Avery, and I in on what they encountered on their little exploration toward the house at the end of the path.

"You guys should have come with, it was pretty awesome. We had to walk for about fifteen minutes to get there. That driveway is long AF. Once we came up to the house, I swear, it was like we were being watched."

"Drama queen," Nikki says. "I didn't feel like that at all. The house was more like a shed. It's falling apart and super old and neglected and literally just one room. I was more nervous to walk in and have it fall down on us than I was of ghosts."

"Well, aren't you brave?" Noah retorts. "I thought it was creepy. Leo agreed with me! Mandy was just holding her dumb little crystal pouch in her hands like a cross."

"They are protection stones," Mandy says flatly.

"Yeah, whatever. Anyway, we walked up to the freaky house and there was no door on the hinges, so we just went right on in. And *get this...*" he pauses to build the tension. "There was, like, some sort of devil shrine in there. No cap. Candles all over the place, pentagram drawings on the floor, buckets of God knows what kind of old dried up fluids, it was fucking disturbing."

"Yeah," Leo says. "There were definitely people getting into dark shit in there at some point. I don't think anyone has been around in a long time though, the dust was super thick."

"Anyone living," Nikki says, amusement in her voice. "Until tonight," she adds in an attempt at a spooky tone.

"There was definitely power there. I could sense it," Mandy says, as she continues to clutch at the crystal hanging around her neck.

"Ok, so you see this Satan shrine and start digging around and actually *take* something?" Kate asks Leo, exasperated.

"Babe, I don't believe in haunted things or the power of devil worship. So, I really don't see the big deal. It's just a book. Aren't you a little interested in what could be written in it? Isn't the reason we came here to see if we could find anything strange? And we kinda did. I couldn't just leave it behind."

"Oh, but you could have." Kate replies, accusingly.

"Can I see the book?" I reach a hand forward for it. I really am curious, and kind of wish I had gone with them to explore.

Noah reaches down and pulls the journal out of the gym bag and hands it over his shoulder to me. It's too dark to read, so I hold the flashlight from my phone down at it for a better look. The deep purple cover is lined with grime, and worn. The name *Heather* is neatly embossed in gold script in the middle. The battery on my phone is running low, so I switch off the light and set the book down on the seat next to me. I want to wait until we are safely back on the surface streets to look closer. The thought of my phone dying this far out in the country makes me feel nervous.

As we are nearing the turn off to get back on Dyer Lane, flashing lights quickly begin approaching to our right. The familiar red and blue of a police car beams bounce around in the darkness as the car speeds forward. "Not another cop," Noah groans. "Do you think someone called in because they saw us parked out here?"

The police car surges forward at a speed much too fast for the narrow country road. There is no siren on, just the whirring lights. The car passes by in a blur and disappears before the turn ahead, vanishing into thin air like it went through a portal into another world. My mouth drops open. I immediately glance up at Avery next to me, and he is also sitting there with a bewildered expression. Noah, Mandy, and Kate all start talking at once in a mix of questions and exclamations.

"How did it take the turn so fast?"

"Where did it go?"

"The ghost cop!"

"There's no such thing," Nikki says. "It must have just taken that turn super fast and went up the road and we can't see it anymore because it's so dark."

"There's no way," says Avery. "Did you not see the speed it was going? There is no way it could have taken that turn like that and not have crashed. Also, lights don't just disappear, we would still see them shining back even after the turn. That just vanished."

"Did anyone else notice that it didn't look like a normal police car?" Leo croaks out. "It didn't have the modern shape of one."

"It's the ghost cop I read about earlier. OMG, OMG, OMG," Mandy starts repeating.

"Shut up," Kate says as she rubs at her eyes in frustration.

"I wouldn't believe it, if I hadn't seen it for myself just now," Avery adds.

I just sit in baffled silence, a little breathless. Maybe the car did turn and fade from view and there is a reasonable explanation for this. It is dark out, we are tired, and have been drinking and smoking. Maybe our eyes deceived us. Despite the excuses my mind conjures, I know what I saw.

I know that the car *vanished.*

CHAPTER 5:

"We should go up the way it went and see if there are tire marks or something. I swear, it just took the turn fast and disappeared around the bend. It's pretty sharp, but aren't cops trained for that shit?" Nikki says.

"I didn't hear any screeching tires," Mandy adds, skeptically.

"Me neither," Leo agrees, "but let's go check. We can follow that road up anyway and get off Dyer Lane at the end and head back."

"Ok, let's make this fast, yeah?" Kate chimes in. "I just want to get home and crawl into bed. This is all too much. Plus, I have to go to the bathroom and there is no way I'm doing it out here."

Leo edges the car back onto Dyer Lane and approaches the turn where the police vanished. "No tire marks." He reports, as he squints in concentration at the dark road ahead of us. I continue to stare at the dense blackness outside the window, unable to discern clear details as we pass by the hulking shapes of the oaks lining the road.

"It's dark though, maybe you just can't see them," Nikki answers.

"Come on, you know what we just saw can't be explained," Mandy says, holding a crystal in her hand like a talisman.

"Yeah, it was pretty weird," Noah adds. "I'm going to go ahead and file that into 'shit I never thought I'd live to see.'"

"I mean, y'all wanted to see ghosts," Avery says. "I think we accomplished that."

"Fuuuuck," Noah says, drawing out the word as he usually does. No one speaks after that. The car is quiet, as the Tahoe smoothly navigates the curves of the road like a predator slipping through water. All of us seem to be sober now, and on edge. Our highs from earlier in the night are gone and replaced by a marked wariness. We sit in prolonged silence until Leo turns the car off Dyer Lane and onto a cross street, heading for the freeway. I shift to turn in my seat, and watch the trees recede into the smothering gloom of the night. The oak branches appear like clawed hands, beckoning for us to turn the car around and come back.

"I'm glad to finally be off that road," Leo says with a nervous chuckle. "I would be down to explore it again in the daytime, though."

"Yeah, we are for sure coming back," Noah responds in agreement.

"You would really have to bribe me to get me back here. This whole experience has given me the creeps," says Kate.

"You didn't even get out of the car," Nikki states, a smirk on her face lights up as we drive under the glow of a streetlamp, which are present again now that we are on city streets.

"I didn't have to. I had a whole freak show right outside my window. And what was up with my car not starting?" Kate says as she turns on her playlist and music fills the car.

"It's working fine now," Leo adds. "Sometimes new cars are touchy."

"That's not what that was," Kate mutters looking out the window. The strangeness of the night continues to hover over us, a miasma of suppressed fear and curiosity.

When we arrive back at Kate's, Mandy and Nikki are

both leaning into Noah's shoulders, resting. He is asleep in the middle, his head thrown back and mouth wide, "catching flies," as my dad would say.

Kate is curled up into herself in the front, head leaning against her door. Even Avery looks like he wants to nap, but is fighting his fatigue and reading something on his phone. Physically, I feel tired, but mentally, I am wide awake. My mind is continuously going over what we experienced, and everyone's description of the abandoned shack at the end of the path.

We approach the gate for Kate's house and Leo reaches forward on the visor to hit the remote that opens it. The gate slowly begins to swing forward and once it is completely open, we drive through and head down the long driveway.

Leo stops the car in front of the house, and reaches over to gently shake Kate awake. Avery leans forward and does the same to Nikki, Noah, and Mandy. Everyone begins the task of grabbing belongings and filing out of the car.

I get out and sling my purse onto my shoulder, still clutching the strange notebook that Leo took with him. I glance around and slip it into my bag before anyone notices that I still have it. If Leo had asked me for it, I would have given it to him...but I really want to know what's written inside.

* * *

Everyone follows Kate toward the front door. Rather than go with the herd, I call out "I think Avery and I will head over to my place." He shoots me a puzzled look and stops in his tracks. Avery glances at Kate and does a quick nod, "thanks for having us over tonight."

"I'll call you tomorrow," I say to her. "Bye everyone!"

The group are all groggy as they pause and manage waves and mumbles of bye and then continue toward the house.

"Okay, drive safe. Text me when you get home," Kate says over her shoulder as she slips her key into the front door.

"I will." I wave and quickly turn to walk toward the car, Avery follows behind me, jogging to catch up. He reaches my side and says "why don't you want to stay the night all of a sudden?"

"I just want to sleep in my own bed."

"Oh, okay. Well, as long as I can cuddle you I don't mind," he says as he unlocks his car and gets into the driver's seat.

"Well, of course," I answer with a grin as I slide in next to him. My pulse beats a fast rhythm as I think about the fact that I just went out of my way to steal some creepy book from a friend. Not that Leo would really care, but still. It's unlike me, and tonight has been so strange. My body is craving sleep and I am thankful that my apartment isn't too far away.

Within fifteen minutes, Avery parks his car in a space close to my front door, and we drag ourselves from the car. It's 1:30 AM. He follows me up to my apartment, and I throw my purse down on the small table by the front door, then head to my room. I go into the bathroom and catch a glimpse of myself in the mirror.

I pause to gaze at my reflection. I have my father's nose, and my mother's full lips. It's always been a comfort to me to spot imprints of them in my own features. I notice that my face is even more pale than usual and there are dark plum colored crescents beneath my eyes from lack of sleep. It must be all the overnight shifts I have been working lately at the hospital.

I push my long blonde hair away from my face and quickly brush my teeth. The foul taste of sour spiced rum and CheezIts are replaced with clean mint. Avery walks into the bathroom shirtless and begins brushing his teeth, too. Once he is done he turns to me and says, "I would love to kiss you now."

"Oh yes, the kiss that was promised," I say with a grin. I wrap my arms around his lean waist and lean in to turn my face up toward his. Our lips part, tongues gliding over one another. The warmth of his mouth is a welcome comfort. My mind is completely blank as I savor the moment with him.

After a minute of kissing, Avery turns away from me and starts the shower, then returns his mouth to mine. Once steam begins to gather, we get in together, washing away the last traces of tension from the night.

Our bodies slip and slide together in the small space as soap suds trail down us. I look at Avery and take in the hardness of his body and the glistening smoothness of his skin as the water runs over him. After we are both satisfied, we dry off and make our way to the bed to fall asleep in each other's arms.

CHAPTER 6

I wake up from a dreamless slumber and can feel Avery's chest rising and falling behind me as he still sleeps. The light from the window across from my bed creates slashes of sun across the honey colored hardwood floor. My mind immediately goes to the purple book I put in my bag last night. I reach out and grab my phone from the dresser top next to me. It's eight in the morning. I've only had about five hours of sleep, and my body aches with the need to shut my eyes and rest some more, but I can't ignore the pull to explore the pages of that journal.

I slowly lift Avery's arm off from around my waist, and shift my body over to the side to half roll off the bed. I feel like I'm moving in slow motion, wading through water, but I don't want to wake him up. Despite my carefully orchestrated movements, Avery senses my absence. He rolls over onto his other side, and I'm relieved to see that he doesn't wake up. He is curled toward the wall, hugging the pillow under his head.

I tiptoe slowly toward the bedroom door, avoiding the floorboard that always squeaks. Once I exit the room, I assume a normal pace and make my way through the kitchen, grab a mug, and start the coffee machine. I like it black, straight jet fuel.

Once I have my steaming mug in hand, I get the purple diary from my bag, and settle into the kitchen table. I set it in front of me, and stare at it for awhile. It's dirty and battered, but is otherwise unremarkable other than the golden name embossed on the cover. The silky letters are still shiny enough to reflect the light streaming in from the morning sun outside.

"Who is Heather?" I mutter to myself as I stare at the script on the cover.

And why do I care?

I sigh and flip the book open, revealing the first page of a diary entry. The writing inside is round and neat with a slight slant to the right. It looks like the handwriting of a typical teenage girl, and is easy to read. I wrap my fingers around my steaming coffee cup and begin.

* * *

September 12, 1997

Today was the fourth day of my Junior Year at Stone Bay High. Or Stoner Bay High, as I think of it. The D.A.R.E. program hasn't done shit to help this place. Not that I'm complaining.

I hate school. It's not like it actually teaches us anything we need to know. The only thing that makes it bearable are Tasha and Liv. I don't know what I would do without them. My teachers suck, the classes suck, this town sucks.

Want to know what else I hate? This journal. My mom gave it to me to write my feelings in because she's "worried" about me. Lucky for her I like writing, so I'll use it, but I hate what it stands for - just another way for her to control another aspect of my life. She probably thinks I will write in it, and then she can sneak looks while I'm gone.

She asked me yesterday if I had written anything yet and I told her yes just to get her off my back. Now I'm writing this in the kitchen while she makes dinner, right in her eyesight, so she will stop nagging me.

SEE MOM, I'M WRITING MY FEELINGS.

As if her trying to tell me what to wear isn't enough. She says I look like a Goth. Well, Mother Dearest, perhaps you're onto something for once. When she gave me the journal, she was like,"look it's purple! Your favorite color."

I had to fight rolling my eyes and tried to force a smile. Purple hasn't been my favorite color since, like, the fourth grade or something. And my name on the cover? Seriously? Barf.

She should have gotten a black journal...with a pentagram on the front if she was really trying to make me happy. She would never, though. Satanic Panic, and all that.

She also bought me some new scrunchies...they have sparkles on them. She says I need to get my hair out of my face. As if.

I dye it black, which makes her mad. She says my red hair is beautiful, but I don't feel the same way. I like it as a long dark curtain. Something I can hide behind and block out the rest of the world.

Mom bought me new clothes, too. It's like she thinks she can purchase my affection and change me all at the same time. It's sad, really.

Ever since Dad left us, Mom has been crazy over how we appear to outsiders. We MUST look like we have it all together or whatever, even though we clearly don't. She works constantly and is at her office more than she's home, and I could give a fuck about what other people think of us at this point. HE LEFT US. That's a well known FACT.

What kind of man leaves his family? Seriously. Dad walked out on us for another woman. An already married woman with a family of her own, too. It makes me wonder how horrible his life with Mom must have been. It's hard not to blame her for him finding love somewhere else. It's probably not fair, but it's how I feel.

I'm the only one in this family who seems to keep it real and have a realistic grasp on the situation. Mom thinks I am crazy for how I dress and talk, but I think she is the crazy one.

My little sister, Jessica, just acts like everything is fine. Not a care in the world. In her defense, she's only seven. I would at least expect her to seem a little sad, though.

I resent Mom so much. Her constant questions, her stepford wife aspirations, her obsession with Jessica and lack of real love for me. She's never accepted me for who I am, and has always tried to change me. She probably did it with dad too, and he just had enough of it.

Want to know who will never leave me or try to turn me into someone else? My friends. They are my family now. Sorry Mom, this journal you gave me has only become a place to write about all the things I do that would drive you up the wall. Money well spent.

* * *

September 13, 1997

So much for the first week going smoothly. I should have known it wouldn't last. Nothing ever does at Stone Bay.

Shane Dodson of course had to ruin it all. He's such an asshole. I can't wait for him to graduate next year and be gone. It doesn't help that his mom is the woman my dad left us for. How's that for some soap opera type shit? Now good ol' Shane has made it his mission to majorly fuck up my life.

Today, right before third period, I went by my locker and saw red spray paint all over it. Someone had written "Witch Bitch" across it. Nice.

I figured whoever did it probably thought I would go postal, but I just went about my day. I am well aware of what everyone thinks of me, and I DON'T CARE. At least that's how I try to appear. If people only knew how much I cared...

I got through my first two classes as normally as possible. Of course Mr. Peters was his usual skeezy self. Staring down girls' shirts as he hovers over their shoulders to "check their work." He is the biggest creep teacher. I just glared at him whenever he started toward me and he turned on his heel real fast. Glad that works. I'm Mr. Peters Proof.

Anyway, I got through all my classes, and at the end of the day met Liv by the front of the school so her mom could give me a ride home. As we waited, Shane rode up to us on his motorbike (such a douchey looking one, too). He threw a can of spray paint toward us and it landed, rolling toward me so that I could see it was red. Clearly, he was happy to take the credit for spray painting my locker.

I stomped on the can with my boot and gave him the same stare I give Mr. Peters. I am disappointed to report that the look doesn't work on this dickweed. Shane just laughed and flipped his middle finger at us while he rode off on that stupid bike.

I cannot stand him. Liv tried to cheer me up, but honestly I wasn't even mad. I was more frustrated than anything. There is a big difference in those two feelings, at least I think so. I am frustrated because my dad caused this mess, and there is nothing I can do about it.

Liv promised she would help me get even with Shane, and then invited me over to her house for dinner. I called my mom once we got there to let her know where I was, and she sounded bummed that I wouldn't be home, but I bet she was actually relieved that it would be just her and perfect little Jessica tonight. I bet she thinks that the less time I'm around, the better. I'm a bad influence. She doesn't need her corrupt older daughter infiltrating Jessica's sweet little mind. I'm happy to give them the space.

Anyway, I love having dinner at Liv's house. Her mom (who only lets us call her Pam and never Mrs. Johnson) immediately opened a bottle of gin and started sipping. She was smashed, dancing around the kitchen and singing the song Honey by Mariah Carey to herself within 20 minutes. Clearly, Pam is a lush.

We didn't even have to eat at the dinner table as a family. Pam just allows us to take fold up trays in the living room and eat microwaved TV Dinners while watching Buffy the Vampire Slayer. It's rad.

Then, Liv and I had Rice Krispie Treats for dessert. Those little gooey squares are the closest thing to perfection I think I have ever tasted. It was everything I needed. If it wasn't for Liv cheering me up, I may have just gone home and cried myself to sleep.

Maybe this diary wasn't such a bad idea. Maybe Mom got something right for once. Maybe I'm not a lost cause and writing this all down will help pull me out of the hole I've fallen into. I don't like to play the victim, but when I am this helpless it's hard not to feel like a crime has been done against me. Parents have no idea how much they fuck up their kids, but maybe Mom knows this and the journal is her way of saying sorry and giving me a place to vent?

It is a relief to get these emotions out. I have too many. I wish I could be as numb as I try to make the world think I am. My friends are the only ones I am comfortable talking to about all of this.

I am grateful that although today may have started out bad, it ended pretty well. There's so many ups and downs in life, but I feel like as long as I have Liv and Tasha, and maybe this journal, I will be OK.

CHAPTER 7:

Avery walks into the kitchen, and his sudden appearance startles me. I jump and slosh some coffee over the side of my hand. It's gone cold, so at least it didn't burn.

"Sorry, I didn't mean to surprise you," he says, frozen in place, holding out his hands with his palms facing me like he's trying to calm a spooked animal.

"Hey," I say, as I stand to grab a napkin and clean the spilled dribbles of coffee off my hand and the table. I pick up the journal and am relieved it didn't get splattered. I feel guilty, like I've been caught doing something wrong.

Avery eyes the book in my hand.

"Is that...?" He pauses, and points a finger at the book. "Why do you have that? Isn't that the creepy book that Leo took from the place last night?"

His eyes are narrowed and I can tell he is thinking his way through this.

"Yeeees..." I stare at him, dragging out the middle of the word, my eyebrows raised, trying to smile. It's an awkward attempt at deflecting how random it is that I have stolen this weird ass book and am reading it over coffee in the morning after all the strangeness that happened last night.

"Okayyy..." He says, matching my expression and tone.

We stand there facing each other for a few heart beats,

and then I slump down in the chair and sigh, my eyes cast down at the floor.

"I don't know why I didn't give it back to Leo last night after Noah handed it to me. I just really wanted to see what was inside, so I slipped it into my bag." I flick my eyes up at him, trying to read his expression.

Avery bursts out laughing. "Wow, that's weird! Why Cora?" He's still laughing as he crosses the room and sits in the chair across from me.

I begin laughing too, and straighten up in my seat. "Not as weird as what's actually in the book. Well, diary, actually. It's some teenager's journal from the 90s," I say, sliding it toward him across the table.

Avery grabs it and flips through the pages. "Damn, she seemed like she had some issues," he notes as he pauses to show me a page of a hand drawn inverted pentagram and strange symbols written around it. There are dark brown smears maring the page.

"Kinda makes sense when you consider that Leo discovered it hidden in a Satanic worship shed," I say as I eye the stains on the page.

"Ooo I like that name for it, 'Satanic Worship Shed,'" Avery repeats, "and yes, I think the shit on this page is probably blood...or mud...or maybe actual shit. But, probably blood given this voodoo drawing."

I let out a laugh, "you're the medical professional."

"Well, I definitely see my fair share of dried blood in the field," he says, "and it has this look."

"Speaking of, when do you work next?" I ask.

"Tonight, one of the medics that normally has the PM shift called in this morning and I woke up to a text from Sam asking if I could cover for her."

"I work tonight, too. So, maybe I'll get to see you."

He smiles and leans in to kiss me. My hand comes up to caress his jaw, and his morning stubble prickles my palm. I pull away from him grinning.

"So, what did you learn in your morning detective work, Nancy Drew?" Avery asks, returning the focus back toward the diary.

"Honestly, not a ton. I only read a couple entries. Basically, this Heather girl was being bullied and seemed to have a broken home life. People called her a witch…"

"I mean, can you blame them?" Avery says cringing and gesturing toward the journal and the drawing it contains inside.

"Yeah, I mean the bullying is sad and her parents had a messy separation, so I think she just needed help to sort through those emotions that came up after all that, you know? I don't know how great mental health services were for kids back then. I kinda want to read all of her journal, now. It's interesting getting this look into something so personal from years ago, and she's not a bad writer. Her grammar is good. She knows the difference between "your" and "you're."

"Oh, I know how that's a deal breaker for you."

"Well, yeah!" I reply with a smile. "I'm going to read the rest of it, then maybe I'll tell Leo I accidentally took it home with me."

"Let me know what else it says. I'm curious," Avery says with a chuckle.

"I will."

Avery stands and leans over to kiss my forehead before he says "I'm going to head out. I have some things to get done before my shift, but I will text you when I'm on my way to work."

"Sounds good," I say as I smile up at him.

"I love you, infinitially," he says.

"Infinitially," I say, feeling warmth bloom inside me. We made that word up to combine *infinitely* and *unconditionally*. We mashed the two words together to make something new and meaningful, our own special word created just for one another.

I watch as Avery grabs his things and slips his black and

white checkered Vans shoes on. He takes his keys from the side table, and opens the front door, turning to say, "bye babe," before shutting it behind him.

I get up to make a fresh cup of coffee, still smiling to myself. I am just finished with buttering a slice of toast, when I hear the ping of an incoming text message on my phone. I go into my bedroom to check it, and see that Kate has texted me asking if I want to come over and study with her and Mandy in a couple hours. We have Nursing clinical shifts coming up next week, and our first exam of the semester is this week. It definitely will help to study together. I respond that I'll be there and then I go back into the kitchen to finish my breakfast.

I sit down and stare at Heather's diary resting on the table across from me. I reach toward it, and then hesitate. I don't have time for distractions right now. I'll have to wait to read more. I'm surprised at the feeling of disappointment that floods my stomach and I glance over at the clock. Well, maybe just one more entry won't hurt.

* * *

September 15, 1997

Last night was amazing. I'm super hungover right now, but it was worth it. Liv and I went to Tasha's after school and got drunk off vodka and cranberry juice. The first few gulps were harsh, but then it was nice and smooth. Like ripping off a bandaid; a little burn leads to fresh air and freedom.

Once we were all feeling good, we got ready for the night and Tasha let me borrow her lacy black dress. I paired it with ripped black tights, my studded combat boots, and my new black lipstick that I got from CVS with a five finger discount.

Once we were all dressed and ready, we snuck out and went to a party at Daniel Wood's house. His parents are always gone, and he's known for throwing hella big parties. He lives out in the country, so the cops almost never get called since his neighbors are so far away. Daniel's house is huge and as expected, the party was packed. There was a wide mix of people there, and of course I scanned the room quickly but didn't see Shane anywhere, so I felt safe to stay and chill.

Daniel basically had an open bar, so we drank a ton more. Every counter in the kitchen was covered with alcohol bottles and everyone was helping themselves. I've only really seen scenes like last night in movies, so it felt cool to actually live it for a bit, you know?

Someone brought a Ouija board, and set it up in the living room. A crowd had formed around it, and Tasha, Liv, and I joined in. I've played with a Ouija board before, but never in such a large gathering. I was sure someone stupid would lead the planchette around and create a fake spirit narrative. It totally happened just as I suspected.

At one point, the board told the room that Linda Green wasn't wearing any underwear. Spoiler alert: she wasn't and showed the entire party. I wonder how drunk you have to be to do something like that. I would never. Anyway, I'm pretty sure Conny was the one pushing it around.

People continued to ask the lamest questions. Like, who would ask who to prom, and if so and so would become a millionaire. It's not a magic 8 ball! That's not how Ouija boards work...It didn't take long for things to go in too dumb of a direction and people started to lose interest in the board. Liv glanced around and gave me a wicked smile before she slipped it into her backpack.

Then, Shane and his group finally showed up. I knew it would happen eventually. He would never miss a party of this size. We left before he could spot me and start anything. I was stoked that we managed to steal the Ouija board and take it with us when we snuck out the back. I bet Conny told everyone that a spirit took the board. She would totally say something like that.

We didn't have a ride so we walked along the road. Well, I guess it was more of a stumble than a walk. It was so dark out without any street lights, and we wandered around the woods near Daniel's farmhouse for a while. We came to a little area with lots of fallen old oak trees and sat down there to play with the board some more. It was so cold out that we could see our breath, but it didn't bother me.

Liv grabbed the board and set it in the middle of us. We tried to contact the dead for real, without Conny around to mess it up. We all lightly placed our fingertips on the planchette, and Liv introduced each of us by name to the spirit realm. Then, she asked if there was anyone with us. It took a moment but the planchette moved to the top left corner to say YES! It was amazing.

Next, we asked if the spirit was happy, and the board said NO. We all paused and looked at each other. We asked if it was sad and the planchette stayed on NO. We asked if we could help the spirit, and the planchette didn't move at all. We sat like that until finally Tasha suggested it was gone. We lifted our hands from the planchette ready to pack it up, when the planchette suddenly zoomed to YES.

I was so stunned to see it move on its own. I thought that was impossible. Liv was clapping her hands and practically squealing with excitement. She interpreted that to mean we could help this spirit. We all placed our fingertips back on the piece and asked for a name. The planchette swooped down to GOODBYE and was still.

It was all so sudden, I had a hard time believing anything had happened at all. We were all buzzed off the excitement, and I felt powerful.

Liv wanted to keep trying to contact the spirit realm but it was near freezing. Tasha and I convinced her we could come back later and should leave, so we packed up and decided to start walking along the path again. We didn't get back home until super early in the morning. We had to walk for a long time until we found a pay phone at a gas station and could call Cole, Tasha's cousin, who came and gave us a ride back to her house.

I can't stop thinking about how fun our time in the woods was, though. We summoned a spirit. I know it. I haven't felt so alive in a long time. Isn't that ironic that it takes talking to the dead to make me feel alive?

I can't wait to go back to our new spot with supplies and try some more. We are planning to meet up later today and use the board again, but I'm not sure we will be able to make it back on a Sunday.

We made sure to remember the name of the street we explored, so we can find it again.

It's called Dyer Lane.

* * *

September 16, 1997

Tasha and I went over to Liv's tonight for "dinner" which consisted of eating Taco Bell on pop up trays in front of the TV while watching Scream. Billy Loomis is so hot. I'm obsessed with this movie. That part when Billy says,"movies don't make psychos, movies make psychos more creative." I felt that. We blasted the volume of the TV at the end of the movie and screamed the lines out along with the characters. It's great what we can do when no adults are around to control us. This is not the way things are at my house. It's one of the many reasons I love going to Liv's.

Her mom was passed out and it wasn't even six in the evening yet, so we could basically do whatever we wanted. Even if Pam were awake, I bet we could still get away with anything. Liv said Pam had started making margaritas after church this morning and then blasted Chumbawamba for hours while she cleaned the house, drunk. What a life.

When we were done eating and watching the movie, we played around some more with the Ouija board. As expected, getting a ride to the woods on a Sunday night wasn't something we could swing, so we hung out in Liv's room with cans of Dr. Pepper and lit a bunch of candles. I was a little worried that Liv's cluttered little room was going to catch fire and go up like a tinderbox. She has dried flowers and pages of sketches all over the place, and that can't be safe. It didn't though, obviously.

Since we couldn't go to the woods, we layed around talking about classes and teachers, and played with makeup, hair styles, and clothes.

We eventually became bored with all that, and attempted to contact our spirit friend from before, which was hard because we still didn't have a name to summon. Nothing happened. I guess it only works at Dyer Lane, or we are doing it wrong. Probably both. We were all majorly disappointed, but we are going to ride our bikes back to the lane after school tomorrow and bring the board. I hope we can get it to work again.

* * *

September 18, 1997

I spent the school day trying to avoid Shane, while also trying to act like I don't care. I'm so tired of the charade and just want to curl up in a ball and cry. The sound of his voice makes every muscle of my body tense and my heart races with anxiety whenever he is near. I can feel it beating so hard in my chest that I worry I may pass out.

Yesterday, Shane wiped some sort of shit all over my bookbag while I had it on the bench during P.E. I mean, not something that merely looked like shit, I am talking actual feces. I don't know where he got it from or how he was able to get away with his plan, I just know that my bag smelled so bad I had to throw it away and no one else would do something like that. I know it was him.

For the rest of the day, I had to carry my books around in my arms with no bag to hold them. I worked so hard to keep a straight face all while sweat soaked through my clothes as my body struggled to control my overwhelming nerves, and my arms ached from lugging around everything. Being at school feels like a nightmare these days.

I did well with keeping out of his way today, though. Shane is always surrounded by his basketball team friends and has such a loud voice that I can usually hear him coming and scramble the other way, like a field mouse avoiding a hawk.

I hate being this person. Always looking over my shoulder, always uncomfortable and on edge. I should be the predator, not the prey.

I was relieved when the final bell rang and I was able to meet up with Liv and Tasha. That was the bright light of today, and what gets me through the hard days.

Also, after school was extra special because we rode our bikes for miles all the way to Dyer Lane. The exercise felt good, and the talks we had as we peddled were cleansing.

I told Tash and Liv all about the anger I have about Shane. They understand. They have seen how he treats me, and they know all about the sordid issues of my family. It makes me want to hurl just thinking about my father creating a new life with Shane's mother. No wonder he hates me....it's still not fair, though. I'm not the one responsible for the actions of his mom and my father. Yet, I am the one being punished the most.

Anyway, it wasn't just the talks that made today better, it was what we did when we got to the woods. Liv told Tasha and I all about how she had snuck out late last night and hitched a ride to Dyer Lane, where she had found a little cabin. She led us to it, and I was surprised to see how cool it was. There is moss growing on the roof and it is surrounded by oaks, like something from a fairytale. Even the way the sun filtered through the trees and shone down on it felt special.

We followed Liv inside and she immediately pulled out the Ouija board and lit our ritual candles. The cabin is definitely tiny, more of a shed or something like that. There isn't a bathroom or a bedroom, but plenty of cupboards and enough floor space to store our things.

It is the perfect chill spot to explore our craft. Also, it has a presence to it. The shed feels full of life, although it's clearly been abandoned for years. There was dust everywhere, but that stuff has never bothered me.

Once we got settled in and had our candles lit and circle drawn, Tasha wanted to tell us what her cousin had told her about Dyer Lane. She said that there are tons of rumors about this place and when his friends smoke pot, they come out here and tell ghost stories. One of the ones that he shared with her was about a woman named Alice. Tasha said that apparently Alice was married to William Dyer, the man who settled this area and owned a slaughter house and farm on the land in the late 1850s.

One night, Alice snapped. She was tired of William's infidelity and domestic abuse. She was pregnant with their first child, and didn't want her husband anywhere near their baby. So, she killed him with a cleaver and then she disappeared. No one ever knew where she went, but some people think she may have committed suicide here after she realized the evil she had done. Some nights, if you listen closely, you can even hear the cry of a baby who's life was stolen floating in the wind.

Liv and I both exchanged skeptical glances at this story. If my husband had been trash like William, I would have gotten revenge, too. It's not too unbelievable. Cheaters are the worst. My dad falls in that category. My mom is too weak to do anything about it, though.

In the version of the story that I have created in my mind, Alice killed her husband but ran away and started a new life somewhere good with her unborn child. I refuse to believe she would kill herself and her unborn baby. That totally sounds made up for the shock factor. Alice is better than that.

I immediately had so many questions for the spirit we have been contacting. Maybe it was Alice? We discussed what we wanted to ask, and then placed our hands on the planchette with a new and stronger purpose.

Tasha spoke, and asked Alice if she was present. Nothing happened right away, and we sat quietly, patiently waiting. Finally, the planchette slowly began to move and spelled out H-E-R-E. I could feel my pulse in my neck, I was so excited.

Tasha asked if she had a husband named William. The planchette quickly jerked to NO. She reassured the spirit we were not here to judge, but wanted to understand and help. Could we do that? The planchette circled around the word YES.

Next, Tasha asked why Alice had killed her husband. Nothing happened for what felt like a long time. All I could hear were the small easy breathing of my friends next to me as we sat and waited. Then, the planchette smoothly began to spell out H-A-D T-O.

When that happened, we all looked at each other with wide

eyes. I was like, holy shit! Were we actually talking to Alice? Tasha frowned as she asked if Alice had committed suicide. The planchette zoomed to the corner that said NO.

Then, Liv interrupted Tasha, eager to get some of her own questions in and asked her how she died. The planchette moved to spell out H-I-M.

When that happened, I was puzzled. Him? We looked at one another in confusion. Tasha asked who 'him" is. The candles seemed to suddently glow brighter, and bathed the small shed in an otherworldly light. The temperature plummeted, and quickly became so cold we could see our breaths in front of our faces. It was the craziest thing.

Then, get this, the planchette slid around the board to form the letters spelling out F-A-T-H-E-R. I mean, what? I felt so confused.

I wondered if it was Alice's father, or William's, that had killed her. Before we could ask, the planchette flew out from under our fingertips, and off the board with such force that it hit the cabinets against the wall. I felt my mouth fall open, and stared at my friends in disbelief.

Tasha's chest was rising and falling as she gasped for air, but Liv looked unfazed. I crawled across the floor to retrieve the planchette, and as soon as I wrapped my hands around it, the candles all went out at once in a coordinated snuff.

That is when I truly believe that we were talking to another realm. It was exhilarating. At least, that's the first word that comes to mind. We are in touch with spirits. We are learning the history of their lives.

When we lit all the candles and tried to contact Alice again, there was no answer. She had gone. I felt a pit of disappointment bloom within me, but I still am hopeful that we will be able to talk with her again soon. We will keep trying. I'll write it all down here.

CHAPTER 8:

I finish reading and then just stare at the wall for a few minutes. It's wild to be learning of someone else's experience with Dyer Lane from years ago. It just sounds like a silly, harmless journal entry of a teenaged girl who is interested in dark stuff, but it makes my stomach do a flip. Could the girls have actually believed they were speaking with spirits? Is that even possible?

Who's to say it's not?

The vision of the police car disappearing before my eyes last night surfaces and makes my mouth go dry. There is definitely something different about that place. It reminds me of somewhere Stephen King would write about in his novels. Somewhere where the veils between worlds are thin and dark things can cross through.

Next, you're going to start seeing Pennywise lurking in the corner, I think to myself. "Want a balloon, Georgie?" I mutter under my breath as I flip the diary closed.

Great, now I'm talking to myself. Not a good sign, I think with a sigh.

I don't know what to believe, but the paranormal doesn't typically fit in with my usual way of explaining things. I chew on my thumb nail, trying to process my way through how I feel. I have to admit that what we saw last night doesn't make sense. Nikki was probably right and there is a logical explanation for what went down.

Goosebumps prickle my arms as I stand and start to get myself ready for the day. I was only supposed to read one entry, but that turned into multiple. I just couldn't stop. Now, I am behind schedule. I pack a bag for work and plan to go straight to my shift from Kate's. I go through the motions in a daze. My mind keeps wandering back to Heather and what else she could have written in her journal, and the events that took place on Dyer Lane in the past and present.

I swing my school bag over my shoulder, grab my work tote, then head out the door, locking it behind me. I'm still lost in thought about spirits, and hauntings as I drive to Kate's.

My mind keeps going back to my philosophy courses and wondering if there is life after death. It's something that will never be completely proven one way or another. I miss learning philosophy and go down these trains of thought from time to time. They are both perplexing and comforting in a strange way. Not knowing is simultaneously unsettling and exciting. Something to think about without having a proven conclusion. Exercise for the mind.

I was a philosophy major until my father passed away from a sudden heart attack. He died in my arms. My mom and I did CPR, but by the time the defibrillator arrived with the EMTs it was too late. I went to therapy for it. I had PTSD after the trauma of losing him so suddenly and the helplessness that I felt in trying to save him. That's when I decided I wanted to be a nurse. I want to help people, and be there to comfort their families.

Kate had already been a pre-nursing major and was a rock for me after my father's sudden passing. She used the medical knowledge she was learning in school to reassure me that there was nothing I could have done to save him. I spent a year feeling like it was all my fault that he wasn't still alive and I couldn't fix him when his heart failed. I still feel that way sometimes, but it's gotten better.

The next semester, I reluctantly dropped my philosophy

classes and joined Kate and Mandy in their pre-nursing courses. I even took summer school to catch up with them so we could all apply together to a nursing program the next year. For some reason, I felt called to it.

I landed a job in the Emergency Room as Scribe, which is basically an Emergency Physician's personal assistant. We go with them to each patient encounter and chart for the doctors in real time, which frees their hands and eyes up so they can focus on patient care, rather than documentation. I wanted this job in order to desensitize myself with health emergencies before applying to nursing school. I needed to feel confident that I could handle it. It's actually been unexpectedly therapeutic. I feel closer to humans through witnessing the fragility of life that we all face.

After all, everybody dies.

The fact that we will one day breathe our last breath is truly the only thing that's ever guaranteed to each and every one of us when we are born and take our first gasp of air, often crying and screaming as oxygen floods our lungs.

I've noticed that death is often actually a more peaceful event than birth.

Not only has my job in the ER helped me on my journey of healing after the loss of my father, but it is also what brought Avery and I together.

* * *

It had been my second week at the hospital, when a code rushed in with a heart attack patient. My stomach dropped. I had only ever seen one cardiopulmonary arrest, and it had ended in the death of my father. I didn't feel ready, but I knew I didn't have a choice. This is the reason I took the Scribe job in the first place. I needed to know that I could handle emergencies like this.

The gurney was moving fast, and a paramedic

immediately began voicing the patient's status and medical history to the doctor. I started scribbling notes on all the pertinent information; the patient's background, what interventions had already been performed enroute, and the times each drug was administered. I would take all this information and return to chart it for the doctor after the code was finished.

A female medic rode on the side of the gurney and was performing chest compressions. Tendrils of her brown hair had slipped away from her bun and fluttered around her face with each downward push. The medic who had given his report to the doctor was providing the patient with ventilations through an Ambu bag. I remember looking at how calm the paramedic was as his dark eyes watched the patient's chest rise and fall with each squeeze of the bag. The muscles on his forearms tensed as he pushed air into the patient's lungs. Everything seemed to slow, although in reality it was all happening in hyperspeed as everyone worked to save a life. I was transfixed by the scene and couldn't pull my gaze away until the patient's gurney rounded a corner and entered a private room.

I followed the doctor as he began to give orders to the nurses, instructing on what meds to push through the patient's IV, and I realized I needed to chart the times of administration and focus on the chart. I noticed as the paramedics left, and watched the man who had been ventilating the patient exit through the back door. He gave one last look back and our eyes connected briefly, before I turned back to the life saving interventions being performed in front of me.

The doctor I was working with did everything he could for the patient, but the man didn't make it. I had to chart the time of death for a heart attack patient for the first time since starting this job. I'd done other TOD charting, but none of them had been for a cardiac arrest yet. My fingers typed in the military time for the chart - TIME OF DEATH: 15:48.

My shift ended at 3:30 but went over slightly so I could finish with the code. My eyes were swimming with tears that threatened to spill over as I clocked out.

I kept thinking about my dad and how the medical staff did all they could for him when he had his heart attack. I wondered about this patient's family. *How are they doing? What will the next few weeks be like for them? What about the next few years?*

It's been years since my father's departure from this Earth, and I still feel an immense ache when I think about losing him. Despite what people say about time healing wounds, that type of pain just simply doesn't go away. It clings to a person like honey to a spoon, but much less sweet.

After I grabbed my things, I walked out the double doors making my way to the staff parking area. I remember the afternoon air feeling cool upon my flushed skin and how the tears silently streamed down my face, coming fast now that they had permission to flow freely. I was walking slowly. More of a shuffle, really. I was looking down at my feet, lost in the labyrinth of my own mind when there was a soft tap on my shoulder, and I turned to see the paramedic who had given the report on the cardiac patient.

"I'm sorry to bother you," he said. "My shift just ended after I dropped that patient off and I wanted to know how he is. I don't normally do this, but usually I have a few drop offs left and can check in on the status of past patients. I always like to know how they..." his words froze in his throat once he saw the tears on my face.

His handsome features immediately took on an expression of comprehension. "Aw, no," he said in a sad tone. "I'm sorry...are you new to the ER? The first death is really hard. Do you want to talk about it?"

I recall wanting to tell him that this isn't my first death. Not even close. It's just the one that reminded me most of my dad. Instead I say, "yeah, I'm new. I started a week ago."

He nodded with understanding, and said, "my name is

Avery."

"I'm Cora."

That was three years ago. Now, I can't imagine my life without him.

❋ ❋ ❋

I snap back from my memories just as I pull up to Kate's gate. I enter the code and it slowly swings open. As I wait for the gate, I realize that I wasn't even paying attention as I drove here. I was fully on autopilot.

How can I drive all that way inside my own thoughts, barely registering the things around me, and still make it here safely? It's startling. I need more sleep.

I sigh with the knowledge that I won't be getting the much needed rest tonight. After this, I'll be headed to my overnight shift. I yawn, and wonder if taking a nap would be better than studying right now.

No, it's best that I take the time to go over the information with Kate and Mandy. I'm nervous for our exam and the quickly approaching clinicals where we will be actually providing nursing care as students. I *need* this time to study, I can't slack off.

I take a deep breath as I park my silver Subaru, gather my things, and swing the car door open. I walk up to Kate's front door, and let myself in. I've been coming here since middle school and it feels like home.

"Coraaa, is that you?" Kate calls down from upstairs.

"Yeah!" I respond as I drop my work bag and start taking off my shoes at the door, then shoulder my backpack full of study notes and climb the stairs. Kate is in the study, which is a huge office/library off to the right. It has a full wall of floor to ceiling books and a ladder that glides along. It's basically every bibliophile's dream.

Too bad Kate doesn't read anything other than the

required nursing textbooks. I can't say I have much ability to read either these days. Nursing school takes up all my time and the thought of reading for fun on top of all our assignments makes me cringe. Then, I realize I literally stole a journal from the 90s to read in my spare time and cringe again.

I take a seat in a plush gray velvet chair next to Mandy at the big cherry wood table. She already has her Fundamentals of Nursing text opened up and her multicolor highlighter out. Nikki is here too, she looks up from her phone and greets me with a smirk. Her platinum blonde hair is pulled up in a messy bun, and the small diamond stud on the side of her nose catches the light and twinkles.

Nikki is pretty in a grunge type of way, and even though she is still wearing the same clothes she had on last night, evidence that she hasn't gone home yet and didn't remember to pack a change of clothes, she still manages to look like her appearance was artistic and purposeful. Even the eyeliner that rims her big hazel eyes looks like it was meant to be smoky and messy rather than remnants from the night before.

"Hey," I say to everyone as I drag my eyes from Nikki, and pull my laptop and books from my bag.

"Glad you're finally here, now we can talk about what happened last night," Kate says as she shifts in her chair and pulls her knees up to her chest. She slides her laptop toward her on the table. "I googled cop cars and finally found one that looked like what we saw disappear. It is from the 1950's like that ghost story that Mandy found," she turns the laptop screen to face me with a photo of an outdated cop car that does seem to closely resemble what we saw speed by last night. "So, I think that kinda clinches it. We saw something paranormal."

"There is no such thing as ghosts," Nikki says as she rolls her eyes.

"How would you know that for a fact? You can't prove that, and after what we all saw, I think it's weird that you're so against it," Mandy responds, crossing her arms defensively.

"There has to be an explanation. It's not like that story

isn't accessible to everyone. You found it online, so anyone could have seen that. Maybe some weirdo thinks it's funny to drive an old police car up there just to fuck with people."

"Nope. I'm not buying that," Kate counters. "Something strange happened. No physical car could have sped by like that and then vanished like it did. That was something supernatural, and clearly other people have experienced similar things." Kate suddenly turns her bright gaze to me, "what do you think, Cora?"

"Ummm." I say as I stare at the picture on the screen. "I don't know what to think. Both of you have valid points." I feel uncomfortable under everyone's stares. Kate and Nikki have always had a strange relationship. They are friends through Leo, who introduced us all to Nikki years ago. He became close with her in his photography class freshman year of college, and she's been a part of our group since. Mandy always takes Kate's side, so I often feel like Nikki's only female ally in situations like this one.

"You're just being nice Cora, you always do this. You know you saw something that can't be explained but you don't want to hurt Nikki's feelings," Mandy insists.

The tension in the room creates an awkwardness among us.

"I really don't know what to think. We smoked and drank, and honestly it all happened so quickly and it was dark out..." I trail off, my feelings of discomfort growing and making me feel itchy. I just wish they would drop it.

"Yeah, you're right. I don't think we will prove anything by a Google search," Kate says with an expression of disappointment. "But I wanted to show you that photo. It's just such a weird thing to have happened, and I can't stop thinking about it. I really do believe it was something supernatural," Kate says stubbornly, "and isn't it a weird coincidence that the diary Leo had has gone missing, too?"

I freeze, feeling guilty.

"He probably just misplaced it, or Noah accidentally put

it down somewhere when we got out of the car and forgot," Nikki says dismissively. "Or are you suggesting the ghost came and stole it? Maybe the paranormal cop was speeding to try and arrest Leo for taking it?"

"You're being rude," Mandy replies coolly, defending Kate against Nikki.

"Um, actually, I have the diary," I confess, with a wince. "I forgot to hand it back when we pulled up to your house. I could give it back to him?" I offer, wishing I hadn't said anything.

"Seriously? Leo freaked out when he thought it disappeared," Kate laughs. "I'm not going to tell him you have it yet, let him try to figure out where it went for a while and see what ideas he comes up with. He is serious about this paranormal stuff right now."

From the corner of my eye, I can see Nikki shift in her chair uncomfortably.

"Anyway, we should probably start on this studying," Kate says, as she opens an orange cylinder with pills rattling inside and palms two small bright blue circles. She pops the pills into her mouth and takes a sip of water.

Nikki stares at her, head tilted down and eyebrows raised.

"What? They're prescription," Kate says, holding the bottle forward with the label out that clearly marks her full name, birthdate and the title Adderall on the front.

"You know that stuff is basically one chemical away from Meth, right?"

"Don't think you're original with that comment, that's literally what almost everyone says when they find out I have a prescription. And no, you can't have any. That's the second most frequent comment. I don't share."

"Didn't want any," Nikki says, holding up her palms.

Kate follows her pills by popping a stick of gum in her mouth. She swears it helps her retain information better when she studies. Then she starts discussing the case notes we were presented in class and formulating NCLEX style questions for us to answer.

"You know we don't take the NCLEX until we graduate, right? Why are you so hung up on this test when it's our first semester?" Mandy asks, pushing up her reading glasses. "I'm more concerned about the first exam. Which shouldn't really be too bad since we've only been in school for a few weeks."

"In case you haven't noticed yet, all our exams are based on this test. Even now. The license exam is a beast and the sooner we prepare for it the better off we will be. It's all about learning the format so we can quickly figure out the correct answer. Usually, all the answers presented will technically be right in their own way, but it's about deciding which one is the MOST RIGHT and what you would perform as a nurse FIRST, and you need to know that quickly. Wouldn't it suck if you answer all your NCLEX questions correctly but take too long and run out of time? You need to be able to choose the right answer and move on, not be stuck staring at the question. It's like that in life too, we need to make the right choice fast as an RN if we want the best care for our patients. I'm setting us up for that."

"Preach" I say, still looking down at my notes.

"Damn, that Addy kicked in fast for you," Mandy teases.

Kate reaches over and playfully smacks her arm. "I just take this all really seriously."

Nikki scooches her chair back and stands from the table. "I need to head out. I have work and still have to go home and change. Thanks for having me over, Kate, and for breakfast."

We all say bye to her and confirm our Thursday meetup plans at the Wheelhouse Bar for drinks later this week. Then, the room falls quiet as we flag questions to quiz each other with. I can hear Nikki's combat boots clunking on the stairs as she descends to the first floor.

"That was awkward. Why do we even invite her to things?" Mandy asks.

"Leo always invites her. I'm not going to say no.

Honestly, I would rather have them hang around with us in a group than on their own. I think she likes him." Kate answers in a flat tone as her eyes trace over her notes.

"I like Nikki. I think there is definitely some tension between you two, though," I say.

"Yeah. I wish she was still dating Noah. Maybe she just needs a good lay," Mandy says with a smirk.

"Don't we all?" Kate adds.

* * *

We spend the next two hours asking one another questions we think will appear on our first exam and practicing how to give a proper nursing report on a patient. My mind is mush by the end of our study session, but I feel much more prepared for the week.

It's 4:00 PM and I have two hours to get some coffee, a snack, and drive myself to work. I gather my things and say bye to Mandy and Kate, giving them both hugs.

Mandy doesn't look like she is leaving Kate's anytime soon. She will probably spend the entire week here, especially since they have this house to themselves. Mandy has basically lived over here unofficially since we were thirteen and Kate and I met her in 8th grade. Growing up, Mandy lived in a rundown trailer park, and was raised by a single Mom, who had little money and was rarely home. She doesn't have siblings, and over time Kate and I became like her sisters.

Kate and I would often share our clothes, makeup, and jewelry with her. There have been so many sleepovers together over the years, so many shared memories. In highschool, we would chant the song *"we're the three best friends that anyone could have"* from the movie The Hangover. We still do sometimes.

With these thoughts, my mind flashes back to the diary, and how Heather wrote about her friends being like her real family. I can relate to those feelings.

CHAPTER 9:

I get in my car and drive away feeling tired but content despite my fatigue. I decide to skip the first two classes in the morning tomorrow, and only come in for the exam at the end of the day. I need sleep. Working a night shift won't allow that, so I'll have to sacrifice Intro to Nursing, and Pathophysiology classes today. Mandy and Kate both said they will send me their notes, thankfully.

I reach a red light and glance at my phone to see that Avery has texted me saying he is starting his shift soon. I let him know I am on my way to mine, too. We will probably see each other at some point tonight.

I arrive at Cross Hospital Emergency Department feeling my lack of sleep from last night all the way down in my bones. I gulped down a Starbucks iced venti quad shot coffee on the way, but all it has done is make me feel jittery, and I'm still tired. It tasted good though, so I guess that counts for something.

I toss my ice filled cup into a trash can, and then use my badge to unlock the door leading into the ER. A rush of coldness from the air conditioning hits me, along with a strong antiseptic smell. I hear the song of beeping equipment and IV pump alarms going off accompanied by the squeak of non-skid shoes as a nurse rushes past.

I make my way to the break room and scan myself in

with my badge. I put my bag down on the back counter, where there are a couple nurses eating boxed salads nearby.

I still have ten minutes until I can log in and report to work, so I take a seat at a nearby table and pull out my phone to scroll through Instagram. As soon as I start scrolling my feed, I think about how I'm looking forward to disconnecting for the next 12 hours. Social media is so useless. I won't have my phone with me once I start my shift, and I'm glad for it.

It's almost 6 PM, so I leave the break room and go to the row of computers surrounded by glass in the middle of the ER. We call it the "Fishbowl." It allows Scribes to sit with their assigned Doctor for the shift and chart while still being able to observe the happenings in the ER.

I scan my badge at the computer to clock in, and I'm excited to see that I am paired with Dr. Sherman tonight. She's my favorite Doc to work with. She's young, sharp, and relatable, which can't be said for all the physicians I've been assigned to. Some are mean, impatient, and suffer from burnout.

I organize my notebook and make sure I have enough pens in my pocket to get through the night. Nurses are notorious for "borrowing" pens and then forgetting to return them. I don't mind, I know they are busy, but I make sure I am well stocked before leaving the Fishbowl.

I notice that my friend, Amy, is also scribing tonight. She is paired with Dr. Lopez, another doc who is fun to work with. Amy scoots over to me so that she is at the computer next to mine and scans herself in. She is a couple years older than me, and has been scribing for a few years longer than I have. She's really great at her job, and was a huge source of information and tips for me when I first started.

"Hey Cora, how's it going?"

"I'm super tired, but otherwise good."

"If you need a boost, I have an energy drink in my bag that you can have," she offers.

"Thanks, but I already drank a quad shot from Starbs

and think I would be tweaking out if I had any more caffeine at this point," I reply with a laugh.

"Oh, yeah. That wouldn't be good. I had too much caffeine last shift and felt so shaky."

Our doctors still haven't shown up in the Fishbowl yet, so we continue to sit and talk while waiting for them to pop in and begin seeing patients. Amy and I are discussing our favorite downtown Sacramento brunch spots when Dr. Sherman breezes in with a coffee in one hand and her work briefcase in the other.

"Cora, Cora, how I adore ya," she says in a singsong voice. "I hope you had a good weekend and are ready for tonight. I think the first patient we are going to go see is this one with ear pain in 12," she states while tapping my computer screen with a short unpainted fingernail. She is pointing to the name Feeney, Linda, and I jot the info down in my notebook.

"Sounds good," I respond with a smile, "I'm ready."

* * *

We approach the patient's room and Dr. Sherman does a brief knock on the door to announce our presence, and then enters the room. I follow behind silently as she explains to the patient who she is, and introduces me as her Scribe. She explains that I will be taking notes for her, and then she asks the patient to describe what has brought her into the Emergency Department tonight.

The patient calmly sits in a chair with her purse in her lap clutched to her soft round belly that hangs over tight black leggings. Her flip flop clad feet are crossed at the ankles and her frizzy bleach blonde hair is pulled back into a messy ponytail at the nape of her thick neck.

"I got an earache on this side," she says, tapping her right ear with a long purple manicured nail.

"It started a day ago and it really hurts. I took some

Advil for it, but it didn't help none," she says in a husky voice suggestive of frequent cigarette smoking.

I begin writing her history down on the notebook paper under her name and room number. Her watery blue eyes flick to me when she sees my pen moving.

"Okay, have you had a fever?" Dr. Sherman asks as she cleans her hands with sanitizer and starts to put gloves on.

"I don't have a temperature taker at home, so I don't know," Feeney replies, shrugging her hunched over shoulders.

"Do you mind if I take a look?" Dr. Sherman asks, as she pulls down an otoscope from the wall and turns the light on at the end, preparing to shine it into the patient's ear and assess the issue. Feeney nods, and Dr. Sherman approaches to the right side and gently grasps the outside of the patient's ear and shines the light down into her ear canal. I stand across the room, watching the assessment.

Dr. Sherman's eyes are narrowed in concentration and then quickly widen in an expression of alarm. She gazes into the patient's ear for a moment more, and then withdraws the otoscope and clicks the light off. She pauses in thought for a moment and then says, "I have found a foreign body in your ear. I am going to get the supplies to remove it, and then be right back."

"A *what* in my ear? Huh?" the patient asks in puzzlement. Her pouchy eyes are squinted and her mouth hangs open revealing tobacco stained teeth.

"Something that doesn't belong. It happens sometimes. I think this is the cause of the pain. I will be right back," Dr. Sherman says. She gives me a pointed look as she makes for the door, and I follow behind her like a shadow.

We turn the corner and head down the hallway in silence and then Dr. Sherman calmly says to me, "that woman has a beetle in her ear."

"Excuse me, what?" I say with wide eyes.

"An earwig is in that patient's ear. You know, the bugs with little pinchers on the end? It's really more common than you think. I believe it's dead, but can't know for sure until I get it out. I'm going to grab some forceps and remove it."

"Wow. Never a dull moment."

"Uh huh. That patient looks relaxed enough, but I don't want to alarm her and tell her what is in there until I get it out. I don't want her panicking."

"Makes sense," I say, as I enter the supply room with Dr. Sherman and watch her gather up the things she needs. She smoothes her hair away from her face as she bends to grab one more tool from a low shelf of the supply room rack. Dr. Sherman straightens up and gives a little shudder. "Nasty little creatures, those earwigs," she mutters, "they love dark wet places. It's not the first time I've had to do this." She holds the door open for me to walk through, "shall we?"

We return to room 12 and Dr. Sherman quickly sets up and explains to the patient that she is going to extract the foreign body, and that it's very important for her to remain still.

I stand to the side and watch intently as Dr. Sherman removes the forceps from the pack and positions a magnifying light over the patient's ear. She pulls back the top to straighten the ear canal and steadily reaches in with the tweezers. Moments later, she pulls out a small elongated beetle and unceremoniously places it onto a tray. The bug isn't moving, so I think she was right about it being dead. The wilted legs are curled in upon itself but the hard shell shines and the pointed forked pincher on the back end glints under the bright hospital lights.

An uneasiness settles over me as I stare at the dead bug. I have the distinct feeling of being watched, but both Dr. Sherman and the patient are gazing elsewhere and there are no other people in the room. I suppress a shudder and try to focus on the scene in front of me.

Dr. Sherman then uses the otoscope again to examine the ear and determine if everything went successfully. Apparently, she is pleased with the results, because she replaces the scope on the wall holder and begins removing her gloves.

"All done," she notifies the patient, and comes around the front to face her. "A small beetle was removed from your ear canal. I believe that was the cause of the pain you've been experiencing and it should subside now. If you develop more pain, loss of hearing, discharge from the ear, or a fever, then contact your GP for antibiotics. A nurse will be in shortly to flush your ear."

The patient gasps and puts her hands on her head in shock. "WHAT?!" She blurts out in alarm. She turns and looks at the dead pincher bug. "That was in my ear?Oh Lord, oh my God." I can see the panic washing over the patient, as her skin pales and her breathing rate increases.

"Yes, but now it's not. You will be fine. This happens." Dr. Sherman reassures her.

I quietly exit the room as the doctor continues to calm the patient and goes over more discharge information. I go straight to my computer to put information into the chart and wrap everything up so she can be released home. A few minutes later, Dr. Sherman joins me and dictates what else she would like me to write about the interaction.

The Fishbowl has filled up since we first started the shift and other scribes and their partnered doctors are working together at computers nearby. We spend the next few hours visiting with multiple abdominal pain patients, a 5150 hold, a drunk man who needs to detox, a patient with a broken finger, and a little girl who needs stitches under her eye from a dog bite.

The hours fly by due to how busy we are, and our scheduled 45 minute break arrives quickly. I wonder where Avery has been delivering emergencies, because I haven't seen him at all this shift. It's common for us to run into one another a few times when we are both working, but apparently that's not the case for tonight.

Since Amy and Dr. Lopez started at the same time as us,

they are also scheduled for a break, and Dr. Sherman and I join them in the staff room. We all sit together at a round table and snack on the food we have brought.

"So, Amy, Cora, maybe you young ladies can help me with something. What does the term 'no cap' mean?" Dr. Lopez asks with her eyebrows raised.

I smile a little and respond "it basically means 'no lie' or 'for real,' my friend Noah says that all the time."

"Is this about that drunk patient you just had before break? The one you saw while I was in the bathroom?" Amy asks.

"Yes, he was a strange one. I mean, the intoxicated ones usually are. I just am not hip with the lingo these days and with you gone, I didn't have my trusty translator. Being in your sixties, like I am, and trying to deal with the young patients isn't always that easy. His friend was trying to describe the bar fight they had gotten in and said that someone bit the patient on the shoulder. Then, the friend said the phrase, 'no cap,' and I felt so confused. I just shook my head, examined the man's shoulder, and then prescribed him antibiotics, of course. Human bites are infections waiting to happen," Dr. Lopez says and then goes on to describe the shoulder wound. "It was like Hannibal got hungry or something. No cap." She pauses with a mischievous glint in her eyes, " Did I use it right?" She asks, grinning broadly.

Dr. Sherman finds this extremely funny and starts laughing.

"Yes, you're basically part of Gen-Z now," I say.

Dr. Lopez winks, and Amy and I exchange amused looks.

"The fact that we can sit here and eat while talking about wounds really says something about us," Dr. Sherman points out with a chuckle and then takes a large bite out of her ham and cheese sandwich.

We spend the rest of our break snacking and discussing random patient encounters, omitting any identifiable information so we don't violate HIPAA. Sharing these stories is always a highlight of hospital breaks. The time flies by, and we clean up our wrappers at the table and head out of the break room to return to the last half of the shift.

Moments after logging back into my computer, I hear the siren of an approaching ambulance and Dr. Sherman notifies me that a trauma is coming in. We will be meeting the first responders at the drop off zone. We stand at the back doors and wait as the sirens get louder, shrieking into the still night air.

The ambulance pulls to an abrupt stop and the rear opens. A coldness quickly descends over me and my heart plummets when I see who is emerging beside the gurney.

Avery looks up at me, and he is covered in blood.

CHAPTER 10:

Avery's eyes are wide and sweat dots his hairline, shimmering in the overhead lights as he pulls the gurney forward. Crimson blood covers his uniform and slathers his gloved hands.

A man with a scraggly gray beard is on the gurney, his skin has a yellow quality and his grimy hands are bunched around the blanket that covers him. The man's mouth hangs open and blood stains the few teeth that he has, jutting up from his gums like crooked tombstones. Bloody rivulets drip down his chin and more is smeared across his face in patchy crusts. His eyes are wide and unfocused, and a round green circle sticks out one of his nostrils, indicating that he has a nasopharyngeal airway placed.

Avery promptly begins his report on the patient to Dr. Sherman as we hurry to bring the man to a room and assess him further.

"Patient is of unknown name and age. We were dispatched to the scene after a call came in from a driver reporting a man stumbling along the road holding his bleeding stomach. Upon assessment, it was a clear abdominal evisceration, and we covered the protruding organs with gauze soaked in sterile saline, established an IV in his right forearm, administered O2, and made sure his airway is stable. He's been in and out of consciousness and received some O neg blood."

As Avery continues reporting, Dr. Sherman peels back the blanket slowly to examine the wound. I lock eyes on the site, and my stomach clenches. Bright ruby blood continues to ooze forth through the wet gauze. A few feet of the small intestine can be visualized beneath the nearly transparent dressings sitting as a mound on top of the patient's lap like long strings of coiled sausage.

There must have been a bowel perforation, as food particles and brown feces can be seen sticking to the bandages and the smell is thick and rank as it mingles with the coppery stench of blood. I gag, and dig a fingernail into one of my palms to focus my attention on something other than the graphic scene in front of me.

"He needs to go to surgery STAT," Dr. Sherman says and gives orders to the nurses to begin further stabilizing treatments. She immediately gets to work on getting the patient transferred to the operating room, as multiple nurses flood the room, hooking the patient up to various monitors and hanging IV bags.

I notice one RN struggling to contain her nausea as the sour fecal smell intensifies within the small room. I don't want to be in the way, so I lock eyes with Dr. Sherman and point a finger toward the computer area, she understands that I am signaling my departure and nods permission before turning her gaze back to her extended patient assessment.

I hurry from the room, and glance around but Avery has already left the Emergency Department and his ambulance is no longer parked outside the double doors. I can't shake his haunted wide-eyed look from my mind, or the image of his arms covered in glistening fresh blood.

I am eager to talk to Avery, but we both still have a few more hours in our shifts, and my phone is currently tucked away in the break room. I am still nauseous as I type up the chart for the unknown patient.

Dr. Sherman joins me at my computer a few minutes later. She looks frazzled. She fills me in on the man's status, and

I wrap the chart up. He is in surgery now, and the outcome is out of her hands. She doesn't think he will survive his injuries, though, and I can tell the knowledge of that is troubling her.

The rest of the shift goes by in a somber blur. Dr. Sherman is in a mood, and looks pale. I let her process her emotions and keep myself busy, only talking when chart clarification is needed. When 6 AM rolls around and it's time to clock out, I am incredibly relieved.

I collect my things and drag myself to my car. The cold early morning air helps to slightly wake me up, and I blast music as I drive home to keep my eyes from getting too heavy.

I pull up to my apartment and practically run to the front door. Once inside, I quickly strip my hospital scrubs off and toss them into a hamper, then start the shower. When the steam starts to collect in my bathroom, I get in to rinse away the heavy feelings from the shift and make the water as hot as I can stand. As I step out of the shower, my skin is pink and clean and I briskly dry off. The sensation of the fluffy towel against my skin is soothing, and I feel slightly better from the comforts of home.

I cross the room to slip under the sheets, and lay my head down on my pillow, not even caring that my hair is getting the case wet. I realize that Kate and Mandy are probably on their way to our first class of the day just as I am crawling into bed.

Despite washing with extra hot water, I still fall asleep with dreams of blood and the smell of rust and rot lingering in my nose.

* * *

Not long after closing my eyes, my alarm goes off signaling that it is time for me to get up, get ready, and head to campus so I can make my afternoon class and take the exam. I roll out of bed, feeling somewhat more awake, but still tired. I vow to go to sleep early tonight and make up for the sleep debt

I am accumulating. I check my phone and see that Avery has messaged a couple hours ago letting me know he got home safe and would catch up with me after he wakes up. I sigh, and try to push the vivid memories of last night from my mind.

I start going through the motions of getting ready, throw on a baggy Nirvana t- shirt, some black leggings, and then pile my long blonde hair on top of my head in a messy bun. I slip my feet into my Chuck Taylors, and grab my school bag before walking out the door.

The traffic on the way to campus isn't bad at this time of day, and I make it there in less time than I expected. Finding a place to park is trickier, and I circle the campus for a few minutes before someone pulls out of a spot, allowing me to finally park. I got lucky, the parking spot search can take hours sometimes.

I grab my phone, and text Kate. She replies right away and tells me to meet her and Mandy at the campus coffee shop.

I enter the shop called The Magic Bean, and savor the rich comforting aroma of coffee. It's an instant mood enhancer. I love this university coffee shop. There are others on campus, but this is our favorite. It has an upstairs area that is a bookstore, which is nice to browse when I have the time. Original art decorates the walls, and there are crystal balls and figurines of owls scattered around the store. I scan my surroundings, which is filled with students studying and chatting at tables. It's always crowded here in the afternoon, but I spot Mandy and Kate easily.

I walk toward my friends, who are seated at a small table in the corner under a large painting of a woman swimming naked in a pool filled with coffee. Twinkling coffee beans cover her nipples and private areas. Glitter is mixed into the paint used for the water, giving off an iridescent shimmer.

"Hey," I say as I drop my heavy bag to the floor and slide into the seat next to Kate. The overhead lights reflect off the table top, creating yellow orbs next to the lattes that are resting there on small black saucers.

"We ordered you a coffee," Kate says, as she scoots one toward me.

The drink sways inside the cup as it is slid on the table, the creamy white milk swirling to blend with the tan.

"Oh my gosh, you're my savior," I say as I reach down and grab the cup in both hands. I take a sip and delicious foam covers my top lip. I lick it away, savoring the sweetness."Thank you so much, I really needed this."

"Well, yeah. We figured. Didn't you just get off work a few hours ago? And after the night we had before…" Kate trails off.

I nod and take another drink. "Yeah. I'm exhausted. I just want to get this test done and end the day so I can sleep a full eight hours."

"I'm going to send you those notes right now from the classes earlier. You honestly didn't miss much. Just Professor Abbot going on and on about how to properly make a bed so that the corners look crisp. I can practically do it in my sleep at this point. I was trying not to yawn the entire time. Seriously, that woman has issues. I want to be a nurse to help save lives, not make military style beds."

I smile imagining Kate's face during this lecture. She has this specific pinched expression that she makes whenever she is not amused. I used to call it her "possum face" when we were kids. I always knew when she was biting her tongue about something because that expression would pop up.

"I agree with that statement," Mandy adds as she pushes her glasses up on her little nose, and tucks her hair behind her ear. Then, Mandy takes a drink of her latte, turns to me and says, "I have a crystal that should help you feel less tired."

She reaches a hand into the front of her shirt and comes out with a fist full of crystals in various sizes, colors, and shapes. She drops her handful on the table and selects a pale honey colored stone. "It's Citrine, perfect for an energy boost. You know, if you find the caffeine isn't cutting it." She hands it to me, and it's still warm to the touch from being near her body.

"Thanks," I say, as I hold the quarter sized stone in my hand and watch it reflect the light.

"Oh my gosh, were you keeping those in your bra?" Kate asks with her eyebrows raised.

"Yeah, they need to be close to skin, I keep a bunch in there during tests," Mandy states, shamelessly. "It works. I swear by it." She picks up a small stone with caramel bands of gold running through it. "This is my Tiger's Eye for focus, courage, and clarity." Mandy stares at it for a moment and then tucks it down into the front of her shirt again. "Oh, and my smoky quartz. I found this one recently…on a walk. I fell in love with it as soon as I saw it." She holds up a stormy looking crystal with swirls of black and gray through it and rotates it under the light. It looks like something is swirling and alive inside, like ink in water. It is stunning.

"Woah! That's so pretty," Kate says, reaching a hand out for the stone.

Mandy quickly slips the smoky crystal back into her top. "You already have my clear quartz for memory improvement, and mental organization. This one is special. Sorry, it will throw off my auric field if I give it to you," she says with an apologetic look. Then, she collects the few dark colored stones left and tucks them into her bra with the rest.

Kate just stares, her features unreadable. "Okay," she says and flips her shiny dark hair over her shoulder. She reaches into the front of her jeans pocket and takes out a clear crystal and tucks it into her bra. I shrug and tuck the citrine stone into my bra, too. "If people knew we were doing this, they would think we are nuts."

"Like we care?" Kate says with a grin. "Let's finish these coffees and then we need to go. Class starts in fifteen."

CHAPTER 11:

I completed the exam feeling confident in myself. We definitely over prepared for it, but I would much rather be ahead than behind. The crystal that Mandy had given me also probably worked as a placebo. It felt like a good luck charm and whenever I was stuck on something, I could feel it near my chest and was reassured. Although Mandy truly believes in the powers of her stones, I never have. Maybe I will rethink that if my test score comes out high.

The three of us exit the Nursing Program building and walk across campus toward the parking lot. They plan on going back to Kate's and invite me to join, but all I want to do is meet up with Avery and see how he is doing after last night at work.

I didn't mention anything about my shift to my friends, it still feels like a nightmare whenever I think of the guts spilled from the man's abdominal cavity like a mangled balloon animal. I feel nauseous when I remember the smell and the blood glistening on Avery's arms.

I dig my fingernail into my thumb to refocus my thoughts and distract myself from those memories as I say bye to Kate and Mandy and walk to my car.

I rub my eyes, which burn with fatigue, but the coffee I had is still pumping caffeine through me and my mind is awake. I pull my phone from my bag and call Avery. He answers after a couple rings.

"Hey."

"Hey," I reply, "are you doing ok?"

"Yeah. I'm fine. Just woke up a while ago and had some food. How was your exam?"

I smile, I love that Avery always remembers the little things. Even when he has had a crazy overnight shift, he still remembers what is going on with me.

"It was good. I think I aced it."

"Well, that's not a surprise. What's your plan for the rest of the day?"

I tell him I just want to go home and rest and ask if he wants to join. He says he can be there in about an hour, which is perfect, because I want a little time to read some more of Heather's diary without any interruptions.

When I get back to my apartment, I drop my bag by the door and immediately settle in on my couch with a glass of water and the diary on my lap.

I open it up, and flip through the first couple pages to where I left off.

* * *

September 20, 1997

This week hasn't been a good one for me. I haven't even had the energy to write in this journal over the last few days. I'm so grateful that it's almost the weekend again.

My thoughts have been dark lately. Shane is still bugging me every chance he gets. I try to ignore it, but it's constant. Like, he stuck gum in my hair on Tuesday morning as he passed me in the hall. He stuck it right in the middle of the back of my head.

I waited until lunch time, then I walked up to his table, reached back, and cut the chunk of hair out with scissors. Then I tossed the hairy gum into his food. It landed right on top of a pool of grease in the center of his pizza slice.

I glared daggers at him the entire time. If my looks could kill, Shane would have fucking choked on his food and died. But they don't and he didn't. Instead, he just smiled at me, totally unphased. His friends were laughing and saying I was going to cast a spell on him. Maybe I will. I hate him so much.

I wish I could make him pay. I WILL make him pay.

Now I have a bunch of hair hacked off in the back of my head, and what I did didn't even affect him. I have been wearing my hair in a ponytail since this incident, and I don't even like ponytails. Maybe if I tell Mom, she can help me get it fixed but I don't even know how to bring it up to her. She will make it a WAY bigger deal than it is and try to get involved. That's the last thing I want. So, ponytails it is.

On top of the Shane sitch, my mom has been on my case about how I dress again. If she knew how much this pushes me away maybe she would stop. I've tried to tell her, but she never listens. I will never be like her precious Jessica, so calm and pure. So innocent. So loved.

This is part of the reason I haven't told my mom about what's happening with Shane at school. I know it will reflect poorly on me in her eyes, even though it's actually her and dad's fault that Shane hates me.

I wonder if Liv's mom could help me with my hair? I'll have to look into that. I need to ask when she's not drunk, though. The thought of her trying to cut my hair after tipping the bottle is a scary one. She can barely keep her eyes open sometimes.

In happier news, after school today, Liv and I rode our bikes to a nearby bookstore that has grimoires and books of spells. If I could live in a store, it would be this one.

I grabbed some stuff on the Occult. My mom would totally freak out if she knew I was researching into black magic, but I want to punish Shane and this seems like the best way. Also, I still can't stop thinking about the night we had in the woods last weekend, and I crave the chance to try and contact the spirit realm again.

In the book I got, there are spells for revenge. Liv said she would try them with me, and if she is going to, I am sure that Tasha will, too. We have plans to go back to Dyer Lane tomorrow with the board and to try some stuff...maybe we can contact Alice again.

There is something there in that place. Something more than just a random spirit. Something dark...something I want to explore more.

* * *

I pause and take a sip of water. I feel like I am reading a fictional story about a young troubled girl who was bullied and lacked parental trust and guidance. I have to remind myself that this was an actual person writing down her real experiences. At least I think it is. Maybe it really is fiction? Maybe she was creating a story? There is something very readable about her writing...but it still makes my stomach knot uncomfortably.

I feel worried for Heather, whoever she was. It seems like she is creating a persona to protect herself from the pain she feels and she is going deeper and deeper down a bad path. I continue on to the next entry, hoping things get better, but I have a feeling that they won't.

* * *

September 22, 1997

Holy shit. We did it. We contacted the spirit realm again last night.

We convinced Cole to give us a ride to Dyer Lane. He picked us up from the arcade by Tasha's house and dropped us off right before nightfall.

It was better to explore the area with a little more light, and this time we dressed warm and brought flashlights and our grimoires. Liv also had a bag with candles, matches, chalk, the Ouija board, and an ornate ritual knife. It is really pretty, she got it at the spell shop along with our occult books.

The woods were so peaceful and quiet. I love it there. It just feels right. It's the perfect place for us to practice our craft. We found the dirt path off the main road and followed it all the way down to the shed we went to last time. It's basically ours now. We have claimed it.

Tasha lit the candles around us in a circle, and we drew an upside down Pentagram symbol in the middle with some chalk, and lit a candle inside of it. We got the board out and crowded around it, trying to talk with the spirit of Alice again. We summoned her quickly, as if she was as eager to talk with us again as we were to with her. I asked if she was the same one we met before and she said YES. I asked if there were more spirits around us, and she said YES.

Liv asked if the spirit was good or bad. The planchette went back and forth between YES and NO. Which makes sense, because is anyone really only just one or the other?

Then, we asked what it was like to be dead and the planchette traced out the letters C-O-L-D. We all looked at each other for a moment. It actually felt like the room became colder after the spirit said that. Then, Liv asked her to prove she was real. Nothing happened for a moment, then one of the doors on the cabinet against the back wall flew open and slammed shut three times.

Tasha looked shocked with wide eyes, I think she was scared, but Liv and I couldn't stop smiling. I have a feeling Alice's spirit is trapped here, and maybe we can help her. I also think there are many more spirits, too. I want to know more.

After the cabinet door slammed, we were all excited to ask the board more questions. I was feeling euphoric in our ability to converse with the otherside. We were about to ask another question when Shane and his friend Chris came and ruined it all.

Those assholes kicked the shack door in, practically ripping it off the hinges. It reminded me of a ragged hangnail the way it was hanging off the frame. I saw red. How dare he come here and trash our sanctuary.

I screamed at Shan as he and his friend started spraying silly string at us and yelling lame things like, "witches are bitches."

Who even says stuff like that? One of them sprayed the silly string too close to one of our candles and the sleeve of Liv's shirt caught on fire. Apparently, the aerosol from the can is flammable. Idiots.

Tasha jumped up and wrapped her sweater around Liv's burned skin and quickly snuffed out the flames. Liv's arm was red and glistening under her charred sleeve. Everyone was screaming and I was repeatedly pushing Shane hard in the chest trying to get him to leave.

It was total chaos. The boys finally ran out laughing, not even caring that they had hurt Liv. We could hear the rev of their motorcycles starting as they sped away back toward the main road. And just like that, our perfect gathering spot felt tainted and our ideal day was ruined.

I don't know how much Shane and Chris saw, or how they found us out there. They must have been following us or something when we got picked up at the arcade by Cole and then dropped off at Dyer. I was so angry but also relieved that Liv's arm was mostly alright. She was definitely burned, but nothing that wouldn't heal on its own in time. Luckily, the thick sleeve of Liv's sweater had protected most of her skin and Tasha had put it out quickly for her, but her arm was still pretty red.

When we walked out of the cabin, we saw that the guys had strung three rope nooses from a nearby tree and left a note stabbed into the bark of the trunk saying "hang all witches."

I stared at the nooses swinging slowly from the branches, appearing to do a slow waltz in the breeze as they dangled in the air. If Shane thinks that calling me a witch will bother me, it doesn't. If anything it makes me want to delve deeper into the craft and learn more. He's lit a flame inside me, and the witch won't burn in this story.

I know there are spells you can cast to bring death upon someone. I want to find those. It's not evil to kill someone if they deserve it, right?

* * *

September 28, 1997:

Things got a little out of hand. I mean, they went according to plan, but I don't think we realized how complicated things could get. I just need somewhere to write it all down and get it out of my brain. It is haunting me. If anyone were to read this, I know I would be so screwed, but I just need to confess it somewhere. It feels cathartic to write. So, I won't leave anything out.

Last night, we did something bad...but it felt good. If something feels right at the time, can it really be all that wrong? I wish I actually had an adult I could talk about all of this with. I am so lost.

Anyway, this journal will have to do for now. Okay, here it goes...It all happened on Friday. Liv, Tasha and I had been carefully avoiding Shane and his friends all week...until yesterday. We wanted Shane to see us, and follow us. We had a plan.

We walked by the locker room area when we knew Shane was getting done with basketball practice and would be around that area. He noticed us right away and yelled some comment about how "witches are meant to be burned, or hung." You know, typical Shane bullshit.

We ignored him, and it made him mad. Of course he wanted a reaction. He stormed after us saying more disgusting things about us being "sluts," and that we will "get what we deserve."

If he only knew.

We continued to ignore Shane as we got on our bikes and rode toward Dyer Lane. He followed behind us stopping to pick up rocks, which he chucked at our backs as we pedaled away from him. The rocks that Shane threw pinged off our bags and the wheels of our bikes. One hit me on my left shoulder, leaving behind a sharp sting all the way to the bone. I just clenched my teeth as tears filled my eyes, and kept moving forward.

It took us over an hour of riding to get there and by the time we reached the start of the road, the sun was almost fully set. Shane was persistent and kept pace a few yards behind us, slowed down by his constant collecting of stones to chuck. He was alone, which was exactly what we had hoped for.

Once we got deeper onto Dyer Lane we picked up our pace to keep some distance between us. It was fully dark by then and a dense fog had rolled in and coated the space between the trees. Shane revved his bike and lagged behind us as we pushed ourselves to ride faster. My legs burned, and I was relieved when we came to the turn off for the shed. The three of us swiveled sharply and veered onto the side road.

Shane wasn't expecting this, and missed the turn. I heard his bike screech as he slammed the brakes to turn around and follow us. I couldn't see his motorcycle but I could hear it gaining behind us and see the light bouncing off of the oaks looming ahead.

We were taking turns at reckless speeds and flying down the dirt path until we saw two small orange flags placed on either side of the trail, which marked our stopping point. We quickly swerved off the road and hid ourselves behind dense bushes. Luckily, the darkness and fog hid our movements well.

We stayed huddled close and waited as his motorcycle rumbled closer. I remember feeling the adrenaline pulsing through me like a living thing as Shane approached. My heart was racing and I didn't want to blink and miss the results of our plan. It was so sudden, that I think if I had let myself close my eyes for even a moment, I would have missed it.

Shane was smiling up until the very moment the piano wire hit his throat at the level of his Adam's apple and his head flipped back like a Pez dispenser.

Shane was thrown like a ragdoll in the air. A flying trail of crimson followed behind him, spraying the nearby tree trunks. He didn't know about the thin metal wire we had hung with care between the trees earlier in the day. What a surprise that must have been for him.

The three of us ran out from behind the brush and stood over his body. Shane's mouth was opening and closing like a fish out of water, and blackish blood gurgled forward. All I could think of was the chocolate fondue fountains that I've shared with my family for dessert when we ate at The Melting Pot restaurant. His blood rippled forward, endlessly, and dark. I stared as a bubble rose between his lips and then burst, leaving a deep ruby foam behind.

Liv glared down at him and said in a flat voice, "look who got hung." When I looked up, I almost didn't recognize her. Liv's eyes were empty of any emotion. I looked at Tasha, who was shaking and staring at the blood painted trees with a vacant expression. Shane's eyes were so wide I could see a perfect white circle around his irises, like an animal caught in a snare. He basically was.

His head was held on by a ragged string of flesh and had been almost fully severed from his body. I saw frayed remains of blue veins and thick arteries peeking through the thick flowing blood. There was an area that squirted like a fountain in a rhythm, as it pulsed along with his dying heart.

It didn't take long for Shane to bleed out. His body jerked a few times as life left him. I couldn't move my eyes away. I know a normal person would feel remorse and fear, but in that moment all I felt was relief and power.

Suddenly, Liv appeared next to me with a small rusty axe. I have no idea where she even found it. It must have been packed in her backpack with all the other supplies. She pushed her sleeves up her arms and then began to hack through the remaining tatters of skin and bone that held Shane's skull to his body.

Liv finally sliced through, and his severed head rolled to the side and came to rest against the toe of Tasha's boot. Her breaths were coming in harsh gasps as she began to panic. Liv told her that if she screamed, she would be sorry. It was clear to me that Tasha was traumatized. The sad part is, I didn't even care. I felt as numb as I always pretend to be.

Liv instructed us to each grab a side of Shane's body and haul him up so that he was at an incline and she could collect the remaining blood that was left in him in the bucket she held. I don't know where she got that either. Liv must have come back yesterday and brought more stuff after we set up the flags and wire. She must have had a plan of her own.

There was so much blood. On the ground and trees, dripping into the bucket like syrup, on our hands and clothes, caked into our hair...I glanced up at Liv who was completely occupied watching the bucket fill and when she flashed her eyes up to mine I saw that they were full white. She had no pupils, as if her eyes had rolled into the back of her head, or like someone had filled her sockets with Elmer's glue. I was so startled that I almost dropped Shane's corpse, but I somehow managed to hang on.

The sludgy trail of blood started to slow, and Liv reached up to the severed vessels hanging from his neck and started to milk them, trying to get every last drop she could. The bucket was almost full by the time we set Shane's body back down on the ground.

Liv reached her fingers into the bucket and then lifted them slowly to her mouth and sucked the blood off. I thought of Billy Loomis in Scream, the movie we have watched together a million times. I thought of the moment in the movie when Billy sucked the fake blood off his fingers. It was like that, but this was real. Fear hit me square in the chest. The suppressed remorse mingled with the realization that I was scared.

Liv continued to dip her fingers hungrily into the bucket and then bring them back up to her lips. She was continually lapping Shane's blood off her fingers, as Tasha and I watched in disbelief. Then, she smiled at me and her teeth were stained a deep shade of red. I screamed.

I heard the smack to my face before I felt the sting of her palm. Liv had reached out to slap me so quickly, I didn't even register it at first. I lifted a bloody hand up to my cheek. It burned from the blow. I knew I had to stay quiet, or else I may end up like Shane.

When I glanced at Tasha, she looked like something had broken inside of her. Her lips were clenched into a tight line, her face was sheet white, sweat dampened her hair, and she was clearly holding in a scream of her own.

Before I could point it out, Liv's eyes had returned to

normal, but I knew what I saw and that her eyes had been different just moments before. I also noticed that the burn on Liv's arm was fully healed. There wasn't one blemish left, which is impossible after the blisters I had seen beginning to form only days ago.

I had so many questions but I kept them to myself as we worked to wrap Shane's headless body in a sheet. Once he was contained, Liv instructed Tasha and I to pull the sheet across the ground toward the shed we had been at last weekend. We moved slowly because his body was so heavy, even without blood. Liv followed behind Tasha and I. She was carrying Shane's head by the hair, and the bucket of his blood in her other hand.

We dragged Shane's body up to the doorway, which still had the door hanging by one hinge. Liv stepped up and set the bucket and head down and ripped the rest of the door from the frame. Then she took it inside and propped it against a wall. We followed her in, leaving the wrapped up body outside. Im not sure any of us had thought through our plan past killing him...I didn't know what would become of his body.

The inside of the cabin was exactly how we left it last weekend. The upside down pentagram on the ground was still there and Liv lit some of the candles that we had left behind to cast some light. Then, she dipped her pointer finger into the bloody bucket again, and every muscle in my body tensed with the fear that she was going to drink it, but instead she traced over the pentagram drawing.

When this happened, the blood glistened in the dim glow of the candles and the wind picked up outside, so that the shed shook forcefully around us. Tasha cried. Not a soft silent cry, but an actual wail. Liv started laughing. I didn't know what to do so I just stood there trying to wipe the sticky blood from my trembling hands onto my pants.

Then, the candles went out all at once and we were in total darkness, and a voice spoke from Liv that wasn't her own. It was throaty and sharp and made me feel cold. It spoke in a language I didn't know, and it seemed to fill the small cabin. It seemed to fill my entire skull.

A hissing sound vibrated through the room and the pentagram outline in blood lit up and caught fire. I can still see the blazing symbol if I pause my writing of this and close my eyes. It is seared into my eyelids even now.

As the flames glowed, time slowed to a crawl, and some of the fear left my body. I felt powerful due to my proximity to Liv, or whatever was inside of her.

As the chanting grew in volume, Liv began to violently shake forward and back so that her head snapped to her chin and then was thrown back repeatedly. I was worried she would break her neck, but when I tried to move toward her to stop her head from whipping like that, I found that I couldn't move. My body was paralyzed. I was frozen in place unable to blink or close my eyes to the terror in front of me.

Then, it all stopped as suddenly as it began. The room was so quiet that my ears were ringing. The fire went out along with the candles and I slowly lifted my arm in relief that I could move again. I relit the candles so we could see and Liv began to speak again. Her voice had returned to normal, and she told us everything.

Liv explained how she came back to this shed a couple nights ago on her own with her Occult book and summoned a spirit. She wanted to find a way to punish Shane. A spirit answered her. He told her that he had been here, waiting for us all along. He promised he could help us, and make us more powerful than we ever thought possible. All he needed was a special vessel. She said that we could all be under the spirit's protection, and that he lived inside her now. We could belong to him.

We sealed our deal with blood.

* * *

I can feel my heart hammering in my chest. What did I just read? It's like I just looked over a screenplay for an American Horror Story episode. *What the fuck.*

I read the last line a couple more times and goosebumps rise on my arms. Suddenly, the front door opens and I tense. I relax when I see that it's Avery. He's holding a big brown paper grocery bag in one arm and a bottle of wine in the other. "Thought we could make some dinner," he says with a grin.

"What's on the menu?" I ask as I run a hand through my hair, trying to act natural despite the frantic dance my heart is performing inside my chest.

"Spaghetti and garlic bread, with a salad."

"Yum," I say, attempting to sound bright, but it comes out flat. I walk into the kitchen to help Avery unload the bag, placing the various ingredients on the counter. I notice he has packed his famous homemade spaghetti sauce in a container. I hold it up at him, "you know how much I love this," I say, managing a weak smile, as I try to keep my hands from shaking.

"I do. I had this night all planned out. We just have to heat that up," he replies as he reaches into a cabinet to take out a saucepan and places it on the stove top.

I hand Avery the cold container of sauce and he opens it, dumping it into the pan before turning to me and saying, "what's wrong?"

His eyebrows are furrowed as he stares at my face trying to read my expression. Damn it. He's so perceptive, which is normally a good thing, but I am still processing what I read, and not sure I feel like relaying it right now. It's probably not even real, and I feel physically and emotionally exhausted from the last few days.

"Am I really that obvious?" I ask, feeling slightly defeated that I wasn't able to better conceal how I was feeling.

"You look pale and your hands are shaky."

I let out a nervous laugh. "Really? Don't I always look pale, though?"

Avery rolls his eyes. "And whenever you're upset you chew on the inside of your bottom lip," his eyes flick down to my mouth, "like you're doing right now."

I immediately stop biting the inside of my cheek and force my mouth into a closed lip smile, and crinkle my nose at him. "Well, aren't you the modern day Sherlock Holmes?"

"Is this about the patient I brought in last night? Because we definitely do need to discuss that."

I sigh. "I mean, yeah, that was not a pleasant experience, but..." I let my words hang in the air as I try to think how best to start updating him on the journal. I remember him telling me he was interested to hear what I read in it, and to keep him informed...maybe the best way to do this is just have him read it himself.

Avery opens the bottle of wine with a *pop* and pours the crimson liquid into two long stemmed glasses. He hands me one, and I accept it gratefully and take a sip. Trying not to think of Liv drinking blood in the entry I just read. I cringe a little, but force myself to take a gulp, letting the wine warm and relax me. It has a pleasant spiciness to it, that helps steady me a little.

"I know that deaths rattle you sometimes," he starts, "and you know I always check up on my patient drop offs, and he did unfortunately die, but that was to be expected based on his condition."

I nod before having another long sip of wine as I take in his words.

"I know, I figured that would be the case. I don't think many people survive those types of wounds," I say softly.

I swirl the wine in my glass and look at it as it whirls around. *Red like blood.* I close my eyes and suppress a shudder. Avery looks concerned as he reaches up to place his hands on my upper arms and rubs them soothingly. "What else is the matter?"

"It's never easy to know a patient died...and seeing you covered in blood like that is something I hope to never experience again. It really scared me when you got out of the ambulance like that. I was afraid some of the blood was yours, and I always worry when you go to work that something could happen to you."

He silently takes in the words I am saying, and nods his understanding. "It's not the safest job, but you know it's only temporary until I get into med school and I am always cautious on our routes."

"I know," I murmur, leaning into him. I take a deep breath and then say, "I also read some more of that journal Leo found. I could try and explain it to you, but I think you should just read it yourself." After a moment add, "I would read it after you eat or you may lose your appetite."

Avery lifts his eyebrows at me, "Okay...I actually have a story for you that I want to share but also think it would be best for after we eat."

I mirror his expression and raise my eyebrows back at him. "Who are we?"

He lets out a chuckle and squeezes me a little tighter in his embrace. Then, we get to work on making the spaghetti, compartmentalizing what we want to discuss after. The act of simple cooking tasks feels calming as I chop some veggies for the salad, and Avery tends to the pasta. We refill our wine glasses as we cook, and have a relaxing buzz going by the time the food is ready.

Avery and I sit at the table and I compliment him on the garlic bread he made. He uses fresh garlic for the spread on top of a soft french roll that he bakes in the oven. His mom taught him to cook at a young age, just basic things, but he never eats frozen food at home and prefers to make things fresh. He doesn't even buy spaghetti sauce in a jar like I usually do. Instead, he pre-made it earlier in the day from scratch using San Marzano tomatoes. This is something I have always found endearing about him. I am not much of a cook and admire the joy he gets from making things.

I have at least two slices of garlic bread to myself, but can't bring myself to eat more than a couple bites of the spaghetti, even though it is my favorite.

The sauce is red like blood. Red wine. Red sauce. Red blood.

I try to push my intrusive thoughts away as I eat, but my stomach is upset after what I read. The color of everything mirrors Heather's writing too much for comfort.

After we clean up the kitchen together, we settle into the couch. I rest my legs over Avery's lap, and turn to face my body toward his, "okay, you tell me your effed up story first," I say.

He cracks the knuckles on his right hand as he thinks through how he wants to start.

I may bite my lip when I am worried, but Avery cracks his knuckles whenever he is.

We all have our tells.

CHAPTER 12:

Avery takes a sip from his wine glass and then begins. "So, that patient with the evisceration we dropped off was one of the strangest calls I've ever been on."

"How so?"

"Well, when we were asked to report to Dyer Lane that day, I thought it was a weird coincidence. What are the odds that I would be called out to the same place we explored the night before, right?"

"But haven't you been called out there before to pick up patients?"

"Yeah, but I guess it just didn't mean anything to me before going there with everyone the other night and reading all that stuff about it online."

Avery stares down at his hands which are clasped in his lap as he continues to describe what happened. "Anyway, Shelley was driving the ambulance and it didn't take us too long to arrive on scene. When we got there, that man was walking on the side of the lane holding his guts cradled in his arms like a baby. It felt like we were in a movie, Cora. Or a nightmare. Shelley pulled over and we got out of the ambulance and assessed the scene. Dyer Lane may be even worse during the day because in the light you can actually see how much trash is dumped around and how isolated it is. Our surroundings seemed safe at the time, but obviously someone nearby had disemboweled him, so we were being extra cautious. Shelley and I approached the man and announced who we were and that we were there to assist him. The man started sobbing and lifted his arms to the sky like he was praying. The sound of his intestines slipping to the ground was the same as meat hitting concrete."

Avery clenches his jaw, "I never want to hear that sound again in my life." I can see his throat bobbing, as he recalls the experience. Avery has always worn his emotions on his sleeve, but it is rare to see him this worked up. I can tell he is close to crying right now.

“It was horrible,” he states in a soft voice. “I don’t think all twenty five feet of his intestine were out, but it was close. There was a blood trail behind him winding toward the road from the field.” Avery’s eyes flick toward my face to gauge my reaction, and I reach out and clasp one of his hands in mine as he continues.

“Shelley and I were stunned for a moment but quickly ran up to him and got him on the backboard and started to assess him and get the saline on his organs and all that. We managed the bleeding the best we could, but his insides were covered in dirt and his hands were filthy, so it was hard to clean him up. He reeked of blood and alcohol.”

Avery’s gaze turns far away and trance-like and he pauses. I can tell that he is processing this experience as he recounts it to me. This is important for him to move past the trauma he witnessed. Avery takes a deep breath and then says, “the entire time we worked on him, the man was wailing about a girl in the woods with three sharp claws on her hand, who lured him over and then attacked him. The horror in his eyes was something I’ll never forget.”

I sit in silence, stunned for a moment. That was not what I was expecting him to say. “That sounds awful,” I say, awkwardly. “I mean, what the actual fuck.”

He releases a small huff of a laugh before continuing, “yeah, right? The man kept muttering strange things as we drove. Which I know was probably due to shock and blood loss, but at one point he grabbed my wrist and when I looked at him, his eyes were wide and he appeared totally lucid. He told me the girl who did this to him had 'all white eyes' and 'wasn't natural.'" Avery holds up finger quotes for the descriptions. "Those were his exact words." Avery shakes his head, a frown creasing the space between his eyebrows. "It was definitely up there for one of the weirdest things a patient has ever said to me."

I am startled by what Avery just told me. "Huh?" I murmur as I take in this information. "White eyes?"

Avery shrugs and runs a hand over the top of his head, "I mean, obviously the man had suffered a major trauma and was hypovolemic, so anything he said would have been delusions... I mean, the claw thing kinda sounds like Freddy Kreuger."

"No," I say, softly. "I don't know about the claws, but the white eye thing...it's mentioned in that girl's journal. Someone had obviously harmed him, but there is a connection to what your patient said and this last entry I read, the one I wanted to tell you about."

I reach forward and snatch the book off the table to hand to him. Avery reluctantly takes it from me. I lean over to flip through the pages, searching for the entry that I just finished reading. When I find it, I tap the section with a pointer finger. "There! This part."

Avery glances up at me skeptically, doubt radiating off him like heat from pavement, and then starts reading. I study his face as he makes his way through Heather's writing. Avery's jaw literally drops at one point. I'm guessing it's the moment that Shane was decapitated. When he finishes, he sets the journal back down on the table and shakes his head. "That can't be real. It sounds like fiction."

"That's how I felt at first, but I have a weird feeling it really happened."

"Well, shit."

I laugh, "yeah, I also felt that way, too." I begin chewing

on the inside of my lip.

"I see what you mean about the description of the girl's eyes going white. That is a strange coincidence..." Avery adds as he flips through the journal pages.

"Right?" I say, feeling excited that he thinks it's odd, too. "Maybe some of those urban legend stories about Dyer Lane have some truth to them."

"Don't all stories start with a seed of truth, though?" Avery asks.

He sets the book down, then leans forward to wrap his arms around me hugging me close. I allow myself to melt into him.

"What a fucked up week this has been," he says. "On a serious note though, there is something really off about Dyer Lane. The stories are one thing, but our experiences there have been real. It's not a good place. I'm not saying it has to be paranormal or anything, maybe the patient I had and the girl who wrote this are just building off of past stories that they have heard and there is an urban legend about white eyes and they both just happened to hear it and bring it up...I don't know. What I do know is that nothing good ever seems to happen at Dyer Lane."

"You really think that this is all just some strange coincidence?"

"Yes? No...I don't know. I guess it sounds like a stretch, but it seems more possible than possession or a female Kreuger or whatever the other option is."

I pull back so I can look up into his face. "You're right. I'm curious now, though. I feel like I need to know more about the history of that place."

"I figured that much. Maybe just finish this girl's diary, browse the Google searches a bit, but will you promise you won't go back there?"

I bristle a little bit at his question. I know Avery is saying it out of love and concern, but I don't like being told what to do.

"I actually wanted to go see the shack where Leo found

the journal..."

Avery is looking at me with a frown. "Why?"

I don't answer and just chew on the inside of my lip, stalling. I honestly don't know why I want to go. I just feel compelled to see the location that Heather wrote about for myself.

Avery shrugs his shoulders, recognizing that trying to tell me not to go will only make me want to do the opposite. "Fine. But if you go, I want to be there with you. Please don't go without me."

I crack a small smile at him, lean in to give his cheek a kiss, and say, "deal."

CHAPTER 13:

The next few days are uneventful and filled with the normal rhythm of classes, work, and studying. Thursday night arrives and it's time to let loose a little and we all plan to go to The Wheelhouse. It's a local restaurant with a great bar that we go to every Thursday as a group for the "Thirsty Thursday" drink specials. The Wheelhouse is trendy and even has an axe throwing area and other games to play, which attracts a lot of college students as the end of the week approaches.

Mandy grabs a lavender colored cashmere sweater from a hanger and holds it up to herself in the full length mirror. It compliments her eyes framed by her tortoiseshell oversized glasses, and her long auburn hair that hangs down to her waist. She has a clear crystal hanging from her neck tonight and matching earrings dangling from her ears. "Can I borrow this tonight?" she asks Kate.

"Yeah, you can have it if you want. I haven't even worn it yet, it's not my style," she responds as she reaches over and rips the tag off that was dangling from the sleeve. "But it looks amazing on you," she adds.

Mandy's eyes dart down to the crumpled tag fisted in Kate's hand and then back up to her reflection. The sweater is most likely around $100 and something that Mandy wouldn't be able to afford for herself. "You sure?" she asks with a hopeful expression on her face.

"Totally. It's the perfect color for you," Kate says with a smile right before she pulls a dark green shirt over her head. It's an off the shoulder knit that displays her fragile collar bones and long slender neck.

Kate has an effortless grace about her in whatever she wears. Her mom is Swiss and her father is Filipino and Kate is a balanced mix of them both. She is naturally stunning in her unique beauty. Her big brown eyes always have the perfect flick of eyeliner drawn on top, which gives her a glamorous look. She has full rose bud lips, smooth tan skin, and dark shiny hair that shimmers in the light.

I turn back to the rack of shirts I've been browsing and finally decide on a red silky top with a deep v-neck.

"Damn, Cora. Breaking out the big guns tonight?" Kate says with an arched brow, her eyes focused on my chest. I laugh and cup my breasts in my hands suggestively, and make a kissy face at her. "Hopefully I don't get a nip slip."

We all laugh and crack jokes as we continue to get ready and do our hair and makeup. Looking through Kate's closet for clothes to wear has always been something the three of us do before going out. It started in highschool and just became a regular bonding ritual.

"Will you help me with my eyes?" I ask Kate as I lean over the sink and tame my eyebrows. I've always asked her for help with my makeup. She's had a talent at pulling everything together. Kate glances over at me and says, "yeah, but with a sexy shirt like that we have to do a smokey eye."

"Sold!" I slide into the clear chair that sits in front of a mirrored vanity, and turn so that Kate can start on my face. Tonight feels like old times. It's been a while since we all have been able to get together like this and get dressed up before going out.

As Kate does my makeup, I think about Heather and her friends. The past and present are so different, yet so similar. Years separate us and our interests are clearly not the same, but I feel a connection in how she and I value our friends.

With each swipe of the puffy eyeshadow brush across my closed lids, I let my mind wander and lose myself in memories.

* * *

People tend to bask in Kate's glow, similar to the way sunflowers worship the sun. She has something exceptional about her that draws others in. I don't recall Kate ever going through an awkward faze, but I do remember the first time I realized that she was truly next level beautiful.

We were thirteen years old, and were shopping together at the mall. Kate's mom, Emilia, would always spoil me and buy me whatever Kate was getting, too. Money was never an issue for her family. We left with some high end beauty products and spent the night in Kate's bathroom trying them all on and learning what looked best on us.

Nothing ever looked bad on Kate. I felt a pang of jealousy when I looked at how effortlessly gorgeous she was with her long legs crossed beneath her as she applied various beauty products to her symmetrical features. I knew I wasn't ugly by society's beauty standards, but I felt that I was plain, while Kate was unique.

I remember hovering close to the mirror and becoming incredibly frustrated trying to make the eyeliner I drew on my left eye match the one I did on the right. Instead, the black line just kept getting thicker and thicker until what was supposed to be a thin line grew to cover almost my entire eyelid.

"Hold on," Kate said, grabbing the liquid eyeliner from my hand. "Let me show you a trick." She took a makeup wipe and gently wiped away the tragedy I had created on my eyes. Then, she fanned my face so my eyelids would dry enough for the makeup to go on again smoothly. Kate patiently showed me how to start on the outer corner, and use my pinky to brace my hand to create stability, so that the line I draw would be solid and not shaky, and need less revision to balance out. The result was a perfect wing.

"How did you learn to do that?" I was in awe of how easy she had made that look, when I knew damn well it was hard to get right. My thirteen year old self tried hard not to squeal in excitement at the winged eyes that gazed back at me in the mirror.

"It was something I started doing when I took an art class last summer, and learned calligraphy. The pinky helps steady my hand, or else it shakes too much. I found out that it would work with eyeliner wings, too."

"I love it, thank you," I said, staring at my reflection, feeling pretty.

Kate gazed at me in the mirror, our eyes meeting there. She smiled a pleased grin, "you look beautiful," she said, and smoothed my hair down.

That's it. That small moment is when I knew that Kate was just as gorgeous on the inside as she was on the outside. Underneath all the designer labels and privilege, Kate is genuine and kind and wants others to feel good about themselves. Unlike some girls I had been friends with growing up, nothing was a competition for her. She wanted to see those around her shine. Maybe that's why she has always tolerated Nikki being around Leo and the close friendship they have. She never wants anyone to feel less than, and goes out of her way to avoid conflict.

I think I had always assumed that when you had looks and money, that stuff didn't matter. I had seen enough catty girls on TV shows to know that female drama is real. But not with Kate. She is always giving her friends things and sharing what she has, without asking for anything in return. It's not only material things either, she's incredibly supportive of her friends goals and desires in life. I've never had a better best friend than her.

* * *

"Oh my gosh," Kate exhales as she finishes the final touches of my makeup. I can feel her warm breath on my face as she leans in to swipe a little bit of highlighter on my brow bone. "I think this is my favorite look you've ever had. You're like a sex kitten tonight, Cora."

I gaze up at my reflection in the mirror. My eyes are framed with sultry dark eyeshadow in a winged shape that makes the blue of my eyes pop. Kate has put false lashes on me that make my eyes look big and glamorous.

"Ooo I feel pretty," I say, smiling wide and picking up some light colored matte lipstick to swipe on my lips.

"You look hot," Mandy adds, giving me an appraising look as she curls the remaining strands of her hair. She turns her gaze to Kate and says, "You're seriously the makeup master. I don't know why you're going to be a nurse when you're so good at this stuff."

"Haven't you ever heard of a side hustle? I can do both," she says with a smirk and starts gathering eyeshadows and supplies to create a look for Mandy.

After we are all finished, we get into Kate's car and drive over to The Wheelhouse, ready for some drinks and a good time.

* * *

The song, Sucker, by the Jonas Brothers blares through the speakers to greet us as we enter the restaurant. The Wheelhouse is decorated in an Industrial Style with a mix of wood and metal surfaces and dark green vintage velvet style couches and chairs. A massive wooden wheel hangs from the ceiling with lights fixed to it, creating a rustic chandelier, and there are a few Buck heads on the wall. Their blank shiny eyes stare out from high positions and their crown of antlers fan out across the wall they are mounted to.

In the back of the restaurant, behind a large circular bar, is the axe throwing cages, where loud cheering and thunks of the axe into the wood can be heard.

The hostess greets us with a bright smile, "do you have a reservation?"

"No," Kate says, "we are just meeting some friends, I think they already have a table," she gestures toward a side dining area where Leo, Nikki, Avery, and Noah are all seated in a huge plush wrap-around booth.

"Oh, you can head on over there, then," the hostess says as she turns her attention to the couple who has walked in behind us and begins to greet them.

I follow Mandy and Kate to the booth and Noah's voice rings out above the surrounding sounds as we get closer.

"Donald Trump is the greatest President we have ever had."

We slide into the booth as Nikki responds to Noah's rant. "Are you on crack?"

"No, I'm just using my brain. He does way more for our country than people give him credit for. Don't you want America to be great again?" Noah responds with raised brows.

Nikki glares back at him. With the amount that these two bicker, it is clear why they could never last in a relationship. The sexual tension is always high, but I never know if Nikki will snap and finally stab him. She looks extra stabby right now, and I glance around the table checking to see if any knives are nearby. Fortunately for Noah, there is not.

"Hi," Kate says with a tight smile. "Hope I'm not interrupting this passionate discussion, but can we not talk about politics tonight?" She leans over and gives Leo a quick kiss on the cheek as a greeting. "I'm going to get enough of that shit during the holidays, which are around the corner, and I don't want to start early with it."

Nikki's fiery gaze flicks over to Kate and she says "Noah

thinks a president that talks about grabbing women by the pussy is worth supporting. I am appalled." Clearly, Nikki isn't planning on listening to Kate's suggestion.

"You can't fault the man for speaking what's on his mind. Don't act like you don't have sexual fantasies," Noah mutters under his breath. Nikki sighs and starts picking at the black nail polish on her thumb, and flicking the flakes to the floor. Which is kind of gross.

I give Avery's thigh a squeeze as a hello and he grabs my hand under the table. A waiter with a big fuzzy beard comes by and drops off plates of garlic fries, roasted brussel sprouts, and chicken nachos.

"Oh my gosh, I am so glad you ordered the brussels!" Mandy says, clapping her hands. "These are the best."

"You're welcome," Noah says with a wink.

Mandy rolls her eyes and then scoots the dish of brussel sprouts in between her and Noah and proceeds to discuss how the cranberries and walnuts combined with the sauce really make the appetizer extra flavorful. I can tell she's trying to reset the mood and steer the discussion in a different direction and I feel grateful.

Everyone begins chatting and snacking on the appetizers, and things seem to be going in a smoother direction. Then, Nikki reaches over with her fork to grab a brussel sprout and Noah, unable to help himself, says "woah woah, are you sure you want to share food with a perverted Trumpkin like me?"

"Noah, can you just drop it?," she says, setting her fork down with a clatter.

"I just feel like you judge me because I support Trump," he replies, his blue eyes locked sternly on Nikki.

"I do," she answers coldly. Nikki and Noah stare at each other while we all look around the table uneasily. This is not how I imagined the night going. "You're really going to act like it's okay for the leader of our country to talk about women that way? Not to mention he's a total racist and narcissist."

Noah picks up his beer and brings it to his lips for a long swig before saying "You're just mad that I'm not a woke little leftist sheep like you are."

Nikki picks up her drink, but instead of sipping it, she throws the amber liquid into Noah's face. Beer drips from his chin down the front of his shirt, and splatters Leo, who was sitting on the other side of Noah.

"Excuse me," Nikki says, nudging Mandy so that she can get up and let her out of the booth. "I'm heading out, see you guys later."

Nikki quickly departs, her blonde hair swaying as she rushes to walk out the double doors of the restaurant without even a glance back to us. We all sit stunned for a moment as Noah wipes at his face with a cloth napkin. Leo starts to chuckle and hands Noah his napkin to use, since the one he has is already saturated with beer. Mandy reaches over to start mopping off the table. The garlic fries are sodden and wilted.

Avery gets up and walks over to the bar. When he returns he has a fresh plate of fries. "I had to get more, these are my favorite and I refuse to eat the wet ones."

"She has anger issues," Mandy says, glancing up at Leo to gauge his reaction.

"Yeah, she really feels her emotions," he says with a shrug. "I think that's what makes her such a great artist."

"She has this angsty Halsey vibe going, and I used to find it endearing. But now..." Noah cringes and drinks some more of his drink. "I wasn't trying to pick on her, I was just saying my opinion. None of you were getting aggressive with me even though you don't like the president either. It's not my fault Nikki's so hot tempered."

"Yeah, but you pushed her there," Leo adds.

"Now I reek of alcohol," Noah whines as he bunches up the beer soaked napkins and shoves them toward the end of the table.

"That's normal," Avery says.

"Ha, you're funny."

"We love you, Noah," Mandy says, "You just have this way of pushing people's buttons. Especially Nikki's."

His shoulders relax and Noah smiles, "I am a good button pusher," he says with a suggestive look.

"Not what I meant," Mandy says as she pops a fry into her mouth.

"Nikki has been kind of edgy lately," Leo says thoughtfully.

"Lately? This is normal for her. I mean, the flinging of perfectly good beer is new, but otherwise, she is always pretty confrontational." Mandy states.

"Yeah, I know. I think she is just stressed. She is applying to a photography program at Cal Institute of the Arts soon, which has been stressful. Also, her grandma has cancer and Nikki is really close with her. She takes care of her and makes sure she is getting all her medications. She doesn't want to put her in a care facility, but might have to."

Kate places her hand on Leo's arm and squeezes. "That would be a lot for anyone. She's lucky to have a friend like you. I didn't know she was planning on moving for art school." It's obvious to me that Kate's interest is piqued and there is a hopeful look in her eyes. I know the thought of Nikki being out of Leo's everyday life makes her feel relieved.

"Yeah, she applied there and one in Maryland, and another in New York. California is her first choice, though. She has family down South she can stay with, which would help financially."

"Mmm, that makes sense, it wouldn't be a far move," Kate responds. I can practically see the gears in her head turning as she tries to work out a timeline of how soon Nikki may be leaving for school.

"That's exciting for her," I chime in with a smile.

"Yeah, she's stoked," Leo replies.

"I'm just glad we weren't doing the axe throwing during this argument or she may have gone Jack Torrance on you," Mandy says, "there are worse things to throw than drinks."

Noah looks at her with wide eyes and slowly shakes his head from side to side. "Terrifying," he whispers.

"Speaking of terrifying, I still haven't been able to find that book I found at the cabin on Dyer Lane. Remember? It's gone," Leo says to the group. "I am telling you, that place was haunted and it's like the book was a ghost book or something." Leo's eyes are wide and bloodshot. High as a kite.

I glance over at Kate and she looks like she's about to explode laughing, and Mandy is smirking while digging through the remaining brussel sprouts for a cranberry. Avery gives me a subtle nudge in the arm, as if he is encouraging me to say something.

"Um, Leo, I have the book. I forgot to hand it back to you the other night."

"Oh my God. Yes! I remember now. Wow. Okay. I'm glad you had it. All this time I was like, am I crazy? Where could it have gone?"

"Sorry," I say with a shrug. "I should have brought it up sooner, but I started reading it and it's pretty wild." I take a sip of my beer, letting it calm my heart which began to race as soon as I thought about the journal.

"Really? What book is it?"

"It's not a novel," I say with a frown, "It's some teenage girl's diary. Honestly, it's super disturbing, but I can't stop reading it."

Leo is nodding and looking at me thoughtfully. "Well, that's to be expected considering where we found it. It was like, nestled in some voodoo hut."

Noah barks out a laugh, "that's an accurate description."

"I kind of want to see it," Kate says.

Noah turns to her, eyes wide with feigned shock. "You?! Princess Kate? I thought you, and I quote, 'never want to go to Dyer Lane again.' What is going on?"

"Well, I pride myself in my ability to change my mind, Noah," Kate responds, lifting her chin and lowering her eyelids in an exaggerated way to suggest superiority. "I want to see the voodoo hut, but in the daytime. I'm not crazy."

"That's right, you stayed back with Cora and Avery that night," Mandy comments.

"Yeah, it was just a bit too much for me at the time, but now I'm curious. Also, I want to know what's in that diary," Kate says, shifting her gaze to me.

"Uh, you may not want to." I say. "It's pretty out there. I still can't decide if what I am reading is fiction or not."

"Huh, it's that crazy?" Noah says, his eyes sparkling with interest. "Now I want to know, too." Noah stuffs a handful of fries in his mouth and chews loudly, then washes it down with a long pull of his IPA. "I've been wanting to go back to that hell hole and check it out in the light anyway. We should go tomorrow."

"I'm down," Leo says.

Mandy looks apologetic, "I can't, I have work."

"You're scared, huh?" Noah says sarcastically as he rubs her arm. She jerks it away. "Nope! I just need money, unlike some people," she gives him a pointed look.

It's no secret that Noah doesn't have to work. Just another member of the privileged college students who attend Stone Bay University, but will never know what it's like to have student loans or debt because his parents take care of all his expenses and even bought him a nice house to live in while he goes to school.

I let my gaze wander over Noah's flushed face. He is model handsome. He has a square jaw, and deep blue eyes that can suck you in when he wants to. Most of the time he acts goofy, but when he is serious, he's not so bad. Even though Noah is an asshole sometimes, I couldn't imagine our group without him.

I manage to shake myself out of my thoughts of Noah and say, "I'm coming when you go, and I'll bring the diary so you can read some of it."

Next to me, Avery looks surprised and a little concerned. "Count me in, too." he adds as he flips his menu closed. "Is anyone else going to order a meal?"

"Hell yeah," Noah says, "and more beer."

CHAPTER 14:

The next day, I go directly to work after I get out of class. My school day ends early on Fridays, so I always try to pick up an afternoon shift. I arrive at the hospital a little before noon, feeling thankful that I don't have to do any more overnights for the rest of the month.

Today, I am partnered with Dr. Manita. He's in his early sixties, and always extremely calm during patient encounters. He has a stern demeanor that commands respect. He actually reminds me a little of my dad, and I like working with him.

"Hi there, Cora," he greets me with his velvety smooth voice. "It's been a S-L-O-W day."

"Oh yeah, don't say the word," I say with a smile as I sit at the computer next to him and log myself in. There is a superstition among Emergency Medicine workers that if you say "it's slow" in the ER, all mayhem will break loose.

He chuckles and says "I promise I won't utter it in your presence."

"What's on the schedule today?" I ask, scanning through the triage list of patients.

"Lots of abdominal pain patients, an armpit abscess, a couple psych evaluations. Oh, and there is a kid with a high fever but I think Dr. Samuel is about to pick that one up."

"I am, indeed," Dr. Samuel says dryly from his computer at the other end of the Fishbowl.

"So, we will probably go see that abscess real quick, and get her home so we can free up some space."

"Sounds good to me," I say as I rub sanitizer into my hands and open the patient chart to jot down the name and information.

We get to the room and greet the patient, and are finished in a flash. The patient encounter is a quick one, just a simple incision and drainage of the abscess, and I am back at the computer entering notes.

I'm finishing up the chart, while Dr. Manita is off using the restroom when I hear a familiar smoky voice coming from down the hallway. It takes a moment for my brain to place it, but then it hits me that it's the voice of the motorcycle cop who had pulled us over a couple weeks ago when we had been on Dyer Lane.

I crane my neck to see if I can glimpse her, and my guess is confirmed when I spot her speaking to an EMT. Her posture is relaxed as she discusses something animatedly with the man.

She senses my gaze and her eyes lift from the person she is speaking with to meet mine. I see a flicker of recognition flash upon her face before she turns her attention back to the technician. He glances back in the direction she had been looking, and when he spots me breaks into a wide grin. The man that the officer has been chatting with is Adam, one of Avery's friends that he is often partnered with at work.

Adam lifts a hand in a subtle wave. I click out of the patient notes that I've finished and get up to say hi. As soon as I approach them, Adam asks "How's it going Cora?" and opens his arms to give me a hug, his kind eyes sparkling as they always do.

"I've been super busy lately, but busy is good," I say with a smile. I can feel the police officer watching this exchange and the prickle of sweat starts under my scrubs. I'm not sure why her gaze makes me feel this uneasy.

"I know nursing school must be hard. We've missed you

and Avery over at the place lately. Next time you get a break in your schedule let's plan to meet up. This is my cousin, Jenna," Adam says, gesturing to the officer.

Jenna stares back at me with an unreadable expression. I turn to her with a polite grin, "hi, it's nice to meet you."

The right side of her mouth quirks up.

Shit. She recognizes me.

"Nice, to meet you," she responds with a short nod, not acknowledging that she has ever seen me before. She holds my gaze for a moment, and then turns to Adam, "I better get going. My break is just about over. I'll see you tomorrow at Nana's."

"Sounds good," Adam says, giving her arm a quick squeeze before she turns and strides out of the ER. "Jenna is always so serious. I try to get her to loosen up, but damn," he says with a playful grin.

Adam feels like sunshine. He's one of those people whose attention is like a warm yellow glow pouring over whoever is in his presence. I feel my muscles relax, and I say "I've actually met your cousin before. She pulled over Leo while a bunch of us were in the car the other night. She was super cool about it, though. She didn't give him a ticket or anything. I guess she didn't remember me, which is probably good."

Adam lets out a deep rumble of a chuckle and his eyes crinkle at the corners. "That's why that whole interaction felt so awkward, huh? She acts like such a hardass, but inside she's a softy. I'm glad she didn't give him a speeding ticket. She has a photographic memory though, I bet she remembered you but didn't want to say anything. She's not big with small talk."

"She actually pulled him over for driving too slow, not for speeding."

Adam throws his head back and lets a full laugh out this time. "No! No way. Leo looks like someone who would speed, not drive like a senior citizen in a Prius."

"Yeah, well, looks are deceiving," I add with a grin. "We were actually driving on a one way country road, so he was going a little slower than usual. Have you heard of Dyer Lane?"

Adam's smile drops a fraction. "Yeah, I've definitely heard of it. Never ventured there myself, though, and thankfully never had to go there on a work call." He lowers his voice and leans in to say, "I heard there are swastikas on the trees."

I nod solemnly. "It's terrible," I reply.

"You should be careful goin' out there, yourself. I know you've heard those urban legends, I don't think anyone who lives around here hasn't."

"Yeah, I have." I glance back to the Fishbowl and see that Dr. Manita has returned from the restroom and is clicking through the patient lists, waiting patiently for me to wrap up my chat. "I need to get back to work, but Avery and I will make plans to get together with you soon, It's been too long."

"That would be great, Cora. It was nice seeing ya," he says as he turns to go back to the ambulance and start making his rounds in the field.

I return to the Fishbowl and slide into the chair next to Dr. Manita. "Dyer Lane," he whispers under his breath, his gaze still roaming through the newest admits.

"Ah, you heard me mention it. You little eavesdropper," I say, teasingly.

"Yeah, well. I've raised a few kids, discretely listening in on conversations has kind of become a specialty of mine." He turns in his seat toward me. "I can't believe people are still going up to there. My friends and I used to go as teens, if you can believe it. That road was a local hang out spot back in my day. People would throw parties there. Even before that, my parents had strange stories about that place. I guess it's just always been somewhere of interest around here."

"Yeah, I've read a lot of the urban legends that are online in forums and stuff. I hadn't ever been there until recently, though. I guess I just never had the guts to go, but my friends wanted to explore it the other night."

"Sounds pretty typical. Remind me to tell you about some of my experiences during our lunch break. Until then, we have to go see this kid with a rash in Room 9."

* * *

The rest of the night continues to be unremarkable, and I count down the minutes until we have our break so I can hear about Dr. Manita's stories. The kid in room 9 has eczema, very non emergent. Then, we visited another kid with a bead stuck up her nose, then a 51/50 patient who refused to speak, and we couldn't get a full history from him.

Finally, after what feels like an eternity, it is time for us to head to the breakroom and my pulse thrums with excitement. My fascination with Dyer Lane has only grown since reading the parts of Heather's journal, and I need to hear more.

Dr. Manita and I settle at one of the tables and begin pulling out our snacks. He has packed a turkey sandwich, and some chips, while I have a butter croissant from Starbucks and a large bottle of water. *Carbs over everything* seems to be my motto as of late.

"So, tell me more about this notorious Dyer Lane," I say nonchalantly, trying and probably failing at not seeming eager.

Dr. Manita chuckles. "Well, I'm sure you've heard all about it being haunted. Tons of people said they could hear voices and whispers when they went there. Some even say that there are shapes in the fog. Have you ever been when it's foggy? It's extra strange up there on those nights. One guy I knew said he was held down on the ground by something invisible and couldn't get up, then there's the phantom police car stories, lots of weird rumors like that."

I nod my head as I tear off a piece of the buttery pastry, immediately feeling cold at the mention of the police car. "What was it that you experienced there?" I ask before popping the flaky piece into my mouth, and hoping that my hands don't look shaky as crumbs tumble down and land on the table in front of me.

"My friends and I went up there practically every weekend while we were in high school. We never saw anything too notably terrifying. By that I mean nothing that would make it into one of those Paranormal Activity movies. One time though, we decided to park and put baby powder on our windows because we heard that if you did, the children who have died on the lane would push your car to try and save you. Morbid, right? Well, we tried it out. My pal put tons of baby powder all over the rear window and we parked right in the middle of the road, which is stupid when I look back on it. But anyway, it worked. Our car started moving. At first I thought my friend was pulling a prank and had the car in drive or neutral or something, but I looked down to confirm, and he really didn't. The car finally came to a stop after it had been moved off the road at the first big turn. We jumped out, and sure enough there were handprints in the baby powder on the back window. They were big prints, not children sized though. That was something of a relief, I think. The thought of ghost children is extra sad, so, yeah. Either way, I'll never forget it."

"No way," I say. "That's such a crazy story." I tuck a strand of hair behind my ear, feeling fidgety and uncomfortable. "I think that is actually Paranormal Activity worthy."

"Yeah. Maybe it is. I still wonder if there was some way that my friend had pulled off a prank and tricked me, though. But I've come to accept that there are just some things in this world of ours that cannot be explained. I had never been one to believe in ghosts, but I do believe in science, and there has to be energy that remains after someone dies. You've heard of the First Law of Thermodynamics, right?"

"Um, refresh me on it," I say as I slowly pull off another piece of croissant. My appetite is gone, but I need something to do with my hands.

"In a nutshell, it says that 'energy cannot be created or destroyed,' so, all energy that is here on the earth doesn't just disappear. It is cycled back in another state or form, but cannot just vanish. I think that can apply to spirit energy, too."

I take a sip of my water and think about what he's just said. "So, you're saying that spirits are possible, and hauntings?"

"I know a lot of people who would disagree and use science to dispute that claim, and if I hadn't experienced some of the things I personally have in my lifetime, I would probably be one of those very people. But I definitely have opened my mind to the possibility. The world has a lot of mysteries. The truth of the matter is, some things just cannot be proven one way or another."

Dr. Manita pauses to take a bite of his sandwich, and then continues on. " I personally don't think that our consciousness ends with the death of our bodies. I think that there is more after life ceases. Our energy has to go somewhere." He shrugs, " it's science."

I stare at my water bottle on the table, trying to process what he's saying. "Hmm," I take a deep breath. "It's all so interesting, and oddly comforting. I mean, the thought that we go on after death explained through a scientific lens is something I like."

A small smile blooms on Dr. Manita's face. "I like it, too."

The subject matter of our conversation changes and we begin discussing his upcoming trip with his wife to Hawaii, and how his daughters are doing. He asks about my Mom, and I tell him all about her travels through Europe.

Before I know it, it's time to go back and wrap up the work shift. As I log back into the computer, my mind is on spirits and urban legends and I decide I want to really commit to researching more about Dyer Lane this weekend, and I need to finish reading Heather's diary.

CHAPTER 15:

When I wake up the next morning, I grab the journal and start on the next entry. I tossed and turned all night thinking about it, but made myself wait until the morning when my head was clear and fresh to start reading. The last thing I needed was to read something that would give me nightmares, and Heather's diary is definitely fuel for bad dreams.

I skip the coffee, because I'm feeling jittery, and make some tea instead. While the lemon tea bag soaks in the hot water, I inhale the steam and flip through the pages of the journal until I come to the entry I left off on, "what do you got for me next, Heather?" I mutter under my breath, almost afraid to find out. Then, I begin to read.

* * *

September 29, 1997:

Mom always makes pancakes on Sunday mornings, and today wasn't any different. I woke up to the smell of coffee and when I walked into the kitchen was greeted with a huge stack of blueberry pancakes, plated and ready for me.

Mom was cheerful with a big smile on her face like some creepy wife from a 50's sitcom. She was humming...actually humming. Who does that?

*I wanted her to go away. I sat down at the table, trying not to make eye contact with her as flashes of Friday night replayed through my head on a loop. I cut into my pancakes and *FLASH* Shane's shredded neck filled my mind. The severed tendons and vessels poking through like ripped cables.*

*My mom handed me a bottle of maple syrup. *FLASH* I saw Liv cutting our palms open down the middle with her ritual knife and instructing Tasha and I to squeeze our blood over the candle in the middle of the circle. My blood oozed like the thick amber sludge that I just poured over my breakfast.*

*I looked across the table at Jessica as she happily devoured her buttery pancakes. *FLASH* Liv's glistening eyes had replaced those of my sister's, and she stared back at me as if the whites of an egg had been shoved into her sockets. Devoid of any pupils. Emptied of the girl that once lived behind them.*

I was so lost in my thoughts that I didn't notice my mom talking to me, asking me if I liked my breakfast. When I looked up, her lips were moving but no sound was coming out. All I could do was nod as I choked down my food. I didn't have the strength to talk to her. I wasn't sure my mouth would work to form words. I ate slowly, and when I was done, breakfast felt like a rock inside my stomach.

Once I was done eating, I somehow managed to say "thank you," and emptied my plate in the sink. Then, I came back to my room where I immediately locked my door and flopped onto my bed to start writing this all down.

Something is wrong with me. Since we did the blood ceremony I feel like a different person. I've been getting fevers at night and having terrible dreams. Life feels more intense now. I see colors brighter, and sounds are sharper, but my mind feels tethered to something or someone who isn't here and the visions are random and all consuming. When the black candle sparked as it fed off of our blood, we made promises to serve the thing that is inside of Liv. I don't even know what that means, I just know that I was swept away in the moment.

I feel so much. Gratitude, reverence…fear. I am both excited and exhausted by what I've become. I know I'm a monster.

I think I like it.

* * *

I snap the journal shut. My stomach feels queasy. I sit in silence for a minute, chewing on my lip. This girl is crazy, she must be. A pact with a demon? Magic powers? Murder? This shit just can't be real.

I take a sip of my tea. It's gone cold. Then, I grab my computer and pull it onto my lap, and flick through the beginning of the journal to find the name of the boy Heather claims to have killed with her friends.

Shane Dodson.

Maybe instead of researching Dyer Lane, I should be researching these kids. All I get is urban legends and ghost stories when I look up the *place*, but maybe researching the *people* will bring some facts. I type his name into the search engine, eager for information.

Some random news articles pop up about a Harvard graduate with that name, there is also a Linked In profile, a Twitter and Instagram account, and an obituary for the year 2008. None of these seem to match with the boy I'm looking for. Maybe I need to go to the library and research there since it is currently the year 2019, and articles from the 1990s may not be posted online.

I am about to give up, but then I notice a link titled *Where did Shane Dodson go?* It was written in 2007, so it may be totally unrelated, but I'm curious. I click the link and my heart rate picks up speed as I start reading.

Where Did Shane Dodson Go?

By Jessica Harper

Ten years ago, Shane Dodson, a sixteen year old highschool student, mysteriously disappeared from the small town of Stone Bay in the Fall of 1997. Authorities continued to search for the sixteen year old for over a year after he was reported missing by his mother, Sherry Dodson, on September 29, 1997. Miss. Dodson stated that she last saw Shane on Friday morning before school, and he didn't return home at the end of the day.

Shane's basketball Coach reported that Shane

attended practice, and his friends said they saw him ride off on his motorbike at the end of the day, only to never be seen again.

Stone Bay Police Department led an extensive search for the teenager but never found a body or a lead as to where he could have gone.

So, what happened?

A few people were questioned in relation to Shane's disappearance, but ultimately no notable evidence was collected. However, the city of Stone Bay is notorious for having a high number of people reported missing each year. This small idyllic town is located near the Sacramento area, which is a known human sex trafficking hub due to the numerous ports and freeways available for transporting kidnapped victims. Sacramento currently has a higher than average percentage for human trafficking in the nation.

Some people speculate that this could have been the unfortunate fate of Shane, but that theory has not been proven.

In ten years, forensics has come a long way. I can't help but wonder if perhaps a vital clue would be found if the Missing Persons Case was reopened and investigated further.

People do not vanish into thin air. So, that begs the question, where did Shane Dodson Go?

JESSICA HARPER COVERS TRUE CRIME, COLD CASES, AND COURT NEWS FOR STONE BAY NEWS

- CONTACT VIA JHARPER@STONEBAYNEWS.COM

* * *

My mouth feels dry, in contrast to my hands, which have begun to sweat. I wipe my palms down the side of my lounge pants as I gather my thoughts. I glance at the journal that is next to me on the sofa, clear evidence of what may have taken place in the Shane Dodson case.

This is real. This really happened.

I urge my mind to slow down. I don't know anything, not really.

What if Shane went missing, and the journal entries are just a sad teenage girl's fantasy of what happened to him? Yeah, that seems possible. My gut tells me that is not reality, though. Should I bring the journal to the police? That seems like the right thing to do.

This is the part in every story where the main character has the choice to "do the right thing" or to make a stupid decision...This may be the evidence that is needed to bring closure and justice to a possible crime.

There's just one problem. I haven't finished reading the journal yet. I'm only part way into it all. I selfishly don't want to give the book up before I'm done, and if I tell the police, they will want it. I could photocopy the pages and keep those to read, but then there will probably be an official investigation, and I want to investigate it myself.

I know it's stupid. I know it's wrong. I am thinking like a crazy person, but instead of contacting the Stone Bay Police like I know I should, I scroll down to the bottom of the article again and click on the link for Jessica Harper's email.

I want information, but I want to get it myself. Maybe once this desire for playing detective is satisfied, I'll give the police a call…maybe.

I pause to collect my thoughts. Then, I type out a

message.

To: JHarper@Stonebaynews.com
From: Corakins22@yahoo.com
Hello,
My name is Cora. I'm a college student who is doing research for a project. I came across an article online that you wrote a few years ago about Shane Dodson, a teenager who disappeared in Stone Bay during the 1990s. I'm writing a report about cold cases and was wondering if I could interview you. I think it would be very helpful. Please let me know if this is possible.
Thank you,
Cora

I send it off, feeling uncomfortable about lying, but also stubborn in my need to look into this more. I want answers, and I think it's possible that Jessica Harper could have some. It's a Saturday morning, so I don't expect a reply from her right away, but a responding email dings into my inbox within minutes.

To: Corakins22@yahoo.com
From: JHarper@Stonebaynews.com
Hi Cora,
When is your report due? If you want to send over some interview questions, I can get those answered and sent back by the end of next week. I'm happy to help.
-Jessica Harper

I sigh in frustration. Of course she thinks it's just some simple school report and I am going to have basic questions about cold cases. I need to make her understand that this is more. I fire out a quick response, not caring if I seem desperate.

To: JHarper@Stonebaynews.com
From: Corakins22@yahoo.com
Thank you for the quick response. The interview is urgent. I also may have some new information that is relevant to the Dodson case that I specifically want to discuss with you…can we please meet in person? My number is 555-897-3899 - feel free to call me.
-Cora

I send it, feeling my scalp prickle with anxiety. *What am I doing?*

I reach for my phone, and as soon as I grasp it, it rings in my hands. *That was quick.* When I see that it isn't Jessica Harper, a wave of disappointment sweeps through me. Of course it isn't her, that would have been too easy. Instead, Kate's name is displayed across the screen. I'm tempted to ignore it. I don't feel like talking right now, but I swipe along the bottom of the screen to answer. Glancing at the time before raising the phone to my ear. It's only 8 AM.

"Hey," I answer, trying to sound cheerful.

"Hey, come over, Leo wants to go to Dyer Lane this afternoon and I figured you and I could get some food first."

"Oh yeah, I do want to check out that cabin or whatever…" I say trailing off, trying to sound less interested than I am.

"Yeah, so go get dressed, and let's grab some breakfast and coffee. Bring that creepy book, too."

I chew on my bottom lip, "Alright, I'll be there in about thirty minutes."

"Are you alright?" Kate asks. "If you don't want to go, I totally get it. That place is most likely cursed."

"No, I want to go. I'm just thinking about how fast I can get ready."

"Are you sure that's it?" she says gently.

"Yeah, I'm fine. Kinda tired, but I'm good." I run my hands through my tangled hair. After all these years of friendship, she knows me too well for me to be able to fool her. She can hear something in my voice that I cannot conceal. "I mean, I am a little anxious. You'll understand when you read some of the diary...and that place just makes me nervous because of all those stories about it, you know?"

"Yeah. That's understandable. I mean, it IS daytime, though, and there will be four of us there. Leo already invited Avery and he is meeting up with him. I figured we could take separate cars so you and I could get our breakfast date in."

"What? No Noah?" I ask.

"No, apparently he has a terrible hangover this morning. Serves him right." I can practically hear Kate's smile through the phone.

I switch the phone to speaker so I can open a text that Avery just sent me. It says he is meeting up with Leo soon and will see me in a few hours.

"Okay. Yeah, that sounds good," I tell Kate distractedly as I type back a reply to him.

"Alright, just let yourself in when you get here."

CHAPTER 16:

The mid-October morning has a damp chill in the air, and the fog blankets everything in an eerie swirl of gray. It's always foggy in Stone Bay during the fall months. I have to drive slower than usual because it's hard for me to see too far ahead, and deer are known for jumping out at cars in the area that surrounds Kate's home.

By the time I pull through the gates leading to her house, it's around 9:00. My stomach is rumbling with hunger, and my head is starting to hurt for want of caffeine. I'm usually on my second coffee at this time of the day, at least.

I walk inside Kate's, welcoming the warmth and feeling instantly cheerful at the idea of getting some time with her, just us two. So often we are in a group setting, and Mandy practically lives here, so time with Kate is never like it was when we were kids.

"Lucy, I'm hooome!" I call out in my best impression of Ricky Ricardo from the black and white I Love Lucy shows we always used to watch together. It's been a joke for me to come over and call out like that since Kate and I were nine or ten years old, and I still do it whenever I let myself in. Kate comes around the corner wearing a frilly looking kitchen apron and holding a spatula.

"What are you wearing?" I say with a mock look of fright on my face. "Lucy you've got some 'splaining to do!" I wag my pointer finger at her, furthering my impersonation.

Kate bursts out laughing so hard that it turns silent. I love when this happens, it immediately makes me start laughing and both of us stand there in her entryway, doubled over and silent-laughing together for a few moments.

Finally, we begin to recover. "Oh my gosh, that was great," she says, catching her breath and wiping tears from her eyes. I gesture to her apron, "but seriously, what's with the apron?"

"Well, about 20 minutes after I got off the phone with you, I realized I was starving. So, I cooked us some pancakes."

A pit opens in my stomach and the endorphins from the laugh fest quickly begin to vanish. As soon as Kate mentioned pancakes I immediately thought of Heather's diary entry and how she ate breakfast imagining the terrible things she had done.

"Uh," I bend over to reach in my bag and grab the diary. I hold it out to her. "Thanks for cooking, but I honestly don't know if I can eat pancakes right now. When you read some of these entries, you'll get it."

She looks at me, puzzled and takes the diary from my outstretched hand. "Okay, I guess we can have some coffee while I make you an omelet instead? I can save the pancakes for Mandy. I bet she will want them when she gets back from work."

"Deal," I say as I follow her around the corner into the kitchen.

"So what exactly is up with this book?" she asks as puts seran wrap over the plate of pancakes and places it into the fridge.

"I honestly think it just speaks for itself. I don't even want to give you any spoilers."

"Ooo cryptic," she says with a smirk.

"I'm serious. Here, you read, and I'll make my own omelet. You're always stingy with the cheese, anyway."

"Am not!" she says, faking offense and throwing a

blueberry at me.

I laugh and dodge the little flying missile.

She sits at the counter and pulls the bowl of fruit over to her and begins to snack as she reads. A few minutes in, she pauses and lowers the book to give me a wide eyed stare. I just nod at her with raised eyebrows and say, “yeah, I know. Keep reading until after the breakfast entry, and then stop.”

“Oh gosh, OK, if this makes me never want to eat my beloved pancakes again, I’ll be pissed,” she mutters as she returns to reading.

Time unravels slowly as I make my food and wait for her to finish reading. I’m sprinkling cheese on top of the eggs when I hear Kate gasp loudly. I whip my head up and she has a hand over her mouth and is shaking her head. “Holy shit,” she whispers. I walk over and put a plate down in front of her, but she pushes it away. “This isn’t real, though. I mean, it’s hard to believe something like this could ever happen. Can a wire even do that? We should Google it." She shakes her head. "Let’s not get started on the witch shit, too.”

I shrug, “that’s what I was thinking. It could be fiction, right?”

Kate nods at me wide eyed, and then goes back to reading as I begin to eat. A few moments later Kate shuts the book, “yup, no longer a pancake fan.” She shudders and hugs herself. “Ugh, that story is so messed up.”

“I know. Now I’m curious to see where Leo found it, though. Maybe there are some more things left behind that will clue us in.”

Kate looks at me with a crease between her eyebrows. “I don’t know, Cora. It kind of seems like something we should give to the police. If this really happened…”

“But we don’t *actually* know that it did. We would just be wasting their time and resources unless we know for sure...”

Kate stares down at the journal sitting between us on the counter, “yeah, but isn’t that for the cops to decide? This could be a homicide confession.”

"It gets worse," I say.

Her eyes flick up to mine, "what does that mean?"

"Um, well, I did some research about that Shane boy. He really did go missing in 1997. No one knows what happened to him."

"No! We are for sure going to the cops with this. Are you kidding? This is a big deal." Kate says, panic etched on her face.

"Kate, please, we can't. I want to look into it more..."

She interrupts me, "what are you talking about? We aren't authorized to 'look into it more,'" she says, making air quotes with her fingers. "We are not law enforcement or detectives or anything even close to that. You're not being logical."

I put my head in my hands and take a deep breath. "I know it sounds nuts."

Kate lets out a huff of air. I look up at her and she's looking at me with concern, her arms crossed in front of her chest and shoulders almost up to her ears.

"Please?" I say, "I know it isn't the best idea I've ever had, but I feel like I need to look into it before getting the police involved. I even contacted this reporter who wrote an article on Shane's disappearance. She works for the local news and I'm trying to get an interview set up with her. I want you to come with me."

Kate is shaking her head back and forth, and she looks pale. "Cora, you're lucky you're my best friend and I trust you. I can't even believe you're talking me into this, but I'll go along with it for now." I open my mouth to begin to thank her and she quickly raises a hand up to me and continues, "but if this even starts to get too sketchy, I will insist on contacting the police. No exceptions."

Kate has that pinched possum expression on her face that she gets, and I almost want to laugh but instead I lean forward and hug her, "thank you." Her body is rigid in my embrace, but she eventually relaxes in my arms and hugs me back.

As if fate was listening in, my phone gets a text from an unknown number. I pick it up and flick to my inbox. Kate leans over to read the message over my shoulder.

"Hi Cora, this is Jessica Harper. Would you like to meet at my house tomorrow around noon? I am willing to do a quick interview for your report, and am interested in the information you claim to have. My address is 308 Maplewood Drive in Stone Bay. Let me know if this works for you."

I quickly type back a reply: "Sounds good. I will be there at noon tomorrow. Thank you."

My heart is drumming at a fast rhythm and I feel a mix of excitement and nerves. It makes me feel more alive than I have in a long time.

Kate sighs next to me, "So, when did you decide to join the cast of Scooby Doo?"

"I just have this feeling..." I shrug. "I don't know if it's real or not, but I feel compelled to find out for myself. I don't know how else to explain it. It just feels interesting and exciting. You know things have been hard for me since everything with my dad..."

I let that linger, feeling a tiny bit guilty for pulling him into this. But at the same time, it's true. Life has been on a loop since he died in my arms. Avery woke me up...for a while. Then, I fell back into a numbness, and somehow this mystery and the proximity to possible danger has awoken a side of me that feels determined and engaged with life again.

Kate looks at me with a thoughtful expression before saying, "fine. I know how hard things have been for you. I don't think this is the answer to those feelings by any means, but I guess I'll be your partner. Ride or die, and all that," she says, rolling her eyes and then smiling at me. "Don't tell Leo, though. Just act like you forgot the journal at home or something. He will for sure make you go to the police if he reads that." She bites her lower lip in thought and then asks, "what does Avery think?"

"He read it, and thinks it's fictional. You know him, he's

so chill about everything. I didn't tell him that I researched Shane Dodson yet, though."

"Okay. Don't tell him. If we are going to do this, it's our secret and stays between us. Oath?" Kate says, lifting her pinky finger up toward me.

I wrap my little finger around hers and we kiss our thumbs and then push them together, in the same promise routine we had as kids.

"Oath," I echo back.

CHAPTER 17:

The fog from this morning is still dense as Kate and I drive to Dyer Lane. There is an accident on the freeway, and traffic is thick. We spend the time listening to Billie Eilish, laughing, and chatting about school and our relationships. It feels so normal, I almost forgot we were headed toward a creepy place in the woods to search for clues about witches and murder.

Once we finally turn onto Dyer Lane, we fall silent. Immediately, we are greeted with the sight of a dead deer on the side of the road. Its body is stiff and contorted, and its tongue swells out of its mouth and hangs to the side.

In the light of day, the road is even stranger than at night. The sun illuminates all the jagged edges of the trees, and the slow ripple of the tall grass that borders the lane. The fog rolls lazily through the trees, but doesn't conceal all the detritus scattered and piled along the road like tombstones in a forgotten cemetery.

I begin to roll my window down, and Kate immediately hits the button for it to slide back up, "let's not," she says with a nervous giggle.

"Why? Are you afraid to let the spirits in?" I ask, raising an eyebrow.

"Um, yeah. That, and flies. There's a lot of dead stuff out here."

I turn my head in time to spot another dead deer decomposing on the side of the lane as we pass by. “There’s no bugs, though,” I mutter under my breath.

“There has to be with all these corpses littering the road,” Kate responds.

“No. There seriously isn’t though. That’s one thing I noticed and thought was weird when we were here the other night. Usually I would hear mosquitoes, or at least see something flying around, but it was silent. It’s like nothing wants to live out here, not even bugs.”

“Well, clearly deer don’t want to live here, look there is another dead one,” Kate says nodding her head to the right, where I glimpse a deer on its back half way into the field between a couple of looming oaks. Its legs are stiff and stretch up to the halo of branches above.

“You have good eyes. I never would have noticed that one since it’s not right near the road,” I say. “I thought maybe the deer were being hit by cars, but now I’m thinking something else must have killed them because that one isn’t anywhere near the street. I guess maybe it could have hobbled away after being hit..."

We come to a sharp bend in the road, and suddenly a gaunt man is standing in front of us. Kate pushes her foot to the brake, quickly bringing her car to a crawl as we approach. The man is still as he stares blankly at our car. His sallow face is sunken in, and his hollow cheeks give him a skull-like appearance. There are open sores blooming on his lips and chin.

“He looks like an extra from The Walking Dead,” I say, as Kate maneuvers her car around him. He doesn’t even blink as our car goes by, and continues to stand facing the road as if he is waiting for something.

“So damn creepy,” Kate says, darting her eyes to the rearview mirror, taking another glance at the man in the road. I turn in my seat to look. He is still facing the way we came, his back to us. I can see the sharp points of his shoulder blades through his thin shirt.

“He didn’t even look at us when we passed. I can’t even be sure he is breathing,” Kate adds with a small anxious laugh. I notice that her knuckles are white as she tightly grips the steering wheel.

“Isn’t the turn off we took somewhere around here?” She asks as she slows the car to search for the path Leo had ventured onto before.

“There!” I point to a small dirt offroad. “I’m pretty sure that’s it.”

“I think you’re right,” she agrees as she turns her Tahoe onto the path. We follow it down and see Leo’s red Ford Explorer parked ahead. Kate pulls up next to it, and Avery glances up from his phone when he sees us. He’s sitting in the passenger seat, and opens the door to get out. Leo is already circling around his car and approaching Kate’s side. He opens the door for her and she jumps down from her car and plants a kiss on his cheek. “Sorry we are late, there was hella traffic on the way here.”

“No worries,” Leo says, “we hit that traffic, too.”

Avery slings his arm around my shoulders and gives my forehead a kiss. I encircle my arms around his waist and lean into him. I’m just about to ask if we are all ready to go check out the cabin or whatever it is, when the back door of Leo’s car opens and a head of bright blonde emerges. Nikki is there holding her camera bag. She has a smile on her face and raises a hand in a small gesture of hello. Kate’s face flashes with a moment of confusion and annoyance, but she recovers quickly, like a cloud briefly passing over the sun. “Hi, Nikki!” she says, with an attempt at excitement.

I also am surprised to see Nikki here, and am glad Noah didn't come today. I reach over to greet her with a hug and can see her shoulders relax with relief at a kind welcoming.

“I hope I'm not party crashing," Nikki says. "I asked to tag along when I heard you were coming here so I can get photos of this area for my art program portfolio." She raises her professional Canon camera out of her bag and begins to adjust the settings.

"I bet you'll get some great shots in this place. It's...a mood," Kate responds gesturing around us.

I look around, and have to agree. The trees are still, there is no breeze. Gossamer tendrils of fog continue to spin around us, and the jutting angles of the surrounding oaks resemble the thin limbs of dancers in pose. There is definitely a strange natural beauty to Dyer Lane. *It's the people who make the ugly parts*, I think as my eyes zero in on a pile of trash discarded on the path.

"Well, shall we proceed to the destination?" Leo asks, clapping his hands together once.

"Let's do it," Avery says, clasping my hand and entwining his fingers with mine.

We walk up the dirt road, heading deeper into the wooded area. "That's not disturbing or anything," Kate says and points up into the sky. Three buzzards are circling in the air above us. They slowly float among the trees, an ominous feathered merry go-round.

"Those are harmless. They are just looking for dead things. So, you know, don't die and we'll be good," Leo says with a smirk.

The sun oversees the afternoon high in the sky, and the trees around us are shedding vibrant leaves, but the atmosphere still feels gray and bleak despite nature's attempt at brightening it. The fog has thinned out, as we continue our stroll along the dirt road for another ten minutes. The road narrows into a single file path the further we go and is lined by a sentry of oaks, until it finally opens up to reveal a small rickety shack-like structure.

The tiny shed has vivid green moss growing along a triangular roof, and reminds me of a sinister version of something I would have built with Lincoln Logs during my childhood. It looks ancient, and the front door has been torn off the hinges, just like Heather described in the journal. The absence of the door leaves an unwelcoming black rectangle. A monstrous gaping mouth into the desolation within. An invitation into the depths of darkness.

I suppress the unease threatening to consume me as we approach the entrance. The wood around the door frame is rotting, and there is a distinct fetid mildew smell that tickles my nose and makes me want to sneeze. Leo pulls out his phone and turns on the flashlight before passing through the gaping frame first. Kate and I follow next, with Avery and then Nikki taking up the rear.

I hear the small click of Nikki's camera from the back and a flash of light illuminates the interior of the shack for a brief moment. Dust particles float in the air, and I have that peculiar feeling of walking through spider webs, just like I did the first night we came to Dyer Lane. Except this time, it's very likely I did step through a web. The shed is a wreck and full of mildew and even in the dim lighting I can see that thick dust coats every visible surface. I can hear something skitter in the corner. *So there is life here after all*, I think to myself as I grab my phone and turn on my flashlight, too.

There are cobwebs hanging down from the low ceiling, and I can see a huge faded pentagram drawn in the middle of the floor surrounded by stubs of cracking burned down candles. The wax has melted into globs, cementing the base of the candles to the ground.

We all stand rooted to one spot, our heads swiveling to glance around the small room. Well, all of us except for Nikki, who scampers around taking photos from various angles. Leo points out the cupboards where he found the journal, and I carefully make my way toward it, attempting to stir up as little dust as possible. I can already feel my lungs becoming itchy and the urge to cough is developing in my chest.

As I walk toward Leo, I feel a distinct temperature change, like I just stepped into a walk-in freezer. The sensation is there and gone within seconds, and I clench my jaw as I try to focus on what Leo is saying to me.

"It was in this exact spot," he says, as he opens one of the cupboards. If Leo felt the strange temperature change, he's not showing it. I shiver at the memory, and bend down to get a better look at the area he found the journal.

The cabinets are short and wide and line the entire back wall of the cabin. I have to stoop to see inside. I can faintly see a rectangular outline in the dust of where the journal must have been, but there isn't anything else in the drawer now. I feel discouraged. I don't know what I expected, but I was hoping to find something more.

"This definitely looks like old blood," Avery says from across the small room, gesturing to a large tin bucket that is crusted with a coat of something thick and rust colored. He shoots me a serious look. I swallow hard, remembering Heather's account of draining Shane's blood into a bucket.

"Maybe we shouldn't touch anything in here," Kate says with an edge to her voice, as she sweeps the light of her phone around the room. She pauses the light in the corner, illuminating an small rusted axe that leans against the rippled and decaying wood wall. Kate's head snaps over to my direction and her eyes are wide. I know exactly what she is thinking - this is a fucking crime scene. *The journal is adding up.*

Disregarding what Kate just said, Nikki begins to open all the cabinet drawers one by one to look inside. Kate rolls her eyes dramatically and gives me a *what the hell* look. Dust is flying around us as Nikki carelessly disturbes the area. Leo comes around behind her and shines his light over her shoulder to create more visibility as she continues to search through the cabinets. There are more candles tucked away and coated in dust in one of the drawers, but the rest are all empty.

It feels like the shadows shift and move inside the cabin. There is a dense solidity to the darkness. I stare down at the pentagram and imagine Heather and her friends here playing with the Ouija board.

I am lost in the conjurings of my imagination and don't notice Avery's approach. He places a hand on my arm, and I jump, startled by his touch. “Sorry,” he says softly, “wanna go outside? I don’t think there is much more to see here.” I nod and tap Kate on the shoulder and point to the doorway, letting her know I’m going out. She follows behind Avery and I to the door, not bothering to tell Leo, who is still looking around the cabin with Nikki.

When we step through the open doorway, it’s like coming out of deep water and emerging into fresh air. I take in a long breath, and my eyes begin to adjust to the presence of sunlight. We were only in the shack for a few minutes, but they stretched out to feel like much longer. “That place is horrid.” Kate says, grabbing some hand sanitizer out of her cross body bag and rubbing it into her palms. “Ugh, it smells so bad in there.”

“There is definitely probably a side of mold along with that thick as hell dust,” Avery comments. “I hope none of you get bad allergies.”

“We’ll be fine,” I say as I stare back at the cabin. It feels like something from within is staring back at me. “It is just like the journal described…”

Suddenly a scream rings out and Nikki comes running out of the opening of the shack. She is slapping at her hair and flipping her head up and down as if she is trying to unlodge something. Leo emerges from the doorway looking grim.

“What happened?!” Kate calls as she runs toward him, concerned.

“Uh, we found something…”

Nikki continues to swat at her hair and takes huge gasps of breath. “I hate bugs!” She screams, “there were so many. Oh my gosh, SO MANY.”

“She was taking a photo of one of those empty cabinets when her camera picked up a gap in the back of one, and we pushed it open. There was a false back and a little space behind it for storing things discreetly, I guess. Nikki stuck her head in there for a better look and freaked because it’s full of those little pincher bugs.”

"Ew," Kate says, and then goes over to Nikki and starts helping her smooth her hair and check for beetles. "I don't see any on you, I think you're fine."

Nikki is panting and struggling to catch her breath. "I just can't stand those things. All those pointy ends," she says with a trembling voice. Her cheeks are flushed and she continues to run her hands through her hair. "I think there was something back there, though, in the cabinet."

My mind conjures up the memory of the patient who had one of those beetles in her ear. Such a weird coincidence. I clench my teeth together at the recollection of the wilted hard shelled body.

"I want to see," I say, surprising myself. Everyone stares at me silently. Probably shocked that I would want to see a bunch of bugs, but I am determined to look and find out if there really is something in the hidden drawer. I start back toward the entrance into the shack. Avery follows behind me, with his phone light already switched to help light the path ahead.

We approach the cabinet and I see a drawer that has been left open. I go straight to that one and duck down to look inside. Avery's light reflects off of the hard shells of what has to be thousands of wriggling pincher bugs. The forked ends look sharp, and they vibrate as they crawl over one another and spill out of the back of the cabinet. I gasp and straighten up.

"Geez, there really are so many," Avery notes and he takes a step back. The bugs continue to spill forth and drop onto the grimy ground below, making small clicking sounds as their bodies tumble down. They crawl over one another in a thick layer, legs and long antennas moving under the glow of the phone's beam. I have never seen anything like this in my entire life.

I take a fortifying breath for strength, and reach my hand into the mass of earwigs. I saw something back there, and I want it. I feel as if I could cry as the sensation of the pincher bugs swarming across my hand intensifies. The small legs climb up over my hand and up my arm, I bite my lip and keep feeling around until I grasp what is hidden beneath. It's a book. I pull it out and shake my hand to dislodge some clingers, and slap the cover to remove more pincher bugs. Then, I run toward the doorway and back into the light.

"Cora, what the hell," Avery says as catches up to me and brushes off the remaining beatles that have grasped onto the sleeve of my shirt.

"This was in there," I say, holding up a battered old book so he can see it.

"Oh no, not another journal," Avery moans, with a look of distrust on his face as he eyes the book in my hand.

"It's not a journal," I reply, turning the book over so the cover is visible. The title on the cover simply says *Dark Occult.* I flip it open and a musky scent is released as little motes of dust rise from the stained and yellowed pages. "It looks like a book on black magic..."

"Oh no. No, no, no. I was cool with the creepy little teenager's journal, but this shit is not alright. This is bad shit, Cora. We should just put it back. We don't want to mess with this stuff. My grandma from the islands has way too many stories about this voodoo kind of stuff."

"I thought you didn't believe in it, though?" I ask in a challenging tone.

"I don't," he replies defensively. "It still makes me uncomfortable, though. Please don't mess with it."

I flip the book shut and tuck it under my arm. "I just want to look at it. It's just a book. It's not a big deal."

"Ugh," Avery says in exasperation, knowing better than to argue with me once my mind is made up. We look around, and don't see Kate, Leo, or Nikki anywhere. "Where did they go?" Avery asks, puzzled.

I scan the surrounding area, and see no sign of them. "Maybe they went around back?" I suggest. Avery takes a deep breath and then reaches his hand out to me, I take it, and we head around the back side of the shed. Once we round the corner, we spot them a football fieldlength away, circled around something .

Avery and I move toward them at a quick pace, and about halfway there I am able to discern what they are gathered around. It's another dead deer.

We walk up to the group, the smell of marijuana greeting us as Leo blows clouds of smoke into the air. Avery hangs back, not wanting to get close to the carcass. His expression is serious and he looks drained. He really doesn't like supernatural stuff after all the Cape Verdean stories his grandma scared him with as a child. I get it. I should be more considerate.

Kate gestures toward the animal splayed in the dirt, "we called the non-emergency police number to report it. There's clearly something making these animals sick and it should get looked into. The person I spoke with said they would contact animal removal services..."

Nikki is hovering around the deer and taking photos at different angles, which seems morbid to me. I stare at the animal's small bone colored antlers, and then startle when I see that the eyes of the deer are a filmy white.

White eyes. No pupils.

"Ew, its eyes rolled back in its head," Nikki says when she notices the blankness staring up from the deer's skull.

I look up and catch Kate's gaze. Her complexion has paled as she nods almost imperceptibly to me. She is thinking of how Heather described Liv's eyes on the night they killed Shane, too. She said that they had gone completely white, with no pupils or irises...just like this dead deer's. Just like what Avery's trauma patient had said of his attacker.

Suddenly Avery clears his throat and speaks up, he has also noticed the abnormal state of the corpse's eyes, "y'all should back up. Who knows what diseases that deer could have, it doesn't look well."

I take a few steps back, and Leo and Kate do the same. Nikki glances up at him, her face in an expression of challenge. “I’ve been holding my breath when I get by it, and I haven’t touched anything, so…” she shrugs and continues to photograph the scene. “It doesn’t even smell or anything, and there’s no bugs. It can’t have been dead too long,” she adds.

Avery shakes his head a little, and cracks the knuckles on his right hand, his familiar sign of nervousness. “Look at those scratch marks on the tree over there,” he says motioning to a nearby oak. Deep cuts are slashed into the wood. “What do you think that means?”

Nikki shrugs, “it’s better than the Nazi symbols on the trees where we parked.”

“Yeah, I noticed those,” Avery responds, looking irritated. “Those were clearly made by assholes, but these look more animalistic.”

Nikki turns and walks up to the oak with the gashes, and starts to photograph the scene. Some of the trees in this area looked like they have been burned or survived a fire in the past. They are charred, dark, and twisted. Nikki continues to snap photos with fervor.

“Well, I think we should probably get going, anyway,” Leo adds, rocking back on his heels bringing his hand rolled joint to his lips and taking a one last long drag before licking his finger and tapping the end to put out the roach. “I’m hungry.”

“How can you eat after seeing this?” Kate says, pointing down at the deer.

“Doesn’t bother me,” Leo says with a dopey smile and squinty blood shot eyes.

We start walking back, and Nikki trails a few paces behind, continuing to photograph the landscape. I take in the image of the trees, the long branches arched to embrace one another, and I wonder what it all looks like through her camera lens.

As we make our way up the path back toward the cars, I show everyone the book I had gotten from the back of the bug infested cabinet.

"Shit, you've got some balls," Nikki says with a tinge of admiration, "I never would have willingly stuck my hand into the hell hole."

"Yeah, well. Nothing can really stop me when I am curious."

"So, It's some sort of witchy book? Figures," Leo says. "Whatever happened to the journal? I thought you were going to bring that today?"

Kate shoots me a quick look. Her possum face is plastered on even though she is trying hard to appear relaxed.

"Oh, yeah. I guess it slipped my mind. I'll bring it to Noah's next weekend." I say with a smile, going for nonchalant. I can see Avery studying me out of the corner of my eye, but ignore his gaze. "He's still having his Halloween party, right?"

"Yup. He's stoked about it," Leo says. "He won't stop talking about how excited he is. You know he lives for parties."

"Oh, we know," Nikki says sarcastically.

"I can't believe you threw a beer at him the other night," Leo says, shaking his head.

"That's, like, the worst thing you could have done to him. Not because you got him covered in beer, but because you chose to waste alcohol," Avery adds, with a laugh.

"Yeah, well, he'll survive," Nikki responds, dryly.

CHAPTER 18:

We say our goodbyes once we are back at the cars. Avery works tonight, but says he will stop by my place tomorrow. He gives me a searching look. "What's going on in that beautiful mind of yours?"

"I promise to fill you in on everything when you come over tomorrow," I answer softly, feeling guilty. He nods, his expression concerned. "I love you," he adds and places a soft kiss on my temple.

"Infinitally," I say in return and we hold each other's gaze for a moment before he climbs into Leo's car. As he shuts the door, I feel a wedge between us form. I don't like that I am hiding the research I did about Shane, and that I haven't told him about the meeting with the journalist coming up. I usually tell Avery everything, and I wonder if I am making a mistake by not confiding in him right now. I make a vow to myself that I will inform him of everything about the reporter as soon as we are alone together.

I circle around to the passenger side of Kate's car and am about to climb in, when she stops me,"uh uh, nope!" She calls from her side. "You're not bringing that dirty nasty book into my car." I stop in my tracks, frowning.

"What do you want me to do? It might have clues. I want to look through it." Kate rolls her eyes, "*clues*...gosh, Cora. Stick it in the trunk, I guess."

She pops open the back of her car, and I tuck the book in. It looks ridiculous sitting in her huge trunk all alone. When I climb into the passenger side she is already holding out a little travel size hand sanitizer and squirts some into my palm. "I can't believe you even took that out of the bug infested creepy as hell shack. So much for your theory about there not being bugs," she says with a smirk, "did you see that axe and the bucket, though? What the hell...and what was with the eyes of that deer? It's like a continuation of that journal...which makes me even more convinced that the girl was telling the truth and we need to go to the authorities with everything we have found."

Kate says all of this without taking a breath and it tumbles out in a rush of words. Her head whips to the side as she sees Leo's car pull out and she lifts her hand to wave with a fake cheerful smile as he passes us and blows her a kiss. As soon as his car is facing the road, her smile drops, and she turns to me again, "I'm serious, Cora."

"I doubt they would even believe us," I mutter, feeling annoyed.

"Well, that's none of our business. We will give the facts and it's up to them to decide what to do with it. Keeping this to ourselves isn't the answer though."

My heart tells me that Kate is right, but my mind is thinking of all the interesting possibilities we could discover. *Why am I like this?*

"Okay, I agree under one condition, we will go to this meeting with the journalist and get more info first, and then bring it all to the police after. We already scheduled a time to meet with her tomorrow and told her that we have information, so I don't want to just ghost her, you know?"

Kate lets out a heavy sigh and runs her fingers through her dark glossy hair. "Fine. After tomorrow, we bring it all to the cops," she says, looking at me decisively.

I throw my hands up in a gesture of surrender, and then reach over and buckle myself in.

Kate pushes the button to start her car, but it doesn't work. "Oh, come ON! Not again," she says, hitting the button another time. "I really need to get this issue checked out. This is a brand new car, damn it," she whines, as she hits the button again, but is not greeted with the start of the engine. The car remains dead, and Kate hits her steering wheel in frustration. She grabs her phone, and scrolls through her contacts, "I'm going to call Leo and see if he will turn around."

In an instant, her car starts. The lights inside begin flashing on and off, and the music blares through the speakers. Instead of the pop song we had been listening to while driving here, the chorus of *The Beautiful People* by Marilyn Manson blares loudly from the speakers. The aggressive rasp of his voice and the thumping rhythm of the drums is jarring as it cuts through the silence that previously pressed down on us.

Kate slaps her hand onto the *off* control for the music, but it keeps playing steadily. If anything, it seems to grow louder. Kate is panting and staring in panic at her car dashboard. My heart feels like it is in sync with the song, and I sit silently in confusion of what is happening as the lights continue to flash above us and the metal music roars. Kate covers her ears and closes her eyes, looking like a child warding off a nightmare. As quickly as it all started, it stops, and we are met with an eerie silence.

Then, in the dense quiet that has chased away the noise of the music, a small voice whispers "help me." Kate lets out a gasp and brings her trembling hands to her mouth.

"Help me, help me, help me…" the disembodied whisper repeats over and over, growing louder and faster, filling the space like smoke, smothering us. "Help mehelpmehelpme," the voice continues, the words rasping and running together. It feels like it's being spoken inside of my skull. Then, the whispered plea makes a choking, gasping sound, and is snuffed out all at once like a candle flame pinched between fingers.

My heart is hammering and Kate's hands visibly shake as she reaches down to shift into drive. She races to circle the car around and turn back onto the main road of Dyer Lane. We sit quietly for a few moments, both coming down from the adrenaline that has flooded our bodies during the surprise of the car malfunction and the frightening whispered words.

"Well…" I say, breaking the silence that feels almost holy after all that just transpired, "that was...something."

Kate allows her solemn gaze to drift to me for a moment and nods her head, still at a loss for words. I wring my hands in my lap, trying to think of what to say next.

Kate finally seems to find her voice and says, "this place is so fucking haunted."

CHAPTER 19:

When I finally get back to my apartment, I am starving, but can't bring myself to eat. I still feel shaky and off balance. I fill a glass with water, and the ice pings against the side of the cup as I quickly walk to the living room to set it on a coaster at the coffee table. Even though I am rattled, I have work to do and need to come up with a plan for the interview tomorrow. I open my laptop, place Heather's journal to the side of it, and grab my newest acquisition, the Dark Occult book next to that. The book has to be the one that Heather claimed Liv used to summon a spirit. I've always been incredibly skeptical of this demon stuff, but can't deny that after everything that has happened recently my mindset is rapidly changing.

Due to Kate's insistence that the book was filthy, I take a Lysol wipe to the cover and have to agree that based on the layer of grime stuck to the wipe, it was in fact extremely dirty. I pause for a moment and wonder if I just tampered with evidence by cleaning the book, and then reason that I am beyond that at this point. I am also not fully convinced that I want to involve the police at all.

Before sitting down, I light a pumpkin candle, because *'tis the season*, and all that. It isn't lost on me that I am delving into a mystery involving murderous witches a mere week before Halloween.

I tap a pencil on the table, trying to think of an outline for the meeting tomorrow. My mind is blank. There has to be something supernatural happening. If I doubted it at all before, I am almost certain now.

Help me. What happened in the car had been a whispered plea. Insistent, and almost angry in its persistence. It has needled its way into my brain and burrowed within the folds of my mind. Haunting me. I take a sip of water to calm myself.

My thoughts wander to my dad's death. I think the reason why I want to solve this mystery so badly is because I felt so incompetent when my dad died. He had been neglecting to take his blood pressure medication, and his uncontrolled high BP was most likely the cause of his sudden heart attack. I blamed myself for not encouraging him to be more diligent with his meds. I felt like it was my fault that the CPR didn't work, and that he passed away. If it were not for the reassuring words of my mom, Kate, and Avery, I would still blame myself for my inability to save him. I think in some ways, I still do.

"If only" is a common phrase that I think about. *If only* I had insisted he stayed on top of his medication instead of ignoring that he wasn't taking it. *If only* I had done CPR better. *If only* I had been able to bring him back when his heart stopped.

I know that investigating a random mystery like this has absolutely nothing to do with the death of my dad, but for some reason it feels like it has everything to do with it. It's a chance for me to piece something together and lose myself in a task. That type of distraction is something that helps when my mind begins to create narratives of all that I lack.

This is something I *can* do. The people involved aren't even alive anymore, so I don't have to worry about my inability to save anyone. I already know I'm a failure at that. Sometimes I feel like nursing is the wrong direction for me. I am so plagued with doubts. I should drop out after this semester is over, and give my placement in the nursing program to someone who actually deserves a spot. At least as a Scribe I'm not responsible for saving people.

I let out a sigh and continue to wrack my brain, hoping that once I've had some food I will be able to think more clearly and focus on what's in front of me instead of ruminating on all my anxieties. I take another long drink of water, savoring the coolness sliding down my throat. Then, I decide that rather than staring at a blank notepad, my time will be better spent reading more of Heather's journal. If I have more content, maybe questions and links will naturally arise.

The condensation from the glass has left my hands cold and wet. I dry them off on the fluffy blanket I have curled up in, and grab Heather's diary. It doesn't take long for me to find the spot where I left off.

* * *

September 30, 1997

I'm supposed to meet Liv over at Tasha's house in a couple hours so we can all ride to school together. The sun hasn't even come up yet, and I am savoring the dusky skyline outside and the chill in the air this morning. I want to stay in and ditch my classes for the day.

I haven't seen my friends since the night we killed Shane, but I feel them close to me. Sometimes I can hear whispers of thoughts that aren't mine being spoken to me in my head. It's both a comfort and a concern. I know if I tell anyone about this, they will think I am crazy. Perhaps I am.

I know I said that I kind of liked this new version of myself, but I don't feel that way anymore. I feel scared. I feel used.

I do not know the demon's name that Liv summoned, but it doesn't seem necessary. I know his desires and needs at all times, like he speaks to my mind with his own. We call him "Father" and he only requires us to be faithful to him, and in turn he will make us powerful. He is ancient. He has lived upon the land for centuries. Father says that Dyer Lane is a special place. One he can thrive upon. He survives by inhabiting the bodies of animals, but they do not last long as hosts for him, and he prefers the bodies of humans. We are the perfect vessels for him. He says it is an honor that Liv has been chosen.

I know that Liv has always wanted to be wanted, and now she is. Her mother's lack of interest has made her crave attention. I always wished my mom were more like Liv's. Mine is always trying SO hard, it's annoying.

I caught her searching my room last night. All she found was some pot, thankfully. I don't think I can keep this journal anywhere at home anymore. I am going to have to hide it in the cabin, in a secret spot where I know it will be safe from prying eyes. I can't let my mom find out these secrets. It would break her.

I hate her sometimes, but she's still my mom, and I love her, too.

* * *

October 1, 1997

Yesterday was the best Monday I have had in a long time. I could finally breathe in between classes and my chest was no longer tight in anticipation of encountering Shane. For the first time in a long time, I felt light and free walking through the halls.

I don't like being tied to Father, but I do think the oath we made with him has given my mind an edge. For example, I somehow knew all the answers for the exam today in Science class even though I didn't do the reading and haven't been paying any attention during lectures. My mind just knew everything. It was insane. I wonder what else I can do now that we have opened the gate with the spirit realm.

At lunch, Tasha, Liv, and I sat at our normal table, but that was the only typical thing about the day. There were zero shouts of harassment across the cafeteria, my locker wasn't defiled in any way, and I didn't have to walk through the halls in anger. That felt good.

One strange thing was that Liv didn't eat anything during lunch time. Usually, she gets a sandwich and some chips from the cafeteria, but today she drank from a little silver flask that she brought from home. Her drink coated her teeth in a dark ruby film. Tasha and I exchanged glances when Liv wasn't looking, but neither one of us mentioned anything. I can sense that Tasha is scared, too.

At times, I catch Liv staring at me with a hungry expression. I feel like she wants to rip my throat out and get fresh blood from my jugular. It is unsettling. She isn't herself anymore.

I know that Father has needs to be met to stay alive within Liv, but seeing her drink blood like a fucking vampire is too much. Also, since Father has inhabited her, Liv has developed a tic. Her head twitches toward her right shoulder in a quick snapping motion. It startled me the first time I saw it, but she assured me that she has never felt better.

When Liv touched my arm today, the pentagram necklace I always wear glowed hot on my skin. It was painful.. a knowing look was in her eyes, like he knew my inner thoughts and that I wanted him gone. This look was a warning.

After school, we all went over to Liv's house. Pam was drunk, as usual, and didn't even notice us come in the door. Her music of choice today was some moody Sarah McLachlan song. Her mascara was running down her cheeks in black smudges as she cried on the couch.

We went straight to Liv's bedroom. We had to discuss what to do with Shane's body. After we killed him, we chopped him into smaller pieces and hid him in two of our backpacks at the cabin. It wasn't too messy with most of Shane's blood all drained from his body.

Axing through bones is a lot harder than it looks in movies.

It took us hours. Shane's parts are still sitting in the bags and we need to go back and get rid of him. No one seems to be looking for him yet, but it's only a matter of time. Tasha's aunt and uncle own a farm. I think we are going to go there later today to get rid of his pieces. I am sickened by the thought.

I am so conflicted right now. While I am grateful to have Shane gone from my life, I think I actually regret killing him. I also regret involving my friends and wish I had figured out another way. I wish we had never played with the Ouija board or gotten dark magic books. I wish we had never done the blood oath. I can't tell my friends this, but I wish we could go back to the way things were before Father was around.

I know I wanted to contact the spirit realm, but not like this. I feel like our friendship will never be the same. We traded a bully for a blood drinking ghost that lives in my friend and I honestly don't know which is worse. I don't need to know all the answers in class. I would happily give back anything that Father has bestowed on me. I don't even plan to go to college, so I couldn't care less...I just wanted to be free of Shane.

I feel unsure of what to do with all of my racing thoughts. Tasha seems like she is swimming in fear and can't come to the surface for air, and I worry that I am not far behind. I worry we are in too deep and Liv is the only one with a lifejacket. I sense that Father is expecting something in return from us and I don't know if I am going to like what it is.

* * *

October 2, 1997

It's been done. Shane's body has been disposed of.

After school, we rode our bikes back to the shed and got the backpacks, which were starting to smell really bad. Tasha tried to fix it by spritzing a ton of cucumber melon scented body spray on the bags, which only made it worse.

We went back into town and called Cole from a pay phone and asked him to come get us. Tasha told him we had a school project on farm life and needed to collect data at his house. He bought it, and took us to his family's farm. We rolled the car windows down on the way there and I crossed my fingers that Cole wouldn't notice the smell. If he did, he didn't mention it.

When we arrived at the farm, we walked over to the pig pen and pretended to observe them and take notes. Cole left us to it, and we emptied our bags as quickly as possible into the food trough.

Those animals were starving and more than willing to tear apart whatever is placed into their pen. Bits of Shane seemed to disappear in minutes, his bones sinking into the slop and mixing in with the other various scraps that had been dumped there. It was horrible to watch. The pigs were nothing like the cute little one in the movie my little sister likes to watch that came out a couple years ago. I think it was called Babe.

Yeah, these pigs were not like Babe. These pigs were in a frenzy. Their squeals made me want to cover my ears with my hands. I don't think anyone will ever find even a scrap of Shane.

Liv's eyes turned white as she watched the pigs feast. She let out a low throaty laugh, that sounded nothing like her. It made me think of boots scraping on gravel. Her smile stretched across her face, creating bloody splits on each corner of her lips, and every tooth in her mouth showed as she watched in amusement. I felt cold and nauseous.

As much as I hated Shane, I do feel sad for his family. Over the last day, the lack of remorse I initially felt has begun to transform into so much guilt. Today at school, they announced there would be an organized search for him. Shane is officially deemed missing. His father was crying, and I felt terrible for the obvious pain we have caused. As if it wasn't enough that my father broke up his marriage and is now living with his wife…now I have killed his only son.

The lack of my own personal pain now that Shane is gone is a relief, school has never been better. But I feel selfish after seeing the suffering I have caused others. I can't go back in time, so I am just trying my best to move on. I mean, I know what we did was wrong, but I felt like I had no other options.

Also, I am majorly worried about Liv. Her thick hair has begun to fall out in clumps. It was once shiny, and is now dull, and becoming sparse. She has oozing sores forming on her lips, and still has that tic that flings her neck toward her shoulder. I worry that Father is killing her from the inside out and I feel helpless.

* * *

I pause my reading and feel a rush of nausea. *Pigs. They fed him to the pigs.* A clenched fist squeezes in my stomach at the thought of it. I get up and begin to pace, then stop to brace myself against my kitchen counter and take some deep breaths. That was one of the most heinous things I have ever read in my life.

How evil does someone have to be to do something like that? Heather's friend sounds physically sick in addition to mentally ill. Don't these teens' parents notice any of this? Then I remember Heather describing how Liv's mother is a depressed alcoholic who neglects her, and that Heather avoids any connection with her own Mother, a single working mom of two...and Heather's father's recent abandonment of his family.

Again, I wonder how much of what Heather describes is fact. She says she is hearing voices in her head...that's something that is common with psychiatric patients and maybe she is an unreliable narrator. It seems like she has lost touch with reality, and has a wild imagination. Not for the first time, I wonder what happened to Heather after she graduated.

Where is she now?

CHAPTER 20:

Kate comes over to my apartment about an hour before we are scheduled to meet with the journalist, Jessica Harper. We go to the Magic Bean to grab a quick breakfast and coffee. I want to tell Kate about what I read in the journal last night, but also think she will freak out and cancel this meeting, so I suppress the urge to fill her in. The comforting aroma of coffee and pastries cheers me as we enter the shop, and it helps to settle my nerves.

"It was so hard to lie to Mandy about where I was going," Kate tells me as we wait in line together to order our lattes and breakfast sandwiches. "I told her I had a pap smear. It was the only way I could get her to not want to join."

"Maybe we should have invited her?" I ask.

"Nah. I already told you. We are keeping this little escapade between us a secret, and then it's time to involve the police. I haven't changed my mind about that part," she says with a challenging look. Before I can answer or object, the barista greets us with a perky "I can take your order now." We halt our conversation and place our breakfast requests. I throw a blueberry muffin into my order because the comfort of carbs is too much to pass on right now.

We make our way back to Kate's car with our coffees and bagged food in hand. Kate begins to tell me about how Mandy came home late last night, and she was thankful to have some time to herself to process all the strangeness of the day. Kate is still spooked from the car incident, and I can't blame her. When coupled with everything else that happened yesterday, it's a lot.

"I felt bad, though," Kate says. "Mandy had a big scratch on her hand that I had to help her bandage. It looked pretty deep and she seemed upset, but she said she was sure she didn't need stitches. Guess how she said she got the cut?"

I shrug, at a loss, and knowing that this was a rhetorical question and how Kate always likes to tell her stories.

"A crystal.. A fucking crystal cut her hand."

I raise my eyebrows at that. "Wow." I'm distracted and kind of don't care about Mandy's crystal cut right now but try to feign some interest.

"Yeah," Kate laughs, "only Mandy would injure herself with a crystal."

I smile at Kate as I open a map app on my phone and plug in the address that Jessica texted. I feel both nervous and eager at the same time, and am grateful that Kate will be with me. I wouldn't want to do this alone. I've never been a skilled liar, but Kate thinks quick on her feet and is good at directing conversations, so I know these skills of hers will come in handy if I start to falter. I begin to wish I had told Jessica the truth, but I know what I am doing is strange and don't want her to think I'm some weirdo and decline a meeting. At least this way, she just thinks I am an interested student who is looking deeper into a local unsolved case. I guess it's not too far off from the truth...

We pull up to our destination in less time than I anticipated. Jessica lives in a small brick house with yellow roses blooming on either side of a white front door despite the cold fall weather. I glance at the dashboard clock and note that we are ten minutes early.

Kate takes a sip of her coffee, "we should probably wait a little bit before we go up, don't you think?"

I nod at her and scan the neighborhood. The houses on

the street are all well kept, the lawns mowed, and porches tidy. It looks like a typical small town suburban street, much like all the neighborhoods in Stone Bay do. Outsiders refer to the town as "quaint." There is a new side, and an older side, and this falls into the latter, but many of the homes have been remodeled and kept up at a high level. No one would ever think less of it for not being as modern as the other area of town.

"So, do you have a plan for when we go in there? What are you going to say?" Kate inquires as she plays with the ends of her long hair.

"Um. Kinda. I was just going to see what information she has, and then tell her we heard Shane liked to go to Dyer Lane a lot and see what kind of knowledge she has about that place..."

Kate frowns, "that doesn't even make sense, Cora," she says. "How would we have heard Shane likes to go to Dyer Lane? That sounds so random, you've got to have something better than that."

I shrug, "I don't know. Do you have a better idea?" She shakes her head and stares out the window at Jessica's house. "Why don't you just show her the diary?"

"What? Why? You actually think that's a good idea?" I'm clutching my bag in my lap and staring at Kate with narrowed eyes, trying to figure out if she is being serious or not.

"No. It's the only thing I can think of that makes any sense, though. She writes about this sort of stuff all the time, maybe she will be able to discern if what is written is fact or fiction and help us decide what to do..."

"I thought your mind was made up and we were going to the police?"

"Oh, it is. I just dont think *yours* is. It would be nice to have another voice of reason on my side," she says with a wink.

I roll my eyes at her, and then glance over at the clock again. It's a couple minutes before noon. I point at the numbers on the clock and say "good enough."

I unbuckle my seatbelt, grab the handle for the door and swing it open. Kate follows my lead and gets out of the car, too.

A thousand wings flutter inside my stomach as we walk up to Jessica Harper's porch. Kate reaches for the doorbell, just as the door swings open to reveal a short woman with impeccable makeup. Her lips are expertly lined and glossy, and her light red hair hangs over her shoulder in a braid.

"Hi, I'm Jessica," the woman says as she steps back, clearing a path for us to enter. "Come in. I have about forty five minutes to chat and then I need to be off for another meeting."

"Okay, that sounds like plenty of time," I reply as I step inside, Kate following close behind me. "Thanks for meeting with us. I'm Cora, and this is my friend, Kate. She's working on the project with me." I gesture to Kate whose eyes are dancing around Jessica's cozy home, taking it all in.

The interior is decorated in a modern farmhouse style. There is a plethora of framed family photos adorning the walls, and bright flowers in a vase on the kitchen counter. It smells like vanilla and everything is kept clean and welcoming.

We follow Jessica to a sitting area near the front of the house. There is a navy blue sectional and a loveseat surrounding a dark wood coffee table. A bright teal briefcase is resting on the sectional. Jessica reaches over and grabs it from the cushions, depositing it on the ground. "Cute bag," I say, "it's such a great color."

"Thanks. It was my mom's," she replies as she lowers herself to the love seat. Kate and I take our places on the now empty sectional, facing her. I place my boring brown bag on my lap and start to pull out a notepad, my fingers brush Heather's journal and I feel a pang of nervousness.

"So, how should we begin? You mentioned you had new information about Shane, and that brings up a lot of questions for me. So, should you interview me first, or the other way around?" Jessica asks, with a smile. She is leaned forward with a neutral expression on her face and her hands are clasped in her lap.

I clear my throat, "Well, I guess I just want to know what you think happened to Shane...from what you mentioned in your article it sounds like you followed the case closely, but there weren't many details shared and not much online about his disappearance."

Jessica purses her lips. "Shane's case wasn't very unique in a place like Stone Bay. Teens go missing here all the time. It's actually quite common. A lot of people thought maybe he was a runaway. A teenager who was bored with the small town life." Her eyes drift over to a framed photo that rests on a side table. "It was never really proven one way or another, as you know from my article. I can tell you that I don't think he was a trafficking victim, but that also is something that can't be said for sure."

I follow the path of Jessica's gaze to the photograph she had been glancing at. It's of a teenage girl with long black hair. She is staring straight at the camera with a challenging expression in her piercing gaze. The girl looks beautiful like a rose. Not in the way that the flower is delicate, but in the way that if you grab it wrong, there will be blood.

When I focus back on Jessica, I see a similarity between the two. Something in the way the mouth is shaped, or the chin. Jessica must have noticed my interest and sighs, "that's my sister," she says, gesturing toward the framed photo. "She disappeared shortly after Shane did. I was only seven years old at the time, but it turned my world upside down. Everyone thought she was a runaway, but if I am being honest with myself, I don't." She shakes her head softly, "I also don't think Shane was, either."

Kate gives me a slight nudge in the arm with her elbow. She is studying the photo, and when I look back and examine it closer, I see the small pentagram necklace around the girl's neck. My flesh breaks out in goosebumps as I hear Kate say, "I am so sad to hear that happened, that must have been so difficult for your family. What is your sister's name?"

Jessica sighs. "Heather. Her name was Heather."

My grip tightens on my pen and notepad as I try to appear calm. "You said she disappeared?" I ask in a concerned tone. I try to swallow but my mouth is too dry. I pull a water bottle out of my bag and notice that my hand is shaking.

"Yes. It was actually a similar story to Shane's. About a month after his disappearance, she and her friends just didn't come home one night. They were deemed missing after a couple days, and there was a search for all three of them. Nothing ever came of it. Since Heather and her friends were... troubled, some may say, I think that people just assumed they all ran off together." Jessica pauses. "Our family had a complicated connection to Shane's, so my mom always thought the cases may have been connected somehow, but there was no way to prove that. The entire thing was a dead end. It's what got me into this line of work, though. I grew up seeing firsthand what these types of tragic mysteries can do to a family. I feel like if I can reveal information and bring about answers for people in any way, I want to do that."

I nod, "I can understand that feeling."

I feel Kate staring hard at me. I know she wants me to hand over the journal and come clean. I take a deep breath. "Thanks for sharing all of this with me. It's helpful." I reach into my bag and pull out the purple diary. "I think there is something you should have."

I hand Jessica the journal, and she looks down at the cover with a creased brow. Her finger traces the embossed name on the cover. *Heather.* She flips it open and starts to slowly flip through the pages, her eyes wide as she realizes this is really the journal of her missing older sister. "Where did you get this?" she asks in a hushed voice.

"It was found in a little shed on a road off Dyer Lane...have you ever heard of that place?" I ask. Jessica's face is grim as she looks up at me. "Who hasn't?" she says, and then goes back to studying the journal. "Heather was into some dark stuff. I was young, but I could still recognize that she was not a typical teenager. She was always so angry..." she trails off, lost in thought for a moment. Then, her voice takes on a hard edge, "I'm sorry, but were you aware when you scheduled this meeting that I am Heather's sister?"

"No. I swear, we had no idea. We just wanted more information on the Shane Dodson disappearance because of some things we read in the journal."

Jessica nods slowly, processing this. "And are you even writing a report for school?"

I shake my head, feeling like a total asshole. "No. We aren't. I'm sorry we lied."

Jessica shrugs and continues to scan the inside of the journal, avoiding looking back at me. Kate nudges me again with her elbow. I think this is the longest she has gone without talking and I am shocked she hasn't said more. I look at her trying to perceive what she wants from me. Her eyes bore into mine. She clearly wants me to tell Jessica about what we have read.

I clench my jaw, I am feeling nauseous from all the nerves. "Um. I do need to warn you about some things...We read parts of the journal and there is stuff that Heather wrote that is linked to what may have happened to Shane."

Jessica's head snaps up to look at me with a questioning stare. "What do you mean?"

Kate finally can't hold her tongue anymore. "Heather basically wrote a murder confession," she says in a fast gush of words. I can feel her body uncoil a little bit as she seems to become more relaxed now that she has shared this news and unburdened herself of a secret.

Jessica looks puzzled, and I feel a surge of annoyance with Kate's lack of tact. "We read some of the journal," I repeat in an apologetic tone. "We aren't sure how much of what Heather wrote is true or if some of it was fiction. There are some details in there that implicate her in Shane's disappearance...but there's no way of proving it." I say in an attempt to salvage the situation and gain more insight without completely disturbing this poor woman. She will get it when she reads this diary for herself.

Jessica stares back at the photo of Heather with a glazed

look in her eyes. "I don't feel like I ever really got to know my sister. She always kept me at arms length, and I was only in first grade. I just know my mom was devastated when Heather went missing. She always tried so hard to make a happy home for us, but nothing was ever good enough for Heather. My mother passed away from cancer a couple years ago, but always kept the hope that Heather would return to her one day. I think all the stress from our broken home really impacted her health and I can't help but wonder if things had been different, my mom would still be here."

I feel sad. Kate and I came to this woman's home and have completely turned her day into shit. "I'm sorry," I say, truthfully. "I wish things had been different. Heather writes a lot about her feelings and family in there," I gesture toward the journal that sits in Jessica's lap. "Maybe it will bring you some closure to know what was going on with her."

I suppress a shiver. I don't think Jessica will actually get any comfort from the journal, but I want to leave her with some hope. Kate and I will go soon, and Jessica can read the journal and decide what she wants to do with it. She can choose to go to the police, or not. It's going to be out of our hands now, and among the sadness, I also feel an overwhelming relief.

Jessica slowly drags her gaze from Heather's framed face back to Kate and I. Her eyes shimmer with unshed tears. "Well, this was not at all what I expected from this meeting. Thank you for bringing this to me. I will read it, and I appreciate you coming to me with it," she says as she stands, our cue that it's time to leave.

I nod, and Kate and I silently follow Jessica to the front door. We step onto the porch, and I turn for one last word, "I'm sorry for misleading you, I just wanted you to agree to meet with us. I had no idea you were related to Heather, but I'm glad this found its way to you." I gesture to the purple bound notebook Jessica still has clutched in her hands.

She gives me a tight lipped smile. "Thanks," she says

softly.

Kate and I continue down the path of yellow roses and make our way back to her car. I climb into the passenger side and look up to see Jessica still standing there looking like a ghost of the woman who greeted us only thirty minutes ago. She slowly raises a hand to me in farewell and closes her front door, shutting the world out. I wonder if she will make it to her next meeting. I wouldn't. If I were her, I would lock myself away and finish that journal cover to cover.

"What are the odds that would happen?" Kate asks me with wide eyes. "Must have been meant to be. I'm glad you gave her the diary. That was the right thing to do," Kate murmurs, pulling me from my thoughts as she starts her car. "I don't think it will bring her any consolation, but she deserves to know. I'm actually a little surprised that you gave it up."

"Yeah, I took photos of the rest of the entries with my phone, so it was an easy choice," I say. Kate looks at me with her mouth hanging open in an exaggerated face of shock. "Wow. Of course you did. I'm just relieved it's off your hands now. It had bad energy, as Mandy would say. We don't need that object hanging around messing with our vibrations, or whatever."

I scoff. "Oh gosh. Are you going to pull out some crystals now?" I ask.

Kate smirks as she reaches into her shirt and takes out a stone. It is a swirl of light blue and yellow hanging from a golden chain around her neck. "Mandy gave me this today when I said that I was nervous for my doctor appointment. Apparently it is a protection stone."

"Oh gosh," I roll my eyes. "Well, maybe it worked because you were super chill in there. I was actually surprised at how calm you were."

"It's the stone, baby!" Kate says, lifting the crystal to her lips and kissing it. "It grounded me," she said in an exaggerated mystical voice with narrowed eyes.

I start to laugh and then after a moment of silence, I ask, "do you still want to go to the police?"

"Nah. Let the sister decide what to do now."

CHAPTER 21:

By the time we have returned to Kate's house, the sun has chased away the morning fog and it almost feels warm outside. Kate slams her car into park and then turns in her seat to face me, "alright, show me the photos."

I pull out my phone and open the photo album app to look at the pictures of Heather's remaining journal entries. I am stunned when I see that every photographed image shows blank journal entries. Nothing is written, although I *know* the pictures I had taken were of fully filled out entries.

So, I do what any normal person would do and freak the fuck out. "No, no, no," I mutter in panicked frustration, flipping through each photo on my phone faster and faster. *How could the pictures all be of blank pages?* That is impossible. I know without a shadow of a doubt that blank pages aren't what I had photographed. I am certain that I had taken numerous pictures of fully filled out entries written by Heather.

Kate leans over the middle console to try and get a glance at my phone. "What's wrong?"

I rake my hands through my hair and feel like screaming. *How can this be reality?*

I hand Kate my phone, and she swipes through photo after photo of blank journal entries, I attempt to wrap my mind around it all.

"There is no way that I took all those photos of blank pages. I swear that I didn't. I can't understand how this is happening," I say in a shrill voice. I feel like crying because this entire situation is insane.

"I believe you," Kate says in a soft voice to counterbalance the panic radiating off me. She has a worried expression plastered on her face as she hands my phone back to me. "This is obviously something way over our heads. It's supernatural. We need to let it go. It's too much."

"I know," I say softly. "You're right. This is crazy. I just want to know what it all means."

"I wish I could match your enthusiasm to find answers to all of this, but honestly, it just scares me a lot and I don't want any part of it. Some things are just better left alone and don't need an explanation. You know?"

Kate's words hang in the air like a feather in a breeze. My breaths are coming faster as silence fills the car. I can hear my blood rushing as if I am holding a shell to my ear. I close my eyes and rest my head back, trying to calm my nerves.

Kate sighs, "I don't want to be harsh...but I only came with you today because I couldn't stand the thought of you going to some rando's house all alone. You need to drop this Nancy Drew fantasy you have going on. It won't end well if you don't. I have a bad feeling about it all. Let's just take this as a win. The journal is gone, and we can leave it at that."

"You know I loved those books growing up," I answer, flatly. My eyes are still closed, but my mind feels more clear now that I have my breathing under control.

"Damn it, Cora! This is real life and we aren't meant to be dabbling in this stuff. The fact that my car wouldn't start both times we went to Dyer Lane, the voices we heard, the bloody axe and the bucket and all the other things...now this shit. You know it's not all just some coincidence."

I make a pouty face at her, trying to lighten the mood.

"That look might work on Avery, but it won't on me," she says with an annoyed laugh. "I'm done with this stuff, and if I'm being fully honest, I am glad that those photos turned up with blank pages. Whatever witchcraft did that, did you a favor."

I purse my lips, feeling irritated, but knowing that Kate is right. She hands me back my phone and I take in a breath and let out a long exhale as I slip it back into my bag.

After a moment of awkward silence passes, she asks me if I want to come in for lunch. A peace offering. "Mandy said she made roasted veggies and grilled chicken. If you want some, there should be plenty. She's been on a meal prep kick and is making all those little fridge packs throughout the week."

"Will there be bread, too?" I ask, raising an eyebrow.

"Ha. You'll have to take that up with Mandy."

I let the tension from a few moments ago slip away, and follow Kate into the house. Immediately, we are hit with the smell of seasoned home cooked food. The aroma of garlic stands out, and my stomach rumbles in anticipation. I hadn't realized how hungry I was until now. "Ahh, it smells so good," Kate comments, mirroring my thoughts.

We kick our shoes off and drop our bags by the door, then walk straight into the kitchen where Mandy is cutting up grilled chicken and depositing portions of it into multiple tupperware containers spread across the counter. She looks up from her task and smiles at us, "Hi! Anyone hungry?"

"What's on the menu?" I ask, coming to sit across the counter from her as she places perfectly roasted brussel sprouts, carrots, sweet potatoes, and onions alongside the sliced chicken into plastic containers. "Balsamic roast veggies and garlic grilled chicken," she says, perkily. "mmm, I knew I smelt garlic. It looks so good."

"Tastes even better," she says. "I already ate, but I'll make you a plate."

I thank her, my mouth beginning to water. "Any bread?" Kate asks.

"Come on, now," Mandy says, shooting her a look that

says *you know better.* She walks over to the oven and pulls the door open to reveal slices of french bread covered in bubbling cheese.

"THAT is what I am talking about! Thanks for cooking all this," Kate says, and wraps her arms around Mandy in a hug. "I am starving and this is exactly what I needed."

Mandy looks proud. "I'm glad you're excited for it. I felt bad that you were so nervous for your doctor's appointment earlier. I could tell you were anxious. How did it go?"

Kate looks away guiltily, I can tell she doesn't feel good about lying to Mandy and wonder again why she didn't just tell her the truth. I wouldn't have cared.

"It went well. I think the crystal you gave me helped," she says as she reaches up to unlatch the necklace. Mandy puts a hand up to stop her, "it's okay, you can keep that one. I'm glad you feel like it worked for you," she says. "So, when did you and Cora meet up?"

"I picked her up after the appointment. I figured we could study a bit for the week ahead. Remember, we start patient care in clinicals on monday."

I'm slightly impressed at how easily the lies roll off Kate's tongue. Mandy has a strange expression on her face, and there is something a little off about her today, but I can't put my finger on it. She is smiling, but it feels forced somehow. Maybe she suspects that she's being lied to, or maybe I am just imagining it. She keeps rubbing at the bandage on her left hand. That must have been the one that she injured last night. I notice the dark circles under her eyes, and the dull pallor of her usually dewy skin. The freckles on her nose show distinctly against her pallor.

"Ugh, I am not ready for patient care yet," Mandy mutters.

"I'm not, either," I add as I scan her face again and wonder if she's been stressed about the upcoming nursing clinicals. That could be why she is looking so drained right now. I haven't been very refreshed lately, myself. I have Dyer

Lane and Heather to blame for that. The worries of the nursing program are just a cherry on top.

I push the thoughts of school out of my mind as I devour the food on my plate. Everything is full of flavor and I almost groan out loud with how good it all tastes. Mandy is an excellent cook. She may even be better than Avery. Mandy had no choice growing up but to learn to feed herself because her parents were never around. When she started staying over at Kate's house more and more in high school, she would often cook dinners for us on the nights that Kate's parents were out of town or working late. Those were some of the best home cooked meals I ever had growing up. My parents were never really into home cooking and we ate out or got delivery a lot, so it always felt like a fun treat to get these hot freshly made meals from Mandy.

"Vegetables tasting this good is criminal" Kate states, as she scoops another forkful into her mouth. "Seriously, I could eat a whole plate of just the veggies. They have no right being this good."

Mandy laughs and then shrugs, "healthy and tasty sounds like a win to me. It's super easy to make. I found the recipe on a blog. I'll send it to you."

"Me too, please," I add as I spear a glazed roasted carrot with my fork. I glance at the time on the wall clock and remember that I had asked Avery to come over tonight after he is off work. I scoot my chair back, "I'm going to go grab my phone," I say, and then walk toward my bag by the front door to retrieve it. When I return to the kitchen, Mandy and Kate are talking about plans for Apple Hill at the end of the week.

"We should get some pumpkins to carve," Mandy suggests. "Also, they have the best apple cider donuts ever. We for sure need to get some of those."

"That's a must," Kate agrees. "So, let's all meet up there Saturday morning before it gets too busy. Should I tell everyone to get there around ten?"

I slip back into my seat at the kitchen island and scroll

through my text messages. Avery said he will be done with his shift in a couple hours and wants to know if he should still come over after. I type back "yes! I can't wait to see you." with a heart and smiley face emoji. He responds with a kiss face emoji, and I smile despite the clenching feeling in my stomach as I remember all that I have to fill him in on.

Kate pokes me in the arm, "Cora, hellooo," I look up at her. "I was asking you if ten works for Apple Hill on Saturday morning."

"Yeah, that sounds good," I say, and swipe out of my messages. "Sorry, I was texting Avery back." I slip my phone into the pocket of my hoodie, and grab the ice water Mandy has set in front of me.

"Make sure to invite him to Apple Hill too, of course," Kate says and I nod back at her.

We clean our plates and flop down full and satisfied on a big plush sofa. It's the kind that just envelopes your body and is so comfortable you don't know how you'll ever get up again. Kate flips through channels until she lands on a house renovation show. I watch as a bearded hipster looking man wearing a blue chambray shirt smashes through the drywall of an old home that he's going to flip. My eyes feel heavy, and I fight to keep them open, until finally giving in to the sleep that my body clearly is craving.

I wake up in the same place hours later with a kink in my neck. I rub it, trying to loosen the tightened muscles that formed when my head fell to the side as I napped. Mandy and Kate are no longer on the couch, but someone has placed a blanket on me. The sky has gone dark outside and I feel a surge of panic as I scramble to get my phone out of my pocket and check the time.

My pocket is empty and I feel puzzled. Then, I see my phone on the table in front of me, which is weird because I thought it had been in my pocket and don't remember taking it out. I shrug the uneasiness off, and look down at the screen so it will unlock using facial recognition. Right away, I see that

I have numerous calls and texts from Avery spanning the past hour. I am over an hour late to meet up with him. He texted me when he arrived at my place around five and I wasn't there. Then, he called a couple times and continued to text asking where I am, his alarm escalating when he wasn't getting any response. I smooth my hair back from my face, and call him back.

He answers after the first ring, "Cora! I was worried. Where are you?"

"Hey, sorry," my voice comes out gravely, and I clear my throat. "I was at Kate's and fell asleep on the couch after we had lunch. I was out for a few hours. I guess I was super tired," I let out a small laugh. "I'm going to head home now."

Avery can't conceal the relief in his voice, "K, I'll see you soon, then. Love you."

"Love you, too," I say and then hang up and haul myself off the cloud-like couch. It's only around six, but the darkness outside is already velvety thick. I turn on the hallway light so I can see better as I climb the stairs to make my way to Kate's room so I can tell her that I'm heading home. Her door is cracked, and I gently push it open all the way and peak my head in. Kate is asleep in her bed, softly snoring, her long hair swept across her pillow and an arm slung over her face.

I don't see Mandy anywhere and walk over to the guest bedroom to see if she's sleeping there. The door to the guest room is open, and the bed is empty. I assume Mandy went to work. She's been working increasingly more hours as a nanny these days. I go back downstairs, grab my bag and slip my feet into my shoes. Then, I realize that Kate drove me here and my car is back at the apartment. I sigh in frustration and call Avery again. I don't want to wake Kate up just to drive me home.

"Hey," he answers.

"Can you come get me from Kate's? I just realized that I didn't drive here and she's asleep."

"Yeah. I noticed your car was here when I got to your apartment. I'll leave now."

"Thanks. You're the best."

"See ya in a bit."

I hang up and open the front door to wait outside. There is a calmness in the air at this time of day. It's dark, but Kate's front porch is well lit with solar lanterns that lead up the path to her front door. I spot Mandy's old Honda Civic parked where she normally does, and find it a little strange since I didn't see her when I looked around the house. I only checked a couple rooms, so I guess she may have been home and I had missed her.

I walk down the long driveway toward the gate that guards the entry and decide to wait on the outside so that Avery doesn't have to deal with it when he gets here.

I exit Kate's property and take a seat on a low brick wall that surrounds the entry code box on the outside. I pull my phone out as the gate clangs shut behind me, and I scroll through Instagram for a couple minutes before getting bored with it. I decide to text Mandy and see where she went.

Your food knocked me out. It was like Thanksgiving but minus the tryptophan. I guess my belly was just happy. Where did you go? I wanted to say bye before I left but couldn't find you.

Three dots quickly appear, indicating that Mandy is typing back a response, and then they disappear. I stare at my screen, waiting. The dots appear again.

I don't know why, but I feel like Mandy is hiding something. It isn't anything specific that she has done, just a weird feeling I keep getting. Also, it's strange that we all fell asleep after eating, but I realize it is paranoid to think Mandy would tamper with our food. Why would she want to put us to sleep? That's a completely ridiculous thought.

Mandy's reply dings into my text inbox:

I was in the bathroom getting ready for work. I am nannying for that family with the toddler and the newborn, and staying overnight there to help when the baby wakes up through the night. I won't be getting sleep, so I'm jealous you two did lol

Okay. So, she was just in the bathroom probably doing

her makeup or hair or something and so that's why I didn't see her...Kate and I have had a strange few days with all this Dyer Lane stuff, so it makes sense we are exhausted. We probably needed a good meal and some rest, that's all.

I hope the baby takes it easy on you tonight. Newborns are wild, but you got this. Thanks again for the food.

I text back with a heart emoji at the end. I hit the send button right as headlights approach me. Avery's car is slowly pulling forward. I stand and start walking his way. The car comes to a stop and I open the door to jump in, and then lean across the seat to give him a quick kiss. "Thanks for coming to get me."

"Was I supposed to say no and just leave you here while I sat alone at your apartment?"

"You'd get bored," I say, as I place my hand on his thigh while he drives. He reaches down and clasps my fingers in his. "How was work?" I ask.

"Nothing notable. Just the usual type of calls, you know how that goes."

I nod, understanding that Avery's job is strenuous and it isn't relaxing to go into details about a typical shift while off the clock. The night we talked about the disemboweled patient was rare, and discussing work is not something we normally do in detail.

"How was your day?" he counters, smiling over at me briefly before turning his attention back to the road.

"Um, it was interesting..."

He waits for me to elaborate, and when I don't he says "how's that?" with raised eyebrows.

I sigh, and then I tell him everything. I explain about the research I did and that I found out Shane Dodson really did go missing. I tell him how Kate and I met with Jessica, who turned out to be Heather's younger sister, and describe how the photos I took of the journal all came up blank. When I am done talking I feel drained, but also relieved to have shared it all with him.

Avery shakes his head from side to side in an expression of disbelief. "It all just gets stranger and stranger."

"Yeah," I say, and then I remember to tell him about the incident that happened in Kate's car with the music and whispered pleas for help. I had forgotten about that for a moment. Probably my mind trying to suppress the frightening memory. When I am done describing it, Avery looks concerned. "I'm glad you're okay, that must have been scary." He squeezes my hand, which I find comforting.

I take a deep breath and nod my head. "I'm just ready to put it all behind me now. I gave away the journal, now it is time to just move on and wipe our hands of it all."

"I think that's smart," Avery replies. He slides the car into an open space near my apartment, and puts it into park so he can unbuckle his seat belt and turn to face me. "I love you. I don't know what I would do if anything happened to you. Earlier today, when all my texts and calls were going unanswered, I felt afraid. I knew you were expecting me over your house and you never don't answer your phone, so my mind immediately started racing with all the terrible possibilities. Working as a paramedic has shown me how fragile life is. Anything can happen at any moment. I know you already know this from personal experience. For me, the thought of something happening to you is my biggest fear."

I put my hand on Avery's cheek and he leans in to place his lips on mine. At this moment, I want to kiss him more than I want to breathe. His love is my air and I am floating, weightless in his arms. I don't know what I would do without him, and losing him is also my biggest fear.

I unbuckle myself and slide across to sit on his lap, straddling him. Our tongues glide across each other, and I start to roll my hips creating delicious friction between us. Avery runs his hands through my hair, and lets out a low moan. "We need to take this inside," he whispers. I look into his eyes, which are black with desire, the pupils huge as he stares back at me with lust illustrated on his face. I lean down and trace his bottom lip with my tongue. “I don’t want to go inside, I want you right here,” I say as I pull my shirt over my head and begin kissing him with increased urgency. My hand goes up to the steamed window and slaps against the cool glass as I brace myself.

When we are finished, my legs are shaky and I stay sitting in Avery's lap. He brushes a loose strand of hair away from my face, “you never fail to keep me on my toes,” he says with a twinkle in his eye.

I slide my clothes back on as he leaves the car and comes around to open the door for me. I slip out of the car, and he wraps an arm around my shoulders as we walk toward my apartment. My emotions are a yo-yo on a string bouncing up and down, but right now, with Avery I feel on a high.

My fears have been overtaking me for the last few days, but right now I know I'm safe. As soon as we are inside, we collapse in bed and begin to kiss again.

My body melts into Avery, and he feels like home.

CHAPTER 22:

I wake to the sound of a woman crying. My eyes fly open. Only it's not what my half awake mind had interpreted, it's my alarm going off playing the song Rolling in the Deep by Adele. I sigh, and sling my arm across my face, not wanting to get up yet. I reach over and grab my phone from the nightstand and silence the music.

Avery stirs by my side, and rolls over to face me, wrapping an arm around my waist and pulling me in toward his body. I inhale the familiar scent of him, spicy with a hint of citrus. "School time?" he mumbles, his voice coming out thick with sleep.

"Mmhmm," I respond, and nuzzle into his neck. I plant a kiss right under his jaw before responding, "I have my first clinical shift. I am supposed to be at the hospital at 6:30."

Avery wraps me tighter in his arms and rubs my back, "awww it's my baby's first day of giving patient care. You're going to be so good at it. You should probably get up soon, so you're not late, though. Don't let me hold you up."

I savor a couple more seconds of the warmth radiating off of him, and keep the mixed emotions I have been having about becoming a nurse to myself. I want to bring it up, but I also know that it's a conversation that deserves time to break down.

A tight band settles around my chest and squeezes at

the thought of having to actually *do* patient care today. I can feel my breath becoming hard to catch, and I try to slow my thoughts and breathe deep in through my nose. Working as a Scribe was supposed to help desensitize me to health emergencies, and it has in some ways, but it also feels like a safety net. While I'm exposed to a busy medical setting full of life or death moments, I'm not actually the one who is responsible for handling the patient. Today should be simple, though. I'll be on a medical surgical floor with stable patients and a Nurse Instructor who will guide me. It's not like I'm being thrown into the Emergency Department and expected to save lives right now. Despite knowing this, I still can't stop worrying. *What if I mess up? What if I'm not good enough?*

I roll off the bed with a moan, feeling disappointed at having to leave the warm cocoon of blankets and body heat. I try to shake off the lingering anxiety as I start the shower and go through the motions of getting ready. I brush my teeth, gather my nursing scrubs and school bag while the shower heats up. I only have fifteen minutes before I need to leave if I am going to be on time, so I rush through my shower and quickly wipe the steam off the mirror. My lips curl up into a smirk when I see the swipe of my hand on the glass and think back to the handprint I left on the fogged up window of Avery's car last night. My heart starts to beat fast at the thought of him and I together, and I feel a comforting warmth inside my chest.

I drag my mind back to the present and try to refocus on getting ready. I rake a brush through my long golden hair and smooth it into a low wet bun at the base of my neck. I don't have time to dry or style it any more than this. I swipe on some undereye concealer and mascara and go through a mental checklist in my head of everything I will need. I realize I haven't packed my stethoscope and rush to grab it off my desk. I hastily throw it into my bag as I speed walk into the kitchen, hoping I have enough time to make some coffee before I need to leave. I smile when I see that Avery is pouring me some freshly brewed dark roast.

"Just when I thought I couldn't love you any more," I say with a grin as I gratefully take the travel tumbler from his hands and add a couple packs of sugar to it before popping on the lid.

"Anything for my Nurse Cora," he says with a soft smile as he gently flicks the Student Nurse badge I have clipped to my scrub top.

"Thank you. For everything," I say, as I grab his hand before he can lower it.

Avery knows that I am thanking him for much more than the coffee. "Anytime," he responds and reaches around to cup his hands on my ass. "You make scrubs look good," he growls into my ear.

"Keep talking to me like that, and I will definitely not make it on time," I whisper back.

"I wish I could be selfish right now and bend you over this kitchen table, but I love you too much and can't let you be late," he leans down and gives me a deep kiss. When he pulls back, I don't want to let go. The thought of dropping out of school and staying home with him crosses my mind.

"Text me when you're done for the day," he says as he backs away and pours another cup of coffee for himself. I sigh, disappointed to be facing the reality that I need to leave.

"I will. Stay here as long as you want to," I reply as I shoulder my bag and glance at the clock. I'm right on time for when I need to go. "Love you," I call back as I open the front door and step out in the frigid early morning air.

"Infinitially!" He calls back, a moment before the door closes behind me.

* * *

As I approach my car, I notice there is a layer of frost covering my windshield. I let out a growl of frustration and rush forward to start the car. Then, I dig through my back seat to locate an old water bottle that I can use to pour over the glass while I run the windshield wipers in an attempt to get it clear enough to see through. By the time I slide into the front seat and blast the heat, the engine has warmed up a bit and the defroster is able to control some of the cloudiness across the glass.

My fingers are so numb from the cold that they sting and I wish I had thought to grab some gloves. I sigh and close my eyes for a moment. I feel overwhelmed but I don't have time to think about it for too long. I glance at the clock and see that the headstart Avery bought me by making my coffee has been eaten away by the frozen windshield issue. So much for a relaxing drive on my first day, I'm going to have to pray I don't hit too many red lights or traffic on the way if I want to make it on time.

"C'est la vie" I say under my breath and back out of my parking space to head the familiar route to the Stone Bay Hospital.

I pull into the parking garage nearest to where I am supposed to meet my instructor to get my clinical assignment for the day. I am lucky to find a parking space right away. I slam my car into park and dash toward the building entrance, hitting my key fob to lock my car as I jog toward the sliding glass doors that open into the medical surgical wing. I'm thankful that working here has given me knowledge of the hospital layout and I know exactly where to go once I am inside. At least I won't waste precious time trying to find my way around.

I am greeted by the familiar antiseptic smell of the hospital as I pass through long generic halls with numbered doors on each side and enter a small waiting room area with chairs arranged in rows. I quickly cut through the space and take a seat next to Mandy and Kate who are both quietly flipping through their notes for the day. Kate glances up at me and gives me a smile as a greeting and then continues to study whatever notes she has in her lap, and Mandy lifts her bandaged hand to give a small wave.

What are they even studying? I think in a panic. *We haven't been assigned a patient yet.* My pulse picks up and my nerves threaten to overtake me.

I grab my bag and haul it onto my lap to look for my clinical folder, desperate to see if I have any notes that would be helpful to go over right now. As I slide things around in my bag, I see a little folded note tucked in between my books and binders. My name is written in Avery's familiar writing, and I instantly feel more grounded.

I begin to open the note, when Professor Clark, our clinical instructor, enters the waiting area. He is a small pudgy man with big blue eyes and glasses that are chronically smudged. I always wonder how he can stand looking through the lenses when there are that many fingerprints stamped across them at any given time. I shove the notes back into my bag for later as my instructor begins to address the group of us.

"Hello everyone, welcome to your first day of nursing clinicals. I won't throw you to the wolves, so try to relax. Some nurses may eat their young, but we don't do that here," he says, with a high pitched chuckle that reminds me of a leprechaun… or a garden gnome who has come to life. Come to think of it, that's exactly Professor Clark's vibe; a living gnome.

Some students let out small laughs along with Professor Clark, and others look around uncomfortably. I can see Kate sitting with her back straight and her hands folded primly in her lap. Mandy is chewing on her nails, and she looks nervous.

"Today is more about getting you all familiar with the nursing process and how the medical surgical floor operates," Professor Clark continues, with a serious expression and his little hands clasped in front of his round belly, which bulges under his dark blue scrub top. "As I am sure you all know, a Medical Surgical floor of a hospital is designated for clients recovering from surgical procedures or who have medical conditions that require them to be monitored as they heal. It's pretty straight forward." I cringe as Professor Clark pauses his speech to crack his neck from side to side, which elicits loud pops.

"I will take time to work through the electronic charting with you, so that you feel confident with that, since documentation is an important part of your day. We will also choose your patient for the week so you can practice writing your nursing care plans, which will include your assessment, a proper nursing diagnosis, goals and outcomes for your patient, interventions, and evaluations. I also expect you to be able to give a solo nursing handoff at the end of the week for your patient, so keep that in mind. Basically we are just feeling things out today, but I do expect things to progress quickly. We covered most of this stuff in orientation a couple weeks ago, but are there any questions?"

A boy with thick black framed glasses and a severe side part in his dark brown hair raises his hand. "Yes?" Professor Clark inquires with his scraggly blond eyebrows raised in a dramatic fashion.

"How do we choose a patient for all this?"

Professor Clark grins, "it's simple. I will give you your student login information for the electronic charts, and you will have access to information on patients in this wing. When you see a medical condition that interests you, let me know, and if appropriate, I will assign that patient to your care for the week. Then, you will be partnered with the patient's nurse and able to enter the chart. I'm glad you brought that up actually, because I have all your papers with your logins right here." Professor Clark reaches into a folder that he had tucked under his arm and pulls out some sheets of papers. He glances at the names on each page and begins to hand them out. "Any other lingering questions?" He asks, as he continues to pass people their papers.

No one raises a hand or speaks up, so he does another high pitched chuckle and claps his hands together with glee. "Great! I've done my job then. You can all follow me through this door and we can begin the day."

We walk as a pack behind Professor Clark as he waddles through the doorway that leads to the computer banks. Nurses in light blue scrub sets are hurrying to various rooms, their shoes squeaking on the shiny linoleum. There are also some physicians in white coats making their rounds, and gathering information on patients.

I can see students looking around, trying to take it all in. Behind the scenes, hospitals always feel like organized chaos. Luckily, it's nothing new for me, and I am unfazed by the busyness. *This is familiar. I can do this.*

Professor Clark shows us the computers we can use to look up the patient we want to provide care for, and we take our seats. The rapid clicking of numerous keyboards begin to mingle with the incessant beeps of the various hospital equipment as we log in and search through the database.

I chew on the inside of my lip as I scroll through the patient list, trying to decide which would be the easiest to build a care plan for. The charts appear different on this wing than they do in the Emergency Room, but are still easy to navigate.

There are patients with hip replacements, a few telemetry patients, some end stage renal and liver disease cases, a MRSA patient with a large wound. I keep scrolling. I want a simple and easy to manage situation. I bet Kate will choose a complicated case, she loves a challenge but that's not what I am going for.

Finally, I decide on a patient who is an eighty-nine year old female recovering from pneumonia, and quickly raise my hand to try and secure her as mine before someone else can request to care for her.

Professor Clark makes his way to my side, and I point to the computer screen indicating the patient I want to work with. He clicks into her chart and nods his head as he reads. "This will make a great patient to care for, Cora. I think you're all set for the week. I'll have her current nurse, Amaya, come by and meet you so you two can be introduced."

"That sounds great, thanks," I say, feeling relieved at getting my first choice. He pats me on the shoulder before he turns to walk down the row of computers toward another student who has her hand up.

I scan through the information on my screen, and make note of the patient's most recent vital signs. I click through the last nursing assessment that was performed and see that she is stable, which is good. I start to worry that she may be discharged home before the end of the week, and I will be left scrambling for a new patient. I chew on the inside of my lip as I click through her physician notes, trying to gather as much information as I can on her current status.

Someone taps me on my shoulder, and I turn to see a tall thin hispanic woman standing behind me. "Hi, I'm Amaya," she says with a smile, revealing a row of white straight teeth; the kind you see in toothpaste commercials. "Your instructor told me you're the student nurse who will be assuming care for the patient in room 9."

"Yes, I'm Cora," I say, as I fumble to log out of the computer and rise from my chair. There is something about the relaxed posture and kind expression on Amaya's face that immediately sets me at ease with her, despite my nerves. "Your patient seems pretty stable from what I've read in the assessments."

"Yeah...well, her labs tell a little more of the story. I can show you those after we go meet her. Basically, we are holding her here for observation until her kidney function improves and her pulse oximeter reading stays above 90%. She was extremely dehydrated when she was first admitted, but that's been corrected. She has moments when she seems confused, so we will be screening her for Dementia. Her tests came back negative for a UTI, which is a common reason for older patients to present with an altered mental state. Anyway, she is the sweetest lady, and very receptive to being educated, which makes her ideal for a nursing student to care for."

"That's great," I say as I follow Amaya down the hall

and we approach room 9. She knocks on the door frame, waits a beat, and then pops her head into the room. "Hi Janet, it's just me, Amaya. I'm here with a nursing student who will be working with me this week. Her name is Cora, is it alright for us to come in so you can meet her?"

A soft voice answers back, "yes, that would be alright."

Amaya glances at me with a smile, "I'll let you two get introduced, and then when you feel comfortable, will you get a set of vitals from her?" she asks. I nod in agreement, and Amaya swings the door fully open so we can enter into the patient's room. I follow behind her, feeling awkward. I glance around and notice that the room is bright with the sun filtering in through a window on the far right wall. There are flowers on the back counter with a few cards displayed, and the overall feel of the environment is pleasant. The patient's bed is in the middle of the space, surrounded by an IV stand, which two bags of fluid hang from. There is also a wheelchair settled against a nearby wall.

The patient, lays in bed at an incline with a thick book resting on her lap and various monitors hooked up to her to continuously record her vital signs. Her eyes are a clear light blue, and shine with interest as she takes in Amaya and I.

"It's always nice when you're my nurse, Amaya," she says, her thin lips pulled into a warm smile, "and your students name is what, again?"

"Cora," I provide, with a smile. I can feel sweat prickle my hairline. *Why am I feeling so nervous?*

"Welcome, Cora," she says, those bright eyes of hers gleaming with a knowing shine. "I love students. I was a teacher when I was younger. Those were the most rewarding years of my life. I'm glad that I can be of help to one again." She fidgets with the book in her lap, and looks like she has something more to say, but appears to think better of it.

Amaya steps away from the computer where she had entered a quick nursing note. "Well, I think this is a perfect pairing, then. If you want to grab some quick vitals and do an assessment on Janet, you can go ahead and start that, Cora. I'm going to go visit my other patients and I'll meet you back at the nurses' station." She turns to Janet and grabs her hand. "Cora is going to take great care of you this week." Amaya gives me an encouraging smile as she passes by to exit the room, her scrubs swishing as she hurries out the door.

I blink a couple times, this is not how I thought this was going to go. I thought Amaya would stay IN the room with me, not leave me on my own the first day just moments after greeting the patient. I let out the breath, and step toward Janet's bedside with a smile, pretending to be much more at ease than I actually feel.

"Not what you were expecting," Janet acknowledges, her chin tilted down and eyes raised to look at me knowingly. "It's alright, dear. You know what to do." She lifts up her arm that isn't attached to the IV, "let's get the blood pressure over with first though, I hate that part."

With her words, I feel the smile on my face become real. "Works for me."

CHAPTER 23:

When I finish my assessment, I record that all Janet's vitals are within normal limits. Her oxygenation has improved, and although this is my first time meeting her, she seems completely normal cognitively. I don't detect any confusion. If anything, I think she comes across as very aware and present.

When I use my stethoscope to listen to her lung sounds, I identify crackling in the lower portions, which is representative of fluid moving around in the tiny air sacs of her lungs. Other than that, she seems to be doing well.

When I finish the assessment and document all my findings, I realize that I don't want to leave Janet's room yet. I've enjoyed talking to her, even if it has only been about the weather and our favorite local restaurants. Her calming presence is a balm for the nerves that I've had all morning. I glance down at the thick novel still resting on her lap. "What are you reading?" I ask as I gesture toward it.

She smiles mischievously at me and flips the book over to reveal the title. "Outlander. I've read it multiple times already. I just can't get enough of that Jamie Fraser. What a man."

A small surprised laugh escapes me, and I fold my lips in on themselves in an attempt to stifle it, but Janet can see my amusement. "Oh honey, you know I've lived a long life. I've seen all sorts of men, but this Scottish Highlander in a kilt from a fantasy historical fiction novel will always take the cake for me."

I nod my head, "I've read the series, and I can totally understand."

Janet's face lights up with excitement. "I think we just became fast friends." She beams up at me from her reclined position in bed. The sheer enthusiasm displayed upon her wrinkled face takes years off her appearance.

I smile back at her, "I think we did."

I glance at the time, and realize that I need to get to the nurse station so that I can check in with Amaya. "I have to get going, but it was a pleasure to meet you. I'll be back to bring in your lunch later today with your scheduled medications." She nods and cracks open her worn copy of Outlander, "sounds good, dear. I'll be here with Jamie until then." Her eyes meet mine, "thanks for the company today. It feels good to see a new face."

I smile and reach out a hand to place on hers in an attempt to squeeze it reassuringly like I saw Amaya do earlier, and Janet's expression suddenly becomes slack. I draw my hand back, feeling puzzled at the abrupt change in her demeanor. Her eyes stare straight ahead in a vacant way that is so different from how she was just looking at me moments before. I grab her wrist to feel her pulse, and it is steady and regular.

She slowly shakes her head from side to side as she comes out of her daze and her eyes begin to regain their sparkle. They slowly trail up to land on my face. Janet is no longer smiling, but looks troubled instead. "I...I'm sorry about that," she stutters. "I get these...episodes sometimes..." Her eyes search mine, as if she is trying to place me. "I think I need a nap, Cora. Thank you again for the good company." she says as she shuts her eyes and puts her book on the tray next to her bed.

I feel unsure of how to interpret what just happened. She

is clearly aware of who I am, she just said my name...but that entire incident was so sudden and strange.

"Okay," I reply, feeling shaken. "I'll be back after you get some rest."

I'm all the way to the door when Janet says in a small voice, "don't go back there."

I slowly turn my head in her direction, one of my hands resting on the door handle.

"Just...stay away from there, Cora."

I feel icy fingers trail up the base of my spine to the top of my neck. "Stay away from where?" I ask, even as every fiber of my being screams with the knowledge of what she is about to say.

"Dyer Lane."

CHAPTER 24:

I rush from the room, not even bothering to respond to what Janet said. I speed walk to the staff bathroom and lock the door behind me. It's a private restroom with a toilet and sink. I want to splash my face with water, but worry it will get my shirt wet and choose to run my wrists under cold water in an attempt to settle my nerves. I feel completely caught off guard. The coolness of the flowing water actually does refocus me and works to calm me down. I turn the faucet off and meet my gaze in the mirror above the sink. The eyes that stare back at me are wide and startled. I inhale deeply and count to seven and then exhale and do the same. I feel confused. How can Dyer Lane follow me here? What the hell just happened?

I take a few more moments to collect myself and once I feel more centered, I leave the bathroom and walk to the nurse station. Amaya is sitting at a computer typing in a patient's chart, and looks up at me with a smile as I approach. Her smile quickly turns to a look of concern when she takes in my appearance. "Everything go okay?" she asks, quietly. Her eyes are searching my face for answers that I don't have.

"Yeah, no issues," I say as I pull over a chair from a nearby computer, so that I can sit next to Amaya. "I added my assessment to her medical chart."

Amaya continues to stare at me for a moment longer

and then sighs. "Did she say something weird?"

I feel the surprise cross my face, and open my mouth to respond, but am unsure of what to say.

"I only ask because she is known around here for saying strange things to the staff. She just tends to know stuff that she shouldn't. I didn't want to say anything to you, because she doesn't do it with everyone and I didn't want to freak you out. I was hoping she wouldn't go there with a student...Janet is the sweetest woman, but she gives some people the creeps because of that sixth sense thing of hers...or whatever it is."

I chew on my inner cheek and nod. "Yeah, she said something...I wasn't sure how to feel about it. It's okay though. No big deal."

Amaya looks at me thoughtfully, before responding, "let me know if it becomes too much. I would understand. We could get you situated with a new patient if you want."

I shake my head and try to make my face look relaxed as I force a smile, "no, really. I'm fine with it. Most of my time talking with Janet was pleasant. I like her. I want her to be the patient I have this week."

"Sounds good," Amaya responds, as she turns back to her computer screen and clicks into Janet's chart to read through what I documented. "This all looks great. You are very thorough with your charting."

"Thanks," I say, feeling pride rise up in me.

"I don't think you have anything else I need you to do until lunch when you bring Janet her meal and record another set of vitals. Did your instructor give you anything to work on during your down time?"

I reach into my bag and pull out my clinical folder, "we are supposed to start on our patient care plan I think."

"Great. You can work on that here, I have some patients to go see, but let me know if you need anything. I'll be popping in here and there to chart."

I nod at her, "okay, thanks."

Amaya jumps up from her chair and heads down the

hall to a room at the end and knocks before entering. I turn to the papers in my lap and sigh as I sort through them trying to decide where to begin. I have three hours until I bring my patient her lunch and then go on my own break to eat mine.

I jot down some notes to begin formulating my nursing diagnosis when a shadow falls over the paper I'm writing on. I look up to see Kate standing over me, a manic look in her eyes. "Hi best friend, I need your help," she says, reaching down to rub circles on my back.

I look at her in confusion, "what do you need?"

"The nurse I am partnered with asked me to do bowel care for one of her other patients, and I need a…helping hand, you could say." Kate's smile is tight as she continues. "She suggested I ask another student to come with me. You know, one of us spreads the cheeks and the other wipes…"

I widen my eyes at her, "you want me to come help you wipe a butt? Is that what this is?"

"Yup. That's what this is."

"Alright, I can do that."

"You're the best ever, follow me."

I trail behind Kate as she heads toward a side hall and approaches a frazzled looking nurse with scraggly gray hair pulled into a low ponytail. The nurse's brow is furrowed as she looks at a computer, her eyes moving back and forth as she reads whatever is displayed on the screen.

"I found a partner for room 16," Kate says softly, and the nurse briefly looks up from what she has been reading and then returns her eyes to her work before saying, "I gathered you some supplies and left it on a cart outside the patient's room. Thanks for doing this for me. Oh, and don't forget to put some of that peppermint chapstick inside your mask before going in there. The smell is pretty bad and we want to preserve the patient's dignity. The mint in the chapstick will help keep you from gagging."

I shoot a quick glance at Kate, who still has that tight lipped smile on her face. "Okay, thanks. I'll come back here when we are done." The nurse nods as she continues to stare at her computer screen.

Kate turns toward a hallway in the opposite direction and leads me to the room of the patient we are going to clean. There is a light above the door that is on, signaling that the patient had pushed her call button. The supply cart the nurse had mentioned is parked outside the doorway, and Kate starts putting on a yellow gown and a hair covering.

"Um, so this patient has contact precautions?" I ask.

"Yeah, and I am embarrassed to admit it, but I have never wiped someone else's butt before. Not even a baby. I feel nervous, but I mean, how hard can it be?" she answers as she swipes some chapstick on the inner portion of her mask and then grabs another and does the same inside it before handing it to me. I put the mask on and my nose tingles with the strong scent of peppermint. It has a cooling quality that makes my nose feel a little numb. We snap on our gloves, and then Kate says "Ruth, that's the nurse I'm working with, said we should double glove for this...you know, just in case it gets really messy, we can just take the top layer off and keep going." I nod my head at her as I snap another dark blue nitrile glove over the ones I am wearing. "Let's do this, then."

Kate knocks on the door before we enter and I see that this room is similar to Janet's, but minus the light filtering in through the window, and the flowers and cards are also absent. The patient is a middle aged woman with long dark hair, and a yellow cast to her skin. Her eyes are jaundiced too, and she lifts a hand to wave at us in greeting from her bed where she lays sprawled out. Her stomach is protruding in a way that indicates ascites from a fluid build up in the abdomen associated with liver disease. When the patient smiles, I can see she is missing a few teeth and the ones that remain are brown with decay.

Kate greets her with a kind voice and introduces us. She lets the patient know we are here to get her cleaned up. The woman doesn't speak, but turns to grab the bed rail and uses it to pull herself onto her side so we can access the soiled pad beneath her. Her rail thin arms are tense and shake with the effort of holding her body up. Kate rolls the pad up so she can remove it as cleanly as possible, and I grab a new one to replace it with, which I carefully tuck under the patient. We work quickly and quietly to get her clean, which isn't easy work. When we are done wiping, the new pad we put down already looks soiled, so we go through the motions of replacing it with a fresh one all over again. Once we are completely done and the patient is comfortably repositioned, we take off all the protective overwear and wash our hands before we exit.

"Thanks for helping me with that," Kate says as we walk back toward where the nurse she was helping is stationed at the computer.

"No problem."

"I was freaking out a little inside when we first started the bowel care, but once we were done, it actually felt rewarding. I know that might sound weird, but...just being able to help someone when they are in need like that with something private, but doing it in a way that feels safe for them...I don't know, it's special. Being a nurse brings you so close to people, and although it certainly isn't glamorous, it's such meaningful work."

"Yeah, I know what you mean," I reply.

"It's good to feel this way. I know it's only our first day doing patient care, but it feels like I'm on the right track, you know? It's reassuring."

I smile at Kate and give her shoulder a squeeze.

"Anyway," she goes on, "I'm going to go back and check in with Ruth. You could probably head back over to your station, you don't need to come with."

"Okay, I'll see you at lunch then," I reply and we part ways as I walk over to where I left my school bag at the computer that Amaya has us working from. I sit back down at my chair and pull my work back out to chip away at. I spend the next hour completing my care plan.

Lunchtime approaches and I grab Janet's tray and bring it to her room for her. She is in good spirits, but quiet as I set her meal down next to her bed and make small talk with her. Amaya meets us at the bedside and gives Janet her blood pressure medication after I take her vital signs and ensure that Janet is in the necessary parameters.

Once the medication has been taken, Amaya excuses herself, and I stick around with Janet for her meal. I'm adjusting her bed so that it is at a more appropriate angle for her to eat when she says "I am sorry about earlier. Sometimes, when someone touches me and their mind is open, I can... see things." She gives a glance from the side of her eye as she peels a small orange. Her hands are shaking slightly, as she continues to explain. "Mostly I see the past, but sometimes the future. I know it sounds insane, but it's just the way things have always been for me. Even when I was a child. It made me one hell of a great teacher, though. I knew which children needed more attention or help at home just based on a simple hug.... I didn't mean to startle you or make you uncomfortable." The look on her face is heartbreakingly genuine, as she looks up at me. She lowers her now peeled orange back onto her tray, and clasps her hands in her lap. The blue veins show through her thin pale skin as she wrings her fingers in a nervous gesture.

"That's one hell of a party trick," I tell her, cracking a smile.

Janet lets out a soft giggle. "You could say that. It gets me in trouble from time to time. There is a physician here who wants to screen me for Dementia now." She rolls her eyes theatrically. " He says I am confused. My mind is sharp as ever, I tell you, but the doctor was feeling my abdomen the other day and as soon as his hand brushed my stomach I just knew he was cheating on his wife. It came into my sight clear as day. So, I told him that she deserves better and he should figure out what he wants instead of stringing a fine woman along. I think my exact words were 'you need to stop straddling the line and make a choice of who you want straddling you because your wife is too good for what you're doing with that woman.' Needless to say, he was not happy with that suggestion."

I open my mouth in a shocked expression and whisper, "oh my gosh Janet, you're bold."

Her face breaks out in a gleeful smile "always have been, dear." Then she takes on a more serious expression before adding, "I am sorry for saying what I did so abruptly. Tact has never been a strong trait of mine. I do mean what I said, though. I hope you stay away from that cursed place. It's not somewhere anyone should ever go..."

I stare back at her trying to decide how much I want to tell her, and then settle on saying, "I realized that recently, and you shouldn't worry. I have no plans on returning."

"I'm glad to hear that," Janet responds before taking a sip of her iced tea and placing a wedge of the orange into her mouth. She chews it with a thoughtful expression. After she swallows she says, "I'm glad you're my nurse for the week, Cora."

I smile at her and say, "I am, too."

* * *

The rest of the clinical day goes smoothly. We have a late lunch as a group, and a debriefing about our first day. Professor Clark is giddy with excitement as we each share stories about our shift and any takeaways or lessons we felt were valuable. After the meeting wraps up, we are all excused for the day, and instructed on what to do when we return to care for our patient again on Wednesday, and then again on Friday. We have Tuesday and Thursday off to attend our other scheduled classes.

Mandy, Kate, and I walk together to our cars and continue to talk about our experiences. Kate tells Mandy about our bowel care patient, and Mandy details her time putting baby powder on a yeast infection that had developed under a patient's breast.

"I didn't know you could get yeast infections under your boob," Kate says. The shock discernable in her voice.

"Oh yeah, you can get that pretty much anywhere, I think. It just has to be wet and dark…"

"Ew."

Mandy laughs at Kate's comment and then continues on, "yeah, but she was the nicest lady. I am glad I chose her for my patient."

"I was just telling Cora that earlier. Even if some aspects of nursing are not ideal, it is still rewarding to do the work. The gross stuff included. It just feels worth it."

I nod my head in agreement with Kate's words, as I look at Mandy, whose expression seems strained. She is clutching at a crystal around her neck, which she always wears but the skin on her hands is cracked and her knuckles are oozing blood. The bandage she is still wearing across her palm looks dirty and in need of a change. Mandy's skin has a pallor to it, and her hair looks greasy and unwashed. I wonder again if the stress of school coupled with work is getting to her. I mean, there are days I feel overwhelmed by it all, too. I open my mouth to say something, but then close it because I am unsure how to bring up the topic.

Hey Mandy, you're looking a little haggard these days. What's up?

Instead, I decide to just drop it and I'll make a point to check in on her more and make sure she is doing alright. Her family life has never been good, and she and her mom have a strained relationship. Maybe it has something to do with that?

Before I know it, we are at the parking garage and parting ways to each go to our cars.

"You're coming back over to my place, right?" Kate calls out to Mandy as she pulls her car door open. Mandy is parked right next to her and looks over her shoulder as she tosses her bag into the passenger seat of her car.

"I think I am going to head home, I want to drop my stuff off there and have work later."

Kate lets out a sigh of frustration, "you've been working so much lately, I barely see you anymore." Her facial expression is pouty as she turns toward me, "what about you, Cora? Wanna come over?"

"I'm tired, I think I am going to go home, too."

"Ugh, I don't wanna go home alone."

"Call Leo," I say.

"Meh," is all she replies. Which tells me they haven't been getting along lately. "Fine. Love y'all," Kate says as she slides into her car, not even waiting for a response from us before she shuts the door. Her car engine starts a second later.

I glance up and see Mandy staring at me from her car. She is studying me intently, and a chill settles in my chest when I meet her gaze. It is like a mask has slipped and I am seeing someone else beneath.

I give Mandy a smile, and her eyes dart away. Moments later, her car backs out of the parking spot, and she drives away without even a backward glance.

That was weird. I think.

I leave the parking garage and go straight home. I really am tired and feel glad that I declined Kate's invite to come over. I just want to lay in bed and rest. I need to decompress and have some alone time.

Once home, I clean myself up and flop onto my bed. The day seemed to go by both quickly and slowly. I don't know how that is even possible, but ask anyone who has had a whirlwind of a day, and they will tell you that it is. I cradle my pillow under my head and rest my eyes. It's not even late in the day yet, but I feel tired from my early morning.

I can smell Avery's scent on my sheets, and it makes me remember the note I had found in my bag earlier. I slip out of bed and locate the folded piece of paper mixed in with my school folders. I open it and see his small boxy handwriting scrawled across a lined page:

Cora,
I know you feel nervous about today, but that's only because you care so much. You are going to make the best nurse. Yes, knowledge and nursing skills are important, and with time you will learn all you need to know to care for your patients at the high standard you've set for yourself. What you already have right in this moment is compassion, warmth, and a kind heart. Those are traits that are often not taught, but come innate within you. You're everything a patient could want in a nurse who is caring for them. I know this. I need you to know this, too. Believe in yourself. I hope you have a great first day, and I can't wait to hear all about it.
I love you, infinitially.
-Avery

His words are melted butter, slipping across my surface to coat me in warmth. I feel so lucky to have someone in my life who loves and supports me this freely. It makes me emotional to know someone cares for me this deeply, and I value how Avery works to show me in little ways like this everyday. I reach for my phone and send him a text to thank him for the sweet note and tell him that my first shift went well.

He responds a few minutes later saying he hopes I read his letter in a British accent, which makes me grin. I told him once that I love the way British men speak, and he never let it go. Sometimes he tries to fake an accent to get me to smile, but he can never get it right and somehow manages to sound Australian, instead. He also tells me how proud he is of me, and asks if I want to grab dinner. Even though I am exhausted, I find that I want to see him. I want to feel his hand in mine, and hear his voice. We plan to meet at our favorite Mongolian Barbecue place in a few hours.

I roll over in bed, allowing myself to rest before I get up to get ready. My mind keeps wandering to Janet. Our conversations today felt surreal. If I were to try and tell anyone about it, I don't think they would believe me. Amaya seems to believe in it and understand, but I think it's something you have to experience first hand to actually accept.

Since my thoughts are swirling and napping doesn't appear to be a feasible option, I decide to go to the living room and switch on the TV to mindlessly flip through Netflix. My mind remains preoccupied with thoughts of Janet, Jessica, Heather, and Dyer Lane despite the action of the *Breaking Bad* episode playing out on screen. I just can't focus on anything, and wonder if Jessica has read through all of Heather's journal yet. I debate texting her, but decide against it. I meant it when I made the decision to leave that all behind me, and I need to stick with it.

I still feel disappointed that I wasn't able to read everything Heather wrote before I turned over the diary, but I also feel guilt for having thoughts like that. It's like I am thinking of this troubled girl's journal as entertainment when really it's a disturbing record of terrible things that have happened in the past. I will probably never know the full story, and I need to be okay with that. The way those pages turned up blank in all the photos even though I know for a fact they had been filled with writing is something that will always bother me. If that's not a scary sign that this is a totally fucked up situation, then I don't know what is.

I switch the show I am watching to Schitt's Creek, ready to lose myself in the silly drama of the Rose family, when a text from Nikki pings on my phone. She rarely texts me, so it comes as a surprise when I see her name. All her message says is *can you talk right now?* I frown down at my phone screen, and then type back, *Sure.* A moment later, my phone rings in my hands. As soon as I answer, Nikki starts talking in a rushed voice.

"Hey, so those photos I took the other day when we all went to that shack on Dyer Lane came out totally weird, and there are tons of orbs and shadows and some are just bright white, and I don't know what to make of it all, and..."

"Hold on," I interrupt. "Take a breath, and repeat this all slower, I don't know what you're even saying with how fast you're talking."

I hear her take a long inhalation on the other end and breathe it out before beginning again, slightly slower this time, "the photos...from Dyer Lane. They are super strange. It's scary. There are...lights and figures in them. I was wondering if you still have that book you found there? Maybe it has some information on...spirits." Her voice has a breathless quality to it, and her sentences are broken as she pauses to take in more air. It all feels overly dramatic.

Whatever she saw, really must have made her feel uncomfortable. I sigh and glance at the time, I only have about an hour and half before I am supposed to meet Avery. So much for watching Schitt's Creek and unplugging for awhile. I close my eyes and rub my forehead. "Do you want to come over? We can look through the book and you can show me those photos."

"Yeah, that sounds good. I'll be there in like, fifteen."

"Cool. See you soon." I hang up the phone and flop back on my couch. An image of the wriggling earwigs flashes across my vision, and I flinch. With all that has happened, I had forgotten about the occult book we had found. *Where did I put it?* I wonder, glancing around my apartment. I hadn't seen it since I brought it home.

I move some stacks of mail on the side table and shift the clutter around as I search. Finally, I spot it sitting beneath some coupons. The cracked black cover still appears dirty even after the wipe down I did, and the binding is splitting at the sides. I open the book, and a musty odor wafts up from the yellowed pages.

I stare down at the page I turned to, which depicts a woman laying in a circle of fire. A knife has been plunged above her left breast. I wrinkle my nose, feeling disgusted and wishing that I had listened and left it behind instead of bringing it home with me. I flip to the next page, which details the sacrifice of a first born female to bring fertility, and I abruptly snap the grimoire closed, not able to take anymore. I want to throw it into a fire, but the book might thrive in there since it seems to have been forged in the depths of hell.

I set it back on top of all the junk mail, and then change into some jeans and a sweater. I toss my hair up into a messy bun, hoping that this meet up with Nikki doesn't take long so that I can leave on time to meet Avery. I'm not hungry, but I could use a beer and the comfort that his presence always brings.

There is a knock at the door, and I open it to let Nikki in. She gives me a tight close lipped smile as she enters my apartment, her heavy looking platform boots clomping on the wood as she strolls straight to my couch. She doesn't greet me or say a word as she slings the tote bag off her shoulder, and pulls out a thick folder. She extends it toward me, and says "I took a shit ton of pictures when we were there, and practically all of them have something strange going on with them."

"Nice to see you, too, Nikki," I say as I take the folder into my hands and sit on the couch to open it. I feel like I am able to be sarcastic with her, since it's her own default. Sarcasm is Nikki's love language.

"Oh, yeah, sorry. Hi."

I shuffle through her photos, not really sure what she's referring to because they all look pretty normal. There are some pictures of the sun filtering through those huge oaks that line the lane. It's artsy, and actually rather pretty. I squint trying to spot something unusual, but fail to see anything other than some great landscape shots. I flip that over and turn to the next photo. This one is of a pile of trash, incongruous with the natural beauty around it, and somehow a strangely pretty photo. It's in how Nikki angled the camera and the lighting, I guess. Only she could get a photograph of trash and make it look like art.

Next, is a photo of Leo's face in profile. His neck tattoos are dark against his skin, and his eyelashes look long. The brilliance from the sun overhead is reflecting off his shoulder length blonde hair. He looks like Kurt Cobain. There are a few more images of Leo that follow the first, and I wonder again if

Nikki likes him as more than a friend. I flip the next one over, and the photo below is of the fog rolling through the trunks of the gnarled trees. It's eerie, but still looks normal to me.

As if reading my thoughts, Nikki says "They all seem ordinary at first...but keep going." She is nervously picking at her chipped black nail polish, like she always does.

I look up at her with the pile of photos in my lap with my eyebrows raised. She tilts her head to the side and purses her lips, "seriously. Don't look at me like that, keep flipping through. I guess I should have separated the regular pics from the fucked up ones." she mutters as she continues to chip away at her black nails. I clench my jaw, fighting myself to not reprimand her for getting her nail polish all over, and make a mental note to vacuum when she leaves.

I flip over the next photo and it's of the abandoned shed. I pause, examining the image closely. It still looks pretty typical, no ghosts or whatever, but the disquieting feeling of being there translates through the photo and an icy chill creeps through me. There is a sensation of eyes staring back through the black rectangle of the doorless entrance. A sinister presence that even a 2D photo was able to capture. I swallow hard remembering the strangeness of the place and the fetid smell that hung around it. When I flip to the next picture, a gasp catches in my throat.

This picture is taken from behind the group as we enter through the doorway of the shack. I remember Nikki being in the back as we filed in through the gaping doorway, and her flash going off and illuminating the interior for a brief moment. The back of Leo, mine, and Avery's heads are captured in the picture as we enter, single file, into the small room. Orbs of white misty light hover above our heads. I count five of them in the photo, and in the far corner, shrouded in deep shadows, lurks a crouching figure. The twisted form doesn't appear human, and its eyes reflect red in the light of the flash. It's startling. I definitely didn't see anything like that when we were there. Somehow, the photo captured these numerous presences that we unknowingly kept company with that day.

I scan the picture a little longer, taking in the strangely gothic scene, and then set this photo aside. I glance up at Nikki and she is smirking at me. “See? Keep going, there’s more.”

CHAPTER 25:

I feel overwhelmed by the time I finish looking through all the photos. I am slightly lightheaded and excuse myself to go splash some water on my face, which usually helps when panic sets in. I comfort myself with the thought that even though the creature was there, we didn't know.

Yeah, there were some cold spots and that weird spider web sensation, but nothing bad happened to any of us. If it wanted to hurt us, then it could have...but it didn't. I wonder to myself why these photos had to happen just as I was intentionally trying to move on from everything Dyer Lane related.

Why can't I get away from it?

I walk back to the living room and see that Nikki is standing from the couch and has packed up her photo envelope. "You can keep those ones, I have copies," she says gesturing to the stack of photos I had set aside. "I'm going to meet up with Leo and Kate later," she says as she shoulders her tote bag and heads for the door. "I'll show them the copies of the ones you have."

I nod, "I would say thanks for coming over but under the circumstances..."

She gives me a single tight nod, "you're welcome for fucking up your night. I just wanted to run it by you first before showing the others. Like, a trial run."

I'm puzzled by the comment, but Nikki says all sorts of shit and some of it doesn't make sense so, that's normal. I shrug and give her a wave as she closes the front door behind her. I cross the room and lock the door, then I lean against it and take some deep breaths as I try to process what the hell I just saw in those photographs.

I go back to the couch and grab my phone. I text Avery asking him to come over, because I no longer feel like going out. As agreeable as ever, he is fine with that and says he will grab food for us and be here soon.

I feel shaky as I sit and wait for his arrival. Nikki had been right, that first photo was just the tip of the iceberg, and there was a whole fucked up block of ice waiting beneath. After that first photo, the pictures became increasingly more terrifying as I went through them.

I pick up the photo on top of the pile. It shows the creature in the corner standing to full height, which is at least seven feet. There is a long curved horn in the middle of its forehead, which practically scrapes the ceiling as the creature hovers over Avery. The shoulders of the beast are boney and hunched, and menace emanates from its posture. I feel sick looking at the image in my hands, and slowly set it back down on the pile.

The thing in the photos had a long horse-like face with wide nostrils, and stringy dark hair flowing down its back. The orbs from the first picture were present in the others, also. They floated around the creature like bubbles of light. In one photo there were so many orbs, the picture looked almost completely white.

I had gasped out loud when I flipped to a photo taken outside by the dead deer. It showed the creature in the light, lingering by the trees that looked burned. It had followed us from the shack. In these photos, it was removed from our group, which was a relief. The creature was even more grotesque in the light of day. It seemed to glow with a misty luminescence, and its lanky arms hung down by its side. There were three curved claws on each hand, instead of five fingers like a human would have, and that scythe-like horn jutting out from its forehead glinted with a deadly sharpness.

I clench my eyes shut, trying to rid my mind of the images. I know these photos will haunt my nightmares, and I can't bear to stare at it any longer. I want a blank slate. My head is too crowded with it all right now. Netflix doesn't seem like an option anymore, so instead I sit on the couch with my eyes closed trying to calm myself with the quiet around me.

* * *

It didn't take long for Avery to show up with takeout Chinese food. Even though I was anticipating his arrival, I flinched when the door opened, popping my silent bubble of calmness that I had finally achieved. I find that I feel centered and somewhat better having spent some time meditating.

"Hey babe," Avery greets me with a broad smile. "I'm actually glad you wanted to stay in. This is cozier. It's freezing out there!"

He quickly crosses the room, sets the bags of food down on the table in front of me, and gives me a soft kiss on the lips. "Congrats on finishing your first day of clinicals." As Avery removes his coat, I can feel the swirl of cold air that came into the room with his entrance, and hug myself. "Sorry for bringing in the chill," he says as he moves to hang his jacket up.

"No worries," I reply softly. I pretend to be fine and begin arranging the boxes of food on the table, doing my best to remain calm and appear relaxed. I want to enjoy a moment with him before jumping into the craziness that Nikki dumped on me. I think about not even telling Avery, but decide that keeping things from him is a bad idea. He would find out eventually and be hurt that I didn't say anything.

I open up one of the boxes, and hot steam rises out. I have been struggling to suppress the shivers, and the moist warmth released from the container of spicy noodles is welcome. The next to-go box is filled with fried rice, another is mixed vegetables, and the third is orange chicken. My small apartment smells amazing and my mouth waters even though my stomach is still in knots. Somehow I find that I feel hungry, despite the weight on my chest that won't lighten up.

Avery and I pass around the containers and share the food as we talk about my first day, which feels like forever ago since Nikki stopped by instead of just earlier today.

The glistening orange chicken is crunchy and perfectly sweet, and for a moment I am able to forget all the strangeness of the past month. I let it roll off my shoulders and live in the bubble of the moment. Avery's warm smile, his genuine interest in my day, his easy way of flipping from serious topics to being light and silly. We discuss our plans to go to Apple Hill this weekend, and Noah's Halloween party that's coming up. When I tell Avery about the patient I have for my first week, I leave out Janet's psychic thing she has going on because it just feels like too much to go into right now.

When we finish eating, we toss our trash and settle back on the couch. Avery begins to flip through different movie options, and I am nestled into his shoulder, wondering when I should bring up Nikki's visit. I can hear the soft thump of his heart beating beneath my ear, and close my eyes soaking in his closeness.

I feel like I am always worried about something these days and even when I try to escape Dyer Lane, it finds a way to come back around. I wish we had never gone there. But if I am being honest with myself, I have had this feeling of dread and anxiety far before visiting that creepy rural road earlier this month. It's been going on since my father died in my arms, and although it fades at times, it is never fully suppressed.

I tilt my head to look at Avery. His face is lit from the light of the television. His expression is content and a small smile graces his lips as he clicks through movie options. I want to have a calm and happy relationship. Avery and I never fight, not really. We fit together so easily, but I tend to bring in sadness on my end like a tide that rushes forward and draws back, only to surge up again moments later. I feel like I always bring darkness because that's all my life attracts.

My mind is heavy with thoughts, and Avery picks up on this subtle shift in energy, as he always does. "What's wrong?" He says softly, and gives me a little nudge.

"Oh you know, just my life being flooded with gloom and despair. The usual."

"Cora, you know that's not true. I'm here. I have a bucket in hand and nothing will flood while both of us control the flow together."

"Awww, you sound like an inspirational card that I read at CVS the other day."

Avery lets out his deep rumbling chuckle that always makes me smile, "Hallmark has got nothin' on me, girl."

I crack a small grin. "But thank you. I really do appreciate you being here for me. I always share bad news, and sometimes I feel like a burden. Even the day you met me...I was crying..." I trail off, and Avery shifts so that he is facing me and takes my hand in his.

"Cora, life is full of dark moments, but who says that's a negative thing? You need the bad times to appreciate the good ones. It's a balance and sometimes there may be more bad...but the good always comes back around, and sometimes the dark teaches us things that the light never could. That's just life."

The look in his eyes as he speaks to me is so sincere. I can feel emotion start to well in me and my nose tingles with the threat of tears.

"I'm always going to be here for you. I don't ever want you censoring anything that's troubling you just because you think that I value the good more than the bad. We are in this together. He tilts my chin up to kiss me. A warmth spreads through my chest and down to my toes. I lay my head back on his chest, and wrap my arms around his middle. "That was a big step up from the bucket comment."

"I thought the bucket line was good…you know, to scoop up the water that's flooding in?" I can hear the smile in his voice, and I turn my head to look up at him, trying to keep a neutral expression even though I want to smile. Teasing Avery for his inspirational comments has always been fun for me.

"Hmmm. Yeah. Like that one saying…" he looks up with his eyes like he is thinking, and then finds the thought, "it goes something like, 'a boat can only sink when the water outside is allowed to get inside and weigh it down. You gotta stay afloat by keeping the water out.'"

I raise my eyebrows at him.

"I will always work to keep the water out of our boat, Cora."

He said *our* boat. It's always him and I in his mind. We are together in everything and I am so thankful for him. "You're the best," I say, and finally let my smile show. "It's just been a rough month. I don't think I have felt this worried or stressed since my dad died," I add.

Avery looks down at me with a searching expression."So, what's going on?" He asks, with a more serious tone, recognizing how upset I am.

I groan. I don't feel like I have the energy to go into this right now. My eyes flicker over to the table where the photos are resting face down. Avery notices this, because of course he does. "What are those?" he asks, glancing over at the stack of pictures.

"Remember those photos Nikki took at…the place that should not be named?"

"Yeah…" His brow is furrowed, as he tries to calculate how these pictures are bothering me. "Are those them?"

I nod, but don't have the energy to elaborate. Avery stares at me for a moment, and then shifts so that he can reach the pile and swoops the photos up before I can warn him further. I feel his body go rigid next to mine, as he looks at the photo on top and then moves through the rest of the pictures. His eyes are wide in disbelief. When he has seen them all, he sits very still. Finally, he licks his lips and says "that's fucked up."

It's not what I was expecting him to say, and I begin to laugh. Avery chuckles, looking puzzled. "Is this some sort of Halloween prank? Did Nikki photoshop those or something?"

Tears stream down from my eyes as I take in his words and begin laughing harder. I am shaking my head at him, but can't get a word out through my outburst. I finally calm down, and wipe my eyes. I take a deep shuddery breath, and a sob escapes from me this time instead of a laugh. I probably look like I've lost my mind. Maybe I have.

Avery sits there quietly, letting me get myself together. Finally, I catch my breath and get my composure. "No, it's not a prank," I say. "At least, I don't think so. I never even considered that, to be honest."

Avery remains skeptical. "Those can't be real," he says gesturing to the photos with a small shake of his head. "No way."

I purse my lips, thinking. "Why would Nikki do that? It doesn't make sense."

"I don't know, Cora. I often wonder why Nikki does a lot of things. The girl has always been off. She's Leo's friend, but why did she come to *you* with these and not *him,* or the whole group?"

"She said she was going to bring copies of the ones she left here to show to Kate and Leo later...I don't know, she didn't really make sense when she explained that part. Here, I'll text Kate and see if she has seen them yet and what she thinks." I grab my phone and write to Kate asking what she's doing, and if she has talked to Nikki.

A reply comes back within seconds, "Studying. No, why would I have?"

I flip my phone to show Avery the screen. "Weird," I mutter. Avery grabs his phone and starts typing on it. "I just sent a message to Leo and asked what he's doing tonight. Let's see what he says."

It takes longer for Leo to reply, but when he responds, he tells Avery that he is at his brother's house watching the Monday Night Football game and would probably just crash there. He even invited Avery to join. We stare at each other for a moment, our wheels turning.

"Well, I don't know what Nikki is up to but this is fucking weird," I say. "The possibility of those pictures being fake is slightly comforting but then the idea of Nikki going through all the trouble to fake demon photos and then come here to scare me raises a ton of new questions in my mind."

"It should concern you, for sure," Avery agrees, looking solemn. "She is unwell up here," he says, tapping the side of his head.

"Well, we don't know that for sure. Dyer Lane is messed up, we have all experienced weird things there, and obviously with all the stories about it, tons of other people have too..."

"Yeah," Avery agrees, "I just find it hard to fully believe in that stuff. Also, wasn't Nikki the one who insisted ghosts aren't real and that the cop car thing could be explained? Something is not adding up." He pauses in thought before continuing,"I actually like to believe there is an explanation for stuff like this and the human mind can conjure some wild things. Sure, Dyer Lane is creepy, that can't be denied, but it doesn't mean it's because of ghosts or a demon or whatever. It's creepy because of the stories and those are just for entertainment. Since it's a scary looking place and it's fun to feel scared and to scare other people, it has just grown to be bigger than it is. It doesn't mean it's all true."

He pauses to take a sip of water, and the room feels quiet as I wait expectantly for him to continue. "My Vovo, you know, my grandma from the islands?" I nod. "Well, she believed in witchcraft and dark spirits and voodoo and all that stuff. She was told stories as a child back when she lived in Cape Verde. She swears there are evil spirits, and she is a very strict Catholic, but that's one thing from those West African Islands she would never give up. But I always thought it was just folklore. Stories told for fun. Some teach lessons and morals, like fables do, and others are to entice people into gathering together. Spoken stories were big there on the islands. Just because something happens and a story is created around it, doesn't mean it is all true. Usually, the tales were so far from the truth they couldn't even be classified as based on a true story. The mind creates connections where there really isn't one and builds upon it to embellish and add interest. I think that's what has happened with Dyer Lane."

"Yeah…I can see your point about the urban legends, but it still doesn't explain the photos or why Nikki would want to fake something like this." I can tell Avery is trying to reassure me, and it is somewhat working, but something he said triggered a discomforting thought. I can't place exactly what it is, but it's bothering me.

It's a nagging feeling at the back of my brain. Water dripping from a faucet that you try to tune out but can't quite shut off. I look around the room trying to place what is niggling at me, when I suddenly realize what it is. The black occult book that was sitting on top of the mail is gone. Nikki never even asked to see it when she got here, but she took it with her when she left. She must have grabbed the book while I was in the bathroom. No wonder she left so abruptly, she wanted to get out before I noticed it was gone.

"What the fuck," I whisper in disbelief. Avery follows my gaze to the stack of mail that I am staring at. I flick my eyes up from the spot I had been stuck looking at and meet Avery's gaze. "Nikki stole that occult book she asked me about. It was on that table when she got here, and now it's not."

"So, do you believe me now when I say she is messing with you? Those photos can't be real. Nikki is a professional at photography and photoshop, she could easily make those."

"The question is why would she do that?"

Avery shrugs and tightens his lips into a thin line. Mischief flashes in his eyes as he says, "maybe she's a witch."

CHAPTER 26:

The next day, I am trapped in lectures for the majority of the afternoon. Avery and I send texts throughout the day guessing what Nikki's deal is. The predictions become more and more outlandish as we go.

Maybe she is setting you up for a secret camera show?

Maybe she is possessed? I send back.

Maybe she has joined a cult and this is her initiation task?

What if she gets aroused by scaring people?

Damn, we getting freaky with this, OK.

I text a laughing/crying emoji.

Maybe she is trying to scare you out of town so she can rent your apartment?

That is the least plausible out of all of the guesses. I text back, smirking. *My apartment is nothing special, and she is planning on moving soon. Remember?*

Oh yeah, I forgot. Anyway, what time are you off work today? Avery sends, ending our streak of strange speculations. I know it will probably begin again later, and am already trying to come up with new guesses to send him when it does.

I tell him I traded my work shift for tonight with someone and will be working overnight on Friday because I need to study. Friday will be the night before Halloween, and I am sure it will be a busy one, but I want to prep for my next day of clinicals without work getting in the way today. So, it seemed like a good trade.

I will be caring for Janet again tomorrow and am eager to make sure I am ready. I have an urge to impress her. The only way I can figure this will happen is if I come confident and competent in my nursing skills.

After the last lecture of the day, I meet Kate at The Magic Bean for coffee before heading home. “Where’s Mandy?” I ask. Her absence lately has been noticeable.

“Oh, she said she wasn’t feeling good so she went straight home,” Kate replies, and then takes a sip of her latte. I nod and take a long drink of mine, my mind still thinking about Mandy and how unwell she has been looking. “Is everything alright with her?” I ask.

“Who? Mandy?” Kate’s eyebrows are raised in question. “Yeah. I mean, I think so. She has been really distant lately, which is weird, but I don’t want to push it. She looks really tired...but so do we,” she adds with a shrug.

“Hey!” I say in mock offense.

“I think Mandy just needs some time to herself with all the work she’s been doing, you know? Anyway, speaking of weird friends, why did you ask me if I had heard from Nikki last night? That was random.”

I take a deep breath and widen my eyes at her.

Kate lets out a laugh. “Okay, spill the tea.”

“Well...” I pause, trying to decide how to explain last night to her. “I feel like whatever I say is going to make you dislike her even more than I know you already do.”

Kate scoffs, “Yeah, well, I don’t know if that’s possible. I try to be nice to her because I know how much her friendship means to Leo, but I just can never connect with her.”

"I know," I reply. I always knew Kate had these feelings even if she tries to hide them, so it feels right to hear her confess.

“Just say it, you obviously have something you need to get off your chest. I won’t tell anyone,” Kate says, the curiosity radiating from her.

I describe how Nikki asked to come over and see the grimoire, showed me photos with a demon creature in it, and then stole the book before she abruptly left, saying she had plans to meet up with her and Leo later.

"What the actual fuck. Okay, she has reached a whole new level of crazy. This girl is like an onion of crazy, just new layers to reveal. Does it ever end?"

I stare at Kate, surprised at her words as she rambles on about Nikki. "Why do you say that, did she do something else recently that was weird?"

"Everyday is weird with her," Kate says. "But yes, actually. Last week, I found her in my house. She didn't even text me or anything to ask. She must have let herself in. I heard something from the guest room and thought maybe Mandy had come over, which you know, is normal. Well, I walked in the room and saw Nikki hunched over behind the bed and asked what she was doing. She jumped up and said she thought she left something behind when she spent the night. I think she was referring to when she stayed over after we went to that God forsaken road. Anyway, she said she couldn't find what she was looking for, and left in a hurry. She seemed nervous. I didn't think much of it at the time, just thought it was Nikki being her strange self. Now though, I wonder why she did that. The only thing on that side of the bed is Mandy's overnight bag. Maybe she really was looking for something she left," Kate adds with a small shrug of her shoulders. "But, I just feel like I can never trust what she says, and it's getting old."

I take another drink of my coffee, feeling confused by Kate's story.

"Now, you tell me about those photos," Kate says with a grimace, "like I said…an onion of crazy."

CHAPTER 27:

I walk into the hospital for my second clinical shift feeling excited and ready for the day. Yesterday, after leaving the coffee shop with Kate, I spent the entire evening learning about Janet's medical diagnosis, going over her labs and what they all mean, and researching how to best care for her. After today, I will only have one more clinical day left with Janet as my patient and I want to make a positive difference for her.

I enter the waiting area that our nursing cohort is required to meet at before going to our patients, and see that Professor Clark is bubbling over with cheer. He is in a good mood. His face is shiny with dots of sweat despite the chill of the hospital. "It's a new day! Another chance to make a difference!" He beams as he glances around the room tallying us up and ensuring we are all present before leading everyone through the doors into the patient care area.

I meet up with Amaya, and listen to her receive the nursing hand-off report from the night shift nurse. Janet has remained stable since I was here last, on Monday. Her labs have improved, and she will probably be discharged home in the next couple days. I guiltily hope that she is still here on Friday so I don't have to choose a new patient in her absence.

When we walk into Janet's room, her face lights up. "Goodmorning, ladies. I'm glad to see you again, Cora."

Amaya and I both say "goodmorning," and Amaya

explains that I will be getting Janet up out of bed for some walking today, and working on deep breathing techniques with her. Then, Amaya excuses herself to go visit other patients and exits the room.

I begin setting up Janet's breakfast tray, and Janet tells me about her day yesterday as I place a straw into her orange juice. She mentions that she misses her dog, a Corgi-mix named Polly, who is staying with her granddaughter while Janet is in the hospital.

"As far as dogs go, Polly is a real gem. She listens better than most people, but isn't that always the way it is with dogs? So much more genuine than half the humans I know."

I smile and nod my agreement, as Janet looks at me with bright twinkling eyes. I gather my things and check her vital signs. As I do an assessment, I find myself hesitant to touch her skin, afraid that she will go into one of her strange episodes and not sure that I want to hear what Janet sees.

She can sense my uncertainty, and says "it's alright, I won't bother you with any visions today." Janet mimes zipping her lips. She reminds me of Betty White, with her cheerful demeanor and an intelligence that simmers below the surface.

I let out a nervous laugh, "oh, it doesn't bother me."

She fixes me with an incredulous stare. "No need to fib now, dear. I can understand how it may be off putting. I won't tell you things unless you want me to. It doesn't happen all the time either, so it's not as if I have a vision every time we come in contact with each other. If it makes you feel more comfortable though, wear gloves during your assessment, that is what most of the nurses do. Then we can try to reduce the risk of any accidental moments of sight."

I hesitate, trying to quickly decide what I should do. "No, it's alright. I'm fine," I reply, certain that this is the best answer. I don't want to be like the other nurses, and deny this woman normal human contact because my fear of what she will find and reveal about me. She's not bleeding, she's not infectious, and I don't have a reason to wear gloves at this moment. I reach forward and start placing the blood pressure cuff on her arm, "let's get this part over with first, right?"

Her smile feels like pure sunshine as she beams back at me from her hospital bed, "yes! You remembered. Thank goodness I have a great nurse today."

And just like that, my entire week is made.

* * *

Janet and I spend the shift laughing and talking about books, and films as we walk through the halls of the hospital. Janet uses her walker, with me at her side, making sure she is stable. We discuss our family life, and her forty year career as an elementary school teacher. She shares stories about her childhood, and how strange it was growing up with her unique gift.

"One time, in highschool, a boy accidentally bumped into me in the hall and I could sense his deep emotional pain. You see, the boy was in love with his best friend, but his father was very close-minded. The boy was afraid that if his parents found out about his feelings for another boy, he would be disowned. It was very sad."

I nod along as she explains, and help her turn a sharp corner in the hall. "Well, I told the boy I knew his secret, and we made a plan together," she continues. "I pretended to be his girlfriend for the rest of highschool and would come over to his house and let him take me on fake dates. This made his parents happy and they were none the wiser that our outings were really just opportunities for him and his partner to spend time together."

"Are you still in touch with them?" I ask, not wanting the story to end. I craved to learn more about her past, and all that she has done in her life.

"Of course. Those boys became some of my very best friends. They were later married and remained very much in love over the years. Thankfully, times have changed for the better since I was a young."

"Your life is so much more interesting than mine," I say. "It's wonderful that you did that for your friends."

"Well, what's life without love? I'm happy that people are not having to hide who they are or who they love these days. Things are finally getting better."

I nod, understanding all too well how special that is. I couldn't imagine if I were not able to openly love Avery the way I want to. I would do anything to be with him, and recognize that our relationship, being one between a white woman and a black man, is something that wasn't tolerated in the recent past.

"Something I can't stand is how people often try to put others in a box. I suppose that it's human nature to attempt to define those around them, but we aren't meant to be in categories. Skin color, religion, sexuality, they all rely on labels. Can't we just be human and leave it at that? No one is just any one thing at all. We are all made of so many differences and deserve to be seen and appreciated for every unique aspect we have, not labeled as something and set aside to be classified and judged."

"Wow, Janet. You're right, I agree," I reply, sincerely. "You should have ran for president," I add, with a small laugh.

This comment seems to perk Janet up and she straightens her back as she continues to push her walker, a smile slowly unfolding on her weathered face. "I should have, huh?" Her face radiates playfulness. "I would have done something in politics, but adults are terrible to manage. I prefer working with children. I believe that many people are terribly dull. That's not a label, it's an observation. People walk through life with unseeing eyes and little interest other than the phone in their hands. Children *see* the world with an enthusiasm that adults lack. But you, Cora, are different from many adults. You are like a jewel and reflect back the light of whoever you are around, shining the best of others back at them. You listen and are present in the moment, and by doing so, enhance it for the rest of us. Don't lose that glimmering part of who you are to fit a box that others have built for you. Not even a box that you have built for yourself."

I am stunned as Janet's words wash over me, a healing tide to soothe the hurting places and insecurities I carry inside. "I think that is one of the most meaningful things anyone has ever said to me." I feel like my response is inadequate to the compliment that Janet has just given, but I feel unable to express how I feel in words and struggle to find anything else to say. She gives me a warm smile, and we continue the last portion of our walk.

When we get back to Janet's room, I settle her in bed making sure she is comfortable and propped up the way she likes. As I pull her blanket up on her lap, Janet asks, "what made you decide on the noble profession of nursing?"

I pause, trying to decide what to say, but something tells me she already knows. "I want to help families who may need support during difficult moments. Nursing seemed like a good option and some of my closest friends were going to apply to this program, so I switched my major and decided to do the same."

I'm surprisingly comfortable with Janet, but the wound of my father's death and how that led me to wanting to be a nurse still seems too personal to share with her right now, despite how kind she is or how familiar she feels. This is still a patient and caregiver relationship and I don't want to make anything too personal.

Janet gives me a knowing look, and then places her hand on mine. "You have a kind soul, Cora. That is a strength of yours. I think that your intentions for becoming a nurse are brave. You've helped me a lot in the last couple of days, just by being a calming presence in this whirlwind life that is being a hospital patient. It is very lonely. You have helped relieve that."

Amaya walks into the room just as Janet is finishing her sentence. We both turn to look at her. She is standing there with a hand on her heart, "that is the sweetest thing any nursing student could hope to hear, Janet. Gosh, that melts me."

Janet smiles, and then gives a shrug, "it's just the truth. Cora, and I are BFFs." Then, she starts to giggle. "I feel young when we are together. Like two girlfriends hanging out." When Janet smiles, the joy is so pure. I can't contain my smile. Maybe nursing is for me, after all.

CHAPTER 28:

On Thursday, instead of going to The Wheelhouse like we usually do, we all plan to meet at Apple Hill, a local group of orchards a few towns away. There are various fruit stands, pastries, pumpkin patches, and drinks for sale. It's basically the Disneyland of apple farms.

When I step out of the car, the feeling of fall surrounds me. The leaves are bright crimson and orange/yellow, small children run around in puffy jackets, girls walk in packs wearing knee high boots and scarves with starbucks cups in their hands. It's the same every year, and sameness brings comfort. I inhale deeply, savoring the crisp, clean air.

Leo and Kate park next to Avery and I, and join us for the walk toward the hillside where there is a pond with picnic tables scattered around. Nikki and Noah are already sitting at a wooden bench together, and miraculously seem to be getting along. There is a big pastry box sitting in front of Noah on the picnic table. I can see it is filled with apple donuts. "These are the best!" He yells, as we get closer. Noah holds a half eaten donut up, "seriously, the blueberry apple ones are next level."

Nikki is grinning at us as we approach. The sunlight shines off her platinum hair, and she seems normal. "He's not lying. They are so good," Nikki confirms, holding an apple crumble donut in her hand, with a few bites taken. I feel awkward because I haven't seen or spoken to her since she came to my house with those photos. If they weren't still sitting in a pile on the side table in my living room, a dark unwanted presence, then I would almost think I dreamed that entire visit. But they are, and I didn't.

"Where's Mandy?" she asks as we circle around the bench and grab donuts from the box. I pick up a classic apple donut, feeling the small grains beneath my fingertips and take a bite. Sweetness floods my mouth, dispelling some of the unease I felt at seeing Nikki. Sugar is a hell of a drug.

"She is running a little late, but should be here soon," Kate responds, as she threads her arm through Leo's. "It's chilly out here," she comments and shivers a little.

"Oh, that's because you need one of these hard apple ciders. They will warm you right up. Noah says, lifting his cup up in a cheers motion at her.

"That sounds delightful," Kate says, grinning, a bite in her tone. "How many have you had so far, Noah?"

"This is my second, going for a third in a sec."

"I'll grab you one," Avery says. He laces his fingers through mine, "I was going to take Cora with me to get one, and we can carry some back."

"That sounds good," Noah responds, with a wide Cheshire Cat smile. He is clearly already feeling the first two. His face is flushed and he is in good spirits.

Avery leads me toward a big barn across from the pond. As we walk we talk about how strange it is for me to see Nikki after the other night and come up with some more wild theories about her. As soon as we reach the barn, I am hit with the pleasant scent of pies, and all other delectable apple treats. The barn is huge, really more of a warehouse, and filled with barrels of apple varieties, apple goods, bottled drinks, and snacks. At the back of the barn, is a window where you can order hot foods and beverages. The line is long and winds through the aisles. Avery and I grab a place at the end. As we wait, he wraps his arms around me from behind and kisses me on the neck.

"You better handle a girl like that right, son," a man in a red flannel shirt with a toothpick sticking out between his lips says to Avery. He is browsing the shelves near where we are standing, and I wish he would move along.

"A girl like that...she deserves the best." He adds gruffly, with a smirk. The man's white bushy eyebrows frame watery eyes staring out of a round ruddy face, and his thinning cotton hair coupled with a long bushy beard give him a rough around the edges Santa Clause look.

I wince. It is always hard to discern when race is a reason that older white men decide to comment on our relationship. He's either a racist or a pervert, I decide. Or both. Either way, it is none of this man's business, yet he feels the need to interject. Avery and I together shouldn't be anything but normal in current times, but people still occasionally look a little too long, and quickly avert their eyes when I stare back, or worse, they say offensive comments. I bite back a sarcastic remark and give the man a tight closed lip smile, but I know my eyes are a cold *fuck you* as I meet his gaze. The man stops lingering and rounds the corner, thankfully. I hope he got the message from my stare; his comments are not welcome.

I turn to Avery and wrap my arms around his neck, "he looked like a hillbilly Santa."

Avery looks back at me with affection, "if he only knew that you're the one on the naughty list, and I'm the saint in this relationship."

I smile and stand on my tiptoes to give him a kiss. "That, you are," I whisper into his ear before turning back to move forward in line.

Avery and I are at the window to order our ciders in a matter of minutes. They serve us, and we stroll back to the tables with full hands. I take a sip of the cider, and Noah isn't wrong, it definitely warms me up. It's hot, sweet, and laced with cinnamon. I can barely taste the alcohol. *This is dangerous.*

When Avery and I arrive back at the spot, everyone is talking excitedly about having a pumpkin carving contest tonight. We hand out the drinks, and Avery lets out an excited whoop when he hears we will be carving pumpkins. He has a very prominent competitive streak and loves any type of challenge.

"I can't believe Halloween is this weekend," Kate says. "Only two days away. This year went by so fast, I feel like I blinked in June and then October was here."

"I feel like that too," I agree. "It's like as we get older, time moves faster."

I look around the group, and notice that Mandy still isn't here.

"Should we go pick out some pumpkins?" Leo says with a grin.

"Hell yes!" Noah jumps up from the bench. "I am going to win this contest. You are all in for a treat."

"I'm going to grab an extra pumpkin for Mandy. She got held up at work so she couldn't make it all the way out here, but will be at my house to carve with us later," Kate explains.

Nikki walks around the back of the picnic table and pulls a small red wagon out from behind a bench. It's the type that people pull kids around in and it already is holding a couple bags of apples."I figured we could use this, so I brought it along. It will work for transporting the pumpkins."

"Genius!" Leo says. "I'll pull it for you." Nikki smiles and hands him the handle to the wagon. "Thanks."

"I think the pumpkin patch is that way," Avery says, and points across the orchard toward a giant haymaze, and a pony ride area.

"Yeah, I think you're right," Leo agrees, and we start traveling in that direction with him, Avery and Noah in the lead.

We pass some kids fishing in the pond, and chasing geese. "Yikes," Kate says, as she notices one particularly vicious goose snap at a child who is running after it with a stick. "I mean, good for that goose. Those kids are brutal." The child, probably no older than five, takes off his beanie and starts fanning at the angry goose. This frightens the giant bird, and it quickly waddles away and slips into the pond.

Nikki falls into step with us, and I tense. Is she just going to pretend like she never came to my house with those photos, and then lied and stole from me?

"It's a perfect day out for this," she observes.

Okay, so she is.

I give her a side eye. "Mmhmm," I respond, purposefully trying to be short with her. She doesn't seem to notice though, and continues on, "How is nursing school going?"

"It's great!" Kate says excitedly, and then goes on to describe all her favorite things about it as we walk. Nikki is clever. She probably asked that question because she knew Kate would latch on to it and talk about it for the entire walk, giving us no time to discuss the pictures and for me to catch her in a lie. Kate seems to have completely forgotten what I told her about Nikki yesterday and has thrown herself completely into talking about nursing.

I'm relieved when we reach the pumpkin patch, and I can break away from Nikki to search for the one I want. Being in her presence is making my skin crawl.

I end up at the back of the patch with Noah and Avery. This is where all the extra large pumpkins are, and Noah keeps us laughing at the most ridiculous jokes as he searches for his perfect pumpkin. He keeps muttering "size matters, size matters" as he jumps around trying to find the one he likes best.

Avery chooses a perfectly round mid-sized pumpkin, and I choose one that is lopsided, but has a cute little curly stem on top. "That might be hard to carve," Avery warns, as he gazes down at my tilted pumpkin.

"Since when do I shy away from a challenge?" I reply, raising an eyebrow at him.

"Gosh, that's hot," he whispers in my ear and gives my cheek a quick kiss. "I'm still going to laugh watching you try to carve that, though. Don't say I didn't warn ya."

I playfully smack his arm. "Hey! I don't want an easy pumpkin."

"That's right, Cora. If they don't make you work for it, it's not worth havin'," Noah chimes in.. He is holding an absurdly large pumpkin in his arms. It's twice the size of Avery's, and Noah's considerably sized biceps are bulging from the weight of carrying it. "I found my baby," he says with pride.

"THAT is not a baby. It is huge," Leo says with a laugh as he gazes at the massive pumpkin Noah is holding.

"Shhh, don't say that. You'll give her a complex," Noah responds in a hushed voice as he cradles the gigantic gourd protectively. "But yeah, I need to set it down before I throw out my back. Can you bring the wagon over here?"

Nikki grabs the handle of her wagon and pulls it over to where Noah is standing. She eyes his pumpkin skeptically. "You would choose one so big that there may not be room for the others," she states in a flat tone.

"This is a competition, Nikki. I came to win. Okay?" He lurches forward and gently places his beastly pumpkin on the wagon. When Noah straightens up he lets out a sigh of relief. "I'm so glad you thought to bring the wagon, Nicksters. You may be a blonde, but you're not dumb."

"Awww, that's the nicest thing you've ever said to me," she says, as she slides her small green and orange bumpy pumpkin over to make some room. Leo drops his dark green pumpkin in, and Kate deposits a light dusty pink colored pumpkin and a white one next to his. "Isn't that shade so cute?" she asks, gesturing to the rose hued one.

"Super cute," I agree as I stack mine on top of the others, focused on trying to make sure it won't tumble off and is secure. I'm oddly fond of the one I chose. I feel connected to it, which I know is weird.

Avery leans over and places his pumpkin next to mine. His is well rounded, and classic in every way. It's a flawless looking pumpkin. There isn't one bump on its dark orange exterior. Avery, himself, is grounded, a perfectionist, and enjoys tradition. His choice is perfect for him. Then, I glance over at mine. It's asymmetrical and quirky with its curled stem covered in small sharp spikes, and it has a little scar on the side. It's strange to me how the things that people select are often a reflection of their personalities.

I wonder how my choice reflects me.

CHAPTER 29:

We drop the wagon off at our cars and unload the pumpkins into the back of Kate's trunk, then circle back to spend the rest of the afternoon, eating, laughing, and exploring Apple Hill. I continue to avoid being around Nikki, and end up having a fun day. Avery and I buy a couple apple pies to take home and we all plan to meet at Kate's later for the carving competition.

I settle into the car with the pies on my lap and start messing with the radio to find some music for our somewhat long drive home.

"Well, that was fun," Avery comments. "Apple Hill never disappoints."

"Never," I agree.

"Did Nikki ever say anything about the other night?" He asks.

"Nope."

"That's so strange."

"Yeah. I just avoided her all day."

"I could tell," he laughs. "Every time she was around, your body kinda locked up and then you would speed walk away in a different direction."

"I did not!"

He glances away from the road for a moment to give me a *yes you did* look.

"Okay, maybe I did that a little..."

"It's alright. I was doing the same thing." He cracks the knuckles on one of his hands using his thumb to push down on his fingers, and then goes on, "anyway, have you thought about what you are going to carve into that wonky pumpkin of yours?"

"I can't tell you and ruin the surprise," I say, as I run my hand down Avery's head and leave it to rest comfortably on the back of his neck as he drives. We break into small conversations here and there but spend a lot of the car ride in companionable silence, listening to the music and enjoying the scenery as we drive past forests of pines, which give way to the familiar oaks of our hometown as we get closer to Stone Bay.

We stop by my apartment to drop off the pies, and grab carving supplies and a bottle of wine. Then, we get back in the car to go to Kate's. We pull up to her house just as the sun is setting, and the sky is stained a glorious mix of orange and pink. I get out of the car and then lead the way inside. As soon as we enter the house, the cloying scent of baking pies engulfs us. Avery takes a deep breath, "if heaven had a smell, this would be it."

I tilt my head back and inhale. "I would have to agree. I wonder what type of pies they got today? Did you see all the flavors there were? I hope someone got a berry cobbler...we should have brought one of ours."

We round the corner into the kitchen and it is total chaos. There are various types of pastries all over the center counter top and pumpkins on top of newspapers line a pop-up table by the back window. Leo is in one corner breaking down weed to roll a joint with, while Noah is arranging rinsed off pumpkin seeds on a lined baking sheet and preparing to put those in the oven. Kate flutters around the kitchen in her frilly apron with a spatula in her hand.

When she sees us enter, she greets us with a brilliant smile, "You're just in time for ice cream and pie before we start getting serious about carving."

"Oh, I've been serious this whole time," Noah says as he sprinkles chili powder on top of the seeds. "Ooo these are gonna be fire! This is the real reason I chose a big pumpkin. I wanted the seeds."

"I'm so glad you're making those," Leo says as he licks the wrap paper and seals the joint. "After I smoke this, I'm going in."

Avery approaches me holding a plate with a big slice of hot berry cobbler and some vanilla ice cream. "Thanks," I tell him as I take the plate from his hands and we sit at the counter to eat. Avery scoops a bite into his mouth, and opens up one of the books of pumpkin carving templates that are set out in front of us, and we browse the various designs. Kate sits next to me with some classic apple pie, the vanilla ice cream on top is melting into a puddle across the steaming slice.

"Noah thinks the cider is the best part of Apple Hill, but we all know it's really the pies that make that drive up there all worth it," she states before spooning a bite into her mouth. "I put your pumpkins on the back table. Noah already broke into his already, as you can see, but after Leo is done with his smoke break and we finish eating we can start the carving." She pauses to lick her spoon. "Do you know what you're going to make?"

I shake my head, "It's a surprise."

"Ha okay, then. Keep your secrets. What about you Avery?"

"I've always wanted to make an owl," he replies, and holds up a page in the template book depicting an intricate owl carving.

"Good choice," Nikki comments, as she materializes next to Kate. "Where's Mandy at? Shouldn't she be here by now?"

Just as Nikki asks, Mandy strolls into the room. She looks different, and then I realize she isn't wearing her large framed glasses like she normally does, and her usual assortment of crystal jewelry is also absent. Mandy's hair is wet like she just got out of the shower, and she is carrying a large bag of tortilla chips in one hand and a jar of salsa in her other.

"Sorry I'm late. Work was holding me back, so I rushed here as soon as I could," she explains as she sets the food on the counter and goes to the cupboard to grab bowls.

"It's totally fine," Kate says, "we haven't started yet, so you're just on time, actually." She crosses the room and gives Mandy a hug. "We missed you today."

"I wish I could have made it, but I'm glad I'm here now," Mandy responds as she gives Kate a quick squeeze back and continues to set up the food she brought. It seems like she is avoiding eye contact, and again I am struck with the sense that Mandy isn't well. She looks sickly and her skin has an unhealthy pallor to it. I look over at Kate, who doesn't seem to notice, but my eyes catch on Nikki standing next to her. She is looking at Mandy with a scrutinizing gaze, like a chemist waiting for an experiment to react. She senses me watching her, and gives me a tight smile before averting her eyes to look out the window.

"How about some pictures?" Nikki says abruptly, pulling her phone from her zip up pocket and snapping her gaze back to the room. My eyes widen as I stare back at Avery, who is also looking at me like *WTF,* and Kate bumps me with her leg.

"Um, no pictures. I heard the last ones you took turned out...well, let's just say no," Kate says in a sickly sweet voice. I see Nikki swallow, clearly realizing I have told Kate about her visit, and her mind is calculating what to do next. "Oh yeah, those were strange. Did Cora show you?"

"No, I was under the impression you were supposed to."

"Yeah, something came up that night, but you will have to see them..."

It's silent and awkward for a second and Mandy just stares at us, clearly feeling out of the loop since she has no idea what pictures we are talking about. I still don't know what to think about the images and my mind goes into overdrive trying to formulate what to say to get some answers from

Nikki, who quickly lifts her phone up and says, "smile," as she takes a photo of Mandy.

"What the fuck," Mandy snarls, "I don't want pictures right now, I'm not even ready."

"It's fine. They are candid," Nikki mumbles, and takes a couple more of Mandy, who lifts her hand in an attempt to block her face. Then, Nikki turns and starts snapping photos of the rest of us. "You'll thank me for these one day," she murmurs.

I feel taken off guard and further confused, but before I can ask what the hell that means, Noah and Leo reenter the kitchen from the back door and bring with them the skunky smell of the joint they smoked outside. Their eyes are bloodshot and squinty, and they are both smiling as they round the counter and start shoveling chips and salsa into their mouths. Noah quickly heads to the oven, puts on mits, and removes his pumpkin seeds. "Oh Yes. These turned out good," he exclaims, giving a chef's kiss after setting the baking sheet down and giving it a good shake.

I'm grateful for the interruption, and can tell that Kate, Avery, and Mandy are just as baffled as I am but we all drop it in favor of moving on from Nikki's weird photoshoot. I continue to do my best to keep my distance from her like I did earlier in the day.

After we snack a bit more, we begin the carving portion of the night. We all stand around our pumpkins at the long table that Kate set up for carving and begin. Other than the music playing in the background, it is quiet in the room as we all concentrate on our carving.

Avery's owl is starting to take shape, and looks cute with the little feathered wings that he has carefully chiseled onto his pumpkin. Kate finishes her carving quickly. She has created a cat face using a template. She grabs some cinnamon and starts to sprinkle it on the inside portion of the top. "This will make it smell so good when you light the candle inside. Trust me."

"Oh, that's a great idea," Leo says, as he glances up from his carving. "Pass me some of that, Martha Stuart."

This comment earns a laugh from Kate and she hands Leo the cinnamon container.

Nikki and Mandy haven't started on their carvings yet, and are still flipping through the template options. I told everyone mine was a surprise, but the truth is I don't know what I want to make and am scrolling through Pinterest on my phone searching for a fun idea. I want to find a design that will complement the unique curly stem my pumpkin has.

I scroll until I discover a photo that shows a pumpkin on its side. It is carved so that the stem is used as a nose. I love it. My pumpkin is perfect for the design. I pocket my phone and start working on carving.

Noah asks everyone if he can have the gunk from inside their pumpkins, which I had assumed was to use for more baked seeds, but instead he has carved his pumpkin to look like it is throwing up and positioned the stringy, slimy, innards so that it's hanging out of the open mouth he carved. He places a beer can next to his creation and stands back to admire his work. "It's beautiful," he murmurs, and Leo starts laughing uncontrollably.

Leo grabs an empty beer can and wedges it in between the sharp teeth of his carving to look like his pumpkin is chomping it.

"Your pumpkin is kind of a badass," Kate notes.

"Yeah, unlike Noah's, which..."

A shrill yelp interrupts Leo's next words, and we all turn toward Nikki who is holding her right hand. Her middle finger is weeping blood, and it drips into a puddle over her carving. Leo rushes forward with a kitchen rag, and holds it out to her. "Thanks," she murmurs, as she puts pressure on her injury. "Will you take a look at this Avery? I just want to make sure I don't need stitches or something. My hand slipped with the knife and it felt pretty deep."

"Yeah, keep holding pressure for a bit, then when the

bleeding slows I'll look at it."

"Okay, thanks." Nikki continues to hold the rag to her hand, which is quickly becoming saturated with her blood. Kate jumps up from the table to grab a first aid kit, and circles toward Nikki with it.

I hear a faint sniffing sound and turn to look at Mandy. Her nostrils are flared like she is inhaling a scent, and the look in her eyes can only be described as predatory. She does another small sniff, and then catches me staring, and quickly lifts her wrist to her nose and wipes. "Ugh, I think I am fighting off a cold," she says softly and shoots me a small smile. The intense expression that was on her face moments earlier, has vanished and I wonder if it was something I imagined. The dark crescents under her eyes stand out harshly under the bright overhead kitchen lights and her lips look pale and bloodless.

"Do you want a tissue?" Kate asks, holding out a pack.

"Sure, thanks," Mandy replies, and takes a kleenex to dab at her nose with. She continues to stare at Nikki's finger intently as Avery cleans and examines it for her. I can still sense something in Mandy's gaze that feels loaded, ready to spring.

Calm, sweet, Mandy is normally so relaxed with her crystals and herbs. Right now though, she has a different energy and I am not used to it. I think back to that day in the parking garage when I caught her staring at me from behind the wheel of the car. Her expression at that moment was also something I had never seen on her face before.

Is everyone going crazy? *Am I?*

CHAPTER 30:

Avery ends up the winner of the carving contest. His elaborate owl looks remarkable when it is lit up.

"That would be perfect for display with all the owl figurines at The Magic Bean," Kate notes. Avery beams at that comment and says he will bring it by there tomorrow and see if the shop wants it.

We hang out for a while on the porch, admiring the glow of our creations and enjoying the cool night air. Nikki left quickly after Avery bandaged her finger and determined she didn't need stitches. When we were cleaning up our carving space, I noticed that her carving was just a bunch of deep gauge marks and slashes. I stopped and stared at it, feeling a chill creep through me. It looked aggressive and angry, no wonder she cut herself.

Leo notices me staring at Nikki's abandoned project. "Maybe she was going for a Michael Meyers victim look," he comments. I turn to look back over my shoulder at him. His eyes are squinty and bloodshot as he stares at the pumpkin with a bemused expression. "Who knows with the artsy types, right?"

"I guess so..." I trail off.

Kate comes up to grab some more trash off the table, and leans in to whisper "onion of crazy," into my ear. I crack a smile, but feel nothing but uneasiness inside.

After we finish cleaning up, we say our goodbyes and Avery drops me off at my apartment before heading home. I feel glad to be alone with my own thoughts. I curl into bed and start thinking about the strangeness of life. I let my philosopher's mind wander, until I fall into a deep dreamless sleep.

* * *

I wake up the next day and quickly get ready for my final clinical day caring for Janet. It's exciting to be almost done with my first week of nursing care, but I have grown attached to her and will be sad to part from her when the day is done.

I pack a duffel bag with my work clothes and supplies. I will have to go straight to my shift tonight after clinicals. It's the night before Halloween, and a friday, so I am bracing myself for injuries and alcoholics to be in the patient rotation.

I get to the waiting area early this morning, and Professor Clark is as jolly as ever. "Good morning, Cora," he chirps. "You look bright eyed and bushy tailed today."

His eyes are always sparkling, like he is holding on to a secret joke and moments away from delivering the punch line.

"Thanks," I say, trying to make my voice enthusiastic to match his energy. He then goes on to talk about the muffins he plans to bake this weekend, and I can feel my mind starting to zone out as I try to listen to him talk about brown sugar versus white sugar.

More students filter in over the next few minutes, and thankfully it is time to go in and start the day, and Professor Clark shifts gears and begins discussing instructions for our final patient care day of the week.

Kate comes to stand next to me as we listen to the various instructions and I glance around for Mandy, but can't spot her. I give Kate a questioning look, and she just shrugs as we follow the group of students trailing behind Professor Clark into the nursing area.

I meet up with Amaya, trying to focus on what I need to do rather than let my mind conjure all the possible reasons of why Mandy is absent today. If I look worried, Amaya doesn't notice, and she is in an upbeat mood and full of energy. I look at the coffee cup she is holding in her hand and wonder how many espresso shots she has in it.

"I'm sad it's your last day!" she says, reaching out to pat my arm. "I know Janet is too, but she will probably be going home by the end of the day, so maybe you two can keep in touch once she is out of here. I've never seen a student nurse bond so well with a patient. It has been so sweet."

I follow her toward Janet's room, where a tired looking nurse with short gray hair is typing on a computer. "Hey Deb, this is my nursing student, Cora. She is going to receive the patient handoff from you this morning."

I face the night nurse with a smile, and pull out my notepad in case I need to write anything. She has a stern expression, but when she opens her mouth to speak, her voice is high and soft like a young girl's. It is totally unexpected and I feel my eyes widen momentarily in surprise. Amaya gives my back a pat and then strolls down the hall to one of her other patient rooms while I listen to Deb prattle on about how uneventful the night shift always is.

Once she is done talking, we part ways and I enter Janet's room. She is laying up in bed reading and her face lights up when she sees me. "Goodmorning, dear Cora. How was your day off yesterday?"

"It was good. I spent time with some friends, and got ready for Halloween. How was your day? I heard you're probably going to be going home later."

"Oh, yes! That is this weekend, isn't it? Yes. I am looking forward to going home and making my own food again. No offense to the hospital cooks," she sticks her tongue out and makes a face of disgust. "I'm just ready to get back to normal life and am feeling much better. Maybe I can even pass out some candy and see the little ones in fun costumes. I've always loved that."

I grin, imagining Janet answering her door with a big candy bowl and doting over the kids who come asking for treats. "That sounds like it would be perfect. I hope you have a costume to wear, too."

"Of course I do," she says, turning up her nose. "Every year, I dress as Winnie the Pooh Bear. This year I will be a 'silly old bear' indeed."

I tell her I love her costume idea, and we spend the morning doing our usual routine of assessments and personal care. We go for a walk again around the hospital halls, and Janet holds on to my arm instead of a walker this time. She seems stronger, and I feel happy to see the quick improvements in her health.

The time passes quickly, and as the end of the clinical day nears, I find Janet seems to be worrying about something. I've caught her falling into a few of her episodes today, but they are short lived and she doesn't address them so I don't mention anything either.

As I am cleaning up her lunch of a turkey sandwich, carrots, and some saltine crackers, I can feel her eyes upon me. I glance up at her, and Janet's expression is thoughtful. "What's on your mind?" I ask, sensing that she wants to say something, but is holding back. "Whatever you want to say, it won't scare me. We are past that now."

She appears grateful to hear me say this. "I always worry..."she trails off, and then begins again, "I always worry that I will say something that pushes people away."

"I don't have the special insight you do Janet, but I find myself often feeling the same sort of things," I say with a reassuring smile. "Go ahead and speak what's on your mind."

She nods, "it wasn't your fault." I feel confused about where this conversation is going as Janet twists her fingers gently in her lap, clearly nervous. "He needed a defibrillator, and it just wasn't there on time," she continues. I let out a little gasp when I realize she is talking about my dad's death, something I have never discussed with her. Janet continues,"and don't start on that medicine excuse about how you should have made sure he was compliant with all his prescriptions, you know deep down that wasn't the issue. You were his child, and he was the parent. It wasn't your fault, and it wasn't his either. Not really. Sometimes there is no one to blame. Just life taking its toll."

I stand tethered in place, as she speaks. Afraid to breathe because I know it will sound labored. My chest is tight, and my eyes burn from the tears I am attempting to suppress.

"You need to stop touching your wound, or else it will never heal. It's important to me that you know you're not the one at fault in the situation, no matter what you tell yourself on your bad days." With those words, Janet looks up from her lap and our eyes connect. Mine wide and shimmering, hers shining with genuine care.

I reach up and swipe at my eye as a tear escapes down my cheek. The taste of salt kisses my lips as another drop follows the first. My father's death is the most painful moment of my life. I have carried so much guilt for not being able to help him when he needed someone the most. I felt like a failure for a long time. I told myself I was a failure…

"Thank you, for what you said. It matters more to me than I can express," I manage to reply.

Janet simply reaches her hand out to me and holds mine in hers. "I know, dear. I mean every word."

* * *

As I am about to leave Janet's room at the end of the day, she hands me a slip of paper with her home address and phone number on it. I know beyond a doubt I want to stay in touch with her. She is someone special to me now. I never thought my first patient would be someone like Janet, and I am sure I will never meet anyone else like her. Her words were the gift I needed to feel like less of an imposter or failure in a hospital setting...and in life. I hadn't realized just how much my fear of being unworthy was holding me back from enjoying what is around me.

I check out for the day with Professor Clark, and say goodbye to Kate before walking toward the Emergency Department to start my scribe shift for the night. It's strange that Mandy never showed up today. Something must be very wrong. I glance at the time on my phone screen, and rush out a quick text to her to check and see if she's alright. I also send a text to Avery to see how his afternoon is going and what his plans are for the night.

He says he is just getting off work, and planning to stay in tonight and study for the MCAT. He is applying to Med School soon, and has been working hard to get a good score on the admissions test. I let him know I'll call him tomorrow. I start work in fifteen minutes and won't be getting off until three in the morning. I grab a protein bar from my bag and eat it as I walk.

While I wind through the corridors of the hospital toward the ER, I reflect on my day. I know my father would have loved Janet. He adored long conversations and good humor, both of which she can provide in abundance. At the thought of him, I find myself wondering again about whether there is life after death. Questioning thoughts begin to sprout in my mind, one after the other. Where do we go when we die? Will I ever see my dad again? How is Janet able to know the things that she does?

I stop at a kiosk to grab a coffee. I'm going to need caffeine tonight. As I wait for my latte to be ready, I continue with my strange existential thoughts. Life holds so many mysteries. Clearly, there are more layers to this world than we humans are typically aware of. I think back to what Dr. Manita said when we talked about energy not being able to be created or destroyed. What about spirit energy? Are lives infinitely recycled? Is there a heaven? My mind feels foggy with the direction my thoughts have turned, and I remember why philosophy appealed to me so much. I could ponder on these subjects all day.

I'm so lost in my own mind that I pass the staff entrance that leads to the Emergency Department, and have to double back. Fortunately, I have a few minutes to spare. I sip my coffee as I circle back to let myself in with my badge. I can already hear the sirens of approaching ambulances, and the sun hasn't even set yet. The night before Halloween, or "mischief night," as some people call it, tends to bring out the wild in people.

I drop my stuff off in the break room, chug my coffee, burning my mouth in the rush to drink it all, but eager to finish it before my shift begins. Then, I go to the fishbowl to log into the computer. I'm disappointed to discover that I am paired with Dr. Brandt today. I've only worked with her one other time, and it was terrible. We don't usually work together since we tend to be scheduled different hours, but because I traded with someone to work tonight I got stuck with her.

Dr. Brandt is all business, sharp words, and harsh tones. The only good thing about working with her is that she likes her space, so I get a little more for myself, too. She often sits at a computer far away, rather than next to her scribe like physicians typically do. It complicates things when I need clarification for a chart and have to get up and ask her, but at least she isn't nearby to snap at me while I work, which she is known to do to people on a daily basis.

"Hi Dr. Brandt." I greet her with a smile, which she doesn't return.

"Cora," she responds tersely, "if I need you, I'll come find you."

I try to keep from rolling my eyes, not that she would have even noticed since she hasn't so much as looked at me since arriving.

"Alright. I'll be at the computer right there," I say, trying to keep my voice pleasant as I point to a work space on the other side of the fishbowl.

"Good," she replies, eyes still averted from me and focused on her screen.

I grit my teeth against saying something smartass and make my way to the computer I will be sitting at.

This is going to be a long night.

Within seconds of me sitting down at the desk, Dr. Brandt is behind me clearing her throat. I turn my head to meet her gaze, my eyebrows raised in question.

"I need to go see the patient in room 7. You can stay, or come. Your choice."

Does she not understand how my job works?

"I'll come with you," I say, as I quickly turn to scan the info on the patient in that room, but she has already taken off and I have to practically jog to catch up with her as she rounds a corner. She didn't even give me a moment to see what the patient was in the ER for or get any information. I can feel myself growing frustrated already, and take a deep breath to steady my emotions.

As I pass through the hall, I hear loud laughing coming from a room, which is unusual for an Emergency Department. The drunks are already coming out and the waiting area will probably be full by nightfall.

I catch up to Dr. Brandt just as she is knocking to enter the patient's room. I follow her in, and see a thin middle aged man lying on his side in the hospital bed. Sweat glistens along his receding hairline, and his cheeks are flushed. The man's shifty brown eyes flick back and forth between Dr. Brandt and I as we walk in. He resembles a cornered rodent.

I can sense his discomfort, so I stop at the door and keep my distance. Dr. Brandt continues toward him and introduces herself, as I remain quiet. She fails to inform the man of who I am, so the patient gestures to me and says, "why is she here?"

"That is just my secretary," Dr. Brandt says with a dismissive flip of her hand. "You can ignore her, she is only taking notes."

"What kind of notes?" The man has a paranoid gleam in his beady eyes as he looks at me so intensely that I immediately have the urge to back out the door and retreat. I've seen this look before when a patient is having a psychotic episode. I still don't know why he is here, and I'm wondering if he is a psychiatric hold. I shift on my feet, feeling awakened under his unwavering gaze.

"Relax. It's alright," Dr. Brandt replies soothingly. "She is taking notes for your medical chart so we can treat you correctly and get you home. It keeps my hands and eyes free to assess you instead of writing it all myself."

Although Dr. Brandt is speaking to him, the patient's eyes haven't moved from me, and he is watching my every move with a harsh expression.

"I want her to leave," he says in a flat voice, his hands clutching the bedsheets like the talons of a large bird. His knuckles turn white as he begins to quake, every muscle in his upper extremities are tensed and his teeth are gritted in a snarl. His eyes begin to dart back and forth between me and Dr. Brandt, like the tail of a rattlesnake before it strikes.

"NOW!" He screams, and grabs the pink bedpan next to his bed and hurls it at me. The bedpan hits the wall to my right and clatters to the tile floor. The outburst is so sudden that I startle and nearly drop my pen. I look at the plastic container, and am grateful it was empty and I am not splattered with urine right now.

Dr. Brandt turns to look at me, her expression grim. I nod my head once and then quickly step out of the room. A nurse is standing at a computer cart on wheels and chatting outside the patient's room. She sees which room I exit from and says, "oh gosh, looks like you've got the lightbulb guy tonight."

I smile and nod like I know what she's talking about. She leans in and lowers her voice, "I mean, I've been an ER nurse for over twelve years and I've seen people stick some weird stuff up their assholes, but a lightbulb is a new one for me." She cringes and then goes back to her charting.

It feels like an hour passes before Dr. Brandt finally comes out from inside the room that I was banished from. She makes eye contact with me, and then keeps walking at a fast pace down the hall toward the fishbowl. I sigh, and speed walk to catch up with her.

She doesn't acknowledge my presence at her side right away, and then in her typical clipped tone of voice says, "the man stuck a lightbulb inside of his anus. Why? I do not know. I did not ask. The exam was not fun. In addition to his self induced medical ailment, he is suffering from extreme paranoia and delusions. I have a psychiatric consultation scheduled. He's booked for X-Rays and will probably need to be anesthetized at the very least to get that thing out."

I fight the urge to gasp at the strangeness of it all. "It's a mess," Dr. Brandt continues, "I'm sorry he yelled at you like that and became aggressive. I'll chart this one myself. I am so sorry."

I'm taken aback by her apology. "It wasn't personal," I say, shrugging the incident with the patient off.

"Yeah, well. It always makes me angry to see men treat women in that manner. Just a personal thing for me, I guess. I won't tolerate it. I put him in his place when you left the room and he now is the proud owner of new bracelets for the time being."

I stare at her for a moment, realizing that she is saying she had wrist restraints placed on the patient for his violent outburst.

"He won't be harming anyone on my watch, especially not my scribe."

"Well, thanks," I say, awkwardly, still unsure of how to interact with her. "In his defense, he looked pretty uncomfortable and I don't know if I would want any unnecessary people looking at my butt with a lightbulb sticking out of it either."

The side of Dr. Brandt's mouth twitches up in an almost

grin. "It wasn't really sticking out. He really shoved it in there."

"Oh gosh, how is that possible?"

Dr. Brandt lifts her hands in an *I don't know* gesture. We arrive back at the fishbowl, and Dr. Brandt is once again clipped in tone and all business. She lets me know that she will inform me of the next patient when she's ready, and then goes to her computer to begin her charting.

I realize that some of Dr. Brandt's coldness could be like a type of armor. A way of making her appear strong and capable, which she is, but the brisk way she deals with others further creates this image. For the first time, I wonder what her story is, rather than what her problem is and think back to what Janet told me about placing people in boxes. I've been judgemental. I need to do better.

CHAPTER 31:

I stare at the computer, waiting for Dr. Brandt to finish her notes on the light bulb patient. I am not accustomed to the doctor writing his or her own chart, and don't have anything to do. I really can't complain because I'm literally getting paid to sit and do nothing right now. I bend down and pull a hardcover book from my bag, Daisy Jones & the Six by Taylor Jenkins Reid, and crack it open to where I left off. It's good, it reminds me a little of A Star is Born, but in the 70s, and no Lady Gaga or Bradly Cooper.

I read a few pages, and then glance back at where Dr. Brandt is meticulously typing. Despite the book being enjoyable, I feel like I can't focus. I keep rereading the same lines over and over again, and losing my place as my mind wanders.

Suddenly, I feel a presence behind me. I turn to see Dr. Brandt standing there. I really wish she would just sit at a computer next to me so she isn't always walking up and catching me off guard like this.

"We have a patient," she says, and then turns to walk away.

I take a deep breath, and rise to follow her. "Who is the patient?"

"Room 14" she mumbles.

"If you sit by me in the fishbowl, you can show me on the

computer who you want to see before we go to the room. Then, I can get information to start building the chart before we even meet them..." I say, hoping that if she knows I would prefer this, maybe we can start working better together.

"Oh. Okay," she replies, curtly. "I'm not the best with social interactions. This feels social. Sorry. I can move closer to your work area if that is what you need."

I chew on my inner lip, and try to hold in a smile. At least it's a start.

We walk into the room and I see a small boy around the age of five sitting on his father's lap in Spider Man pajamas with mittens on his hands. The boy's hair is sticking up in various directions like he just rolled out of bed and he is holding an iphone that is playing Peppa Pig full blast. He is covered in a bright red blister-like rash, and although the kid looks uncomfortable, the father looks far more upset and is near tears.

He lowers the volume on the phone slightly, so he can be heard over the excited squeals of Peppa jumping in muddy puddles, and explains to Dr. Brandt that he never had his son vaccinated for chickenpox. He didn't think it was a big deal, but now he feels terrible and is worried. He has placed mittens on his kid to try and prevent his itching from breaking the skin, but he isn't sure what else to do and is concerned about the high fever.

I watch as Dr. Brandt navigates the situation. She is awkward in her delivery of information, but thorough in her assessment and at providing education for the parent. When she is finished answering all the questions, and giving discharge instructions to the patient, I follow her out of the room.

She releases a deep breath. "Parents always make me nervous for some reason. They are one of the reasons I didn't go into Pediatrics. That, and I am hypersensitive to touch, and kids tend to be clingy."

With those words, it all falls into place for me, and I

realize that Dr. Brandt is neurodivergent. Her organized mind doesn't do well with overstimulation.

"You look like a lightbulb just went off," she observes.

"Better my mind than my butthole," I say before I can stop myself.

Her jaw drops and then she lets out a tittering laugh. It is one of the funniest sounds I have ever heard and I start laughing, too. And just like that, the wall between us breaks a little more. We pass Dr. Manita and his scribe as we walk, and he shoots me a puzzled look of amusement. To see Dr. Brandt smiling at work is rare, let alone laughing in the halls, so I know this looks like a strange miracle.

Once we are back at my computer, Dr. Brandt gazes longingly toward her work area before saying, "I like my space. I am going to continue to sit in my seat, but I will give you time to look up the patient before we go visit them from now on, if that is something you find helpful."

Okay, so a compromise. I think. *I can work with that.*

"Thank you, that would help," I reply, as she turns to cross the room and settles into her isolated seat to review the patients waiting to be seen. I am still smiling a little after seeing the joy bloom on Dr. Brandt's typically stern face. I crack my book open again, hoping the shift picks up. "It's so slow," I whisper to myself. These words would come back to haunt me later, I knew, but at that moment, I needed some excitement.

Five minutes later, Dr. Brandt approaches to notify me that in a couple minutes, we will be seeing the patient in room 2. I thank her and start to look at the patient chart. The person is a twenty nine year old female with stomach pain. We go to the patient's room, and she is doubled over and dripping sweat, her face in a rictus of pain. Dr. Brandt gently pushes on her abdomen and the patient screams out as the pressure that was placed on her stomach is released. Tests and scans are ordered to rule things out, but Dr. Brandt suspects acute appendicitis is the cause and believes surgery will be necessary. The visit is brief and we exit the room, just as a swirl of nurses and a couple physicians in white coats rush past. They quickly head for the emergency drop off area, and the shrill melody of an ambulance arriving hovers in the air.

I glance toward the back double doors where paramedics bring in patients. There are already a couple nurses waiting, prepared for the arrival of the trauma. They have yellow PPE gowns over their scrubs, and gloves on their hands. They are soldiers ready to handle whatever comes through those doors to them.

The sky outside is the faded plum hue of evening with inky clouds. The sound of the siren grows in volume as the rig pulls to an abrupt stop in the drop off bay. Two paramedics jump out and yank a gurney from the back. They are moving fast and have the patient inside the hospital and swiftly wheeled toward the designated room for treatment as they give a detailed report to the physician jogging next to the gurney.

Dr. Brandt watches as the emergency workers rush past us. “I think I am going to see if Dr. Chan needs any help,” she says. “This looks like a big trauma.”

I crane my neck to get a better look from where I am standing. I can’t see her face, but I can tell that the patient is female and that her skin and hair are painted in dark red blood. Her skin has been entirely scraped off of one arm, revealing the raw weeping nerve endings below. One of the woman’s legs is twisted in an unnatural way and her foot is facing the bed instead of the ceiling as she lays on her back. Long jagged wounds are visible down the front of her chest and torso, and she whimpers in between full body shudders.

I stay out of the way and watch the familiar dance as the nurses, techs, and physicians gather to rapidly stabilize the patient and prepare to transfer her to surgery. Dr. Chan draws up medications and hands them to nurses to add to her IV and try to raise her plummeting blood pressure while Dr. Brandt helps where she is needed. In a matter of minutes, the woman is rushed away in a swirl of hospital scrubs.

When Dr. Barndt returns, there is blood on her white coat.

CHAPTER 32:

It's time for us to go on our break. It is already ten PM and I am looking forward to having an hour to myself. Dr. Brandt likes to take her breaks in her car, where she can be alone and rest her mind in peace. I don't mind this, especially now that I am starting to understand her personality more, and know that it's not anything personal against me.

I am about to leave the fishbowl to get water and use the bathroom when a frazzled paramedic runs in. He is carrying a bag in his hands. When he spots me he holds it out and says, "this was for a patient that was recently dropped off. It was found next to her body when we picked her up and was left behind in the ambulance during transfer. Can you make sure it gets to her?"

The bag, which is more like a briefcase, swings in his hand as he holds it out to me. I pause, frozen for a moment as my eyes lock in on the familiar teal color. It looks like the same bag that I had complimented the reporter, Jessica, on when Kate and I went to her house for the interview. I reach out and take it from him, "yeah, I can do that," I manage to croak out.

The paramedic turns on his heel as soon as the bag is in my hands, and rushes for the door, probably racing to get to his next call. My legs feel shaky. I glance around and make sure no one is around to notice me, and then I duck into the bathroom, clutching the bag to my side like it's mine. I need to figure out if this is really hers or not.

I lock myself behind the privacy of a restroom stall, and start to dig through it. My stomach plummets when my eyes land on the familiar purple cover of Heather's journal. *It is Jessica's bag,* I don't need to open her wallet to confirm it, but I do so anyway. I flip open the soft leather of a camel colored wallet, and Jessica Harper's face stares back at me from a California driver's license.

Realization hits me hard. Jessica was the trauma patient who was just brought in. I hadn't realized it during the commotion and with all the bodies crowded around her working on saving her life, and all the blood concealing her features. Her hair didn't look her shade of red when she was rolled in on the gurney because it was saturated in clotting blood. Suddenly, it's hard for me to swallow. I know deep in my core that it has something to do with Dyer Lane. I gave that woman this journal, and it led her to harm. I chew on my inner lip and try to not allow the guilt and panic overwhelm me.

I open Heather's diary and flip through the pages. *I knew it.* All of the journal is filled with writing. There are not any blank pages. The photos I had taken that showed the journal as blank are a mystery to me. *How is that even possible?*

I stuff the journal into the back waistband of my scrubs before exiting the restroom. I quickly walk to my work space, glance around to make sure I am unseen, and then sneak the journal out of the back of my pants and deposit the book into my work bag, which I then sling over my shoulder. My hairline prickles with sweat, as my heart rate starts to increase from the nerves I'm feeling. I know what I'm doing is wrong. I just don't care right now. My curiosity can't be suppressed at this point.

I leave the fishbowl with Jessica's briefcase in hand, and approach the Charge Nurse. I tell her what the paramedic said to me when he dropped off the bag, and then hand it over to her. She thanks me, and then begins the steps of getting it to the proper destination.

Then, I sneak back to the fishbowl and try to find Jessica's chart. I know I can be fired for this. Technically, although I have access to all the patient charts in the ER, I am only supposed to look at the patient charts the Dr. picks up. It is part of the HIPAA laws, and the hospital is very strict about this when they audit. They won't see that I have been snooping for a few days when computer use is reviewed, though. The fear of being caught sits on my shoulders and presses me down, but I push back. I want to know what happened. I *need* to know.

I feel a flash of panic when I don't see her name right away, and worry that since she was sent to surgery for her wounds, maybe she will no longer be displayed on the ER board. I keep scrolling, and then I spot her. I had missed it the first time through because I was going so fast. I take a deep breath, I need to slow down. I click on Jessica's chart and scan the notes.

My pulse pounds in my ears and becomes a rush as I process what I am reading. According to the report given by the paramedics, Jessica was found on Dyer Lane. *Of course she fucking was.* She had lost most of her blood volume, and had suffered deep lacerations to her chest, abdomen, and head. The dermis of her left upper extremity had been ripped off, an injury known as "degloving." Jessica's right leg had been severely fractured and nearly torn from her body. The cause of her injuries is unknown. Jessica was unconscious when she was discovered and unable to answer any questions. I try to swallow, but my mouth has gone dry. There is more written in the physician notes tab, but instead of opening that, I quickly close out of the chart. I've seen enough to have a basic idea of what could have happened. The less I click around, the more believable it will be if I say that I accidentally clicked into her chart if I am questioned later about this unauthorized computer activity.

I hurry out of the Emergency Department and decide to be like Dr. Brandt tonight and spend my break inside my car. I need the privacy. I need to calm down.

The cold air slaps me as I exit the hospital, making my muscles clench as I speed walk toward my car. I feel jumpy, like at any moment I will be caught for stealing from a patient. *What am I doing?* Jessica is probably dying, and I'm horrible for this.

I unlock my car and slide inside. I start the engine to get the heater on, and sit in the silence for a moment, gathering my thoughts. I pull my phone out and set a timer for thirty minutes, to remind me when my break is coming to an end and it's time to go back in for the remainder of my shift. Then, I reach a shaking hand into my bag, and slowly withdraw the journal. I am ashamed at how excited I am to have it back. *Who am I?* Gollum from Lord of the Rings? This isn't "my precious" and I shouldn't be feeling this way...but I do.

This thing is cursed. It has to be. I must be too, since it found its way back to me.

I open the journal to where I last left off, and hold my phone light over the pages so I can read.

* * *

October 6th, 1997

Liv needs help. I don't know what to do yet, but I will do whatever it takes to figure out how to fix this. The power Father provides isn't worth what is happening to her.

Liv is dying. She looks like a corpse. The light in her eyes grows dimmer with each day.

I tried to find a time to meet with Tasha so we could plan, but Liv has some sort of awareness since we made the blood pact, and she can sense when we are together. She doesn't like when we are with each other without her, and will show up wherever we are.

I can feel her emotions. When she is angry, I feel it. When she is joyful, I feel it. When she is hungry, I can feel it. At times, her hunger is all consuming.

Since I can sense Liv's strong emotions, I assume she can probably sense mine, also. Or rather, Father can sense mine. I feel violated.

I know there has to be a way to get him out of her for good, but I do not think it will be easy. I came across some information about the use of crystal energy and chanting to draw a spirit forward. Maybe something like this could work to summon him from out of her? Obviously magic works and spirits are real, or else we wouldn't be in this situation. So, there has to be a solution. I need to keep researching, but I need to hurry.

I'm running out of time.

* * *

October 13th, 1997

I was up all night reading. I've spent the past week searching through numerous books. I went to the library and even bought a second occult book that has more details on dark entities. This one has proven to be helpful. Here is a diagram of a pentagram crystal field that the book details can be used to harness spirits and energy. There is also a special spell to chant.

I really think I am getting closer to figuring out what I can do to reverse whatever Father has binded us with. Liv and Tasha asked me to hang out tonight, but I told them I was feeling sick. I need to find the answers. I am so close, I know it.

It's strange, sometimes Father seems to leave Liv's body, and she is herself again. When that happens, I am afraid each labored breath she takes will be her last. It's like he has drained every last bit of health from her and left her as a husk. I know she can't sustain him much longer and he will be looking for a new vessel. Most likely Tasha or me...

I can't let that happen, and I refuse to lose Liv. I think my best chance at banishing him is to strike in one of those moments that he leaves her body. I need to prevent him from reentering her and then maybe I can get rid of him and get our lives back.

I think it comes down to drawing his energy into something else...it sounds complicated and dangerous, but I am willing to try anything at this point. I am desperate to have my friend back. If I knew murdering Shane would bring us to this point, then I wouldn't have done it. It wasn't worth it. Not only because of what it has done to Liv, but Tasha is traumatized and hasn't been the same since that night, either. I feel my insides clench whenever someone mentions Shane's name now.

I have nightmares almost every night. Sometimes, when I close my eyes and am on the brink of sleep, I can hear the shredding sound the piano wire made when it sliced into his neck. It is loud and wet in the silence of my room. I can smell the blood.

When we killed him, it felt like a vital release. Anger flew from my body like a caged bird glimpsing freedom for the first time. It was revenge, pure and simple. Now, I feel like my soul is damned and I have ruined everything in my life that has value.

My sanity is slipping, my best friend is dying, and nothing will ever be the same.

* * *

I am about to start the next entry, but when I glance at the time I realize I only have a few minutes until my phone alarm will sound. I turn the engine off and hastily shove the journal under the driver's seat. I don't want any evidence of my theft with me when I return to work. Once again, the corrosive feeling of guilt settles into my stomach.

I exit the car and hit the button to lock the doors just as my phone goes off. Perfect timing. I turn and face the cold as I jog toward the hospital entrance. As soon as I am inside, I rub my hands together trying to get some warmth into my fingers. It is freezing outside tonight. Halloween is going to be a cold one tomorrow. The girls in their skimpy costumes are going to probably regret it, I think as I stroll back toward the fishbowl. I only have a few hours left of the night, and I hope it goes by fast.

* * *

As the shift progresses, more people wearing costumes start to filter in as injuries at bars and the night-before-Halloween parties happen. There is an Egyptian Pharaoh sitting in the waiting room holding his shoulder in apparent pain, a college aged girl wearing lingerie and angel wings who is holding a tattered bloody towel against her forehead. Blood is splattered on the girl's white feathers. She is surrounded by three of her friends, who are also all wearing lingerie and an assortment of animal ear headbands. Her group consists of a sexy cat, a sexy mouse, and a sexy bunny. There is also a Darth Vader doubled over in a chair holding his stomach, his lightsaber tucked under the waiting room chair. All these patients need to wait while truly emergent patients coming in with stroke symptoms or chest discomfort have been seen first, and the time could range from minutes to hours.

Dr. Brandt and I jump right back into the swing of things. We visit a patient with a broken arm, followed by a little girl with an upper respiratory infection. Next on the list for us to examine is the Egyptian Pharaoh, who has been to get X-Rays, received some pain medication from a nurse, and has now been moved into a room to be evaluated.

It is a strange dynamic when we enter. The man's costume and makeup is a high quality, and he looks regal and historic. It's surreal to see someone dressed this way surrounded by modern medical equipment. The gold on his headpiece shines under the bright hospital lights, and he is wearing gold wrist and arm cuffs that glint as he shifts in the bed. It makes me want to laugh and I fight back a smile as Dr. Brandt greets him. She looks a little flustered by his appearance, and I can tell she is distracted by his bare legs under his tunic, which is short and reveals his large muscular thighs. It looks like he must wax, too.

The patient greets us and then tells us about participating in an Ancient Egyptian vs. Ancient Greek Halloween tennis match at a party he was at tonight. He describes how when he went to serve the ball, he dislocated his shoulder, which is something that happens often to him. Dr. Brandt nods along, and lets him brag about his past tennis career for a few minutes. Apparently, he was a professional player for a while, and loves to relive his glory days.

It doesn't take long for Dr. Brandt to review the X-Ray findings with the patient and conduct an assessment of his shoulder, which needs to be manually manipulated to get it back in place. She has the patient lie flat on his back on the hospital bed, and then she positions her body next to him on the side of his injury. She places both of her hands on his wrist, and keeps his arm straight and level with his body, his hand and forearm facing down. Then, she slowly raises the man's arm toward his head. While she does this, she makes a small circular up-and -down movement, which she continues to do as she raises the arm, working the joint back into the proper place. Once the ball is back in the socket, Dr. Brandt bends his arm at the elbow and helps the patient sit up.

"Feels better already," he mumbles, holding his arm secure to his chest.

I notice the skirt of his costume has risen up, and quickly glance away. This man was playing tennis *commando* in a short Egyptian tunic…never a dull moment here in the E.R.

"Yes, it should feel better now that it's back in the proper place but you will still need to care for it and allow it to heal. You may eventually consider surgery since this sounds like a frequent occurrence for you."

The patient grunts in response as Dr. Brandt places a sling on him to support the arm.

“A nurse will be in soon to go over your discharge instructions, any questions?”

“No, thank you,” the patient says, fiddling with the sling.

Dr. Brandt gives me a pointed look and we exit the room. We get back to the fishbowl and I wrap up the Pharaoh's chart, and then we go to see the lingerie angel with the bleeding face. She has been moved from the waiting area into room 8.

When we enter, the angel and her friend are in a heated argument. We can hear their raised voices through the door as we approach. The bickering stops abruptly as Dr. Brandt knocks on the door signaling our presence.

“Come in,” the patient calls out. She is still holding the bloody rag to her head, and mascara is running down her face like spilled ink. There is not only blood on her costume wings, but also matted in her platinum blonde hair and dried on her ample cleavage, mixing in with the body glitter she has applied to her exposed skin.

Her friend is standing next to her in black lingerie with animal ears sitting like a crown on her long brown hair. Her arms are crossed as we approach.

Dr. Brandt goes through the usual motions of introducing herself and asks the patient to describe what brought her to the Emergency Room.

“Well,” the patient begins, and then takes a shuddery breath. “Basically, I was at a house party and, like, my friend got in an argument with a girl there and I was just standing in the kitchen minding my own business and a friend of the girl my friend was fighting with came up and hit me in the face with a bottle. Like, she just swung it right at me. I wasn’t even in the fight or anything. It broke on my forehead and now, here we are.” She pulls the rag from her head and winces. The gash is deep, and most likely will need butterfly strips or maybe even stitches. “It’s not going to scar though, right?” The patient’s pleading eyes begin to well with tears.

Dr. Brandt applies gloves, and takes a step forward to examine the wound. “It’s hard to tell. It will need sutures because it is deep, but it looks like a clean line, so with the proper followup care there is a chance you will have minimal scarring.”

Her friend shuffles forward, her heels clicking on the linoleum and the smell of vodka wafting off her like perfume. “I take the blame. I’m the one who started making out with that one girl’s boyfriend. I didn’t know he had a girlfriend, but he was dressed like a cat, and…I’m a mouse, duh,” she says gesturing toward the big round ears on her head with her pointer finger and cocking out her hip. She finds this funny and lets out a little giggle. Dr. Brandt’s expression is flat and I think the *Mean Girls* reference was completely lost on her.

“Anyway, I just thought it would be cute, you know? To get some pictures kissing a cat, dressed like a mouse? So, I did. Obvi it was a bad idea…”

“Right…” Dr Brandt says under her breath, as she continues to examine the laceration on the patient’s forehead. She moves over to some nearby drawers and gathers the necessary tools to close the injury, and pulls over a metal tray to set everything on. The patient’s friend hovers over Dr. Brandt’s shoulder, breathing heavily and she teeters precariously in her stilettos.

“Can you please step away? I am going to use sterile instruments and do not want you near this area while I work.” The expression on Dr. Brandt’s face is grim, and I can tell she is trying hard not to have one of her famous temper outbursts.

The friend stumbles over to where I am standing, and leans in to whisper, “she's a cranky one.” She sways forward and back, and her breath reeks of alcohol. I wonder if I should offer her water. I shift away and pretend to not have heard her.

With the mouse away, Dr. Brandt begins the process of numbing the area and closing the wound. She makes quick work of the process and we are out of there faster than I expected.

"I was just seconds away from telling that friend of hers off. How obnoxious," Dr. Brandt mutters as we walk back to our computer spaces.

"I could tell, and I don't blame you."

"I feel like this has been one of the longest nights…I am ready for it to be done."

"Yeah, it has dragged on a bit," I agree, as my eyes dart to the clock on the wall. Only an hour left.

"Let's get this chart done, and then check the board. If it doesn't look too busy, I would be fine with you taking off early if you want. I can handle the last bit of the shift on my own."

"Are you sure?"

"Yeah," she responds with a stiff shrug. "It tends to quiet down after two in the morning, usually. I can handle it."

"Thank you. Not just for that, but for the whole night. I had a good time working with you…"

She smiles at me, it doesn't fully reach her eyes, but I still feel happy that I am getting this expression from her rather than her usual stare. "I had a nice time working with you, as well," she says softly.

After I wrap up the chart for the bleeding angel, we look over who is waiting to be seen. Dr. Brandt was right, and the ER has cleared out a bit since a couple hours ago. Most of the patients on the board are already being seen by other docs, and there is only one waiting. It is a pregnant woman who has come in because she no longer feels her baby moving.

"This is a sign that you should go," Dr. Brandt says, tapping the woman's name on the screen. I frown.

She sees my expression, and elaborates, "I usually don't take scribes in for patients with possible fetal demise. It is very emotionally charged and personal for the patients. I like to do my own charting for cases like these, and the less people in the room for exams, the better."

I nod, understanding. "That makes sense. Okay, I will head out then."

"Drive home safe," she says, as she opens the patient's

chart and begins to read through her medical history, her eyes never leaving the computer screen.

"Thanks," I reply before turning toward my computer to log out and grab my things. I brace myself for the frigid air as I leave the hospital and walk to my car. My pulse picks up when I think about what I have stashed beneath my seat. I was feeling exhausted moments ago, but the thought of reading the journal has created an adrenaline surge and brought forth new energy.

CHAPTER 33:

I play my music loud like I always do as I drive home at this hour. Old Town Road by Lil Nas X blasts through my speakers as I mumble along. A fog has settled over the streets and the moon above is nearly full. My mind whirs as I think about all that has transpired today. I never would have imagined I would end up with this journal again. I was convinced that I didn't even want it, but my actions prove otherwise.

I am not someone who believes in fate. I think life is chaos and everything is random, nothing is destined or meant to be. But at this moment, I am questioning that reasoning. It almost seems like I was meant to have Heather's diary again. Everything fell into place too perfectly. The chances of the paramedic handing *me* Jessica's bag and not someone else seems too slim to ignore. The fact that she was brought to the hospital I work at while I was working...*Fate.* What a strange concept.

I pull up to my apartment feeling wide awake, despite it being 2:30 AM. I reach under the seat and grab the journal. I stuff it into my work bag, and exit the car. As I approach my doorstep, a figure sitting on my porch rises to a standing position. It's Nikki. She is bundled in a black puffy jacket, with a bright red beanie on her head. Her breath billows in front of her face with each exhalation, and despite her warm clothing, she is shivering.

"What are you doing here?" I ask, puzzled. I slow my pace, not really wanting to be close to her.

"Obviously, I'm waiting for you."

"Well, yeah. But you're aware of what time it is, right?"

"Yup. And you're aware of how a phone works, right? I texted you a bunch and called a few times, too," she replies.

I reach into my bag and withdraw my phone. Sure enough, there are five texts and two missed calls from Nikki. I hadn't even checked my phone since I used it earlier to read Heather's diary in my car.

"See? At least I know now you weren't actually ignoring me on purpose," she observes.

"I was at work. What do you want, Nikki? It's late." I cross my arms, trying to ward off the cold that is permeating through my jacket and thin scrub bottoms.

"Can we go inside? It's freezing."

"The last time you were in my house, you stole from me."

"I had a good reason, I swear. It will all make sense, I promise."

I stare back at her. My jaw clenched.

"It's important...please?" she implores.

"Fine," I sigh, and push past her to unlock my front door. "I'm surprised you didn't pick my lock and let yourself in," I add, sarcastically.

"Thought about it," she replies in a flat tone as she follows me inside.

I lock the door behind us, then wheel around to face her. "So, what's so important that you stole from me and then decided to show up at my house at this hour? Doing what you did with those photoshopped pictures and the lying was really fucked up, by the way. And then you acted like it never happened. That's a weird flex, Nikki" I say, feeling myself becoming increasingly annoyed at the entire situation.

"I know. I can explain," she utters, holding up a hand in an attempt at calming my increasing emotional state. "Those photos I showed you were not photoshopped. They are real. I swear. I brought them to you because I knew I could trust you, and you have always had an open mind about things...and you had that occult book from the shed."

"Which you wanted to steal," I add, staring at her with narrowed eyes.

"I didn't plan to take it. You seemed overwhelmed by the photos, which was understandable. So, I thought maybe it would be better for me to do the rest of my investigation by myself. I *borrowed* the book. Here, I brought it back." Nikki swings her backpack off one shoulder and around to the front so she can access the top zipper. She opens it and takes out the book. The thick cracked spine drops flakes of binding down to the wood floor below. She holds it out to me, but I find that I don't want to touch it. Instead, I gesture to the coffee table, "just set it over there."

Nikki takes a step and deposits it down next to the Dyer Lane photos she brought last time. I stare at it, wishing that it would just dissipate and vanish. It feels like a heavy ominous presence in the room.

Nikki sighs. "You can't tell me you haven't noticed that something is wrong with Mandy."

My head snaps up at her. "What did you say?"

"Mandy. Something is fucking wrong with her."

I don't reply right away. I frown at Nikki, trying to puzzle out what she is getting at. Finally, I respond, "yeah, she seems like she hasn't been feeling well. She wasn't at clinicals today, either. I texted her, but she didn't respond..."

"Yeah, because she's fucking possessed."

At Nikki's words, I feel like the walls shrink in around me. "Huh?"

"I mean it. There is something wrong with her and I think it is possession. No joke. I didn't alter those photos, and I didn't alter these either," Nikki declares, as she again reaches into her backpack, this time withdrawing another stack of pictures. She holds them out to me, a dare in her eyes. I take them from her. They are the pictures that she took from the other night when we were carving pumpkins. The photos look normal, just us hanging out in the kitchen. Most of the shots are candid. I shuffle through them all, examining the images.

"And what am I supposed to be looking for?"

"You'll know when you see it."

That's when I do. It's a candid up close photo of Mandy. Her face is turned to the camera and at first glance she looks perfectly normal, but then I realize that her eyes are completely white.

"If you are messing with me, Nikki, I swear," I threaten as my hand begins to slightly tremble. I set the photo down and flip to the next. It's Kate and I smiling at each other with pies in front of us. The next is of Avery scooping some ice cream, the muscles in his arms flexed as he digs into the carton. We all look normal. The next is a photo of Mandy again, she is glaring at the camera, and her eyes appear as if they are rolled back in her head. There are no pupils or irises, just a milky opaque shield as if she has thick cataracts. Just like how Heather described Liv's eyes, and how the eyes of the dead deer looked.

"This is so fucked up," I whisper between lips that have gone cold and numb.

"I know," Nikki answers. "Do you believe me?"

I nod and grab the journal from my bag and hand it over to Nikki. "If it wasn't for this, I probably wouldn't."

She looks at me with a confused look on her face. "Is this that journal Leo found the first night we went out there?"

"The very one."

She shakes her head slightly, "but...I thought you and Kate gave it to that journalist?"

"Wait, how do you know that?"

She lets out a sharp laugh and shrugs. "Kate tells Leo everything, and he tells me. We are best friends."

I feel anger swell inside me. *So much for keeping secrets.* I push down those emotions and press forward. "Well, yeah, we gave it to her but I got it back."

Nikki's gaze is questioning, but she doesn't ask me how, which I am thankful for. *Small mercies.* The adrenaline that I was feeling on my drive home has been replaced with fatigue and I feel a headache setting in.

"You need to read this up to the entry written on October 13th. That's where I left off. I think you'll understand why I believe this crazy bullshit you've brought to me once you see what is written in there. While you do that, I'll get us drinks. I think we need one...or two," I say as I cross the room and go to the cabinet in my small kitchen where I keep the alcohol. I grab a bottle of vodka and pour us both shots. I carry the glasses back over to the couch where Nikki is sitting.

We tap our shot glasses together and then take them, no chase. Both of us grimace from the burn. Then, Nikki slides me the occult book across the table. "Browse that while I read. I found some useful info about possession in there. That's how I knew to take photos of her to expose the entity within. It describes it all in there. Something about the true self being revealed through film. I knew I loved photography for a reason. Also, I cut myself on purpose that day when we carved pumpkins. I wanted to see how she reacted to blood. I was expecting more, but she didn't really give any obvious signs."

I think back to that moment when I heard Mandy sniffing, like she was savoring the scent of the blood, and the hungry look in her eyes that she tried to conceal.

As Nikki begins reading, I flip open the book. I realize that this is probably the text that Heather looked for answers on how to help Liv. It's like history is repeating itself. I shudder a little remembering how creepy this manual was the last time I looked through it, but I make myself continue anyway.

There are pages upon pages about various demons, discussions of blood sorcery, and detailed instructions on how to seek deities. Some chapters include spells and the accompanying rituals. Others inform practicing witches how to use magic to conceal secrets, control others, and even impact the weather. It's all so unbelievable.

I hear Nikki gasp next to me as she turns a page in the diary and continues to read. She is chewing on her nail and staring intently at what she is reading. I think I know what part she is at, so I grab the shot glasses and get up to pour us another.

I set the filled shot down in front of her, and she lifts it to her mouth and downs it without taking her eyes from the journal. "Thanks," she mutters.

I sit back down, and resume scanning through The Book of Darkness, as I've come to call it in my mind. The drawings in the text are incredibly disturbing. Eventually, I can't take anymore and I snap the book shut. I stare at the wall as I wait for Nikki to finish reading. I sit there like that for what feels like an eternity. Finally, I murmur "hurry up," under my breath.

"I'm going as fast as I can," Nikki snaps. "This shit is so messed up, so forgive me if I have to take little breathers, alright? I haven't gotten to the stopping point you wanted me to, but I did get to the white eyes comment and the fact that her friend is possessed. I think I get the gist of it. She just fed that guy's body to pigs," she says, sliding the journal away from her. "I don't think I can handle reading any more, especially with you breathing down my neck telling me to dive into this abyss faster. Like, what the fuck did I just read?" She puts a hand to her forehead and stares back at me with wide eyes.

I chew on the inside of my lip. "I still haven't finished all of it, but only have a couple entries left." My eyes flick to the spot on the table where the journal rests. "Assuming Mandy really is possessed by something…"

"She is," Nikki interrupts.

"Okay, well then we need to know what to do to help her. Since Heather was going through the same type of thing with Liv, maybe the answer is at the end of her diary. We need to read it to find out. There's not that much left, only a few pages."

"Ugh. Then let's do the damn thing," Nikki says, as she pours us both another shot.

* * *

October 28, 1997

I had to stash this at the cabin on Dyer Lane, so I haven't been able to write like normal. I couldn't go there to get it until today. It feels good to record my thoughts again. I am relieved to report that I have a plan now. It took me a few days to work it out, but I think it's solid.

My book described a ritual that can be performed to bind the entity to another energy source and contain it there for some time. It involves the letting of my own blood over the energy source that I want to be the new vessel, and repeating a specific chant. Since I don't want to sacrifice another person to Father and have it inhabit someone else, I want to use a crystal. The book described the various energy properties of crystals, and I think this plan will work. I just need to figure out what the best stone is for trapping powerful dark energy.

A few days ago, I went to a small shop that sells items that deal with spirituality and the metaphysical. This is the same place I had purchased my new Dark Occult book. It's called The Stones. Lame name, but good store. Anyway, the shop owner, Maggie, is always helpful when I visit. I asked her for a crystal that could help absorb bad energies and remove the darkness from inside someone. I didn't know how else to describe what I was looking for without actually going into detail...which for obvious reasons I did not want to do. Maggie told me she had the perfect crystal for cleansing dark energy.

She handed me a medium sized jagged rock, about the same size as my palm. It was cold in my hand and I watched as the light reflected off its smooth glass-like edges. There were dark swirls of gray and black obscuring its otherwise translucent quality. It was beautiful.

The shop owner told me it was called Smokey Quartz, and that it has the ability to help one move on from a painful past. The stone can absorb and remove unwanted negative energy from someone, and cleanse the spirit. I thought it sounded promising and could work, so I purchased it.

This all feels so hopeless. I have been trying to act normal around Liv and Tasha. I need them to trust me so I can put my plan into action, but I am not sure if it will work. I asked them if they wanted to spend the night on Dyer Lane at the cabin on Halloween. I played it up like it would be fun, and we could practice our craft. I kept talking about how it is a day when the spirit realm and ours connect and spirits and humans can interact more freely. I am hoping this works to my benefit and Father is more susceptible to what I have planned. Liv went along with it, but I sensed warmth in my necklace again, which I think happens when Father feels an intense emotion...or wants to give a warning.

I've never been more scared in my life.

* * *

October 31, 1997

I have been preparing for tonight for the past few days. I have the ritual chant memorized, and a sharp knife ready for when the time comes and I need to cut my palm and squeeze my blood over the quartz. Tasha and Liv are both going to meet me here at the cabin after sunset.

Yesterday, we sent notes back and forth in class about what we should pack and bring with us. They both seem excited, and I wish I could tell Tasha about what I have planned, and that I could get through to Liv without Father knowing. I can never tell when he will overtake her, so I have to be careful about what I do and say around her at all times. He is always watching and prying in my mind. I try to keep my emotions as calm as I can, so I don't alert him to anything at all.

My stomach has been in knots, and I haven't been able to eat. My mom has noticed, and of course she is worried about me. She keeps bringing my favorite snacks to my room and trying to hang out. I don't mind for once. I think I understand that she just loves me, and I almost appreciate it. I even gave Jessica a hug today, which I never do. She smiled at me and asked if she could sit on my lap at breakfast. I wanted to say no, but instead I let her for once. It was actually kinda nice. I ate a bowl of Lucky Charms and gave her all my rainbow marshmallows because she says those are her favorite.

I noticed at school that people are already moving on from Shane's disappearance. It's sad how fast someone can be forgotten. I looked around campus and watched all the happy faces, oblivious to any of the real dark in the world. They think they have problems in their life, but they don't. Not really.

I know that after tonight, I may never make it back here, and I will be forgotten just as easily as Shane. Just a lost soul, here for a short time and then gone. I don't know what life after death holds for me. I am a sinner and therefore most likely not going anywhere good, but I chose this path, and I accept it. One thing I do know is that I do not want to die on Dyer Lane. The spirits that are taken there cannot leave. They become tethered to the land. Father collects souls like trophies, and he never lets them go.

I am not the praying type, but if I were to pray, it would be that this all goes well and we survive. If it doesn't, I just hope I make it off the lane before I die.

I heard a saying once, it went: "Some women are lost in the fire, some women are built from it." I guess tonight, I will find out which one I am.

* * *

"That's it. That's the end?" Nikki mutters in disgust. "That can't be all she wrote." She grabs the book and shakes it like she thinks some secret pages will fall out.

"Well, we know that her and her friends went missing… so it doesn't seem likely her plan worked."

"The fuck! What do we do then?"

I shake my head. "I have no idea." I really don't even know what to think. It's late and my head hurts. Those shots took the edge off a bit, but now I feel incredibly tired. I rub my eyes, which have started to burn with fatigue. I pick up my phone and stare at the time: 4:25 AM. "I think we should sleep on this and talk about it in the morning after we get some rest and have clear heads," I say with a yawn.

Nikki yawns back. It's so weird how seeing another person yawn often triggers someone to do the same. A strange contagious social behavior.

"Okay," she replies, and gets up to gather her things. She grabs the occult book off the table and stuffs it into her bag. I am actually happy that I don't have to sleep in the same place as that messed up text, so I don't say anything about her taking it back. Nikki repositions her beanie on her head, takes a swig of water from her canteen, and then fixes me with a serious expression. "Text me when you wake up or if you figure anything out. I am going to keep researching. I stole some addys from Kate the other day, so I'll be up a while longer."

"You're a thief," I say, as I walk her to the door. Once she is out, I lock it and run a hand through my hair in dismay. I am confused and my mind feels foggy with alcohol and exhaustion. I still don't know if I can trust Nikki, and I wonder if she could have photoshopped those pictures of Mandy. She clearly isn't the most honest of friends. Also, she seems to know more about things than she should…and then there was that time that Kate caught her snooping around her house and in Mandy's things.

Why did Kate tell Leo about the journal and Jessica? Something isn't adding up for me. Also, there was something in the journal that has been bothering me. It had to do with the crystal. Mandy has always had crystals, but for some reason my mind was latching on the one Heather described but I can't quite figure out why it feels important to Mandy.

I flop onto my bed and close my eyes. Maybe I can get

clarity in the morning.

CHAPTER 34:

The morning does not bring clarity. If anything, I wake up with a hangover, dehydrated, and feel even more confused than I did last night. My mouth is dry and I struggle to swallow as I drag myself from the bed to get ready for the day.

I change out of my scrubs, which I am still wearing from the night before, and shuffle to the kitchen to chug water. Then, I make coffee. I need all the caffeine I can get.

I sit at the table with the steaming mug in front of me. I chose my favorite coffee cup today, a small white one with a hummingbird painted on the front. The bird's sharp beak is tilted up toward the rim, and the jewel green wings are spread in flight. This cup once belonged to my dad and always comforts me.

I take a sip, and try to go over all the important points in my mind so that I can try and process it all. I twirl the cup on the table in small circles, the dark liquid inside ripples from the movement as I go over my thoughts.

Do I believe Nikki? *Nope. Not fully, at least.* But why would she go through such pains for an elaborate prank? *I don't think this is a prank.* What do I do if this shit is real? *We are so fucked.* My mind continues to pingpong around.

It is true that Mandy has been strange lately. I try to pinpoint when I first noticed a change in her. I'm still staring at the coffee in front of me as the heat rises up from the cup in a swirling vapor, when it hits me. I recall sitting with Kate and Mandy at the coffee shop before our first exam a few weeks ago. Mandy gave us some crystals for luck...but there was one that she held and wouldn't let Kate touch. She had pulled it away suddenly when Kate had reached a hand forward for it. She had said that crystal was a Smoky Quartz.

Didn't Mandy say something about finding it? I wrack my memory trying to recall exactly what had happened and been said. At the time, it wasn't significant, but now I think it may be the link to what has happened to Mandy. Theoretically, if that entity had somehow been placed into the crystal, and Mandy had picked it up and taken it home with her...could it have left the stone and entered her? Then I remember the cut on Mandy's palm that appeared about a week after she showed us that new crystal of hers. It all has to be linked somehow.

I put my head down on my arms and slump over the table in defeat. *This entire thing sounds completely crazy.* If someone were telling me this, there is no way I would believe them. *No damn way.* It sounds fabricated. Like a horror story. Just like how I thought of Heather's journal when I first began reading it, until there were too many coincidences to ignore the possibility of it being true. I groan.

My phone rings from the bedroom and I go to retrieve it. It's Kate. I answer, and her upbeat voice greets me and asks if I want to get ready for Noah's Halloween party together tonight. My mind is still whirling from everything that happened last night and I don't even know where to begin explaining it to her. Also, I don't feel like I can trust her. I've always trusted Kate, but knowing that Leo is privy to our secrets makes me feel guarded now. But can I really blame her? I broke our pinky promise oath too and told Avery, so I'm being a hypocrite. I understand how secrets often work in relationships, but still. It bothers me.

I tell Kate I have some last minute costume things to do so I'm just going to get ready at home and will meet her at the party. I need space to think things over right now. I'm about to say my goodbyes and get off the phone when she says, "Have you talked to Mandy lately? I've been worried since she wasn't at clinicals yesterday and I haven't heard from her at all. I've been trying to call her and she won't answer."

"No, I was wondering the same thing..." I trail off.

"Oh, okay. I thought maybe she was mad at me or something. I couldn't think why, but since you haven't talked to her either I guess she just isn't answering calls right now? Or she's mad at us both," Kate laughs at that last part. "Anyway, call me when you head to Noah's later. I think Leo and I are planning to get there around seven. I'll keep trying to contact Mandy. I'm worried."

"Yeah, I am too," I reply, "and that sounds good. I'll let you know if I hear from her, also." We say our goodbyes and disconnect. Then I text Nikki to tell her that no one has heard from Mandy still. She texts me back saying we will talk more about it at the party tonight. That is the exact opposite of what I want to do. I don't want to see Nikki later. I chew on the inside of my lip and then send Avery a text to see if he wants to come over. One person I *know* I can trust is him, and I need someone right now.

Avery shows up about an hour later. The sight of him instantly calms me down. He is carrying a small pink box full of donuts, which is pretty standard. Whenever Avery comes over, he brings food. It's like an unwritten rule of his.

His smile is bright as he sets the box down on the kitchen table and bends over to hug me. I inhale his spicy citrus scent as he wraps me in his arms. Avery takes the chair next to mine and opens the box, "I've been wanting to try this place for so long," he admits. "They inject their donuts with a syringe of filling and you can control how much you want to put in. How smart is that?"

"Brilliant," I say, getting up to make him some coffee.

Avery grabs a round donut covered in powdered sugar and picks up a big syringe filled with a chocolate fudge. He pokes the tip of the syringe into the side of the fluffy pastry and pushes the plunger so that the entire content of the syringe floods the inside of the donut. He lifts it to his mouth and takes a bite that is the size of half the donut. His eyes widen as he chews, "that is good."

I can't help but grin. Avery relishes in the simple things of life and lives in the moment; good food, good weather, good movies…anything that can be taken in and enjoyed by his senses lights him up.

"You need to try one," he says, reaching back into the box and grabbing a rainbow sprinkle donut for me. "What type of frosting do you want inside?" he asks, as he holds up three different syringes. One is brown, one is cream, and one is red.

I slide back into my chair and place his coffee cup in front of him. "Hit me with the cream," I say.

"You got it." He injects the contents of the vanilla syringe into my colorful donut and hands it to me. I take a bite, and my mouth immediately floods with intense sweetness and a dopamine surge hits my brain. "Damn," I mumble as I chew, savoring the sugary flavor. "I needed that."

"Yeah? Rough night?" Avery inquires as his eyes skitter over the counter and takes in the shot glasses next to the sink and the vodka bottle still sitting out from Nikki's visit.

"Ugh, hurricane Nikki came back last night. I got home from work a little before three in the morning and she was sitting outside my door asking to come in and show me more pictures."

Avery pauses mid chew of his second donut. "What?"

"Yeah. I know."

"Why are you just now telling me this?" He swallows the food quickly and continues on, "okay, so what were the pictures of this time? Flying monkeys? Dragons? Oh, let me guess, the Loch Ness monster was found in Lake Tahoe again and she has proof."

I let out a small laugh. "You're not far off."

"I'm surprised you let her in."

"I know, I didn't know what else to do...but I think she may be onto something. I wanted to run it by you actually because it sounds crazy, but it kind of fits, too..." I let those words hang in the air as I gather how to approach the topic before continuing. "So, have you noticed anything off about Mandy lately?" I decide to start with that and work my way forward.

Avery continues to eat his donut. His brow furrows as he thinks. "I mean, I noticed that she has looked a little rough around the edges lately. Usually she is always over at Kate's but she seems to be spending more time at her own place now. That's about it, though. Why? What does that have to do with Nikki?"

"Well, because Nikki thinks that Mandy is possessed like Heather's friend was."

Avery's eyebrows shoot up.

"And I think she might be right."

Avery cracks his knuckles, and nods his head. "Alright. Why? Why do you believe anything Nikki says?"

"Well, because I saw some photos of Mandy and..."

"But she could have altered those images to make them look that way," Avery interrupts.

I shake my head. "I really don't think so, Avery. Also, that's not the only reason I think it's possible. Mandy really has been different lately. Sometimes I catch her with this intense look in her eyes, and it's scary. I noticed this all before Nikki said anything, and I was already worried about her. But these new pictures...look." I lean over and snatch the images of Mandy and place them in front of Avery. He glances down, and his frown deepens at what he sees.

He taps the photo and then slowly looks up to meet my gaze. "The white eyes...like what my evisceration patient described. She couldn't have known about that...Okay. Shit. Okay," Avery puts his hands on either side of his face and slowly shakes his head. "It's just unbelievable. Everything in me says she is making this up, but I also don't know how to explain it."

"I know, and no one has heard from Mandy in the past two days. She's MIA."

"Should we go by her house? Noah's party is tonight but maybe we could head there on our way and see if she is home?"

I shrug, "I mean, we could go check in on her and see what's happening."

Avery sits silently thinking, and rubs his thumb against his bottom lip. He raises his hands in a gesture of surrender. "This is crazy, but I'm in."

I reach across the table and take his hand in mine.

* * *

For the rest of the day, Avery and I lounge around the house and discuss possibilities but nothing seems plausible. I try to go about my day as normal as possible, doing normal household chores and attempting to have a relaxing day. I'm in the kitchen rinsing dishes, when my phone pings with an incoming text. I dry my hands and scroll to my messages. It's from Kate:

I finally heard back from Mandy! She had the stomach flu. Thinks she caught it from clinicals last week. She is coming over to get ready with me for Noah's party later. Wanted to let you know she is okay so you wouldn't keep worrying.

I walk into the living room and show my phone to Avery. He looks as confused as I feel as he shrugs and says, "well, that changes things...sorta."

We decide to drop it and see how Mandy acts tonight. Then, we can figure out if Nikki is messing with me or not. Why she would do that, I do not know, but it sorta seems less strange than our friend being possessed. I'm still holding on to some denial if only for the fact that it's less scary than the other option.

Avery and I make sandwiches for a late lunch and share

a bag of chips while watching Netflix for awhile. We settle into a calmness, and I find myself wishing we could just stay in tonight. Why bother going to a party, when I am so content here, with him? When it's just us, I don't have a care in the world and everything feels right.

As evening approaches, Avery and I shower and start to get ready for Noah's Halloween party. We are dressing up as J.Lo and P. Diddy from the 90s when they were dating and are recreating an iconic fashion moment that the couple had with our costumes. I am wearing a white crop top with white jeans, a sparkly belt, and big diamond hoop earrings. The costume is complete with a white folded bandana secured across my forehead and my hair worn long down by back. Avery puts on a navy blue baseball hat with a white tee, sunglasses, a oversized fake diamond cross, and baggy dark wash jeans.

After we are dressed, we stare at our reflections in the full length mirror that hangs on the back of my closet door. Avery puts his hands on my hips, "Okay, Jenny from the Block, lookin fire tonight."

I wrinkle my nose at him and slap his arm playfully. "Thanks, Puff Daddy."

Avery lets out a full laugh and wraps his arms around me, pulling me in close. I give him a quick kiss on the lips and then turn to fix my lipgloss.

"I'm curious to see how Mandy is tonight. You've hyped her up to be so creepy."

I turn to face Avery, "because she has been lately. You didn't see what I saw. She has this hungry feral look in her eyes."

Avery lets out a short laugh, "I believe you, alright. I am just interested to see for myself, I guess." He grabs the big costume jewelry cross he has hanging on a long chain around his neck. "Are we going to need an exorcism or what? Because if so, I got the crucifix right here." He raises the cross up "I will 'the power of Christ compels' her ass until she is normal again."

"If we are dealing with what Heather described in her journal, and if those images from Dyer Lane that Nikki showed me are real, then I don't think it will be that simple," I say, feeling like we are joking about something too serious to play around with. "Heather tried to save her friend and then the journal doesn't really give an answer if she did or not but those girls vanished and were never seen again."

Avery steps toward me and places his hands on my upper arms. "We are in this together, though. Whether it's Nikki latching on to this urban legend shit and trying to make some sick joke, or something really is wrong with Mandy, you're not going to face this alone."

I lean into his shoulder and let him hold me. "I know."

"I love you," he says in my ear and then kisses my cheek. "Now let's go try to have a good night. We don't have to stay out late. We will just scope out what's going on. I bet Mandy is normal and just getting over the flu like she said, and Nikki is pulling another photoshop prank for whatever twisted reason she has, and all this worrying is for nothing. Then, we can come back here and have our own after party, just you and I."

I smile up at him with my arms draped around his neck and in that moment, as I look in his eyes, I know I will never love anyone the way that I love Avery.

"Why do we have to wait for after?"

My words bring a smile to his face, and we fall back in bed together.

CHAPTER 35:

We arrive at Noah's house a little after eight and are about an hour later than we expected. The street is already packed with cars, so we have to park down the block. I can hear bass thumping from Noah's house as we walk toward it. There are still a few children running around in costumes trick or treating up and down the street. Some of the kids are carrying plastic baskets shaped like characters or pumpkins to collect candy. They screech and giggle as they run past, hurrying from door to door. One kid dressed as Ghostface from Scream pops out of the bushes to scare a friend, who is startled and then immediately starts to hit the little Ghostface with his pillowcase full of candy.

Seeing the kids infuses the night with nostalgia, and I remember when Kate and I were young, running around trick or treating together. Now, we are dressing up and partying as adults on Halloween. Times have changed so much, but are still the same in many ways.

When we walk into Noah's, we enter a scene from a frat party. There is a girl doing a keg stand in a school girl costume in the middle of the living room, her plaid skirt is hiked up revealing her purple lace underwear beneath. A group of guys dressed like ninjas are taking shots from shot glasses attached to a ski, so that they all have to take it at the same time. I see a girl dressed as a cowgirl grinding on a guy dressed as a chef, and there are some girls in full lingerie snorting lines in the corner. Basically, it's complete chaos.

"It's too early for it to be so wild, this is going to get broken up soon, I'm calling it now," Avery yells into my ear, struggling to be heard over the bumping of the bass and the loud talking of the party.

"You're probably right," I shout back to him. "Someone will call the cops."

He takes me by the hand and pulls me through the crowded living room toward the rear of the house. The music is just as loud back here, and there are more people in costumes doing questionable things. A shirtless man wearing a deer head, complete with a large rack of antlers is cooking up stir fry. I am struck with a feeling of unreality. Halloween is a strange time.

Avery grabs us each a beer from the fridge, then we head straight for the door that leads to outside. We step into the backyard and the cold air is a relief after the stuffiness from inside the house. The night is crisp, and the full moon above is surrounded by a rippled halo of clouds. Steam rises from the heated pool in the middle of the yard and market lights zig zag above a deck setup with chairs and tables.

"There you are!" A familiar voice shouts from the other side of the yard. I hear the clacking of heels across the pavement, and then Kate is standing in front of me. She is dressed as a 70s disco girl, in a shimmery gold bodysuit with a deep V, flared bell bottoms, and white platform boots. She's holding a light pink drink in her hand and thrusts it toward me. "You have to try this."

"What is it?"

She raises a perfectly arched eyebrow, "does it matter?"

I shrug and take the cup from her, drinking a small sip. It has a sweet, tangy flavor, and is refreshing. So, I go in for another drink and take a gulp this time.

"I knew you would like it," she says with a smug smile. "It's called a 'pink panty dropper,' I know, don't come at me about the name, I didn't give it that title. It has a shit ton of alcohol in it, but you can't taste it."

"It's good." I hand the drink to Avery and he tries it.

"It's just beer, vodka, and pink lemonade, right?" he asks as he passes it back to Kate.

"Basically. I put a couple CBD drops in there too, because I have been anxious as fuck today. So, you're welcome. It won't get you high or anything, there isn't any THC, but you'll feel a little extra relaxed. Just don't eat the brownies in there, THOSE will get you high. Leo made them earlier, and he is heavy handed with the ingredients."

"Noted," Avery says, smiling.

"So, where's Mandy?"

Kate sighs, "she bailed on me after I sent you that text. She said she was coming, and then didn't show up. I haven't even heard from her." A frown forms on her glittery face as she thinks over the fact that Mandy ditched her.

Avery and I exchange subtle glances.

"She's just been so off lately, you know? I guess friendships do this as we get older...people grow apart. I just never thought Mandy would be one of those people for me," she says, crossing her arms. "I'm worried about her, but everytime I try to talk with her, she puts up a wall. Do you think she's on drugs? Like the hardcore stuff her roommates do?"

I shake my head and shrug as Leo comes up behind Kate and puts an arm around her shoulder. He's dressed like a male disco dancer, with a polyester collared shirt, unbuttoned in the front to show off his mural of chest tattoos. Kate reaches up to lace her fingers through his hand that is dangling over her upper arm.

"Hey guys, I was wondering when you two would get here," Leo says. His gaze shifts to me, "who are you supposed to be?"

Kate shoots him a disgusted look, "they are Jennifer Lopez and Puff Daddy. Obviously!"

"Oh, shit, yeah. I see it now," Leo says breaking out in a grin.

Avery reaches out to pat Leo on the arm, "You been tapping those brownies of yours tonight, man?"

Leo starts to giggle, "you know it. You want some?" He gestures toward the house, his eyebrows raised in anticipation.

"Naw, I think I am gonna stick with beer tonight. We are going to find Noah to say hi and hang for a bit then probably head out earlier than later."

I reach over and take Avery's hand in mine and give it a squeeze, signaling that I agree. I've been scanning the party for Nikki but haven't spotted her, thankfully. I'm not ready to address this thing with her until I've seen Mandy and have made up my mind on what I believe.

"Oh, okay, that's cool. Kate and I are gonna be up all night raging. Right babe?" Leo gives her a twirl.

"We'll see about that," Kate says with a laugh. "I think you're gonna get so stoned that you pass out before midnight, just like you do most nights." She gives him a wink.

"Have a little faith in me! It's Halloween. Anything is possible, and Noah has shrooms."

"I'm not doing those," Kate replies, bluntly.

"Babe, you're dressed for a disco, let's get a little psychedelic tonight."

"I'll think about it," she concedes with an eye roll, and then smiles back at him. "You make for a cute disco guy, you might convince me with the right hip moves."

"Tell me more," Leo says, pulling Kate toward him by her waist.

"Alright you two, we are going to go see if we can track down Noah," I say, as I start to pull Avery away with me.

"I don't think they heard you," Avery says in my ear. I look back and see Kate and Leo making out in the middle of the backyard like they are the only ones around.

"She's already drunk. Remind me to bring her some water before we leave. She hates being hungover."

"I think that's Leo's job now," Avery states. "He's going to have to watch out for her because we are not staying much longer. I can't stand all the craziness, it's too much stimulation for me."

Just as he finishes his sentence, a girl dressed in a long black dress runs past barefoot, holding pink heels in her hand. She is laughing and screaming in mock terror as a guy in a werewolf costume chases after her howling.

"My point exactly," Avery adds as he gestures to the couple who have now cannon balled into the swimming pool and are starting to remove their clothes. In a matter of seconds the girl's dress is billowing in the water next to her like a inky jellyfish.

Avery and I cross the lawn toward the side of the house where we hear people shouting and cheering. There is a long fold up table set up with red solo cups half filled with cheap beer and placed triangle formations at either end. A team of two players stand at opposite sides of the table and are trying to throw a ping pong ball into one of the cups as a group of people watch.

"Good ol' Beer Pong," Avery says under his breath.

"And of course Noah is playing."

Noah stands with his broad back to us and is getting ready to launch the ping pong ball across the table. He throws it in a perfect arc. The ball sails through the air like a comet through the sky, and lands in one of the cups on the opposite side of the table with a small *thwack.*

He raises his arms in victory, "ohhhhh! Drink up!"

The guy at the other end grabs the cup that the ball landed in, and chugs the beer.

Avery walks up behind Noah and wraps his arms around him from behind in a bear hug. Noah turns and his handsome face lights up. "Hey! When did you get here?"

"A bit ago," I say, moving in to hug him, smelling the strong yeasty tang of spilled beer. "It's kinda crazy inside..."

Noah has a dopey smile plastered on his face as he nods

at me, "yeah, yeah it is. Just the way it should be. It's a party."

He's dressed in a nice dark blue suit with a tie, and had a little American Flag pin attached to the collar.

"Who are you supposed to be?" I say gesturing to his outfit.

"JFK," he replies, smoothing his gelled hair. "It's more obvious when Nikki is next to me. She's dressed as Marilyn Monroe. She's got her hair curled, the white dress, the mole, and everything." He wiggles his eyebrows at us suggestively and cups his hands in front of his chest like breasts.

"Are you two a couple again?" I ask.

"Nah. We just bang sometimes. So, you know, the costume seemed to fit."

Thwack.

Noah spins around at the sound of the ping pong ball sinking into one of his red cups. "What? It was time out, I was clearly talking!"

"It wouldn't have mattered if you were looking or not, the ball went in. So, it's your turn to drink up," the player on the other end says with a self-satisfied expression on his shiny red face. Noah grabs the cup, and the ping pong ball bobs in the beer as he lifts it off the table. He takes the ball out and flicks his wrist to get the foam clinging to it off. Then, he drinks the beer in three big gulps. He wipes his lips with the back of his hand, "I'm coming for you now, Jack," he says, pointing across the table.

Avery claps him on the back, "alright, we will let you get back to it."

"Have fun, go drink whatever you want, I'll find you when I'm done here," Noah responds, as he eyeballs his next shot, not taking his gaze off the cup he is aiming for.

Avery leans in to me and whispers in my ear, "let's get out of here."

"Already? It's been less than an hour."

"Do you want to see what's going on with Mandy, or not?"

I nod my head once, and we sneak out the side gate, hand in hand.

CHAPTER 36:

It doesn't take long to get to the apartment complex that Mandy lives in with her two roommates. She found the girls in a Facebook group, and always complains about living with them. There was a time when she was rarely at her own place, but since she hasn't been staying at Kate's lately, I assume that she has been staying here more often.

We have to circle the complex to find a parking spot. Finally, we get lucky when a car pulls out and we can swoop the one that they vacate. Once parked, we get out of Avery's car and walk toward Mandy's apartment. My breath unfurls in front of my face in the icy air and the sky above is an angry bruise.

Mandy's building looks rundown and seedy. The complex is poorly lit, and my arms prickle with goosebumps. A fluttering sensation builds in my stomach as we walk. Mandy lives in an upstairs unit, and our steps reverberate on the metal stairs as we climb up to her doorstep.

"Is this the one?" Avery gestures toward an unlit doorway at the top of the steps. I nod. I've only been here a couple times, but I remember where to go. There is a dried up plant withering in a pot next to a doormat, which says "I hope you brought wine." The leaves of the plant are mottled brown and curled in upon itself. I think at one point it may have been some sort of palm.

Avery knocks on the door, and we stand in silence waiting. No one answers. “It’s kind of late, maybe they are asleep,” I comment, as I run my hands up and down my arms for warmth. I put a gray zip up hoodie over my crop top when we left the party, but the cold is still seeping through and making me want to shiver.

“It’s Halloween, and a Saturday,” Avery says. “I doubt they are sleeping.” He raises a fist and knocks again, louder this time. The tapping of his knuckles echoes in the small space.

“Yeah, I don't know then,” I say through my clenched teeth, trying to keep them from chattering, "maybe they went out for the night?”

“That is more believable, but then where is Mandy? Flying around on a broomstick somewhere?”

I tilt my chin and look up at him with an unamused expression, “that’s not funny.”

Avery sighs. “Well…we tried.”

We turn toward the stairs, and I am eager to get far away from this apartment complex, when Avery stops midstep. He turns around, and walks back to Mandy’s door. He grabs the handle of her front door and twists. The door creaks open. Avery turns to me, an apologetic expression on his face, “I had to check and see if it was locked…”

“I think you’ve answered that now,” I gesture toward the partially opened front door in exasperation.

“Let's do a welfare check, shall we?”

My mind screams *NO* and my stomach flutters intensify, but instead of listening to my gut, I reply, “What the hell, let's do it," and follow Avery into the darkness.

* * *

Immediately, we are hit with a rancid odor. My nose burns and I pull off the white bandana that I am still wearing around my forehead from my costume, and put it over my nose and mouth like a mask as I begin to gag. I can hear Avery fumbling along the wall to try and find a light switch. He knocks into a side table, and some junk that sounds like books or magazines topples to the floor. The interior of the apartment is pitch black and I can't see anything. I reach into my sweater and pull my phone from my pocket. I try not to drop it as I use one hand to search for the flashlight icon, while my other hand continues to press the bandana over my nose and mouth. Avery beats me to it, and before I can engage the flashlight, he has the overhead living room light on. I blink as my eyes adjust to the sudden brightness, and try to take in my surroundings.

The place is a dump. There are old fast food cartons littering the table tops, and half filled cups scattered about. Despite the clutter, it looks like a normal, poorly cared for living space. "This rotten egg mixed with shit smell can't just be from this stuff," Avery says pointing to the trash. His expression has quickly changed from one of curiosity to one of concern. I nod my head, not wanting to open my mouth to speak. I already need fresh air. I look longingly back at the doorway leading to outside.

Avery notices my discomfort and says, "do you want to go out there? I can look around on my own real quick."

I shake my head. We are doing this together.

"Okay then," he replies and moves deeper into the apartment. I follow him down a narrow hallway that leads to the bedrooms and a small bathroom. There are three bedroom doors, the first two are closed and the last one is slightly ajar. Avery opens the first door, and it's easy to see that it's empty.

The room is so tiny, all that it can fit is a double bed and a narrow dresser. The walls are bare other than a photo collage depicting a girl and who I assume is her boyfriend in various tropical places. The girl in the photos is thin and pale with shoulder length black hair and a sharp beaky nose. I recognize her from one of the times I stopped by here to see Mandy in the past. I think her name is Melissa.

Avery spins in a small circle, taking in the perfectly

ordinary room. The dresser by the bed is dusty and has a small bible resting on it, which is dusty too. I guess Melissa doesn't read it much.

We back out of that room, and Avery opens the next door to the room closest to the one we left. It is also small, but unlike Melissa's room, this one has more personality. The walls have boho looking woven decorations hanging, and there are tons of house plants, some of which are wilting or dead. The succulents are still going strong, and so is the snake plant in the corner. When all the plants were alive, I bet this room looked like the cute little spaces photographed all over Instagram.

The room is tidy and organized in a way that optimizes the small area. A row of well loved Book of the Month book club novels are colorfully arranged on a shelf hanging over a tiny desk in one corner. A light pink bong rests on top of the desk next to a stack of school books. There is a photo of a blonde girl with long hair wearing a Stone Bay Highschool graduation cap and gown. A man and woman stand on either side of her, beaming proud smiles. I assume these must be her parents. I turn from the photo and scan the room, but see nothing out of the ordinary.

That rancid smell permeates this room, but it's clear this isn't where it originates from. Avery and I back out of the room and turn to the final door, the one that is slightly cracked, the one that must belong to Mandy. I can sense the intense tang of decay stronger now, and know it has to be coming from the other side of this doorway. My hands begin to sweat. My knees feel weak and I struggle to keep myself from locking them. The last thing I need is to faint right now.

Avery and I quietly stand there for a moment, our eyes meet and hold one another's gaze. A silent communication saying *there is something bad behind this door.* My glance shifts back to the small black sliver of space between the door and the frame. For a moment, I imagine a figure with white eyes ripping the door open and rushing toward us from the dark, its rotten flesh glistening and dripping, its putrid breath hitting me as it envelopes me in its arms and sinks its jagged teeth into my throat.

I shake my head to clear my thoughts, and before I can change my mind, I reach out a trembling hand and gently push the door open with my fingertips.

Creeaak.

The light from the hall filters into the darkness before us, illuminating two silhouettes on the floor. Immediately, I am slammed with the smell of rot. This room is just as small and plain as the first, but it is clearly not empty. Avery and I rush forward toward the bodies sprawled on their backs across the floor. Both girls are going through the decomposition process. Their skin is bone pale, other than the flaking crusts of dark red blood that has dried from multiple lacerations, which crisscross over their bodies like a sick game of tick-tac-toe. Small white maggots squirm inside the deep incisions that mar the skin of the corpses. The girls' lifeless eyes are both open in wide death stares at the ceiling.

I spin from the room and vomit on the hallway wall. I am on my hands and knees heaving as the smell of death burns my eyes and the image of the bodies sears my brain. Avery backs away and puts an arm around me to pull me up. "We need to get out of here right now and not touch anything, this is a crime scene."

I allow him to lead me back out through the front door. I gasp in the fresh air, letting it cleanse me as I shake and sob on the stairwell. Avery has his phone out and is calling 911. I hear him talking to the police, but my mind isn't computing what he's saying. All I can focus on at the moment is taking breath after breath of clear night air.

Once I have my breathing under control, I slump down on the stairs and let my head fall back to rest on the cool metal railing. I look out at the night sky, and come to terms with the fact that my friend, or whatever is inside of her, most likely murdered those girls. I can't deny the reality anymore.

* * *

The police arrive quickly, and everything after that is a blur. Avery and I are taken into the station for questioning, and kept there for a couple hours.

Prior to the cops arrival, we had both agreed to say that we went to Mandy's apartment because we had made plans for tonight with her and she told us to walk in when we arrived. We thought this was a good idea so that we wouldn't get in trouble for entering a residence without permission. I don't even know if this trivial aspect would matter in the grand scheme of things, but it seems smart to have our bases covered, so I go along with it.

By the time we are released to go, it's almost midnight. I feel drained and am looking forward to going home. I also feel scared. Apparently the police had found containers full of blood in Mandy's fridge. It will need to be analyzed, but they believe it to possibly be blood that was drained from her roommates. I feel sick to my stomach upon hearing that, and my head feels like mush after answering hundreds of questions backwards and forwards and in every little detail possible.

When Avery and I are being led through the station to the exit, I catch a glimpse of the female officer who had pulled us over on Dyer Lane, what now feels like an eternity ago, but was only earlier this month. I see her in profile, as she looks through a file that rests on the counter. She senses my gaze, and her eyes raise to meet mine. I catch recognition pass behind her stare, and then see it quickly replaced by curiosity. She tracks us with her eyes as we cross the office space and leave through the door at the back of the room.

Since we were brought in for questioning by the police, a vehicle is waiting to take us home. An officer places us inside, and apologizes for the wait but lets us know a officer will be out shortly to bring us back to Avery's car.

We sit in silence as we wait, neither one of us has the energy to speak. I try to unlock my phone, but the battery has died, so I slip it back into my pocket. Finally, the front door of the car opens and the female officer I noticed from before, slides into the vehicle.

"Hello, we meet again," she says in her velvety smooth voice. "I am Officer Jackson and I will be driving you where you need to go."

"I met Officer Jackson at work one day. She is Adam's cousin," I explain to Avery.

His eyebrows subtly raise at this information, but he remains silent. Officer Jackson asks where we want her to bring us, and I give her my address. I just want to go home, and then we can go pick up Avery's car from Mandy's apartments in the morning.

We ride in silence, with no sounds other than the car moving down the road. Then Office Jackson asks, "So, how do you know my cousin Adam?"

"I work with him as a paramedic," Avery replies.

I can see her nod her head at his answer. "He's a good guy," she adds.

"Yeah, he is," Avery answers.

I see her look back at us through the rearview again before she asks, "what were you two dressed up as tonight?" I can see her dark almond shaped eyes studying us in the mirror. A thoughtful intelligence gleams behind them. She is noticing our body language and taking notes on how we are acting, and something tells me nothing goes unnoticed by her.

I clear my throat, "we are J.Lo and P. Diddy."

"Oh, okay. I can see that now. I was wondering if that was his normal outfit choice," she says with a chuckle.

Avery looks down at his ridiculous blinged out costume jewelry and XXL white tee.

"It's Halloween. We expect the people who we come in contact with to be in some costume form or another." Officer

Jackson adds as she maneuvers the car through my apartment complex and pulls up outside my door and puts it into park. "Everything checked out for you two for now. We will be in touch. Stay local and have your phones accessible. We have a BOLO for your friend Mandy, and will hopefully find her soon and get some answers."

"Okay," I say, "thanks."

"Thank you for your cooperation."

Avery and I exit the car and shamble to my apartment in the freezing cold air. I can feel the officer's gaze on our backs. I unlock the door, feeling physically and emotionally exhausted. We move into the warmth of my apartment, and I place my phone on the charger. Then, I join Avery on the couch. He has a dazed look in his eyes and is staring at the assortment of photos on the table that depict horrors we thought could only be fabricated, but now know must be true.

"Well, fuck," he mutters.

"Yeah. I feel the same." I move close to Avery and lay my head on his shoulder.

I wish we could go back to before this, when the only worries in my life were passing an exam, or moving past my anxieties. My problems from before seem so small compared to what we face now. We just found mutilated dead bodies and know that our friend was responsible, and have no way of helping the situation. Definitely not something I ever imagined I would be facing in this lifetime.

I get up to fill a glass with water, and notice that my phone is lit up on the counter. It has charged enough to get texts, and there is an influx that has come in. I have a couple from Noah, a ton from Kate, oblivious to the horror Avery and I just witnessed.

I unlock my phone and go straight to my text messages. Noah sent a text asking where we went, and then another saying that the police broke up his party but if we want to come back, Kate, Nikki, and Leo were still there and we could join.

I open the messages from Kate, which basically repeat

what Noah sent in her own words. I keep scrolling through her messages, and my stomach plummets when read the newest one:

Text me back! Where are you? Mandy finally called me. She said sorry for being a no show, but her phone had died and her roommates talked her into going to a party. Guess where it is? Dyer Lane. Ew. I know. Apparently it's a thing to party there on Halloween. Noah wants to go super bad, and of course Leo is down since he took shrooms. Nikki and I don't want to, but we are being dragged along. Call me xo

"Avery!" I call as I rush toward him on the couch, clutching my phone. His head was tilted back and his eyes were closed, resting. He looks at me with alarm when he hears my tone of voice.

"What?" he asks with concern. He leans forward as I tilt my phone screen toward him so he can read the last text Kate sent. I see the muscles in his jaw clench.

"Oh, fuck," he whispers, "she sent that almost an hour ago."

"I know, I need to call her." My panic is rising as I tap Kate's name and push the speaker button. The phone rings out loud before going to voicemail. I hang up and immediately try calling her again. No answer.

"We need to go there," I declare, running both my hands through my hair. A feeling of panic has settled over me like a shroud. "We have to at least drive by and see what is happening. Obviously there is no party with Mandy's roommates going on." I fight back a sob as hysteria threatens to take me over.

"Don't you think we should tell the police that we know where Mandy is? They could go there and break it up and at least get her into custody."

I chew on my lip, trying to decide what the best course of action is. "Okay, let's call them on the way. They may take too long. We can tell them what we know, but still go there and get our friends."

Avery is looking at me like he is going to disagree and before he can speak, I press on, "come on, I can't just sit here knowing that our friends are out there at that fucked up place in the middle of the night with a fucking monster. I will go crazy." I grab his hands in mine, "please," I plead. "I need to do something."

Avery is tense, and I can see his jaw clench again, a ripple beneath his skin. Finally, he nods, "Okay, we will go."

CHAPTER 37:

The car ride toward Dyer Lane is solemn. My stomach is in knots as I drive us toward the last place I ever want to go. I know that sitting at home and passively wondering if Kate and everyone are okay isn't an option, though.

When we had first gotten to the car, I sat behind the wheel and Avery called the police station and updated them on what we know about Mandy's whereabouts. The officer that he spoke to sounded distracted, and said something about sending a unit out there to check it out. Nothing about the conversation made me feel reassured in any way.

My hands squeeze the wheel tightly as I navigate us toward the freeway exit that will lead us to the backroads and the rural area of Dyer Lane. I feel jittery and on edge as we get closer to our destination. The darkness outside the windows of the car is heavy. I can't see our surroundings any further than where my headlights illuminate as I slowly roll onto the turn off for the lane, which has no streetlights. It is completely deserted here, and I don't see any cars parked nearby. It certainly doesn't look like a party is happening. *Maybe Kate ended up staying in and isn't answering her phone because she fell asleep? Maybe the cops already broke up this supposed party and there is nothing to see here?*

I bring the car to a crawl, straining my eyes to see into

the oak guarded fields that surround the road.

"I can't see shit," Avery comments, echoing my thoughts.

"I know. I wish there were lights. I don't think anyone is out here, though."

"Yeah. I don't see any cars or anything. At least we checked so you can stop worrying." He reaches over and places his hand on my thigh, in an attempt at comforting me. "The police will come and do their own search. We should head back home and wait, that's really all we can do at this point."

We come to a sharp turn, and up ahead parked on the side of the road a couple yards away, is a car. My headlights cast light upon its large boxy shape. It's Kate's Tahoe. I pull up behind it, and cut the engine. I take in a deep shaky breath, and turn to face Avery who is staring straight ahead at Kate's car with a grim expression. His eyes are unblinking. The silence stretches on between us for a moment that feels like minutes but could only have been seconds, until he breaks it by saying "maybe we should wait for the police?"

Avery asks this with a hopeful inflection in voice. My heart aches at this glimpse of fear. Avery is someone who saves people's lives for a living and works in a constant state of danger, seeing him nervous feels wrong. He stares at me, imploringly, even in the darkness I can see the desperation on his features, but I know he is aware of what my answer will be even before it escapes my lips.

"That could take forever. Who knows when the police will get here, or if they even follow up on it tonight at all. We know our friends are here right now, and I cannot leave without finding them." I'm practically whining, but I don't care. I need to make sure they get home.

"I won't be able to forgive myself if I leave like a coward right now and something happens to them," I add. I know it's harsh, because leaving is what Avery wants to do, and he is not a coward, but I also know that these words are what he needs to hear to agree and let me have my way.

Avery slowly releases a long breath. “Fine, we can look around for a moment, but if anything feels too off we have to come straight back to the car. We can call the police again and make sure they send someone out.”

“Deal,” I say, already unbuckling my seat belt and grabbing for the handle to open my door. Avery is slower to exit the car, and I come around to his side. I have a flashlight in my hand, which I grabbed from under my seat as I got out. It has a decent beam, and lights up the path ahead of us so we don’t trip.

Avery turns to look around us, and then points to a footpath that is off to the side of where Kate parked. “Since they stopped here, maybe they took that little trail. I don’t know where else they would have walked. Most of this is tall grass and oaks…” He gestures to our surroundings. I agree and we set off down the pathway.

The darkness has a pulse. It is alive around us, although the absence of sound is profound. I feel like I can hear my own heart thumping inside my chest as the dense shadows shift around us.

Lub dub.

Lub dub.

It beats quickly against my ribs, in contrast to the slow deliberate pace Avery and I are walking. The sound of our shoes crunching over twigs punctuates the acute silence around us. Our breath billows in front of our mouths as we exhale. The cold is numbing. My nose starts to run, and I swipe at it, noticing how icy the tip feels against the back of my hand.

We walk for what feels like maybe five minutes, until we come to a small clearing with large boulders arranged in the center. On top of one of the massive stones, a body is draped in an unnatural position. I can tell that it’s a female, and her long hair flows down the side of the rock. Her back is bent so far back, it looks like it must have been snapped. My heart is hammering in my chest so hard now that I can feel it in my throat, blocking my air, constricting my breaths.

My fears solidify as I climb the rock toward the body and see that the broken unmoving figure is Kate. I let out a sob as I bend forward, and set down the flashlight. I reach for the side of her throat to check for a pulse. Kate's skin is gray tinged and cold. There is a halo blood outlining her head. I can't find her pulse, so I reposition my fingers again and again hoping that I am feeling for it in the wrong spot, although I know that I'm not. I start slamming my palms in the rock in frustration as tears stream down my cheeks. *We were too late.*

I reach forward to take Kate's head onto my lap and my fingers sink into a squishy patch of wetness. I can feel a spongy sensation that can only be her brain, and sharp shards that I know are the fragments of her bashed in skull. I can no longer see through the blur of tears that won't stop coming.

Avery is quickly at my side, and reaches out an experienced hand to feel for himself. Unlike me, he only has to touch his two fingers to Kate's throat once to know the answer. As a paramedic he has done this very thing to strangers hundreds of times, but he never has done it to a friend. Avery's breath comes out ragged and choked. He shakes his head, confirming what I already know. Kate is dead. A heavy teardrop falls from his eye and lands on the blood crusted stone.

Before we can collect ourselves, a thick fog rolls in around us. I look at Avery, startled. The mist has moved in rapidly. It smells earthy and acrid. Avery grabs for my hand, and I lace my fingers through his as I watch in wide eyed horror as figures begin to emerge from behind the looming oak trees. They move unnaturally toward us, and give off a faint milky glow in the dark night. The feet of the glowing forms hover above the ground, their toes lightly scraping the earth as they glide forward.

There are at least ten, if not more, materializing through the fog to where we sit next to Kate's fractured body. The ghostly shapes are dressed in clothing from various eras. The one closest to me is a man wearing a leather jacket. There is a bullet hole in the middle of his head that a single line of thick black liquid seeps from. My breath comes in short gasps and I am frozen where I sit, unable to take my eyes from the apparitions, as they close in on us from all angles.

Suddenly, Avery pulls me to my feet with a swift yank. He is holding the flashlight, and shines it down the side of the boulder. Then, he guides me forward and helps me to the ground, following closely behind me. Once our feet touch down, he whispers in my ear, "run."

CHAPTER 38:

I take off as fast as I can in a full sprint, not looking where I'm going, just wanting to flee the horrors behind me. I feel a sharp sting on my cheek as a low hanging branch hits my face. I can hear Avery running next to me, keeping pace, his breath coming in sharp pants.

He takes an abrupt turn to the left. "This way!" He yells, and I follow his lead. We wind through the closely planted oaks, trying to keep upright and not trip. The fog is winding through the trees following us from where we escaped.

I try to ignore it and keep running as a stitch begins to develop in my side. Avery is a few paces ahead of me, shining the flashlight ahead of us. I keep pushing myself to run harder, as the fog swirls around my ankles. It has caught up, and feels like a tangible thing instead of vapor. The fog wraps itself around my legs and begins to pull me back, hindering my progress. Avery is still sprinting, unaware that I am being slowed down.

I open my mouth to scream, but the breath gets caught as the fog pours into me and constricts my ability to take in air. It is pressing in from all sides. I can feel it slithering down my throat, gagging me. Thoughts that aren't my own flutter through my mind, and I feel immense despair flood into me. I'm choking on it. I stop moving, and double over with my hands braced on my knees as I cough, loud barking hacks that rack my body. I gulp, and struggle to catch my breath. An image of a man dressed in a 1920's suit and holding a shotgun swims into my vision. His face is austere and lined. He is aiming the gun into the distance at an unseen presence. He pulls the trigger.

FLASH

Next, I see a teenage girl dressed in a prom dress that looks like it was made in the 1960's. She is walking down Dyer Lane barefoot, holding her shoes. Her hair is styled in a beehive updo, and wisps of it are escaping the pins. Tears stream down her made up face. A car pulls up behind her, the bright headlights like solar eyes.

FLASH

The next image that floats across my retinas is of a farmer. He is wearing a plaid shirt and jeans, and holding a dead piglet by a leg. It dangles upside down. He shakes it violently and blood streams, small crimson rivers to the earth below.

I scream, heaving everything I have into rejecting whatever has entered me. The fog pours out of my mouth, riding the breath that I am expelling. I dont inhale until I am sure the mist is entirely gone. Then, I take a deep rasping breath. My lungs burn from the violation of the spirits, or whatever that was.

The dense mist surges on, and rolls past. Soon, the atmosphere is clear again and I force myself to continue to breathe deeply and steadily. I focus on the act of oxygen exchange, imagining the small air sacs called alveoli in my lungs puffing up and then deflating. This distracts me from the images I just saw, and helps to calm me. After a few more in and out breaths, I begin to stabilize, the panic receding, but only slightly. My entire body is shaking.

I stand up straight, feeling exhausted and weak. I am more scared than I have ever been in my life. I scan my surroundings, and have no idea where Avery is now. I look around in bewilderment. Everything appears the same. It's dark, and I can't see very far ahead because Avery has the flashlight. I fumble into my pocket for my phone, it has no signal so I can't make any calls, but I am thankful it is charged as I turn on the flashlight. The beam is weak in this dark of an area, but it works well enough for me to see the ground in front of my feet.

I wipe at my face, and my hand comes away bloody from the numerous tiny cuts that riddle my cheeks and the rusty scent of blood hovers around me. I try to focus my mind on figuring out which way Avery went. I look at the ground for clues like footprints or broken branches that may help me find his path. Thick twisted roots of the looming trees weave up through the soil like partially concealed snakes.

I see bright splotches of blood staining the earth ahead toward the right. Alarm rises within me. I cautiously make my way toward the trail of blood, and bend down to touch it. I don't think it is very new. I feel relief at the thought that it isn't Avery's. *But then, who's blood is it?*

My skin prickles, and I scan my surroundings the best I can. Trying to see through the impenetrable dark isn't easy, but I can make out basic shapes. I begin to slowly follow the line of dried blood on the ground as it winds further into the oaks. I keep tracking the stains until it ends at the base of a tree. I slowly lift the light of the phone and raise it up the thick trunk. As I lift the beam higher, it illuminates shoes dangling above the ground. I quickly scan up from there, and gaze up at the body of a man nailed into the bark. He is shirtless, and thick nails have been hammered into each shoulder, pinning him to the trunk. There are three long gashes that run down his torso and weep blood that shines black in the light from my phone. The man's head is leaning to the side, and all the skin has been stripped from his face and scalp leaving behind glistening muscle over the the bones of his skull. The pink and white striated tissue of his cheeks shine in the light from my phone and the nerves running along the surface look like frozen worms. His lipless face reveals long straight teeth, in a permanent death grin. Without a face, it is hard to truly discern what the corpse looks like, but I would recognize those tattoos adorning his chest and neck anywhere. The body nailed to the oak can only be Leo. I let out a scream as terror and grief flood my body, and then I run.

I don't even know where I am going, I am blundering through the oaks in a daze. I just know I need to get away from the gruesome scene behind me and find safety. Leo and Kate are both dead. I don't know where Avery has gone. I haven't seen Nikki or Noah yet, but I'm scared to know what may have happened to them.

My vision blurs and tears spill down my face, but I don't slow down. Somehow I must have circled back toward the main road. Hope surges up inside of me as I pick up my pace toward the street that is now visible through the trees ahead. I don't see our cars, but I think I'm just a little up from where we were parked and if I follow Dyer Lane down then I will find the right spot.

Now that I am out of the wooded area and on the lane, I let myself slow down to catch my breath. I am still moving quickly, but no longer running in a panic. Cold sweat soaks through my clothes, making me shiver. My mind feels numb as I mentally block out the images of Leo and Kate. I wrap my arms around myself and press forward.

As I turn a corner, I can see red and blue lights flashing on top of a police cruiser ahead. I feel lightheaded with the amount of relief that floods through me. I run full speed toward the cop car, and approach the driver side window.

The officer is sitting with his head turned toward the direction of the trees on the other side of the lane, facing away from me. I reach up to bang on his window, but notice it's rolled down. I reach a hand inside and grab at the officer's shoulder. My hand sears with pain as it makes contact with the figure sitting in front of me and a cold like I have never felt before freezes my blood. I pull my hand back and cradle it to my chest as the officer's head slowly turns to face me. There are deep bloody caverns where his eyes should be. Decaying flesh is peeling from his face in strips.

He opens his mouth and earwigs spill out from inside him. I can hear the small *tap tap tap* as the hard shelled bodies tumble forward landing on top of one another, writhing in a wave as they continue to surge forward out of the officer's rotten gaping maw. The bugs roil beneath the surface of the officer's skin like water coming to a boil. The beatles burst through the tattered shreds of his face and continue to seep out, ripping forward from within him.

Tap tap tap.

I stand frozen in horror at the sight in front of me before someone grabs my arm in a tight grasp. The sudden contact shakes me into action and I scream, a shrill alarm that pierces the night. A broken sound of despair.

I spin toward the person who has my arm in their hands, and come face to face with Nikki. Her cheeks are flushed and her chest is heaving.

"Come on!" She shrieks, and leads me away from the police vehicle and the monstrosity within. I follow her, shaking with fear, and struggling to keep up with her pace. I can feel my chest tightening with panic as she pulls me around the backside of a wide tree and whirls around to face me. Nikki holds a trembling finger to her mouth, urging me to stay quiet. Her bright red lipstick is smeared across her cheek. I nod spasmodically back at her. We stand there for a minute, catching our breath as silently as we can manage. Finally, she whispers in a shaky gasp, "they are everywhere."

"Who?"

"The spirits," Nikki's eyes look crazed as she rasps at me, struggling to gain her composure. "There are so many." Her chest continues to rise and fall quickly. "I've been running, trying to find Kate's car, but I can't." Her tone is panicked as she looks back toward the road.

"We parked right behind her," I whisper.

Even in the dark I can see a frown form on her face as she

asks, “why are you here?”

I want to groan as I think about everything that has happened tonight. I think of the bodies of my best friends I just found and stifle a cry. I place a hand over my mouth and muffle any sounds that might escape. I take a few shaking deep breaths and then when I feel certain I won’t make any involuntary loud noises, I move my trembling hand from my lips and whisper, “Kate texted me and said you all were coming to a party here with Mandy and her roommates. But Avery and I went to Mandy’s apartment earlier and her roommates are dead.”

Nikki is chewing on her fingernail and staring at me in abject horror. The surprised expression is quickly replaced by a stern glare. “I knew I was fucking right about her,” she snaps. “That bitch was standing in the middle of the road when we got here. Kate pulled the Tahoe over and Noah got out to see what she was doing. He was so drunk and had taken shrooms with Leo so I think he thought it was perfectly normal for Mandy to be standing in the middle of the lane. He walked up to hug her like she was the welcoming committee for this nonexistent party and she slit his throat. I didn’t even see a knife in her hand or anything," Nikki palms her mouth to stifle a sob, and then when she has it under control, she continues. "It happened so fast. Noah was facing away from us, and when he turned back toward the car, he had his hand up to his neck. He looked so confused, and blood was pouring out from between his fingers...then he collapsed.”

She takes in a shaky breath and swipes at the tears flowing down her face with the back of her hands. She is silently crying, her shoulders shaking as she struggles to finish her story. “Mandy crouched over him there in the middle of the road, and drank his blood like a vampire or something. She’s evil, Cora. I saw this all with my own eyes.” Nikki is still shaking with grief as she speaks. “Leo ran out of the car toward her and Noah. I think maybe he thought that he was hallucinating the whole thing. He went up to Mandy to pull her from Noah's neck and she grabbed Leo by the head and twisted. I heard his neck snap before his body hit the pavement."

Nikki pauses again and puts her hands over her eyes. She wipes hard at the tears leaving black streaks of eye makeup behind. "Kate was screaming and ran out of her car into the trees. I ran, too. I didn't know what else to do. I don't know where she is now. I kept running and I feel like I've been going in circles. The fog confuses me and sometimes I feel like hands are grabbing me and slowing me down. I was about to give up and sit down, then I heard you scream and thought you might be Kate, so I ran that way. I found you at that fucked up police car and now here we are." She lifts her hands up in gestures to our surroundings then lets them fall back to her side.

I stare at the ground with wide eyes. I feel like I am in a trance and this entire thing is a nightmare.

"Where's Avery?" Nikki asks.

The question snaps me out of it, and I look up and narrow my eyes at her, "how do you know that I came here with Avery?"

"You said *we* parked behind Kate, and you also mentioned you were with him earlier. I know you wouldn't have come by yourself."

I nod slowly at her. I am still having a hard time trusting Nikki, but I guess her response makes sense. "We got separated," I answer, "we found Kate...she's dead." My voice cracks with emotion as I say those words, and my nose stings as tears form in my eyes again. I can't even bring myself to tell her how I found Leo's body. It's all too gruesome to try and put into words right now.

Nikki is silent. She stares at me with a blank expression, then she murmurs, "we are so fucked."

I slump down with my back against the tree, and curl my knees in toward my chest. I rest my head down and hug myself. I need time to think. I am so cold, and I am beyond exhausted. My mind feels like the fog swirling around us has entered it again and trying to grasp my thoughts is like trying to hold smoke.

"We need to get out of this place without crossing paths with Mandy. If we do meet with her, we might have a chance. I can try to do that spell that Heather and her friends attempted. I brought the occult book with me," Nikki says, holding up a purse that I hadn't noticed was in her hand until now. "I had a feeling we were going to end up here tonight, so I made sure I had everything with me for the ritual in case we needed it. Also, I have a crystal. It's not the same one Heather used, it's obsidian. I did a lot of research and think it may be the right one. Maybe the quartz or whatever Heather had wasn't strong enough to absorb the negative energy, but I bet obsidian is." Nikki is babbling now. She's not even breathing between her run on sentences.

I skoff and let my head fall back against the tree. "I'm serious," Nikki continues. "Those girls didn't have Google back in the 90s, but we do, and I looked specifically for a crystal that was powerful at absorbing bad things and cleansing, and I think this is it."

"In case you didn't realize, those girls fucking died. Their little witchcraft or whatever didn't work. This is a demon or something, not something that can be solved with a little stone and a chant."

"Do you have any other ideas? Because if so, I'd love to hear it." she demands.

I don't respond, choosing to close my eyes and swallow down the nausea that is clawing at my throat.

Nikki taps my arm, "we can't stay here. We need to try to find the cars."

I glare up at her. "No shit."

She puts her hands on her hips and lets out a breath of frustration. "I refuse to die tonight, so you better get off your ass and start moving, because I also refuse to leave you here. One thing I feel pretty certain about, is that we can't just sit around if we want to survive."

I grab my head and clench my hair in my fists. I want to

scream. I don't answer Nikki, but I do push myself up from the ground and stand. She turns and starts weaving back into the woods, using her phone for a flashlight. I take mine out, and do the same. I still don't have cell service, but keep checking it periodically to see if a bar shows up. I doubt one will.

We walk in silence for some time. There are sounds of crunching twigs around us like something is keeping pace and stalking us. I try to keep my mind focused on not tripping or hurting myself in the dark as we walk. Eventually, we reach the dilapidated shed that Heather's journal was found in. "I never wanted to see this shithole again," I mutter bitterly.

"At least we know the path to take from here to get back to the main road," Nikki comments. "It's this way."

She shines her beam toward the trail that will take us toward Dyer Lane, and something scuttles out of the bushes on all fours. It stops on the path, and Nikki flashes her light in that direction. Mandy is crouched there, blocking our way. Her skin is scabbed over with sores and patches of her hair are missing, exposing areas of scaly dry scalp. Her eyes are completely bleached white, and dark blood is crusted over the lower half of her face and neck. Her head does a sharp tick to the right and then slowly tilts to the side, as she studies us like a curious predator. The sight is revolting, and I feel like I am about to faint. My head is light and I wonder why they call it "fight or flight," because I don't feel capable of either of those things. My vision is starting to tunnel and I struggle to keep myself steady.

Next to me, Nikki slowly starts to lean to the side in an attempt to grab hold of a large fallen branch, which I'm guessing she could use as a weapon. Mandy bares her blood stained teeth in an animal snarl and her stooped body tenses, ready to spring. Nikki freezes, and everything feels suspended in time, balanced precariously between sudden death and the possibility for escape.

Then, Avery is unexpectedly there, slamming into the side of Mandy and tackling her to the ground. His momentum is enough to get her pinned beneath him, but he is straining to contain her. Without any further thought, I run forward to help hold her down. I grab on to Mandy's legs, which she is kicking repeatedly into Avery's side. He has her by the wrists, and we are breathing heavily as we push her onto her stomach and pin her limbs to the ground. She is emitting hissing noises and thrashing at us. I get her legs together and place my knees on top of them, using my body weight to try and hold her in place the best I can. Avery has her arms behind her back like a police officer would do when they detain someone.

"I need something to secure her with," he pants. Sweat glistens on his forehead next to a deep gash that is weeping blood, but he appears otherwise unharmed.

I look back to Nikki, who has stripped off her nylons and is hurrying over to tightly bind it around Nikki's wrists. She ties it so tightly that it digs into Mandy's skin, and a thick pus like fluid leaks from the cuts the bindings have made.

"What about her ankles?" I ask, dragging my eyes away from the sap-like trail dripping down Mandy's hands and trying not to gag.

Nikki shakes her head, and glances around us, searching for something that could work.

Avery bends down to take his shoes off, and removes his calf-level socks to begin to tie them together and make a rope of sorts. "I hope this doesn't slip," he thinks out loud as he secures his makeshift restraint around Mandy's ankles. He tugs on it to make sure it will hold, and it seems to work.

As soon as Avery straightens up, I fling myself into his arms and hug him close to me. My heart is pounding and I can feel his doing the same through his chest, pressed to mine. I grab the sides of Avery's face and pull his lips down to kiss him. My tears reappear and slide down my face. He wipes my cheeks and then pulls me back into his chest. I whimper, leaning against him as he holds me. I feel the vibration of his voice against my ear as he explains to Nikki and I that when he became separated from me, he wandered in circles. He didn't know which way to go, but then he heard a scream and headed for that direction. Eventually, he saw Nikki and I but we were up ahead and he didn't want to call out and attract any attention from the ghostly things that were in the woods with us, so he followed behind until he could catch up.

"Good thing you got here when you did," Nikki notes.

A deep rumbling chuckle escapes from Mandy's mouth. All three of us turn and look at the thing that was once our friend. Its face is in the dirt, and it suddenly whips up to the side to look at us. Instead of the white opaque eyes that resemble thick cataracts, Mandy's eyes have returned to normal and shimmer with tears. She looks at me with a pleading expression, "help me," she utters in a gravelly voice. "Cora, it's me. Please…help."

I start to tremble, and Avery tightens his hold around me. My heart breaks looking at the face of my friend, but I also know this isn't Mandy anymore, not really. I look into her desperate eyes and see a flicker of darkness flash across them, like some large beast swimming below the surface of deep water.

"Help me," she croaks, again. Her lips split as she speaks, and blood seeps up from fissured skin. A sob pushes its way up my throat as I rush toward her. Avery grabs my arm, and I rip it from his grasp and hurry to kneel next to Mandy's prone body. I put my hand to her cracked cheek, trying to keep her, the real her, grounded here with me.

"Please…untie me," she whispers in a pitiful voice.

"Don't!" Nikki screams out.

"You can't listen to her, Cora, that's not Mandy." Avery says in a measured tone, and takes a step toward me.

I start to cry and shake my head back and forth, "you know I can't."

Mandy starts to cry, too. Snot runs down from her nose and collects in the dirt beneath her face. My heart breaks seeing her this way, and just as my resolve begins to weaken, the cries emitted from her suddenly turn into mocking laughter. Then, her spine arches violently and she appears to be having a seizure. Her jaw is clenched and the cords in her neck stand out with strain as her body writhes and rocks. Eventually, the tension in her muscles release and her head rocks down as if she is asleep.

I inch a little closer to check on her, and her head unexpectedly shoots upward with sudden purpose. Mandy's eyes are fully white again and her expression is set in a stony cast of determination. I scramble backwards away from her as her face regains a cunning expression, her mind calculating what to do next.

Avery comes up behind me and helps me up from the ground. We watch as Mandy twitches and jerks, and the nylon holding her wrists begins to shred. The evil unnatural laugh starts again and grows in volume. A deep guttural voice comes from Mandy's mouth and seems to surround us as it reverberates inside my skull.

"This has been fun," the thing inside Mandy growls. "You are all pathetic. You thought you could hold me." When the last word is spoken, the thing breaks all of the bonds with a sudden *snap*, and swiftly rolls over to stand. Shock and disappointment overtake my senses as I watch Mandy's body clamber to her feet. Avery, Nikki, and I edge backward, placing more space between us and the creature.

The entity inside Mandy continues to speak in an unnatural rumbling voice, "I wanted to give you a chance to choose, Cora," it says, pinning me with its white stare, "you could have helped your friend, and been suitable to join me, but you did not choose wisely."

Mandy's head shakes from side to side and tuts her tongue, a smile twisting her mangled lips. "I could have broken those bonds the minute you placed them, but I wanted to see where your loyalties could lie. You're weak, all of you. Because of that, you're going to die tonight." With the last sentence, Mandy clasps her palms together and holds them to her chest, like a schoolgirl, a warped grin still plastered on her distorted face.

My entire body tingles with chills. *The thing inside Mandy was playing with us this entire time. This whole thing is just a sick game for it.* My mind whirls, trying to figure out how to respond.

Before I can answer, Mandy lifts her arms into the air, and ghostly figures surge forward from the woods around us. Spectral forms of women, men, children, and animals of all types flow closer, their toes grazing the earth as they hover. They move in until we are surrounded by phantom light. Many of the spirits have gruesome wounds visible on their figures; blown open heads, protruding bones, slashed abdomens with the viscera glowing in the darkness like bioluminescent creatures shining under the sea.

My eyes catch on a figure to my left. I immediately recognize her solemn face from the photo I had seen in Jessica's living room, even though her shimmering skin looks blistered and burned. I can tell that it is Heather. I see other familiar figures in the crowd. I spot the farmer from the image I had earlier, as well as the girl wearing her prom dress. I shudder remembering the violation and fear I felt when I was stranded in the mist.

Then, I hear Nikki gasp. I look at her, she has raised a shaking finger to point at an area of trees. I follow the path of her gesture with my eyes, and see Kate and Leo standing among giant oaks, glistening with their own otherworldly glow. They are now souvenir spirits, claimed and bonded to the land by this demon. I feel angry tears of despair trace paths down my cheeks.

The entity makes a choking sound, and I drag my gaze back back toward Mandy, who has crept closer while I was distracted with the ghosts surrounding us. She is doubled over, panting and shaking. She slowly lifts her head to look at us. For a brief moment, the real Mandy has emerged from beneath the being that inhabits her.

"Go," she gurgles, wetly like she is speaking underwater. Then, her expression twists into a grimace. The immense pain emanating from her is visible from the tightening of her muscles as she struggles to suppress the demon within. Her eyes are bulging and sightless, but not glazed over. She continues to make violent choking sounds and twitches sporadically, her neck snapping to the side repeatedly. It is clear that this moment won't last for long. The entity inside her is too powerful, too desperate, too hungry for blood.

CHAPTER 39:

Avery grabs my hand and pulls me after him as he races for the path. Nikki follows behind us. There are apparitions everywhere, but we burst through them as if we are running through smoke. For a moment it feels like my heart has stopped. Moving through the wraiths is like plunging beneath a frozen lake. The cold takes my breath away. Then as quickly as it appears, it's gone and replaced by the normal chill of the night.

All I can hear is the blood pounding in my ears and our ragged breaths as we run down the dirt path. I can see Dyer Lane ahead of us now, and sprint faster as we near the road. Once we are on the pavement, we stop to glance up and down the street trying to determine which way the cars are parked.

"I think we should go that way," Nikki says, pointing to the left. Avery shakes his head, "We passed the turn off for the path before we parked, so we gotta be the other way," he asserts, gesturing in the opposite direction. Nikki nods and is about to speak when Avery abruptly lets out a yell of pain and drops to the ground. He rolls onto his back and is clutching his leg. There is something silver gleaming from the back of his upper thigh. Alarm floods me when my mind finally recognizes that the thing lodged in Avery's leg is a hilt of a knife. I drop to my knees next to him and put my hands to his leg as it weeps crimson tears.

"Don't take the knife out, it will make me bleed faster if you do," he says through gritted teeth, biting back the pain. Nikki is standing next to me digging through her purse, and I am trying to think and decide what to do to help Avery. He moans, sweat shimmering on his face, blood flowing, and I am failing him.

Then, I hear the booming chuckle of the demon. A figure steps out from the oaks at the side of the road. A tattered mask of skin is draped over its face. Those blank white eyes stare at me from the other side of the skin it is wearing. I gasp in horror when I realize the creature is wearing the skin it flayed from Leo's skull. It is wearing Leo's face.

"Where did you think you were going to go? You know I can't let you leave my Halloween party," it says, gesturing to the mess the entity made of our friend's displaced features. "Do you like my costume, Cora?"

I struggle to keep from vomiting, as my entire body shakes. Next to me, Avery is wincing in pain, and Nikki is screaming long, crazed shrieks.

The demon continues to slowly stalk toward us, the dangling ends of the ill fitting skin mask sways with each step. It reaches up and grabs Leo's face and tosses it to the side. It hits the ground with a wet *plop*.

Mandy's mangled image is revealed, covered in glistening clotted blood. Her white eyes gaze sightlessly, yet seem to be all-seeing. My stomach clenches and Nikki continues to be hysterical. Her screams fill the night air. I sway on my feet, and clench my hands into fists.

The entity pauses as if considering its next words. It stops to look at Nikki and tilts its head in that predatory way it did earlier, then says, "that knife was helpful Nikki."

Nikki stops screaming like a switch was flicked and stares at the demon with wide eyes. Her breath comes hard in ragged gasps. A wicked smile forms on Mandy's gruesome face, opening the cuts in her lips so that fresh blood mingles with the dried crusts that formed earlier.

I whip my head over to look at Nikki, her face is pale and she is shaking her head. "What? How did you get it?" she whispers. Her eyes are frantic and her tearstained face is flushed from exertion.

"You need to be more careful with your things. You're careless," the grating voice says with an air of smugness.

"I brought that knife for the ritual in case it came down to that," Nikki whimpers, glancing at me, an apology written on her features. "I need it." With those last words, she takes two large steps forward and abruptly yanks the knife out of Avery's leg. He screams in pain, and I gasp in shock and immediately move my hands to the opening the blade has left behind.

My hands shake as they press on the gash in his leg. Avery is in agony as a runnel of ruby blood surges forward, free to flow now that the knife is no longer helping to seal the vessels. Panic claws at my throat and I swallow it down. I grab at my waist, and quickly unbuckle the glittery belt I wore tonight for my costume. I sinch it above Avery's stab wound, and pull it as tight as I can get it. He groans in pain and his hands are clutching his shirt in fists.

"I'm sorry," I sob. "You're going to be okay." I think back to the last time I said those words to someone I loved. It was my dad when he was dying.

I bend over Avery's leg, trying to keep pressure and hoping that this coupled with the makeshift tourniquet, will prevent him from bleeding out before help comes. Then I am hit with a terrifying thought, what if the police didn't take our call seriously?

What if no one comes?

I hear the demon hiss, and glance up and see Nikki using the knife that she took from Avery's wound to cut a line down her palm. She raises her fist and drizzles blood over the shiny black stone that she is holding in her other hand. Nikki drops the knife, and it clatters as it hits the pavement. She quickly bends down to swoop the occult book from her bag, and flips it open. Then, she begins to chant. The creature within Mandy starts to screech in anger like the whistle of a teakettle coming to a boil. Nikki raises her voice louder as she continues to read off the spell in a strange unfamiliar language.

I watch in horror as Mandy's forehead begins to split and a curved horn juts out of her skull to rise toward the night sky. The sharp point glistens in the light of the full moon. Mandy's face starts to elongate into a horse-like shape and those white unblinking eyes stay trained on Nikki as Mandy's form grows in height until it towers over her. The hands of the creature twist and bend until they are replaced by three hooked talons. Nikki pauses in her chant, shocked at what she is seeing and that split second is all it takes for the creature to surge forward and ram its scythe-like horn through her chest.

Nikki sputters and coughs up syrupy blood as a red stain unfurls across her white dress, a blooming rose in the night. She tries to talk, but all that can escape her lips is a gurgling sound as blood oozes forward like thick crimson honey. She drops the book and the crystal, and I scurry forward to retrieve them from the ground at her feet. I grab both objects and then scoot myself backward to return to Avery's side. He is passed out, and I feel his neck for a pulse. I am thankful when I feel the soft thump of his heart. It is faint, but it's there.

Nikki had folded down the corner of the page that has the chant, and I quickly flop the book open to the correct place. I hold the obsidian stone in my hand. It is sticky and hot with Nikki's blood and feels like it is pulsing within my palm.

When I look up, Mandy, or whatever she is now, is suddenly before me. I can smell the intense rust from the blood that stains her face, mixed with the cloying scent of a decay. She has returned to a more human form, but there is a hole in her forehead from where the horn had broken through. It is weeping a black gelatinous sludge mixed with milky white fluid that gives off steam in the cold air.

A scream dies in my throat as her hands encircle my neck, and tighten. All I can see is the film-like white of Mandy's possessed eyes inches from my face as the edges of my reality fade to black. I struggle to pull oxygen into my constricted airway, and my grip on the obsidian crystal and the book slackens. I allow the items to fall so that I can raise my hands in an attempt to pry Mandy's fingers away from my throat, but I am weak, just as the demon said.

Through the murky depths of my oxygen deprived mind, I think I can hear a man softly speaking. The words grow in volume, and I realize it's Avery's voice. Somehow he summoned the strength to try a last ditch effort and complete the chant himself. Stars burst in front of my eyes like bubbles, as the hands around my throat continue to clench. I stop moving, stop struggling, and allow the darkness to envelope me, a black tide surging into the shore.

Then, intense pain and heat engulf me as a shrill screech breaks through the night air and the hands cutting off my life are abruptly removed. I gasp and suck in oxygen through my aching airway. I open my eyes to a sea of flames dancing before me. Mandy is on fire and thrashing on the ground, her form shifting back and forth between human and beast.

I am also on fire and the smoke stings my crushed throat as my skin burns. I drop to the ground and roll, trying to extinguish the flames. The smoke coming off of the creature is black and pungent. It thickens around us, obscuring my vision. I keep rolling until I am no longer aflame, but I can see that Mandy is continuing to burn. Suddenly, there is loud *POP* and she explodes, raining blood down over us in a mist. The rancid smell of rotten meat permeates the air as her vaporized body converges into a murky cloud of smoke.

I scream, but it only comes out as a hoarse yelp. My throat aches and my eyes sting. I watch through the haze as the thick black fumes circle around the obsidian stone and are slowly pulled within the crystal.

The entity's energy is confined, for now.

I feel around the ground, trying to locate Avery, who is no longer speaking. The smoke is so thick I can barely see my own hands, but from what I can tell they are blistered and raw from the flames. The nerves of my burned skin are stinging and I am in excruciating pain. I finally feel Avery's shoe, and pull myself toward him. He is unconscious again, and his leg is continuing to steadily bleed.

I muster every ounce of my strength and get my hands under Avery's arms so that I can drag him backward to get us out of the fire zone. Struggling to breath and gritting my teeth through the pain, I exert all of my energy to move him. My throat is tender and beginning to swell. Every breath is a struggle. For some reason, my mind goes back to what Janet said to me about being capable and believing in myself, and I push forward.

Keep swimming, or die.

CHAPTER 40:

I somehow manage to pull Avery's unconscious body across the lane to the other side of trees, where the smoke is thinner. My eyes and lungs are aflame, but not nearly as bad as my throat, which is raw and agonizing with every breath. I let out a cry when I see that Avery's lips have a bluish tinge to them. He still has a pulse, though. There is hope.

I sit on the side of the road, with Avery's head in my blood stained lap. A siren wails in the night as it approaches. I pray that this is a real police and not another phantom. Tears stream down my face and land on Avery's cheek, mixing with dried flecks of blood and dirt. I feel myself growing weaker.

A police car slams on its break in the middle of the road, and it looks like a real person, not a ghost this time, but I don't have the energy to call out to the officer. My throat hurts too much, and I am wheezing with each breath. The flashing lights bounce off the trees around us, and my tears make the world shimmer in a kaleidoscope of colors. A fire truck and ambulance come to a stop behind the police, and people exit the vehicles with flashlights.

The firefighters get out to start tending to the flames, which have spread to the oaks across the street, and the police officers sweep their beams around the area. Finally, someone spots Avery and I, and rushes forward. "We need medics over here!" he calls out.

Paramedics race toward us, carrying backboards and their equipment. They assess Avery and strap him to the board as they ask me questions and do their own assessment on me. Everything is blurry, everything hurts. I try to focus and nod my head, but I can't talk, my throat is too damaged from being strangled, burned, and all the smoke. I am quickly loaded into an ambulance and they attach me to O2 and start an IV. I feel my eyes getting heavy, and the world goes dark.

* * *

I stand next to Avery's bed in the hospital and run a hand down the blanket that covers him. As if he can sense my presence, he opens his eyes. It takes a moment for him to focus on me. His pupils are small from the painkillers he is on, and his skin color is still not back to normal, but he looks better.

"How do you feel?" I ask, gently.

"Better now that you're here," he replies in a scratchy voice.

I smile sadly at him. "I'm glad you pulled through."

"Thanks to you."

"No, I don't think anyone would have survived if you hadn't done what you did."

"Do you think it's over? Is that thing gone?"

I shrug. "For now." The truth is, I don't ever think the thing we faced on Dyer Lane will be gone. It's just energy that can be transferred from one thing to another…like all energy. It will regroup and be back. It just lost its vessel. It is good we didn't die on Dyer Lane, or else we would have been trapped there. Part of its collection. A human memento.

"I love you," I whisper to Avery.

"I love you, too," he answers softly. "Infinitially."

I gaze back at him longingly, amazed that he survived. I'm about to speak again, when a middle aged nurse with fluffy blonde hair walks in, cutting off my line of communication.

She is wearing hot pink scrubs with matching lipstick. Avery's gaze shifts from me to the bright visitor in the doorway.

"You're awake!" The nurse comments, energetically. She has a subtle Southern accent. "What would you say your pain is at right now on a scale of 1-10?"

"Um, a six right now, I guess" Avery answers, shifting uncomfortably in bed. Then he turns to look back to me, and his gaze becomes puzzled. "Where did Cora go?"

The nurse stops in her tracks. "Oh, honey." Her face falls, "I thought you knew..."

"Knew what?" His expression is concerned and confused.

"She didn't make it. They lost her in the ambulance on the way here. I am so sorry. I thought someone had already discussed this with you, but maybe you were not coherent enough when they explained all that. You've had quite the recovery journey. You lost a lot of blood and had some issues from the smoke inhalation."

Avery's face crumples as his hands twist into fists, clutching the blanket that is draped over him. "What do you mean? She was just here." He lifts a hand and gestures next to his bed, where I had been standing just before I floated up and masked myself in the corner of the ceiling. When you're a spirit, you can choose when and who sees you, and you're not bound by the rules of a body.

I had to talk to Avery one last time, and tell him I love him. Now, witnessing how much emotional pain he is in, I almost regret it. *Almost.* At least I was able to say "I love you," and hear it back from him before I fade away from his life.

The nurse is by his bedside now, muttering about the dose of his painkillers causing hallucinations and apologizing profusely for his loss. I don't think I can stand to watch any more of this, so I float up through the ceiling and into the brilliant blue sky.

EPILOGUE:

When I died in the ambulance, we had departed from Dyer Lane and were almost to the hospital. As my soul left my body, a chemical release took place and every synapse inside me put on a firework show. Neon colors glimmered across my eyelids in brilliant bursts. Then, I felt nothing at all, but I was still there. I could see everything as the paramedics performed CPR. I watched as they injected various medicines in an attempt to resuscitate me. From above, I viewed the lifesaving measures they wholeheartedly administered. Eventually, I left, and floated along the hospital like a dandelion seed, invisible to those around me but present all the same.

I followed the medics along the familiar hallways of my work as they rushed Avery into life-saving surgery to repair the vessel damage that the knife blade had caused and give him much needed blood. I witnessed it all. A passive observer.

After hours of surgery, they brought Avery to the ICU and I watched the nurses care for him. I didn't know what to do or where to go next, so I stayed, lingering in the corners. I kept watch over the man I loved as he slept and the staff cared for him. Then, at some point, I felt a warmth radiating from the side of me.

When I turned toward that feeling, I looked up at the familiar face of my dad. Or, the spirit of my dad, rather. He was next to me for the first time in years, something I wished for everyday since his journey in life came to an end. I know I should have felt immense joy, but I felt almost nothing at all. I think that emotions like that are reserved for the living and without a physical body, I could feel only a tiny fraction of what I could experience when I was alive.

"Hello Cora," my dad said. The familiarity of his voice a comfort, like coming home. His smile was radiant. Every line etched into his face a map of his past, and his image was preserved to be exactly as he looked the day that he died.

"What are you doing here?" I stammered.

"I will be your guide," he said, and wrapped his arms around me. Instead of a solid warm embrace, his hug felt like sunlight filtered through a window. It was an unexpected, but pleasant sensation.

We floated up above the world together, into the clouds. The sky felt cool and misty. We hovered there, suspended in air, weightless and transparent as wind moved through us. Then, he told me everything.

* * *

I learned from my dad that everyone has an energy guide when they die. It is someone who cares about you and has passed on before you, who can help lead you in the afterlife. My father explained that my spirit is free to stay and linger in the world as it is. I can go anywhere, see anything, but I am not tangible, I am only energy. I will not be able to feel emotions as I did in life. I can no longer experience all the wonders that being human holds. However, if I want to live again, that is also an option. I can be reborn and my soul will go on in a new life. The choice is mine, and I can choose at any time.

I guess it is true that energy really can't be destroyed, just altered into a different state. I finally have my proof. I wondered about this but it took dying to find out the burning question that I always would ruminate on the most while alive.

Although as spirits, we have control over who and when someone can see us, my father went on to warn me about contacting the living too frequently. Doing so could create problems and threaten the sanity of the people I visit. I understood what he was saying. Witnessing the confusion and torment that my visit to Avery in the hospital had caused could not be repeated. I can't risk his stability for the sake of my own selfish wants. I need to leave my family and friends alone if I don't want to harm them psychologically.

I chose to remain a spirit for now, afraid of what starting a new life would entail. I like the idea of being able to check on my loved ones from afar. At least they are part of my existence, even if I am not part of theirs.

Over the next few days, I watched as my mother received the news of my death. I couldn't stay to witness very much of that. Even without feeling the full human level of sadness, it is too heartbreaking. My emotions are a stormy shade of gray, but seeing this type of sadness turns my feelings into the gray of dust and decay.

I watched as Avery recovered his health. I wanted so badly to sit and talk with him, but I made myself hold back. I watched my coworkers grieve. I watched the police conduct an investigation. They gave up quickly. Shit just happens on Dyer Lane, was their reasoning, I guess.

I watched people I don't know do things I don't care about. I watched all the little things about life that people take for granted and often don't notice in the busy rush of day to day activities. I watched and I watched...and I began to feel dissatisfied quickly with this strictly observant form of life.

Something that I did value about this time floating around as energy is that it allowed me to speak with my dad about his death. Of course he never blamed me for not being able to save him, but having his forgiveness spoken to me was soothing. I asked my dad what would happen if I decided that I want another try at life. He told me I will be reborn. I could feel something stir inside me when he said that, like the bud of a rose beginning to unfurl.

"So, would that be like reincarnation?" I asked.

"Essentially," he replied, nodding his head. "But you will need to be sure of it. When you start a new life, your old one will be lost to you and there is no going back."

"Why have you stayed a spirit?" I asked.

"Because I wanted to see you again," he says, with a small sad smile. "If I had gone on, we never would have met once more like we are right now. I am going to wait for the day I can see your mother, and then we can decide together what we want to do."

I nodded my head in understanding. The thought of waiting for Avery is appealing, but that could be a very long time in this bland in-between life. Avery is young, with so much time remaining. Of course the end of life wasn't the end of tough decisions and complications.

After the discussion with my dad, I spend the next few days continuing to watch my loved ones do mundane day-to-day things that I can no longer partake in; eating good food, enjoying a movie, crying. It's *nearly* painful. Just nearly. I yearn for any deep emotion but I only find emptiness planted in hollow longing and watered by ennui.

Months pass, and finally I come to a decision

* * *

I find my dad's spirit watching my mom drink coffee on a restaurant patio. She has lost weight and there is a weariness about her. His spirit sits across from her at the round metal table. He gazes at her longingly as she raises the cup to her lips and takes a sip. A breeze surges and flutters strands of her hair across her face. I see my dad lift his hand as if to brush it back and tuck it behind her ear, but he stops himself and lays it back down on the table.

I take a seat next to him. It's strange sitting here with my parents, like I have done so many times in the past. Except this time, only one of us is truly alive. I wonder how many times my dad has done this. How many times has he sat with her? An invisible observer of her life. Someone who loves her long after death. Long enough to wait in silence until they can meet again.

"I think I want to live," I tell him.

He nods, his watchful eyes shifting from my mother and landing on me. "I would want that for you." Although I cannot fully feel gratitude like I once did, I feel lighter upon hearing him say this.

"She would want it for you too," he says nodding toward my mother. We are so close to her, yet it feels like a world away. Another realm. Because it is.

I sit with my dad for hours as we spend the day side by side. When I am ready, we say our goodbyes and embrace for a long time. The sunlight through glass sensation is present as our spirits intertwine. Then, I allow myself to float away.

My father told me, all I have to do is *want* to live again. If I focus all my energy on being alive, I will find my way.

So, I do.

* * *

I am being pushed through a dark tunnel and there is a bright light at the end. I am squeezed forward, and then rock back again into darkness. *Squeeze*. Up half an inch. *Light*. Rock back half an inch. *Darkness. Squeeze.* Up a little more. *Squeeze.* I am compressed on all sides, wrapped in a full body hug until I am pushed through into brightness.

For a brief moment I can remember every life I have ever lived before. I see dunes of sand, ice caps, forests, huts, castles, and seas. I hear numerous languages all being spoken at once, and I can understand them all.

I blink my sticky eyes and can only see blurry outlines. A soft narrow instrument is shoved into my mouth and fluids are suctioned out. My tiny fists are balled next to my cheeks, and I roll my tongue along hard smooth gums.

I release a strangled wet sound as I am placed into warm arms, and I stare up into a blurry unfamiliar face. A woman looks down at me with sheer love and her tearful eyes shimmer with joy.

"Welcome to the world, baby girl," she says in a voice choked with emotion.

A gloved hand firmly pats my back, encouraging the fluid out of my lungs. I gasp the first breath of my new life.

Then, I scream.

ABOUT THE AUTHOR

Marie Aitchison

Marie Aitchison is a former Registered Nurse, and earned her BSN and Public Health Nursing credentials from Sacramento State University. She currently works as a freelance writer, but fiction is her favorite. When she isn't conjuring scary stories, you will find her reading and reviewing books on Instagram @topshelfbookreviews. Dyer Lane is Marie's first novel, but she has plans to contribute many more to the horror/thriller genre in the years to come. Marie lives in Northern California with her husband and two daughters.

ACKNOWLEDGEMENT

Thank you, readers, for giving my debut novel a chance. I hope you felt something from it - whether it was fear,
disgust, entertainment, or any range of emotions in between. I had fun writing this strange and dark story and appreciate you all.

I have often wondered what happens after death. Haven't we all?

This story was my way of exploring those feelings and thoughts. Much like Cora, my dad died suddenly and
unexpectedly. I too dealt with the grief, guilt, and anxiety that was the aftermath of such a heavy loss. My dad is the person who helped shape my love for literature and I know he would be proud of me for writing this book.

Although Cora did not survive Dyer Lane, she did see her dad again and get much needed closure as she learned of life after death. Which I hope is comforting in its own way.

When I was writing this novel, I tried to think of what scares me and aimed to scare myself. There is something about possession that has always been particularly frightening for me, so I went there. The Exorcist movie still haunts me, and I wanted to create my own twist on that feeling. Thanks for taking this disturbing ride with me.

I also want to take time to thank my husband, Matt, for endlessly encouraging me to follow my dreams of becoming an author and for supporting my love of writing over the years. I am incredibly thankful for you and the many hours and nights you listened to me read bits of my manuscript over and over again. I love you, infinitially.

Also, thank you to my friends, especially the
Bookstagram group who read my rough draft word doc manuscript. You all got the raw version and some extra scenes that didn't make it into this final copy...but you also got the massive errors which I also hope didn't sneak into this final edition. (But who knows, they are tricky) Thank you to all who offered feedback and advice, and those who always supported my work during this self publishing process. I am so grateful.

Stay tuned, I have more thriller and horror novels
coming your way.

* * *

Up Next:
A thriller/mystery novel set in Lake Tahoe involving the 1920's, gangsters, and a haunted estate with far too many secrets.